Totally Bound Publishing books by Roxanne Blackhall

Bristol Park
Abbeydon Attraction
Abbeydon Academy
Abbeydon Abandon

Logan County Love
Rekindled

Logan County Love

REKINDLED

ROXANNE BLACKHALL

REKINDLED

Dedication

To my amazing Pitch Wars mentors—Laura Brown and Tif Marcelo. Y'all gave me the encouragement and direction I needed!

And...

With unending gratitude to the professionals who helped with my research—law enforcement officers, firefighters, forensic and arson investigators, veterinarians and more.

Finally...

To all of those whose lives have been touched by the hills and hollers of Appalachia.

Chapter One

Flames leaped and crackled, tearing up the side of the makeshift building inside the Fire Research Lab, casting shifting orange-and-yellow light on the walls of the warehouse. Drea swallowed against the lump in her throat. Even through her respirator, the ashy air was sickly sweet from starter fuel mixed with the scent of burning pine. She clenched her fists and forced herself to watch as the ATF fire crew hauled out hoses. When the first hiss of water produced a cloud of steam, a tendril of panic coiled in her chest. She sucked in a sharp breath, refusing to give in to the rising tide of fear.

"Hey, Hidalgo!" The shout came from her side, and she tore her gaze away from the flames to Gabe Mattix, who had her mask pushed back, eyebrows knitted together. "I called your name three times. You okay, kid?"

Drea flipped her off — she'd known Mattix for years, their communication ranging from high fives to the bird — and shoved her mask back.

"I'm good." She steeled herself and turned to the group of trainees. "The purpose of this little exercise, aside from giving those hose jockeys an excuse to impress us all, is to encourage observation. You'll see things during the active phase of a fire that are clues."

She ignored the scoffing laugh of one trainee. Peter Adams was an incurable smart-ass, but Drea thought he had the makings of a good investigator if his ego would stop getting in the way. She cleared her throat and addressed the group.

"What color were the flames? How about the smoke? These things can tell you a lot about the fire. What suppression methods were used? How long did it take?"

"I know all this shit. When are we gonna get in there and do something?"

Drea turned to face the trainee, and he had the sense to shut up.

"Well, Mr. Adams. Since you know it all, perhaps you would be so kind as to turn your back."

He blew out an exaggerated sigh, but she waved her hand at him and waited until he turned around.

"Good. Think about the perimeter. Anything combustible?"

She didn't have to see his face to know he had no clue. The uncomfortable shifting of his shoulders told the story.

"No, ma'am." His response came out sounding confident.

"Turn around and look again," Drea replied.

Adams turned and glared at her, then at the building. Drea pulled out her stopwatch, punched the button and waited for the ah-ha moment. It came nearly a minute and a half later when his eyebrows rose, and a muttered, "Shit," escaped his lips.

"There's a gas grill on the northeast side." He mumbled the words, barely audible in the noisy warehouse.

"Thank you." She turned the stopwatch, showing him the numbers, and Adams cringed.

"I'll repeat myself." Drea addressed the class again. "The purpose of this little exercise is to encourage observation. If you rely on what you know, or think you know, you will fail to truly observe, and you will miss things. That's true whether you're fighting a fire or investigating it. We're going to break for lunch and let this thing cool down, then we're going to get messy. Adams, c'mere."

She expected attitude. Instead, he looked down at his shoes as he shuffled over to her. She waited until all the other trainees were well out of earshot before she turned to him.

"I'm sorry, ma'am," he said before she could say anything. "I mouthed off."

Drea blinked in surprise. She'd been ready to give him a piece of her mind, but here he was apologizing.

"Did you learn something?" She waited for his nod. "Good. That's the point of all this. I'll be blunt. Questions are fine, attitude is not. You got a problem, you come to me one-on-one, like I'm doing with you now."

When he didn't smart back at that statement, or give her any other grief, she cracked a wide smile. "Instead of telling me how much you know, show me how smart you are. You wouldn't be here if you weren't, and I believe you've got the potential to go somewhere with this. See you back here in an hour."

Adams ambled off. Steam billowed off the burn, and the shouts of the fire crew faded, replaced with the roar of uncontrolled flames. *It's in my head. This is a controlled burn, not the house fire.* Drea forced herself to look at the fire crew — hoses spewing water, the flames nearly out. The concrete floors of the warehouse were so wet they looked like glass. She breathed, in for five, out for five, then shoved her gear into her bag and hustled to the door, desperate for fresh air.

"I hear you're headed back into the field soon." Mattix leaned her nearly six-foot-tall frame against the big roll-up door, arms crossed over her chest. Her dark eyes drilled into Drea.

"Yep. Final eval with the psych is next week." Drea did a little happy dance. "You gonna miss me when I'm gone?"

Mattix chuckled. "Shit no, Hidalgo. You've been a pain in my ass since your first day as a student in my fire science class. Seriously, you should switch to teaching. You're good with these guys."

"Oh, hell no," Drea said. She adored Mattix. The older woman had quickly gone from teacher to mentor, and finally, friend. But after months of being in the classroom, Drea was itching to get back in the field. "I'm not staying. I got into this job to chase bad guys, not teach the good guys how to do it. As soon as I get my walking papers, I'm outta here. Love ya, but not that much."

"No bullshit." Mattix fixed her with a pointed stare. "How are you holding up?"

Drea waggled her hand so-so. Class time was easy. She could stand in front of a group of students and talk fire theory and investigative techniques all day. Being here, next to a burn, with soot and ash and smoke billowing was a different story. She swallowed hard and forced a smile. She'd be fine. She had to be if she was going back into the field.

"The occasional nightmare still," Drea said, and blew out a breath. The flashbacks still happened sometimes, too, but they were getting easier to control, at least. "Even I'll admit I wasn't ready to get back in the field so soon the first time."

Mattix shook her head, sending her short braids bouncing. "I don't know why the doc cleared you."

Drea shrugged. "I seemed good. Everything seemed good. Then the ceiling caved in and landed on me, and yeah, I had a flashback, on a cold scene, with only my partner around. Not a huge deal. I got lucky. It could have been worse."

Mattix gave a sharp laugh and leaned back against the wall again. "And you're good now?"

Drea flashed a bright smile. "Hey, I held it together today, didn't I? At a live burn. I'm coping."

"Tell that to someone who doesn't know you so well." Mattix grinned. "Promise me you'll be honest with the psych, okay? If you're not ready, then you're not ready. There's no shame in that."

Drea wanted to be ready. Needed to be ready. Fire investigation was her career. Not teaching.

Her cell buzzed. Unknown number. West Virginia area code. All thoughts of fires and investigations and her upcoming psychiatric evaluation disappeared. Drea had only one thought... *Gramps*. She drew in a trembling breath and tapped the screen to take the call.

"Hello." Her voice was far steadier than she felt.

"Ms. Hidalgo?" The unmistakable lilt of Appalachia came through in that short greeting. The caller waited until Drea identified herself, then continued. "Your grandfather requested we call. He was hurt while helping clean up after a fire..."

Drea sagged against the wall, and her fingers clenched around her phone. Mattix shifted, her tall frame shielding Drea from any curious looks. The rest of the conversation passed in a haze of half-heard information as Drea's mind whirled on what she had to do next. She hung up the phone and stuffed it into her pocket.

"You're gonna eat before you go tearing off to West Virginia," Mattix said. "No arguing. Gimme your keys, I'm driving."

Mindless, Drea dug her keys out and tossed them to her friend. She didn't care about food. She wanted to get on the road.

Mattix drove, ordered burgers, and pulled into an isolated parking space at the back of the lot. Drea's hands shook as she unwrapped the burger. She tried to hide it, but Mattix didn't miss things.

"It's a six-and-a-half-hour drive to West Virginia, kid," Mattix said. "You could fly." Her eyes narrowed as she peered at Drea. Always assessing.

Drea swallowed and shook her head. "Still an hour from the airport. If I hurry, I can get to the Regional Medical Center before visiting hours end."

"What did the doctor say?"

Drea took in a shaky breath. "Gramps had a heart attack. The doctor wouldn't say much, only that he's stable, but they're keeping him for more tests."

They finished their burgers in silence. Mattix had never been one for filling every moment with idle chatter. When she spoke, it meant something.

"I need to pack," Drea blurted as she tossed her wrapper into the bag. "It's the end of this session, I've got a couple days. The Deputy Director will understand."

Mattix's hand closed over Drea's. "Don't worry about Wilkes."

At her apartment, Mattix helped her pack, then pulled Drea into a tight hug before she headed out the door. "Call me if you need anything." Mattix glared at her. "I mean that."

"Yeah, yeah." Drea waved her off and shouldered her bag. She didn't allow herself to think until she was past the sprawl of Manassas, on her way back to Orchard Creek and the home she hadn't seen since her grandmother's funeral.

* * * *

Whispered conversations and the chirp of medical equipment blurred into the background as Drea's footsteps echoed in the wide hospital corridor. She wiped her palms down her jeans, steeling herself for what was about to come.

"Andrea? Andrea Hidalgo?" A young woman in pale green scrubs came around the nurses' station. "We've been keeping an eye out for you. I recognized you from your picture."

"What? Sorry, I was woolgathering." *Where did that word come from?* Jesus, she'd just rolled into town, and she was already sounding like a local.

"I'm Missy, the charge nurse. Paul told us you'd be coming. We didn't expect you this quickly. He's in four-nineteen, down the hall." She pointed before turning to the nurses' station. "Visiting hours end at nine. You've got about an hour."

Drea's feet felt like lead as she walked the rest of the hall to Gramps' room. She stepped through the door and into a world that felt at once foreign and familiar.

The beeping of his heart monitor and the hiss of the oxygen made an unpleasant symphony, calling up memories of her own time in the burn ICU after her accident. Noisy and hushed at the same time. And the smell. Hospitals all smelled the same — over-bleached linens and heavy antiseptics mixed with the cloying scent of flowers. In the bed, a gray old man sat staring at the television. Lush white hair swept back from a forehead that was more lined and creased than she remembered. He seemed so small and frail.

Paul DeJarnet had been a big man when he was young and healthy. Strong and agile. He'd taken Drea hiking and fishing, and taught her to climb trees and rocks, despite Abuela's protests that girls shouldn't be getting their knees dirty and scraped up. Drea chuckled at the memory of the two of them standing on the back stoop, washing the mud off after a particularly messy excursion while Abuela stood in the kitchen doorway, hands on hips, trying to look angry.

His head turned at the sound of her soft laugh, and his face lit in a broad smile that dimpled his cheeks. Still handsome at eighty-eight. He patted the bed next to him, muted the TV and beckoned her over.

"Little one." His pet name for her. His voice was whispery, like dry leaves rustling in the breeze. Drea sat on the edge of the bed, drawing in a shaky breath. She squeezed his hand and forced a trembling smile before looking away, unable to face the man her grandfather had become.

"What happened?" Drea asked.

"I've been around a long time and I'm worn out." He patted her hand. "I got out of breath."

"The doctor said you were helping clean up after a fire. Why were you out there? Never mind. Don't answer that." She knew the reasons. Orchard Creek was his home, and people took care of each other. "I'm glad you're okay. How long will you be in here?"

He lifted a shoulder. That noncommittal gesture spoke mountains. "A few days, at least. They have tests to run. And some procedure — an angioplasty. I'm sorry you had to come all this way, but I wanted to see you. Just in case."

Angioplasty. This is no minor heart attack.

"What did the doctor say, exactly?" Drea demanded.

"That I'm old." There was no laughter in that statement. "He said I have arteriosclerosis. They'll do this procedure, and that should be it."

He didn't look at her when he answered. His gaze roamed the room, settling on anything but her face. She knew that trick. She'd tried it herself, on him. It never worked.

"Uh-huh. What else?"

He let out a slow sigh. "The doctor said he didn't believe a bypass would be necessary, but he'd know more…" His eyes brimmed with tears, and Drea choked back tears of her own. A bypass meant surgery. She gripped his hand, her fingers curling around his.

"I should have come sooner," she whispered, "but I'm here now, and I'm staying until you're back on your feet."

His eyebrows knit together in a frown as he turned his gaze back to her. "What about your job?"

"I've got time off," she replied. "I took a few days leave to come see you and I can take extended family leave. It's not a problem. The last class session finished, and I haven't started my new assignment yet."

He didn't need to hear that she was uncertain what that assignment would be. She was eager to get back into the field, but also terrified. The psychiatrist said she was ready, but she had one last review before being cleared. Mattix believed in her. None of that mattered when she woke up at two in the morning, covered in sweat, a cry of pain and fear on her lips. Still, she was ready. *Maybe.*

A soft knock sounded, and a nurse came in. Gramps joked with her as she took his vitals and made notes on the chart. *Same old Gramps. Always a charmer.*

Drea sat with him while he talked, slowly, of everything and nothing. His breathing was labored and painful to hear. All too soon, his eyelids drooped, and his head nodded.

"I think you need rest," she said. "I know I do."

"Your room is still set up." His voice was a soft whisper. "You'll stay there?"

"Of course, Gramps." She kissed his cheek, then rose to leave.

* * * *

The door swung open to her childhood home and Drea swallowed hard. Nine years, and she'd bet she could still find her way through the place in the dark. She'd last been here for Abuela's funeral, when the little house had been overflowing with people and food. Speaking of food... She sniffed the air. *Vanilla and coconut. Cookies.*

She dropped her bags at the steps and made her way to the kitchen that took up the entire back of the house, then clicked on the lights. Boxes of buttery, jam-filled shortbread *mantecaditos* and chewy-crispy coconut *besitos* covered the kitchen table.

Every week, Gramps baked dozens of the traditional cookies, as his wife had done for years. And every Friday, he made the rounds, leaving boxes of cookies at nursing stations, the bank, the mechanic's. Anyone who deserved a thank-you or needed something to brighten their day.

Drea groaned and searched for Gramps' delivery list. She found it stuck to the fridge, his once-neat handwriting grown shaky with age. He'd never missed a week of cookie deliveries. Not even when his wife was sick. Abuela hadn't let him. Drea fingered the list.

The boxes of cookies sat neatly stacked on the table. Drea groaned again. She couldn't, didn't want to see all those people. Talk to all those people.

The sugary scent of vanilla and coconut filled the kitchen. Her stomach knotted and roiled. She should have insisted Gramps move to DC after Abuela died. Maybe then things would be different. Drea shook herself, dropped into a chair and skimmed the list again.

Suck it up, Drea. It's the right thing to do and you know it.

Tonight, she needed rest. She'd deal with the cookies in the morning.

Chapter Two

After breakfast at the hospital with Gramps, Drea climbed into her Jeep and checked the delivery list for the umpteenth time. She left the lot without looking up directions. She knew where she was going. The easiest, and the hardest delivery.

Stop number one, retired Police Chief Mack Lawson. She'd known the man her whole life. When she'd become enamored of horses, Chief Lawson had loaned her Hwin, his daughter's paint pony, on the stipulation she was to come over every day to feed and care for it.

The house still looked the same. A long walk to the broad porch, the roof of a small stable visible through the trees. Drea grabbed a box of cookies and made her way up the walk — each step familiar, taking her closer to the small-town life she'd left behind. The Chief would want to talk about Gramps. And he'd ask how she was doing. And he'd know about her accident. Gramps would have told him when he came to see her in the hospital.

The door opened and Drea gulped. His salt-and-pepper hair had faded entirely to silver, but Mack Lawson still looked like he could keep up on a football field.

"Andrea!" He stepped onto the porch and wrapped her in a crushing hug. Moments later, she was perched on his couch, cup of coffee in hand, nodding in all the right places as he reminisced and caught her up on who was doing what these days. His kind eyes soothed, the rhythmic cadence of his voice made her feel at home.

"Now, you know Wilma Davis came back, oh, I guess about five years ago. She's over at the high school now."

Drea chuckled and nodded. She had known that. Gramps had told her, and though Drea should have called her, sent an email, or reached out on Facebook, she never had. Wilma had been her best friend, her saving grace all senior year. Then college and life got in the way. Well, that was a fixable mistake. Drea would take her cookies after all the other deliveries. It would be good to catch up.

"CeeCee came back about this time last year."

CeeCee, her other close childhood friend. Drea's head popped up. Gramps hadn't told her that. Of course, this time last year, Drea had still been in the hospital recovering from burns, so he might have thought it best not to share. Gramps knew the history between the two of them—their friendship had ended over a boy. She wasn't sure what to feel about CeeCee.

"You three were thick as thieves back in the day," Chief Lawson went on. "If anyone wanted to find you, all they'd have to do would be find those two girls. Them or Danny Parsons."

"Oh, that's ancient history," Drea replied. Danny was the last person she wanted to reminisce about.

They'd been friends since they were children. He was her first love and her first heartbreak. She hadn't dated again until after college, too fearful of losing her heart the way she had with him.

Eventually, she made her excuses and got on with the other deliveries. Each visit got a little easier. The heartfelt well-wishes, the comments of how long it had been, the questions about how she was doing. By the afternoon, she was numb, overwhelmed by the outpouring of love and support for her grandfather.

"So good of you to come take care of Paul."

"Our prayers are with him."

"Let us know if there's anything we can do."

Each time she smiled and nodded, said the appropriate things, too dazed to do anything else. When she was finished, she had one more stop — Wilma Davis.

She pulled into the high school and grabbed two boxes of cookies. Gramps always made more than he needed, and she couldn't go in there with cookies for Wilma but not for the rest of the office staff.

It was late afternoon. The halls were deserted but walking through the entrance felt like taking a step back in time. The faded floor stretched ahead, and spirit posters covered the walls, a 'Go Cats Go' banner hung over the office door. The lingering smell of cheap perfume and body spray told the story that the students hadn't been gone long. She pushed through the office door and smiled at the first woman who looked up.

"Drea Hidalgo. As I live and breathe!" The plump woman stood and embraced her. "I am so sorry about Paul. He'll be fine, sugar. I'm sure he will."

Miss Mabel. Her name was Mabel something or other. She ran the office staff. Drea offered up the extra box of cookies and took a step back, out of arm's reach.

"I brought cookies." *Nothing like stating the obvious.* "Is Wilma still here? I mean, did she go home already?"

Standing in the school office, looking at Miss Mabel, who appeared as if she hadn't aged a bit, made Drea feel like a teenager again. Awkward and uncertain.

"Well, look what the cat dragged in." The rich drawl carried across the office and brought a smile to Drea's lips. Wilma Davis was not known for mincing words, but she could tell you to go to hell and make you look forward to the trip. Faded blonde hair fell from a side part into sleek waves, framing a round face and steely gray eyes that peered out from behind black cat eyeglasses. Same Wilma, always a pinup queen. "Come on back."

Wilma turned and disappeared into her office, leaving Drea to follow like a wayward teen. Once the door had closed behind them, Wilma enveloped her in a tight hug. "I'm sorry, hon."

With one hug, the years melted away. The tears that had seemed so close to the surface the last twenty-four hours spilled over. Wilma gave her another squeeze, then handed her a box of tissues and pointed at a battered red chair. Drea sniffed and wiped her eyes.

"I can't stay long, but I wanted to pop in and say hi. Are your folks still around?"

Wilma's mother had taught at the elementary school and her father had been the football coach. Wilma laughed, thumbed her phone and flipped it around to show Drea pictures. "They retired a couple of years ago. Sold the house and bought this monster RV."

Even after all the years, Drea would have recognized them on the street. Coach Davis wearing shorts and a tight tee, his wife in denim capris and a tank top, standing in front of the Grand Canyon.

"They travel. They've got their retirement, plus Mom writes for some RV websites." Wilma slid the phone back into a drawer. "You brought cookies." She gave Drea a sad smile. "I remember those from when I was in the after-school program. And visits to your house. The coconut ones are still my favorites." She offered a shrug. "How long will you stay?"

"I'm not sure." Drea sighed. She'd have to talk more with the doctor. And with Gramps. And with her boss. But none of it mattered. She'd stay until she was no longer needed. "Until he's through the procedure, back home and settled. At least until mid-March."

"Just a couple of weeks." Wilma didn't seem surprised. "He's very proud of you. He talks about you all the time and the trips he takes to visit you in DC. He shares pictures."

Drea felt the heat rise to her cheeks and looked away. Of course Gramps talked about her. But she'd never thought about him sharing their pictures — making silly faces at the Smithsonian or posing to look like they were holding the Washington Monument. She cleared her throat, suddenly uncomfortable at the idea of half the town knowing her life. She'd left this life behind. The small town where everyone knew everyone. It was too much.

"I need to get back to the hospital." Drea's voice was a whisper. "I said I'd be there for dinner."

"It's good to see you again." Wilma scribbled something on the back of a business card and handed it to Drea. "Come back any time you need to talk. My door is open. That's my cell phone. Call me if you need anything."

Drea took the card, not trusting her voice. She rushed from the office and drove back to the hospital in a blur.

* * * *

The elevator doors slid open, and Drea stepped out, almost colliding with a man waiting to get in. She looked up to apologize and took a step back. Danny Parsons' bright blue eyes widened, then immediately crinkled as he smiled.

"Drea, it's good to see you. I just left your grandfather."

She swallowed the lump in her throat and forced herself to look at him. Tall and lean, with sandy hair that fell over his forehead, he was still as good-looking as ever. No, better. Ten years ago, at high school graduation, he'd been cute, boyishly handsome. The years had broadened his shoulders and carved him into marble. The man standing in front of her was nothing short of gorgeous.

"Hi, Danny. Thank you for visiting. I'm sure he appreciated it." The polite, meaningless phrases fell from her lips and his smile faded. "I'm sorry. I spent all day delivering cookies, and I'm fried."

"Of course." He stepped to the side but captured her hand before she could flee down the hall. His touch seared into her flesh and rooted her to the spot. Heat spread from his hands, and she was suddenly too warm. And far too aware of him for comfort. "If you need anything, Paul has my number," Danny said, his voice soft and low. "It really is good to see you again. I'm sorry it has to be for something like this."

He squeezed her hand, and Drea tensed, fearing he would hug her. She wasn't sure she could handle him being that close. If a touch of his hand could turn her into quivering goo, she didn't want to think about what a hug would do. He reached out and patted her shoulder instead, then he was in the elevator and gone.

She blew out a breath, uncertain what had just happened, and turned for her grandfather's room.

Gramps sat propped up in bed, laughing and chatting with a young nurse. He waved Drea over, and she sat in the bedside chair, waiting for the nurse to finish taking his vital signs.

"That young man you always liked came by." Gramps dropped a wink at Drea. "Maybe you saw him on the way in?"

"I saw Danny Parsons, if that's who you mean. We spoke briefly at the elevator."

Gramps fixed her with a stare that made her look away, blushing. He was right, of course. She had more than liked Danny. They'd made plans to leave and attend university together after graduation. Then his brother Jake had decided to join the Navy, and...well, plans had changed. Everything had changed then.

"Why don't you visit a little," Gramps said, mercifully changing the subject. "Don't worry about needs or some gotta-do list."

The arrival of his dinner tray brought the conversation to a halt. Drea kept him company while he ate. He told her stories of the neighborhood kids and what everyone was up to. Gramps wasn't a gossip, but he listened, and people talked to him.

He pushed his half-eaten tray away and gave her a stern look. "Tell me what's going on with you."

Her fingers twisted in her lap. She couldn't hide from him. She never could. He normally came to visit a couple times each year, but since her accident, she'd never found the time for him to come out. Plenty of excuses though. "I don't want to bother you with all of that. It's no big deal."

"Andrea." In that one word, his voice lost the brittle dryness of age and the hissing sound of the oxygen faded away. Steely determination flashed in those green eyes and his brow knit in a rare scowl. He no longer seemed like a shriveled old man. This was her grandfather as she remembered him. A kind and gentle soul with a will of iron.

And she told him. Most of it, but not everything. Not the deep fears she held secret, the ones she barely admitted to herself. She could tell Gramps about the skin grafts that covered half of her back—he'd seen her in the hospital. She couldn't tell him how she'd cried the first time she saw the scars. Or about her ex-fiancé's hurtful words, uttered before she'd fully recovered. She talked about going back to work after the accident. She told him about falling apart while investigating an office fire in Georgetown—her first time back in the field. And about being forced to transfer to teaching. She chalked it up to not being ready yet, she'd be back in the field soon.

She didn't voice the fear that she wasn't ready. That fear spoke in whispers on the heels of the nightmares that woke her in the middle of the night. And she didn't speak about being uncertain about her entire career now. This was who she was. What she'd always wanted. She couldn't say she no longer felt the pull of it. Still, Gramps seemed to know there was more.

He reached out, took her hand, stroked her knuckles. "You'll find a way through this. In the meantime, being back home will be good for you. Time to focus on something different and go back to work with a fresh mind."

A nurse came in to administer meds, and Drea once again saw the age on his face. Deep gray shadows hung under his eyes and that brief flash of steel had disappeared, replaced by a faded weariness. She leaned down and hugged him, then dropped a kiss on his forehead.

"Get some rest. I'll see you tomorrow."

"Smuggle me in some coffee." A bout of coughing cut his laughter short. The nurse gave Drea a reassuring nod, and she turned into the hall. Her feet carried her to the elevator as her mind drifted. *Gramps looks old and frail.* She pushed that thought aside, willing herself not to cry. There had been enough tears today.

* * * *

Danny Parsons turned down the lane and drove past the upper paddock, empty now in the early evening hours. Going straight to his place was tempting, but Ma would have a fit if he didn't stop and talk for a minute. He parked in the drive and climbed the broad steps, reaching up and slapping the Parsons Acres sign that hung over the porch as he'd done time and again since he was tall enough to jump up and reach. Annette Parsons was in the kitchen, brewing a fresh pot of coffee.

"How's Paul doing?" She slid a steaming mug across the counter in his direction.

"As well as can be expected, all things considered." He tossed his keys down and reached for the coffee mug. "He's gettin' up there, and he's not been doing well for months. He didn't have any business helping clean up after that fire." He ran a hand through his hair. "He looks old and tired. Paul won't say it, but I think he's more worried than he lets on." He took a deep swig of coffee before continuing. "I saw Drea." He eyed his mother over the rim of his mug.

"Well, that's not surprising. She's his only family. Of course she came back to take care of him."

He sipped the coffee, uncertain how much he wanted to share with his mother. Seeing Drea step off the elevator had twisted everything in him. Until that moment, if someone had asked, he'd have said he was over Andrea Hidalgo. Now, maybe not. "I'm not so sure. She never wanted to stay here. Barely came back for her grandmother's funeral. I can't imagine she'll stick around. Probably send Paul off to a home, then go back to city life."

"Daniel Parsons, don't you dare be uncharitable. I did not raise you like that."

"Yes'm. That'd be Daddy's influence." He drained his coffee, rinsed the mug, and set it on the rack, then grabbed his keys. If he stuck around, he'd have to listen to his mother's lectures on how he should be living his life.

"There was a time when you were in an all-fired hurry to leave as well. Andrea figured heavily in those plans, if memory serves." She laid a gentle hand on his arm.

"Ma." He pulled away with a sigh. They'd been having some variation of this conversation for years. "That was a long time ago. Another lifetime. Things change. Drea couldn't wait to head off to college. I wasn't gonna be the one keepin' her here."

Drea had been hellbent on leaving, and he'd been right there with her. The two of them had had plans to build a life together outside of Orchard Creek. Then his brother Jake took off, and their mother spent an entire week crying. Their dad had stormed around in a constant state of anger and frustration. And seventeen-year-old Danny hadn't had the heart to ask Drea to stay — he couldn't have handled it if she'd said no.

"Well, don't go blamin' her for doing what you both planned. I never understood why you didn't talk to her…"

"Ma!" The word came out sharper than he intended, and she looked at him, wide-eyed. "I'm sorry. It's been a rough couple of days."

She fussed over hanging the kitchen towel, straightening things that were already straight. "Have you eaten?" Her voice was gentle, softer than he'd heard it in years. Her default question whenever there was tension. A universal offering – of truce, love, support, whatever.

"Yes, ma'am." It wasn't a lie. He'd grabbed a sandwich at the hospital. That had been hours ago, but she didn't need to know that.

"Do you have groceries at that bachelor pad you insisted on building?"

"Of course I do. A man's gotta eat, and I can't be takin' all my meals with my ma." Smartest move he'd made, getting out of the main house. He'd built the cottage behind the lower pasture the year after his father had passed. With both her older son and her husband gone, his mother had decided he needed to hurry up and get married and start producing grandchildren. For months, she'd brought friends over to dinner. All had daughters of the right age. Never mind that he'd gone to school with half the women and had no interest in any of them. Most of them only saw the dollar signs attached to the ranch anyway. She'd finally given up, but she'd still nag every chance she got.

"You did tell Andrea to call if she needed anything?"

Danny chuckled. "Of course I did. You didn't raise me to be rude, now did you?"

She lifted an eyebrow. That look had always stopped him in his tracks when he was younger. "How's she look?"

He cleared his throat. "Who? Drea?" She'd looked...beautiful. Amazing. Wrenchingly sad. "She looked stressed, Ma. What would you expect?"

"You are full of sass tonight."

"I'm tired. It's been a long day. And Drea's back to take care of her granddaddy. I don't need you playin' matchmaker."

Because Drea wasn't hanging around. She didn't want this life, and for better or for worse, this was the life he'd chosen. For a long time, that thought had made him bitter, and he'd felt stuck. He had resented his brother for leaving, then his dad for being sick and eventually dying. He'd resented his mother for not being strong enough to do it all herself or hire someone from outside the family. In the end, family was what had made him stay. First, he couldn't leave. Now, he didn't want to.

He kissed the top of his mother's head and slipped out the door before she could reply. Fat lot of good it would do to offer Drea any kind of help. She wouldn't take it. Never would.

He put his truck in gear and headed down the drive to his cottage tucked near the tree line. He poured a glass of iced tea and flopped into his favorite chair, glaring out the window. The lights in the main barn were still on. No text from the staff on duty meant it wasn't an emergency.

Things were about to get busier than ever. The first half of the season was booked full with mares coming in for covering, and they had a few mares of their own due to foal in spring, plus plans for major expansions coming up. He didn't need to be dwelling on what could have been with Drea or fussing over how long she'd stick around. It wouldn't do him any good, and it certainly wouldn't change things.

She hadn't been back in town since her grandmother's funeral. Paul always went to visit her in DC. Danny had hoped to see her the last time she'd visited, but he'd been with his daddy, hauling a new stallion home. Drea had already left town by the time he got back.

A short whistle escaped his lips. Ten years since high school, and she still made him weak in the knees. When the elevator doors had opened, and she'd looked up at him with those emerald-green eyes, his stomach had clenched into a tight knot and his mouth had gone as dry as bone. Her greeting had been cold. Perfunctory. Dismissive. Same Drea. Focused on what she wanted to get done and too stubborn to look to her friends for support. Nothing had changed.

Chapter Three

Silvery rain lashed the window, and Drea lowered the blinds, making the room feel cozier. Gramps sat propped up in the bed, plucking at the blankets as if he were a child who'd been caught being naughty.

"I thought the angioplasty was scheduled for today?" Drea tried to keep frustration out of her voice. She'd spent the weekend getting the house cleaned up, preparing for Gramps to come home the day after the procedure.

"They moved it to tomorrow." His fingers still plucked at the blankets, making Drea wonder what he wasn't telling her.

A knock, and a tall, older man in a lab coat entered.

"You must be Andrea." He shook her hand. "I'm Dr. Jarvis. If you'll forgive me, you look very much like Isabel."

Drea forced a polite smile. It wasn't the first time she'd heard that. She had her grandmother's olive skin, crooked smile, and hair as black as a raven's wings, but instead of Abuela's rich chocolate-brown eyes, Drea's were green. She always felt she looked awkward, while Abuela had been an absolute beauty.

"You knew my grandmother?"

"I treated her briefly before she passed. She was a strong woman, I must say." He cleared his throat and tapped on a tablet. "Let's see... Paul DeJarnet." He glanced up at Gramps, who gave a short nod. Drea looked back and forth between them, uncertain what was going on.

"Your grandfather was diagnosed with pneumoconiosis—coal miner's lung—two years ago. Unfortunately, that made early detection of the real problem difficult. We found lesions in both lungs..."

The doctor's next words echoed in Drea's head, whirling and swirling into a confusing mess. "Advanced lung cancer...not much we can do... palliative measures."

"Cancer..." The word stuck in her throat. She grabbed a tissue, dropped into the chair next to Gramps' bed and reached for his hand. "Oh...Gramps. How long?"

The doctor sighed and leaned back against the wall. "Hard to say. If we'd caught this earlier, we'd have more options."

Drea lifted her head and caught the doctor's gaze. She held it and repeated her question. "How long?"

"We're talking advanced lung cancer here. It has spread to his lymph nodes and both lungs." He shook his head and sighed. "It's hard to say, but I have made a referral for hospice care."

"Hospice usually means six months." Drea felt as if she were spinning out of control. The little room swam in her vision. She cleared her throat and gripped the sides of her chair, willing the whirling to stop. "What are the options?"

"Andrea." Gramps tugged her hand.

"Why didn't you tell me sooner?" Guilt tore at her. So many could-have-beens.

"What good would come of it?" He'd given up the gentle tone for one of sharp reprimand. "What good? To add another burden to your already heavy load? One that can't be changed or fixed?"

She held her grandfather's gaze, refusing to look away. "Doctor, what are the options?"

"I think that's a conversation you two should have alone." Dr. Jarvis pushed away from the wall. "We'll do the angioplasty tomorrow. With the cardiac system performing better, you should feel some relief."

Icy calm spread through Drea's veins. She felt as if she were viewing the entire situation from a distance — as if she were both in her body, listening to the conversation, and outside of it, above it, somehow detached. She swallowed hard and thanked the doctor before he walked out of the room.

She took a deep, shuddering breath and asked the questions she didn't want the answers to.

"Well? Chemo? Radiation? Surgery?"

Gramps shook his head and reached for her hand. The tears she'd been fighting spilled over.

"Nothing?"

"I'm old, little one." His voice was soft, gentle. "And I'm tired. There is no winning this fight. All it would do is buy me a little more time. And not very comfortable time at that."

Drea blew her nose and sat up. She could focus on the practical. Leave the emotional stuff for later. Doing something was always easier than doing nothing.

"Fine. I'll stay as long as you have." He started to argue but she shushed him. "Don't even think about it. We'll turn the living room into your space. You've been sleeping down there anyway, don't deny it. I found your shoes in the downstairs closet—you never keep shoes downstairs. And a pillow and blankets behind the couch."

She caught his hand in hers and held it, his dry, papery skin warm and delicate under her touch. She waited until he drifted into a nap after lunch. Still, she was reluctant to leave, reluctant to let go of his hand and walk out the door. Finally, she kissed his forehead and slipped silently from the room, telling the nurses she'd be back after dinner. She had to get back to Gramps' place, call her boss and tell him her leave was going to be more than a few days or even a few weeks, and start figuring out how to get Gramps home and settled.

Later, at the worn kitchen table, Drea sat, coffee in hand, glaring at her cell phone and dreading the call she was about to make. She pulled up the contact, then waited while she was connected to Deputy Director Wilkes.

"How's your grandfather, Hidalgo?" the man said with no preamble. No pleasantries. Just his usual prickly self.

"Not good." She closed her eyes and pressed her lips together. *Keep it professional.* "He's been diagnosed with lung cancer. I'm going to stay…" The words stuck in her throat. "I'm going to stay until…"

"I understand." Wilkes' voice softened, a bit. A keyboard clicked in the background, and he cleared his throat. "You'll take extended family leave. When you come back, you'll report to the Fire Research Lab."

Dismay ripped through her, and Drea struggled to remain calm. Expressions of anger or frustration never swayed Wilkes. In fact, they guaranteed the opposite effect. "Sir, I was due to be cleared. I assumed that meant I'd be returning to the field."

His sigh carried through the phone. She could picture him in his impeccable gray suit, leaning back in his chair, long fingers steepled as he glared over his glasses. "Yes, and taking a week or two off for family is not an issue. But we have a department to run, and we need every field agent. You are entitled to take all the family leave you need, but I cannot guarantee placement in the field. You'll return to the FRL and move back into the field when an appropriate position opens."

"But, sir…"

"That's all, Hidalgo." Another deep sigh sounded through the phone, and when he spoke again, his voice was softer than she'd ever heard it. "My condolences on your grandfather."

The call went dead. He'd hung up.

Dammit.

Back to the FRL. Back to teaching.

Maybe she could move Gramps to DC… She looked around. The little house was filled with signs of a life lived—framed pictures on tables and shelves, a postcard from friends stuck to the fridge, even the cookies. Connections. This was his home. She couldn't, wouldn't, take him away from here.

Drea fumbled the hospice coordinator's information from her pocket. It was time to get to work. She had a lot of research to do and phone calls to make. She could rearrange the living room so the far side was screened off and at least semiprivate. That would have to work, and he'd like that better than being in some convalescent home.

* * * *

Drea wiped her hands on a rag and surveyed her handiwork. Sturdy safety rails lined the shower stall, and another was anchored on the wall by the toilet. The list of things that needed doing before she could bring Gramps home had seemed endless at first, but getting everything ready the last couple of days had kept her from dwelling on the fact that her grandfather was dying.

She tossed the tools back into the box and headed to the living room. Something fluttered by the window. Drea paused, waiting to see if it would happen again. There! A blur of movement in the front yard. She yanked open the front door and nearly ran into Emma Tanner, who was standing there with a chicken under one arm and waving a dish towel at a bird pacing around the porch. More chickens scratched and pecked around the yard. The Tanners lived next door and made most of their living selling eggs from their hens.

"What in the world?" Drea closed the door before a hen could slip into the house. Emma lost her grip on the first chicken, and it went fluttering to the porch steps before walking off as if nothing had happened.

"Oh, Drea! I'm sorry. All this rain! Mudslide came right down on the coop." Emma flapped the dishtowel at the other bird, but it ignored her. "We'll get these hens outta your yard."

Drea bent and scooped up a hen, quickly shifting her grip as it began pecking at her hand. "Where are you putting them? I'll help out."

Emma's mouth dropped open and her eyes went wide. Drea had hated chickens when she was younger. She'd been more than happy to help out, so long as it didn't involve going near chickens. The birds always seemed fussy, pecking and flapping at the slightest disturbance. It made Drea worry she was hurting them.

Now, she couldn't care less about ruffling some hen's feathers.

Emma snapped her mouth shut and pointed to their yard. "Will's got a temporary coop set up in the carport."

Drea carried the hen up the muddy hill to the makeshift coop Will Tanner had erected. His eyebrows about met his hairline when he looked up and saw her toss the bird into the coop.

"Thank you, you don't hafta…"

"C'mon, Mr. Tanner, I'm not a scaredy-cat kid anymore. Have you got a spare pair of gloves? I can help get these birds rounded up."

Will silently handed her a pair of worn blue floral gardening gloves. Hands protected, she went back to Emma, and the two of them quickly scooped up the rest of the birds.

"What happened?" Drea sat on the Tanners' front steps a half hour later, picking at the dusting of feathers on her sweatshirt and eyeballing the chickens now happily scratching around their temporary coop. The mud covering her pants was another story. Will came out with cups of coffee, and she nodded her thanks, grateful for something hot and caffeinated.

"That fire up the hill that your granddaddy was helping with left a coupla dead trees." Will shrugged. "Had a buncha rain, and whoosh."

"The whole mess came down on the coop." Emma picked up the story. "Tree rolled right down the hill with mud and rocks and all, took out the whole coop. Lucky I'd already got the eggs today. Don't guess we'll get any tomorrow though."

Drea finished her coffee and looked around. The house was small, much like the one she'd grown up in, the side yard given over to a vegetable garden and the remains of the chicken coop spilled around the other side of the house. Herding chickens and cleaning up the mess wasn't her idea of a good time, but at least it had gotten her mind off Gramps for a while.

"Still got some daylight left." Drea turned to Will. "I don't know much about building a new coop, but I can shovel mud and shift fallen tree branches. And I do know how to shore up that slope so it doesn't come down again if the rain starts back up."

Her offer was met with stunned silence before Emma broke into a wide grin. "Why, that'd be nice, Drea. Thank you!"

* * * *

A beautiful bay muzzle popped over the stall door as Danny dumped a scoop of stabilized rice bran into Raphistra's grain bucket. She nickered at him when he tipped the bucket into her feed trough. Any one of the crew could have done this, but he had a soft spot for the pretty bay.

"Hi, girl." He ran a hand down her withers, then scratched her growing belly. His eyes roamed the open box — water trough clean, salt available, door open into the small yard where there was plenty of forage. She was due in mid-April, and little things could make big differences, especially in the last month of gestation. Raphistra lowered her head into her grain, and Danny gave her one last scratch before letting himself out of the stall.

He spotted Larry Gable's hardware truck coming down the drive. Lately it seemed there was always something that needed fixing. Fortunately, they had an account at the hardware store, and Larry delivered. Danny met him as he pulled up.

"Hey," Larry greeted as he hopped down from the truck.

"Yeah, hey yourself." Danny laughed and called over a hand to take the boxes of roofing supplies to the main barn.

Larry leaned into the cab and pulled an invoice from under an open box with a single cookie in it.

"You've still got old cookies in your truck?" Danny chuckled. Larry was usually neat as a pin.

"Hell no. Those things would never last, and you know it. You're welcome to it. I already ate too many." He grabbed the box and handed it to Danny.

The lone coconut cookie was a misshapen lump, but when Danny bit into it, the texture and flavor were perfect. Not too sweet, crispy on the outside and a chewy middle. It was a little bite of heaven.

"Drea brought those in this morning."

Danny nearly choked on the last bit of cookie. He swallowed hard and cleared his throat. "Seriously? Why was she in the store?"

"She's been in a few times this week," Larry replied. "Installed some handrails and stuff at the DeJarnet place, getting ready for Paul to come home. Helped the Tanners rebuild their chicken coop yesterday. Will said you coulda knocked 'em both over with a feather when Drea showed up and started helpin' round up the chickens. I don't know how she found the time to make the cookies with all she's been doing. Where've you been, man?"

Danny raised his hands in surrender. "It's the first week of March. We've had two covers a day all this week, and it's only gonna get busier. One mare foaled early, and two more are due within a month. Where do you think I've been?"

His head was so deep in the business of the ranch he hadn't paid much attention to other goings-on. He'd heard Paul had had a longer stay in the hospital, and that Drea seemed to be hanging around. At least being busy had saved him from thinking too much about her.

"Well, when you come up for air, we can grab a beer. I've got two more stops today." Larry clapped Danny on the shoulder and climbed into his truck.

Danny looked down at the empty box in his hand. Drea had made cookies. And she hadn't sent Paul off to a home. And she'd gone out in the mud after all the rain to help the neighbors. Like she was thinking of sticking around. Maybe he should ask her out. For old time's sake.

That thought twisted him into knots. He shook his head. He'd made his choice back when they were seventeen. He'd let her go, even though it had nearly killed him to do it.

Chapter Four

Drea pressed her hands into her back and stretched. Getting Gramps home had taken a lot of work, but it was worth it. The first week had sailed by with seemingly constant visits from hospice nurses. The second week had been tougher. Gramps got tired so quickly and visitors had had to be limited. He hated feeling cooped up and not seeing anyone. Drea took to finding little projects for them to work on together.

Over the weekend, she'd hauled a chair out to the backyard so he could sit with her while she worked on cleaning things up. Today, they sat at the kitchen table, Abuela's recipe cards spread out in front of them. Gramps pointed out favorites, telling stories about each one while Drea made notes on the backs of the cards and took pictures of each recipe.

"She had such a hard time when she first came here." Gramps tapped on the recipe for *tostones*. "Sunday Mass was in English, and she couldn't find plantains anywhere."

Drea chuckled. Eventually, Abuela had found plantains — *tostones* were always one of Drea's favorite treats. She pulled another recipe out. *Panetela.*

"The first cake I baked." Drea laughed at the memory. She'd dumped all the ingredients into the mixer and turned it on.

"You covered the kitchen with flour." Gramps chuckled. "You wanted to surprise Abuela on her birthday. Instead, you made a big mess."

"But the cake was good." Drea took a picture of the card and set it aside.

"Yes, it was. Why do you want pictures? You could take the box."

Drea snapped her head up to look at him. His expression was sad, wistful looking.

"Do you see all the stains on these? The splatters from years of cooking — Abuela, then my mother, then me. Those are special. They're history. But they make the cards hard to use. If I take pictures, I have them, always. I can make a digital album or have them printed into a book. I think that would be nice." She paused, scratching her fingernail along a stained card. "You don't talk much about Mom. I mean, after she grew up. All I know are childhood stories."

Gramps looked down at the cards spread across the table and a heavy sigh escaped his lips. "She went to college, became a nurse, moved to San Juan to be with Luis, they had a beautiful little girl and a few years of happiness. And then they were gone. What's to tell?"

Drea rolled her eyes. That was the same story she'd heard all her life. "Why won't you tell me more?"

He looked up at her, a flash of steel in his normally gentle eyes. "They had a good life. They both loved you with all their hearts. Luis was a good man, a police officer, and Victoria was happy. Those are the important things. The rest..." He waved a hand in the air. "Smoke on the wind."

"At least tell me more about how they died," Drea whispered. It had been a fire. She knew that. And it had been deliberate. She'd never pushed before. When her grandparents had changed the subject, she'd accepted it.

Gramps closed his eyes and leaned back in his chair, his face screwed up in a mask of anguish. At first, Drea thought he was in pain, then a trickle of tears trailed down his cheek. She'd lost her parents. She was so young she could barely remember them. But he'd lost his only child that day. She reached out, placing her hand over his. "Gramps, I'm sorry..."

He squeezed her hand. "Your father was a police officer. He angered the wrong people. It was terrible and senseless." He wiped his eyes on the back of his hand and tapped a card heavily splattered with cooking stains. "*Pernil.*"

Message received – change the subject. She'd always known there had been something awful about that night, something that had made her normally forthcoming grandparents go silent. She plucked the recipe card from his fingers.

"Every Christmas. The best pork ever. Where's the rice recipe?" She dug in the side dish pile until she found it. *Arroz con gandules* – rice with pigeon peas. "I'm sorry for bringing up a difficult subject."

He chuckled and shook his head. "You are so like your abuela." His fingers trembled as he pulled another recipe card. *Flan.* One of his favorites. "Always practical, but full of fire and spice. That firefighter you were engaged to would never have been able to handle you. He didn't deserve you."

Drea blinked at him in surprise. He'd never mentioned Frank before. They'd met when Gramps had visited DC, but she'd never talked to her grandfather about their relationship. Not really talked.

"Why do you say that?"

He kept his eyes on the pile of recipe cards, and Drea thought he wasn't going to answer.

He pulled out the recipe for the *mantecaditos*—the little jam-filled shortbread cookies he baked every week. They were another of her childhood favorites. "When you fill the dimples, a half teaspoon of guava in each. Not too much. My hands aren't steady enough, I make a mess these days. Like you as a child." He rubbed his thumb over a new stain on the card. Guava paste.

He sighed and fixed her with a kind smile. "You're too hard on yourself, and sometimes you're too hard on others. You're strong, and fiery and driven. That man was not right for you. You need someone just as strong, who can balance you and not be overwhelmed by you."

Drea gave him a smirk over that comment. "Frank was..." What was he? *A jerk. A cheater. So many things.* "He was an adrenaline junkie. He'll never be satisfied with one person, or with a stable life." She winked at him. "Besides, any man in my life has some awfully big shoes to fill."

They finished cataloging and photographing all the recipe cards, and Gramps stifled a yawn. Drea raised an eyebrow at him, and he shuffled into the living room and sat down on the couch. "I think I'll watch some television."

Drea tucked a blanket around him and kissed his cheek. "I told Annette Parsons I'd stop by today. I ran into her at the grocery. They're extra busy this year, and she was asking for help with lunches. Will you be okay for a bit? Emma Tanner can come over if you need anything. Got your phone?"

He scowled at her. "I'm not an invalid, and yes, I have my phone."

Drea chuckled. "Of course you're not. You just get cranky when you get tired."

"And you don't like being cooped up in the house all day with only me to talk to," Gramps said. Drea opened her mouth to protest, but he cocked his head and winked. "I wish you and I could be doing things — like we used to. I'm glad you're getting out, getting involved. You always loved helping at the Parsons'. Annette and your mother were like sisters when they were younger."

Drea leaned down and kissed his cheek. "I'll be back in a bit."

She didn't like leaving him, but he was right. She needed to be doing something. Her grandparents had raised her to be active — if she wasn't outdoors, she was helping in the kitchen, or loaned out as an extra pair of hands to neighbors in need. And Annette wasn't just Danny Parsons' mother. She'd been like an aunt to Drea — an older woman she could turn to the few times she and Abuela clashed.

* * * *

"Seein' you at the ranch is getting to be too regular a thing." Danny pushed back from the desk and handed Larry a check. "I'd offer coffee down here, but Ma would kill me if I didn't haul your ass to the house to say hello."

"What are moms for?" Larry smirked. "How're plans for the wind farm comin' along?" He dropped the paperwork at his truck and followed Danny up the hill.

"Slowly at the moment, but that's not a bad thing. Figurin' that's gonna get finished up this summer..." Danny stopped as the front door swung open, and Drea stepped onto the porch. He sucked in a breath as his chest tightened at the sight of her. Tight jeans and a soft sweater showed off every curve. Curls of hair tumbled down from a messy bun to frame her face.

"Hi, Danny, Larry." She dug into her pocket and waved a phone in the air. "I'm trying this new idea. You wanna say hi to Gramps?"

Larry nodded, and Drea propped the phone on the porch rail. "How about you?" She looked over at Danny. "You wanna say hi, too?"

"Wait, what?" Danny was too busy enjoying the view of her bent over fussing with the phone, he'd only vaguely paid attention to what she was talking about.

"Gramps hates being all alone. He's used to being social, but he can't do that anymore." She waved her hand at the phone. "And now, through the magic of FaceTime..."

Paul's smiling face filled the phone screen. He chatted with Larry for a few minutes, asked how business was going and inquired after his parents. Danny chuckled. *What an amazing idea.* He stole a glance at Drea. Her eyes were glued to the phone screen and an expression of mixed sadness and joy painted her features.

"Danny, how are things at Parsons Acres?"

The words came out slowly, and Paul's labored breathing came through when he paused, but his voice was strong, and he sounded cheerful.

"Doing well, sir. It's the busy season. Breeding and foaling. Same as every spring."

Paul laughed, a broad grin crossing his features. "Your daddy always said busy meant business was good."

"Yes, sir, he did." Danny swiped his hand through his hair.

Paul doubled over with a coughing fit, and Drea picked up the phone, concern etching lines into her face. She had a brief talk with her grandfather, then slipped the phone into her pocket.

When she looked back up at Danny, her emerald eyes sparkled with unshed tears. His fingers twitched, and he fought the urge to reach out to her. She looked so forlorn, so lost. When they were barely teenagers, before their first kiss, Drea had cried over the loss of her cat. He hadn't known how to comfort his friend then. Now, he wanted to cup her cheek, pull her against his chest and whisper soothing words into her hair.

"He can't talk for long." Drea's voice was tinged with sadness. "It tires him out and he gets short of breath. Thank you. Both of you. He needs to see people, talk to people."

Larry muttered about needing to go in and say hi to Annette and pushed through the door, tugging his handkerchief from his pocket as he went.

"How are you holding up?" The words left Danny's mouth before he could think twice. Dammit. She was gonna clam up.

Sure enough, Drea's expression changed. Her eyes hardened, and her full lips compressed into a line. "I'm managing, thanks." She shouldered her bag and headed for her Jeep.

Danny jumped down the steps to catch up with her before she could get into her car. "Today's Monday. Cookies are Fridays." It was a stupid statement, but apparently the best his brain could come up with under the circumstances. "You drove all the way out here so your grandfather could talk to people?"

"It seemed like a good idea," she replied. "But no, not just for that. I wanted to talk to your mother. See you tomorrow." Drea slipped into the driver's seat and slammed the door before he could wrap his head around what she'd said.

"Wait, what?" It was no use. She'd already put the car in gear and headed down the drive.

* * * *

Danny groaned as he lowered himself into the bubbling hot tub. One of the best investments he'd made. His entire body ached after the long day. He'd been so tired and worn out he'd subjected himself to dinner with his mother.

Then she'd dropped the bomb that explained Drea's parting shot — she would be coming by during the week to help out with lunches for the crew. Ma seemed pleased as punch, making noises about it being like old times when Drea used to work at the ranch. He closed his eyes and leaned his head back on the edge of the tub. *Damn, she looked good today.*

His eyes snapped open, and he stared up at the stars. He couldn't get the image out of his mind. Drea, back on the ranch. Wearing a peach sweater that made her eyes look even brighter than usual and brought out all the golden tones of her skin. Her hair a riot of black curls that called up memories of his fingers tangled in it and the kisses they'd shared.

"Thought I'd find you out here."

He sat up abruptly at the sound of his mother's voice. Water sloshed over the edge, and he had a moment to be thankful the bubbling tub concealed the fact that he was without a swimsuit.

"You took off rather quickly after dinner." She sat on the edge of the deck and looked up at the sky before turning back to him. "I'm not getting any younger, you know."

He rolled his eyes. *This old argument again.* "Ma, I'm not in a hurry to find a woman and get married."

"This isn't about you, Daniel." She gave him a sad smile. "Lord knows you've stepped into a tough job. One that you never intended to take on, and you've done it well. The plans you've got are good ones." She sighed and her expression turned hard. "This is a family business, son. You don't need to be in a hurry to do anything, but you do need to realize I won't be here forever."

"You're still young." Though they disagreed on many things, the thought of his mother passing was not something he wanted to dwell on.

"What will you do when I'm no longer able to help as much? Will you hire someone local? You know as well as I do how that will work out. You got lucky with Brian, but he'll eventually leave when he's done with veterinary college. The wind farm and the camp are great ideas, and I'm not suggesting you need to propose to some young girl tomorrow, but it's high time you start thinking about more than the bottom line."

"Are we gonna have a business meeting while I'm sittin' here in my hot tub?"

She arched an eyebrow at him. "If you'd hung around after dinner, we'd be talking at the kitchen table."

"Ma, everything we've talked about—diversified breeding, letting the power company put up windmills, developing an equestrian camp—every single bit of it is about more than the bottom line. The thoroughbred business isn't gonna die in my lifetime, but it will eventually slow down, and probably die out. What then?"

He'd feel much better having this talk if he were dressed. But she'd come out here and started the whole thing. He was damn well going to finish it. "Everything I've got planned is about preserving Parsons Acres for future generations."

"That's assuming there is a future generation." She stood and brushed imaginary dirt from her pants. "I've said my piece, and we'll leave it at that. I don't want to fight with you. I never do." She was down the steps when she turned back to him. "If you insist on skinny dippin', you could at least build a fence around this thing."

Danny shook his head. "That'd block out my view. Besides, that's why I put it way back here against the trees. No need for a privacy fence. If I'd known you were coming, I would have put on shorts."

He waited until she was around the other side of his cottage before standing and reaching for his towel. One good thing about her visit—it had knocked the dangerous thoughts of Drea right out of his head.

Chapter Five

Drea pulled up to the main house at Parsons Acres for her first day helping Annette and scowled. A beat-up Bronco with a police logo sat in the drive, and Drea's stomach clenched. The Orchard Creek Police Department had only one officer since Chief Lawson had retired — Robert Moore. He'd been a shy, awkward teen who'd hung around the fringes of Drea's group of friends.

She pushed through the door into the sunny kitchen. Annette leaned against the counter, arms crossed over her chest. Robert stood nearby with his thumbs hooked in his belt. Heavier than Drea remembered, but still baby-faced with a shock of brown curls, looking uncomfortable in a rumpled police uniform.

Drea's eyes settled on Danny, grim-faced and haggard-looking, sitting at the kitchen table.

"Is everything okay?" Drea asked.

Danny rose, pulled a chair out and put a cup of coffee in front of her, then sat back down.

"There was another fire early this morning," Robert spoke up. "An old cottage out on the far end of Parsons Acres."

"Was anyone hurt? How did it start? What happened?" Drea's mind churned into work mode, ticking through the standard list of witness questions. A second fire could mean a firebug, or arsonist. Her fingers itched for a notepad or her tablet. She had the notes app open on her phone when she realized they were all looking at her as if she'd walked over someone's grave.

"Hey, it's what I do." She stuffed her phone back into her pocket.

Danny shook his head. "We don't know much. Probably would just be findin' it, but one of the mares foaled early, and Brian was up before the ass-crack of dawn." He cleared his throat after his mother shot him a harsh look. "Pardon my language. He called the fire guys and Robert. By the time I got there, it was pretty much burned down."

Robert picked his hat up from the table. "I think I've got everything I need. Thank you for the coffee, ma'am." He nodded at Annette. "I'll call y'all with the report number and everything. Guess you'll need that for insurance. Soon as they say it's good to go, y'all can tear it down or whatever."

"That's it?" The words were out of Drea's mouth before she could think. "You've had two fires and you don't know how either happened and that's it? Were they possibly connected? What was the cause of the first fire?"

Robert put his hands on his hips and turned to face her. "Not everything requires an investigation. It was an old building. It burned down. Same as that old shack up the hill from y'all. Coulda been a vagrant, or some kids campin' out, and their fire got outta control. Coulda been our friendly neighborhood pyro back in town after her last stint in the hospital. Coulda been a lot of things and none of 'em worth investigatin'. Don't go stirring the pot for no good reason."

Drea's mouth dropped open in shock, then closed with a snap. She had no idea what the hell he meant about a pyro, but that opened up a whole new line of questions.

Robert nodded at everyone and headed out the door. Drea waited until he was backing around in the drive, then turned to Annette.

"I apologize for that outburst." This was a small town, and she didn't want to be seen as rude. Robert could go piss up a rope as far as she was concerned, but she respected Annette, and she had to stay here to take care of Gramps. Making life unpleasant wouldn't accomplish anything.

Annette shook her head and smiled. "Robert thinks his badge makes him the boss in any situation, and he's never liked anyone questioning his decisions or judgment. You did nothing wrong."

Drea sat back in relief. "What did he mean about a pyro?"

Danny muttered something under his breath and looked away. Annette sat and shook her head. "Oh, that's Penny Elkins. You know Lily? She helps with the horses. Her younger sister is… Oh, she'd be eighteen now, I guess. She had some…well, I don't rightly know what to call it. She was a bit of a handful."

"But was she setting fires? That could be significant." Drea remembered Penny and Lily and the entire Elkins clan. Ten kids. She had occasionally babysat for them, though not often. The older kids were usually pressed into that service.

Danny leaned his elbows on the table. "Penny was cutting and burning herself. One night, things got out of control. She set fire to her curtains. Accidentally. Lily got the fire out, and the family got Penny into treatment. She's about as quiet as a church mouse, and every bit as threatening."

Annette rose and snatched up her dishcloth. "Enough of that. I've got to clean up from breakfast before we get these lunches made. You two, shoo for a bit." She waved Drea and Danny out of the kitchen.

"I hope I didn't upset your mom," Drea said as they crossed the broad planks to the porch steps. "Sometimes my mouth gets ahead of my brain."

Danny stood with his hands stuffed in his jeans pockets, squinting in the sun, his expression unreadable. "Don't worry about Ma. She's none too fond of Robert." He waved a hand north where a haze of smoke still hung in the air. "Insurance'll need more than a bunch of coulda-beens, but I'll cross that bridge when I get to it."

He paced the porch, not looking at her. "Much as I hate to admit it, he's probably right about it bein' kids, or Penny. I keep sayin' we should tear those old places down, but Ma wants to keep 'em. Daddy said they were part of our history and should stay to remind us of the past."

He stopped in front of her, head tucked down, looking at his toes, and stuffed his hands back into his pockets. "It's good of you to come and take care of Paul."

Drea took a deep breath and let it out on a sigh. "He's my gramps. Of course I came back for him."

Danny rocked back on his heels a bit, chewing on his lower lip. He looked like a nervous little boy. "So, with you helping Ma, I'll be seein' you around? Just like old times." Danny cleared his throat and straightened up. All traces of the nervous boy disappeared. "Ah, hell, Drea. We can talk, right? We were friends once. More than friends for a while."

Drea gulped air. She didn't want to think about what they had once been. And damn him for bringing that up. She flashed a bright smile and called up the playful banter they'd always enjoyed before they'd started dating. Before Jake left. Before CeeCee.

"You look like crap, Dan-the-man. Get some rest." Drea gave him a wink and yanked open the front door. She was inside before he could respond, thankful he couldn't see her hands shaking. She went to the hall bath and wiped her face, surprised she wasn't bright red. Everything about him made her feel crackly and tense, like the air before a big thunderstorm — so full of electricity it could no longer be contained.

She pushed damp hands through her hair and cast one last glance at the mirror before heading to join Annette in the kitchen, where she had set up what looked like a lunch-making assembly line. It took them most of the morning to make everything, and Drea would be fixing sandwiches in her sleep later.

"What does a fire investigator do?" Annette handed Drea another sandwich. "Peanut butter and jelly. That's the last of them."

Drea labeled a brown sack and tucked the sandwich in alongside an apple and chips, then slipped it into the bin with the others.

"Well, it depends on what type of investigator, and where they work, and..." Drea stopped when she saw Annette smirk. "Oh, you mean me."

The smirk turned into a chuckle. Annette sat back in a kitchen chair and folded her arms over her chest, giving Drea the strange feeling she was looking at an older, female version of Danny.

"I'm a Special Agent with the ATF — the Bureau of Alcohol, Tobacco, Firearms and Explosives — and I'm a Certified Fire Investigator, but my degree is in criminal justice. Until last year, I was part of the ATF's National Response Team."

"Uh-huh." Annette nodded. "You're speaking Greek to me. What does all that mean?"

"Short version — a CFI is specially trained to figure out what caused a fire, and agents with the NRT are sent all over the country to investigate suspicious fires."

Annette rose and checked the bins against her list. "Your granddaddy is mighty proud of you, and rightly so." She closed the bins. "He said you were in a fire about a year ago. Was that work?"

The air rushed out of the room and the sunny kitchen went gray. Fire roared and crackled as bits of flaming debris dropped around her. Drea fumbled for the back of a kitchen chair — fingers curling around the smooth wood as she struggled to catch her breath and remain grounded in the present. *Deep breath in, hold for five, slowly blow it out.*

"No," she whispered. "It was my apartment. Started as an electrical fire in the middle of the night. Nobody noticed until it was too late."

Annette's hands covered hers. Drea looked up into blue eyes, so like Danny's.

"It's okay." Annette smiled, gentle and kind. "I'm sorry, I didn't mean to bring up painful memories."

Drea gulped air. "No. I'm okay. It's just sometimes still…"

"Of course." Annette straightened. "If you need to talk to someone, I can shut my mouth and listen."

"It was a freak accident," Drea replied. "I'm lucky I got out. Not everyone in the building did. And yeah, it's left some scars. Not all of them physical."

"They never are entirely physical." Annette grabbed a bin and headed for the door. "Thank you for helping out. I know you've got your hands full with Paul, you don't need to be working yourself to death."

That was it. No pushing for more. No prying. No lingering on Drea's reaction. Just acceptance. Drea took a deep breath.

"It's no trouble. Gets me out of the house. I loved the summers I worked here." She grabbed a bin and followed Annette to the truck outside.

Annette chuckled. "I always figured you were here for Danny."

Drea's cheeks heated. Danny had been the reason she'd hung out at the ranch so much — she'd loved the horses, loved riding the trails, but especially loved the time with him. "Gramps and Abuela always taught me to lend a hand where I can."

"Sensible advice." Annette stretched and wiped her hands on her kitchen towel. "I'll take care of cleanup if you can handle all the deliveries. You got time for that today?"

"Yes, ma'am," Drea said. "Ms. Tanner comes and sits with Gramps when I'm out. She reads to him, and he likes that. She won't mind staying a little longer."

Drea hopped in the truck, gave a wave and shifted the old thing into gear. She dropped the first bin of lunch bags with the crew at the upper paddock, then headed to the arena. The main barn, mare's barn and breeding shed all sat grouped together around the arena. She eased the truck behind the outermost building, careful not to let the gears grind lest she spook the horses.

Lily ran up with her five-year-old son Kyle in tow, and a young woman who looked remarkably like a tiny, far more fragile version of Lily — her sister, Penny. Drea blinked in surprise. She hadn't seen Penny since she was a child, and the girl might have been eighteen, but she was small and slight, with eyes that looked too large for her face.

Drea handed Kyle the basket of paper napkins and cups while Lily and Penny grabbed the bins and coolers.

"No school today?" Drea asked.

"School break." Lily hefted a bin onto a table. "And Penny can't be left alone. I checked with Brian first — he said it was okay. To bring Kyle and Penny, I mean. Kyle, you take out each bag and line it up nice and neat, you hear?"

"Yes'm." His blond curls shook with the vigor of his nod, and Drea stifled a laugh, then went back to grab the rest of the lunches.

"I'm gonna take Penny to the upper paddock," Lily said when everything was set. "She likes to watch them workin' the horses."

Penny hadn't said a word. She'd kept her head down and her hands stuffed in the pockets of her hoodie if she wasn't actively doing something. Robert had called her a pyro, but Danny had said she self-harmed and just happened to use fire. The two were nowhere near the same thing. Still, if Drea were investigating, she'd be looking at Penny. She couldn't blame Robert for considering it.

Drea tossed the bins into the back of the truck and sat on the tailgate, watching as the staff trickled through to get their lunches.

"Thanks for helping out."

Drea jumped at the voice and turned to find Danny leaning against the side of the truck, watching her intently. Her mouth went dry at the sight of him. Even in worn jeans and an old button-up shirt, he looked good.

"I'm serious, Drea. You've got enough goin' on. It's nice of you to lend a hand."

She didn't recall his voice being that deep. She shook her head. The last thing she needed to do was get caught up in lust with Danny Parsons. Again. She waved a hand at the near empty tables. The crew had already cleared out most of the lunch bags.

"You planning to eat?" Drea asked. "Better grab something while it's still there, or you'll have nothing to choose from."

He didn't move. He stood there, leaning on the truck with an odd expression on his face. His handsome face.

"It seemed the right thing to do," she continued. "Gramps doesn't need me every minute of every day, and sometimes I need to be out. I never was good at sitting still." She stopped. Thinking about Gramps made her want to cry, and she didn't want to cry in front of Danny.

"Will you be okay?" Danny cocked his head to the side. "Without work, I mean?"

"We'll make do." Drea kept her voice even. "House is paid off, and Gramps has his retirement. I've got paid leave, and vacation time, and a good savings. I'd rather things be a little tight and be able to be here for Gramps than be juggling work and everything."

Danny leaned forward, his hand snapping out and snagging a brown missile as it sailed through the air past her face.

"Sorry, Drea! I was aiming at the boss man there." Brian French, the ranch manager, offered a cockeyed smile of apology. "You're stuck with peanut butter and jelly, boss man. I got the last ham and cheese." He grabbed a napkin and hopped up on the tailgate next to her. "Hey, Drea, I'll split mine with you if you like."

"No thanks, I've got mine in the cab."

"Don't say that too loud." Brian laughed and pointed at Danny. "Boss man there will swap your lunch for his PB and J."

Even at noon, there was a hum of activity around the barn. While some were sitting with their lunches, others set theirs aside and continued with work. Drea tapped Brian's elbow. "Is it always this busy?"

He quickly swallowed a mouthful. "That fire put us behind schedule today, the smell has some of the horses spooked — one of the busiest days of the season, too. And it's spring. Happens every year, but this year's a bit more than usual. Someone thought we needed to expand." He rolled his eyes.

The truck shifted as Danny sat on the tailgate next to her. She sucked in a breath at his closeness. He smelled of grass and sweat and soap. Not an unpleasant combination at all.

"Brian's being melodramatic," Danny said. "What he means to say is he's damn grateful to be working for an outfit that has such a keen eye on the future." He looked down at the lunch bag in his hands. "What grown person eats peanut butter and jelly?"

"Me," Drea replied. "And about a quarter of your crew. Your mom takes requests. I'm guessing someone changed their mind, leaving you stuck with the All-American kiddie classic."

Brian coughed and feigned an innocent look. Danny opened his mouth but was quickly interrupted by one of the hands rushing up.

"Sorry, guys, gonna have to cut lunch short. Raphistra is foaling."

Danny and Brian both hopped off the truck. Brian quickly followed the hand to the barn, but Danny lingered, the odd expression back on his face. His hands twitched, and he shoved them into his pockets like a shy kid, but his eyes bored into hers.

"I've missed you." The words came out in a rush. "Drea, I—"

"Hey!" Brian's voice cut in. "Your favorite mare is about to foal, and you wanted to be there for it."

Danny nodded at Brian, then turned back to Drea. "See you tomorrow." With that, he grabbed his lunch bag and hurried into the barn. Whatever he'd been about to say left to mystery.

Drea sat blinking in confusion, her heart pounding. First, he had to go and bring up the past, and now he missed her. That thunderstormy feeling surged into a swirling cyclone of emotions she didn't want to deal with. She gathered up the remains of lunch and headed back to the main house. She had to get cleaned up and back to Gramps before Ms. Tanner's patience wore out.

* * * *

Raphistra's foaling had taken up Danny's entire afternoon yesterday. He hadn't gotten to bed until late and his morning had started before sunup. Then Robert had called right after lunch, saying it was urgent. Danny was not in the best of moods as he pulled up to the police station.

It was just a storefront in a run-down strip of buildings bracketed by a gas station and a coffee shop — where Robert was often to be found at a corner table, nursing a coffee and a pastry. Town tax dollars at work. Mismatched filing cabinets and a pair of desks sat behind a low counter divider that still bore signs of its former life as a dry cleaner's.

Robert looked up from his computer as Danny leaned on the counter.

"I'm sorry for that cryptic call." Robert gestured for him to come back. Danny lifted the counter flap and pulled up a chair. Robert mopped his face with a handkerchief, though he wasn't sweating. He was pasty white and had the look of someone who was about to throw up — chin drawn back, mouth clamped tight, swallowing hard.

Robert turned his computer screen so Danny could see the picture on it — the burned cottage on his property. "Grace Kimmel snapped a bunch of pictures the morning of the fire."

"Her brother's captain of the fire crew, isn't he?" Danny was confused. Grace taking pictures was pretty normal. She worked at the family's garage and took night classes. An avid photographer, she was pursuing education in forensic photo analysis. *Whatever that means.*

Robert nodded. "Amos. Yep. She went out with the crew, took some pictures of the guys in action. When she gets around to putting them on her computer screen, she sees something funny. Of course, she doesn't call us. Instead, she hightails it back there to take more pictures."

"That sounds about like Grace," Danny replied, then caught his breath as Robert stopped clicking through the images. Danny's stomach turned over. A blackened claw of a hand stuck up from the charred remains of the building. That explained the nervousness and pasty face.

"At first I figured kids," Robert said. "Y'know, spring break, camp at the old cottages. New moon and all, dark enough to get up to no good. I've asked around. Nobody's missin'. Not here or in any neighboring towns. I'm guessin' vagrant. Or some druggie friend of Penny the Pyro. If it were summer or fall, I'd think migrant farm worker, but it ain't the right time of year. You ain't missin' any crew, are you? Or got any disgruntled ex-employees?"

Danny swallowed against a dry throat, unable to tear his eyes from that clawing hand. He wished Robert would change the picture or turn the computer.

"Not that I know of," Danny replied. "We've had some up and quit, but they came around to pick up their pay. I don't think Penny's allowed anywhere without supervision." He cleared his throat, sat back in the chair and focused on Robert's face. Anything to not look at that hand.

"I know y'all need a report for the insurance. I'll email you a copy by tomorrow." Robert scribbled a number on the back of a business card. "This is the report number. It'll be in the email, but the number may be all you need to start a claim."

"Won't you need to investigate? Someone died."

Robert shrugged and turned the computer screen away. Danny's breath came a little easier. "No identification. When Grace got those pics, she called Bruce Talbot to come out and take a look. He said it looked like someone had a camp stove or somethin' like that." Robert mopped his face again, his hand shaking. "He called me, and I'm tellin' you, it wasn't pretty. Had to get the county out to get the body. They'll take it from there and give us cause of death, when they get around to it. Meanwhile, a preliminary report should do for insurance."

Danny slipped the card into his pocket. "Not tellin' you how to do your job or anything, but..." He paused. He was pretty sure Robert would blow him off, and equally sure Drea wouldn't thank him for opening that can of worms. "Bruce was a county firefighter for twenty years, not an investigator. Drea's got experience in this stuff."

Robert shook his head. "She's got enough on her mind, and I'm sure the medical examiner will tell us this is some vagrant who died in their sleep. We've got our own fire crew here. We don't need another firefighter thinkin' they're a cop."

Danny shrugged. "Have it your way. Let me know if there's anything else, will you?" He rose and headed to the door. "I think she's an investigator, not a firefighter. With the ATF."

Robert's eyes narrowed and he made some 'harrumph' noise. "All the more reason not to ask for her help. Folks around here wouldn't want some big city federal investigator sticking their nose into town business. I'll send that report over and keep y'all posted if anything comes up."

Danny slid into his truck and glanced at his watch. Dinnertime. He texted his mother to let her know he'd be late. She'd be upset, but she'd understand. He thumbed open his contacts and called Drea. She deserved a warning that Robert might be calling her — or not.

"I'm sorry to intrude," Danny greeted when she answered. "I think I mighta stepped in a hornet's nest and figured I should give you a heads-up." Her warm chuckle quickly turned to ice when he told her about his conversation with Robert.

"I hate to say it, but give him a chance," Drea said as they were wrapping up. "He may have been unwilling to give too many details to a civilian. And you might be a suspect. Or Brian. He is the one who saw it first."

Danny choked back a foul-mouthed reply to that idea. He couldn't imagine Brian harming anyone — he was too nice. But Drea was right.

"Give Robert a week," she continued. "If he still hasn't done anything, and you need more info, you can request copies from county records. Someone died. This isn't just a local matter. Probably have to request in person."

He was willing to put money on Robert doing nothing. "What good will getting a copy of the records do?"

"There was a fatality, so your insurance company may be a little prickly," she replied. "They'll likely want more than a report number. If Robert isn't forthcoming, you can get all of that from the county. Your property. Your claim. You have the right."

Danny shoved a hand through his hair and blew out a frustrated breath. The image of that hand still echoed in his brain and twisted his stomach into a knot. He needed this cleared up—the right way. He had too much at stake with the plans for the ranch to be worrying about what was and wasn't being done right.

"I know I'm asking a lot," he said, "but can I call you if I need help on this? I'm outta my element here, and..."

"Of course." Drea's quick reply loosened the worried knot in his gut. He thanked her and hung up, then texted his mother to let her know he was on his way home.

Chapter Six

Drea pushed up from the flower bed, brushing dirt from her knees. Gramps shaded his eyes and peered down the drive.

"Looks like Danny Parsons," he said.

"I told you Danny might stop by today," Drea replied. "He asked for help on his insurance claim."

"Oh, that's right." He settled back in his chair, tilting his face up to the warm April sunshine as Danny's truck came around the last bend. He hopped out, still dressed for work on the ranch — worn jeans, faded long-sleeved shirt and boots so old they looked like fabric rather than leather.

Not that Drea was paying that much attention.

"Paul," Danny greeted. "Good to see you up, sir." He shook Gramps' hand, then turned to Drea. "Thanks for takin' the time for this."

Drea smiled and pointed him at the porch. "Gramps, you want to go in, or would you rather sit in the sun for a bit?"

He held a hand out so she could help him up. "Think I'll go watch a bit of TV."

Drea got Gramps inside, then she and Danny settled into chairs on the porch, and she took the thin stack of papers he offered.

"This is it?" she asked, then rolled her eyes when he nodded. "A week ago, somebody died in a fire on your property, and you've got a half-page police report and a preliminary autopsy report. That's it. Wow."

She flipped through the meager pages. Not surprisingly, Robert's report was scant at best. The County Medical Examiner's report was as expected — basic. Without cause to spend much time on the case, it had got the bare bones treatment. The claim form Danny gave her was pretty standard. All he needed to do was fill in the report numbers and attach copies of the relevant documents.

"This is pretty straightforward stuff." She eyed Danny over the top of the insurance form. His eyes went wide in a look that said he was about to claim innocence — she hadn't believed it when they were teens, and she didn't believe it now.

"Yeah, it is," he said. "I'm also...ah, hell." He leaned forward in his chair and tapped the sheaf of papers. "Someone died on my land. Robert hasn't done shit about it. That's bothersome. I don't like unanswered questions."

Neither did Drea. And there were a lot of them as she scanned the reports. "A dead body isn't a problem that will magically go away or solve itself. But this is Robert's jurisdiction."

She skimmed the sheet again and shook her head. "That wasn't a John Doe, but a Jane Doe, age twenty-five to thirty-five, probable smoke inhalation."

Danny leaned in to read over her shoulder, and she lost her place. He radiated warmth, but it was the stubble on his cheek and the throb of the pulse in his neck that turned her brain to mush.

"Says she was likely intoxicated, passed out, and didn't wake during the fire." Danny turned his head to her, his face inches from hers. Drea swallowed hard. He leaned back in his seat and folded his arms over his chest. A classic Danny move that had her picturing him as a teenager, tipping his chair up on its back legs, looking like he thought he was king of the world.

"Don't know why Robert didn't ask your help on this," he said. "Seems odd."

Drea tore her eyes away from the corded muscles of his forearms. "Not odd at all. Why would Robert want me stepping in his territory? He sure as hell doesn't want anyone second-guessing him."

Danny rolled his eyes. "Robert's never been too keen on actually workin'." His expression turned serious. "Why don't you believe Penny did it?"

Drea waved a hand at the police report. "It's not that I don't believe it's possible. It's that it doesn't fit. Self-harm, even with fire, is not necessarily the same as pyromania. Setting fires is a particular behavior. Self-harm is different."

"Okay," he persisted. "I don't want it to be her, but could she have been out there, doin' who knows what?"

Drea shrugged. "Unfortunately, there's not enough information in these reports. This has got to be the sloppiest police work I've seen." She tossed the papers to the table. "It's possible it was Penny. That would mean at least two people were out there—Penny and Jane Doe. When the fire started, Jane was out so cold that she slept right through it and died. And Penny, who isn't supposed to be left unattended and who doesn't drive, somehow got herself back home before sunup, without anyone noticing anything."

She shook her head. "It was dark out and the back half of Parsons Acres to the Elkins' place is a long walk, especially on a moonless night. Possible, but not plausible. Maybe it was an accident. The scene still should have been processed for evidence. Robert's so convinced Penny's to blame that he's not looking at other, more likely possibilities."

"Such as?" Danny asked.

She leaned back and eyed him warily. Most civilians didn't like hearing real possibilities. They wanted to blame someone for a crime, but they wanted it to be a bad guy.

"I don't have enough information to guess," she replied.

"Gotcha." Danny leaned forward, elbows on his knees. "On the phone last week, you suggested Robert might not wanna talk to a civilian. Is that what you're doing here? Avoiding giving details I might not like?"

Drea took a deep breath and blew it out slowly. "Standard logic. Always suspect the person who reported the crime. Especially in fires." She ignored Danny's scowl and continued. "Next would be looking at the property owner and any former employees who might have axes to grind."

"Robert did ask that," Danny said. "And you'd seriously suspect Brian? He's not the type."

"Not necessarily," she replied. "But this reaction is exactly why law enforcement plays things close to the vest. People get emotional about someone they know, love and trust being considered — even if it's to eliminate them as a suspect. But without cause or invite, this isn't my territory, so what I would do is irrelevant."

"So, what's next?" Danny asked.

Drea lifted her hands. "You complete this ridiculously simple claim form and you wait. Did you really need help with this thing?"

Danny reached past her, gathered up the papers and stuffed them back into their envelope. The spicy, woodsy scent of his aftershave filled her senses. *Not the same thing he used in high school.* Danny had worn Polo Sport—for years, she would turn her head, searching for him any time she caught the uniquely summery scent. This was more complex, warmer and downright intoxicating. She stopped herself before she buried her face in his neck.

"No," he said. "A bunch of us play darts at Oak Bridge on the weekends. Ask Wilma, she's there a lot. You should come out some time."

It was his sudden change of topic that made her catch her breath, not his proximity. At least, that was what Drea told herself. "I keep hearing about that place." Drea slid her hands under her thighs to stem the urge to touch him.

"It's kinda the local hangout, and what passes for a pub around here. Opened about five years ago. Decent food. Darts, couple of pool tables." He dropped a wink. "Still play?"

Drea arched an eyebrow. She and Mattix had played weekly games for years, but Drea had stopped when she and Frank got serious. He'd claimed he hated the game.

"C'mon," Danny said. "May as well do what the locals do, right?"

"Yeah, I'll think about it. I've got to check on Gramps. He likes dinner early these days." She needed space. Someplace where Danny wasn't. Her body and her mind were on completely different tracks. Her body thrilled at every smile he gave, every twitch of a muscle. While her brain spouted the same lines — *he didn't ask you to stay before. You left and built a life of your own.*

Danny winked at her. "Wouldn't be the first time you sat out here with me when you shoulda been doin' chores."

Drea sputtered, unable to come up with a quick response. She was too busy fighting back memories of the two of them kissing in the porch swing.

His smile turned into a wide grin as he stood. "I'll go pay my respects and get outta your hair."

* * * *

"You look nice." Gramps sat propped on the couch, watching the news with Emma Tanner. "It's good for you to get out on a Saturday night. You going to see that young man?"

"I'm grabbing drinks with Wilma." Drea bent to fasten her sandals.

"You should be going out with Danny." Gramps wagged a finger at her. "You two always seemed happy together."

She ignored that comment, thanked Emma and gave one last glance in the mirror to check her appearance, forcing herself to not touch her hair for fear of it turning into a pile of frizz.

Drea had agonized over what to wear. She hadn't brought a lot of clothes with her, certainly nothing for a night out. She'd finally settled on black jeans paired with a turquoise silk blouse and her one pair of black high-heeled sandals. It made a passable outfit. She'd let her hair curl, pinned half of it up and put on a touch of makeup.

She grabbed her purse and headed out the door. After Danny's comment about getting out, she'd called Wilma and suggested a girls' night, and she was looking forward to it. She pulled into the lot and chuckled. Oak Bridge. *Cute.* The place straddled a creek, made to look like an old-fashioned covered bridge. A big oak tree marked the front entrance. *Gotta give them credit for creativity.*

Inside, it looked like a wide-open barn with a bar area to one side, darts, pool tables and a ping-pong table. Drea spotted Brian over by the dart boards, surrounded by a group of guys from the ranch. She scanned the room for Danny but didn't see him. Wilma sat perched at a table front and center — she looked up and waved Drea over.

"Have a seat," Wilma greeted as she slid a full glass across to Drea. "Just got a beer delivered, and we can see all the action from here."

"Who knew you were such a busybody?"

Wilma pushed her glasses up and smiled. "I'm queer and a high school counselor in a small town. Honey, it goes with the territory. Danny's not here yet, so you can quit lookin' around. Besides, this table's prime real estate. He'll see you the moment he walks in." She tipped her head toward the bar. "Wanna catch up with CeeCee? Bury the hatchet?" Her eyes practically rolled back in her head as she mentioned their former friend.

Drea shook her head. "It's been ten years. I don't have a hatchet to bury. Why?"

Wilma picked up her beer and pointed a finger across the room. CeeCee, cute and blonde as ever, wearing a pretty pink dress and matching lipstick, sat at the bar near the darts.

"Maybe later." Drea shrugged. "I'm surprised you two haven't patched things up since she moved back."

Wilma's lips pursed into a sour expression. "Let's just say the little streak of mean girl CeeCee developed once she made varsity cheer has turned into a big streak. But that's a story for another time."

They sat watching the crowd around the dart board, and every few minutes, Wilma pointed out someone else and added a little tidbit of gossip. The door opened, and Danny stepped in, all long legs and broad shoulders.

Holy hell, that man is nice to look at. A thin white T-shirt stretched over his biceps and chest and tight jeans clung to his body as if sculpted there. A battered straw hat and well-worn cowboy boots completed the look.

And just like that, it was the summer before ninth grade. They had been cleaning the mare's barn, and Danny sprayed her with the hose. Within minutes, they were both sopping wet and laughing. His white tee had clung to him, and he wasn't a skinny kid anymore. Somewhere over the last year, he'd grown muscles. Then he'd looked at her, stammered something about needing to dry off, blushed, and walked away, hands stuffed in his pockets. It wasn't until he'd gone that she'd realized her shirt was as revealing as his.

"You want a napkin to wipe that drool, honey?"

Wilma's voice snapped her attention away from Danny. Drea's face got hot, and she pushed up from the table. "I need... Uh... I need a minute." She needed to think, to breathe. In the wake of that water fight, Danny's parents had laid down a new rule—the two could no longer go on rides alone together. They either had to stay in the arena or have someone else with them. She hadn't understood it at the time.

She came to understand it a week later, when they broke that rule and Danny had kissed her for the first time.

Danny scanned the room quickly. The usual crowd — Brian and the guys in the corner playing darts. CeeCee perched on the same barstool as always. A head of dark curls caught his eye. *Drea. Heading out the door.*

He turned to go after her, and ran into CeeCee, standing there with her pink lips stuck out in an exaggerated pout. She'd made her interest abundantly clear when she'd moved back to town. And he'd made his disinterest as clear as he could without being rude. Still, she was always to be found, hanging out and being mildly flirtatious.

"Hey, handsome, aren't you gonna come say hi?" She looped her arm through his before turning to the dart boards. "I was hoping we could play a game."

Brian stepped up and fanned out a set of darts to CeeCee. "C'mon, I'll show you some tricks." Brian shot him a wink over her head and nodded toward the door. "We can play doubles later and trounce his ass."

Danny mouthed "I owe you one" at Brian and hurried outside but didn't see Drea in the parking lot.

"Looking for someone?" Her voice came from behind him. She was leaning back against the building, outside of the circle of light by the door, looking up at the night sky.

Danny swallowed hard. Her hair gleamed blue-black in the moonlight. *Damn, she looks good.* "What had you leaving in such a hurry?"

She lifted a shoulder. "I needed fresh air. Why'd you come after me?"

He wanted to see her. Talk to her. Someplace that wasn't the ranch. Someplace where he could get reacquainted with the real Drea.

"I wanted to spend time with you," he replied. "Every time we see each other, it's business. I'd like to get to know you again. Maybe go out."

"I don't know why I came here tonight." Her voice was a whisper carried on the breeze. Danny opened his mouth, but she stopped him. "You chose to stay. I'm just visiting, and my life is complicated at the moment."

Her words twisted like a knife into him. He stepped close, propped his hand on the wall next to her. She smelled like soap and jasmine. His fingers itched to plunge into the riot of curls around her face.

"We're not kids anymore," he said. "Complicated goes with the territory. And it doesn't scare me."

She turned her face to him, her chin jutting forward, and her face set in an expression he knew from years before. The same look she'd get when someone would tell her she couldn't do something. Stubborn. Determined. That look said "Try me." *Oh, to hell with this.*

He closed the little distance between them. He slid one hand into her hair, curled the other around her hip and pulled her close. Her lips parted in a surprised gasp, and he paused inches away.

"Should I stop?" He hadn't asked the first time he'd kissed her, years ago, but he wasn't about to press his luck now.

Curls twisted in his hand as she shook her head and tipped her face up. He lowered his mouth to hers. She froze for a split second, then she melted against him with a soft moan that set his entire body on fire. Her hands slid up his chest and twined around his neck, holding him close.

Her lips were silk and honey, and he wanted more. He'd always wanted more. From their first kiss, he'd never wanted to let her go. And yet he had. Because she'd had dreams that took her away. He pressed her against the side of the building, both hands caught in her hair. Loud laughter carried on the breeze, and Drea pushed him away with a gasp. He glanced over his shoulder as a couple got out of a car across the lot.

Danny took a slow breath. "Can we go somewhere and talk?"

Her eyes settled on his, a gentle smile on her face. "I'm going to go say good night to Wilma, and then go home. Alone."

He reached for her hands, wanting to touch her again. She squeezed his fingers, then pulled away.

"You're right," she said. "We're not kids anymore. If you want to talk, Mack Lawson comes over every Sunday after Mass to spend time with Gramps. It's going to be nice weather. We can sit on the porch."

"Okay." He leaned down and kissed her gently. "I'll see you tomorrow."

Chapter Seven

The smell of garlic and roasting pork permeated the small house as Drea checked on the *pernil* for the umpteenth time. Keeping busy kept her mind from dwelling on last night's kiss. She'd tossed and turned all night as old memories and feelings surged through her. It was just a kiss. She shouldn't be losing sleep over it.

She stowed a cooler full of bottled water on the porch and sat a pitcher of water and glasses near Gramps in the living room. She wiped her hands down her apron and tried not to think about Danny. He'd crushed her heart once — she wouldn't let that happen again.

"That smells like your Abuela used to make." Gramps' voice was strong today, and he was sitting up in his favorite chair, his color good and a smile on his face.

"I hope so." She laughed. "I know it's a Christmas dish, but after we took pictures of Abuela's recipes, I wanted it. Besides, I thought it would be good for company."

"You were always a good cook."

Tires crunched on the gravel outside, and moments later the retired chief of police was knocking at the door. Mack Lawson took a seat near Gramps and looked expectantly at Drea.

"Will you be joining us today?"

She smiled at him. "No, thank you. I've got to keep an eye on the pork, and I'm expecting a friend to stop by." She ignored the wink Gramps shot her way and headed to the kitchen, half hoping Danny would hurry up and arrive, and half hoping he'd never show up.

She paced the kitchen, then finally gave up and went out the back door to avoid going through the living room where Chief Lawson and Gramps were. She'd rounded the house when Danny's truck pulled into the drive. She smoothed her hands down her sides and realized she still had on Abuela's apron. She whipped it off and tossed it over the porch rail, feeling like a nervous kid. Danny ambled up the steps, and they stood inches apart, an awkward tension between them.

"Come on and sit. Chief Lawson is in with Gramps, so unless you want to get roped into that discussion, save your greetings for lunch."

Danny laughed and shook his head, sat on the porch swing, and patted the seat next to him. Drea leaned against the rail instead.

"Really?"

One word and an arched eyebrow sent shivers through her entire body as memories of last night's kiss still tingled on her lips.

"You said you wanted to talk, and I'm assuming it wasn't a euphemism for making out. Especially with my grandfather and the retired police chief just inside the door."

He smiled and looked down at the empty space next to him, then at her. "It wasn't a euphemism. Though I like that idea as well. Wouldn't be the first time Chief Lawson caught us kissin'."

Heat rose to Drea's cheeks. The chief had, in fact, caught them kissing more than once. And every time he'd had the same response—he'd shoo them on their way with the admonition to be careful.

"I was hoping we could spend some time together." Danny leaned back, his arms spread across the swing, as if inviting her company.

"We see each other all the time. I'm at the ranch more days than not."

"That's not what I meant, and you know it. Stop being obstinate."

Drea swallowed past the lump in her throat. This wasn't the boy she'd adored throughout high school, and the kiss they'd shared hadn't been the explorations of teenagers. Last night, the years had melted away, but Danny wasn't that sweet young man anymore. Last night, his kiss had been raw, fierce, demanding. And it had left her torn—wanting more and terrified of what that meant. She tucked her shaking hands into her pockets and forced a smile.

"I know what you mean, but I've been gone for ten years. This isn't my home anymore."

The words hurt to say. They echoed in her ears and pierced her soul. She no longer knew where she belonged. During school, she couldn't wait to leave small-town life behind, but the city hadn't offered happiness either. Ten years away, and all she had to show for it was a broken engagement, a horrific injury and a career in shambles.

"You're not the same person you were, Drea. None of us are. I know why you're here now and I know you'll likely leave as soon as..." He cast a glance at the door, then looked down and cleared his throat. "Well, y'know. I don't see why you and I can't spend some time together while you're here."

She took a deep breath and let it out on a sigh. "You're right. I'm not the same person. I'm not certain I'm ready to have this discussion. Can we be friends? Like we used to be, I mean before...well...before."

He leaned forward and captured her hand. His fingers stroked along her wrist, sending shivers up her spine.

"That wasn't a just-friends kiss last night." His voice was low, seductive, and made her skin prickle in anticipation. "But sure. If that's what you want."

A beeping alarm saved her from a response. "I've got to check on lunch. Will you stay?"

He nodded, and she bolted from the porch, eager to get away from the intensity of his gaze. In the safety of the kitchen, she pulled the pork from the oven, then leaned against the counter and tried not to think about Danny's lips on hers.

Her hands shook as she set a table on the back porch for lunch.

"How are things going with the insurance claim after the fire?" Mack Lawson arched his brow at Danny and scooped up another helping of the roast pork.

"They've said they need more information," Danny replied. "Robert's happy to blame Penny Elkins but claims there isn't enough evidence to arrest her. It's almost two weeks, and he figures it doesn't need any further investigation than that, so we're having an argument."

Drea looked down at her plate and bit her tongue. She didn't need to be inserting herself into a local disagreement.

"That seems silly," Chief Lawson said. "He's got someone here with the appropriate expertise." He looked at Drea.

"Oh! I'm on family leave—for Gramps. Besides, unless there's cause for me to get involved, local law enforcement has to request ATF assistance. And I don't think Robert knows what I do. I'm sure he's got it under control, and…"

"I hate to say it, because I hired that boy, but Robert isn't capable of having anything under control. As much as I love Amos Kimmel and how he's stepped up and done something remarkable with the fire crew, they are still barely trained volunteers." He leaned back and shook his head.

Gramps cleared his throat and waved a hand at Danny. "It's the busy time for you. Y'all doin' okay otherwise? You'd said something about expanding."

Drea smiled and mouthed a silent "thank you" to her grandfather for changing the subject. The insurance claim and lack of investigation were clearly sore subjects with Danny. And she couldn't blame him. Something wasn't right. There was no excuse for Robert's attitude. Whether it was Penny or not, someone had died, and they deserved more than he was giving.

"Yes, sir," Danny replied. "We're good. We've been pushing a bit over the last few years, and now we're seein' it pay off. We've got a wind farm goin' in this year, and we've already started diversifying breeding."

He leaned forward and gave a sheepish-looking smile. "Some other plans are still too early to talk about, but we're set to take Parsons Acres into the next stage and feed some jobs into this town. It's exciting, and exhausting. We've got a bigger crew this year, and Drea's been a huge help. Though I'm worried we're taking her away from you."

Gramps shook his head. "Don't worry about that. I talked her into bringing in some outside help."

Danny sat back, his eyebrows raised in question. Drea reached out and squeezed Gramps' hand. The truth was, he hated relying on his granddaughter for help bathing and using the bathroom. After a tense couple of days, they'd called the hospice coordinator.

"I was convinced I could do it all," Drea said. "But we need to do what's best for Gramps. The aides start next week."

Danny's keen blue eyes bored into Drea, as if he knew there were more to the story. She cleared her throat, searching for something, anything to change the subject. "Does anyone need a refill on their drink?"

Chief Lawson took his leave shortly after lunch, and Gramps pushed away from the table after he left. "I'm wore out. Hope you kids don't mind if I take a nap."

Drea rose to help him lie down, and when she came back out, she found Danny had already cleared the table and neatly stacked the dishes.

"I'll help carry all this in. You got a tray?"

A lock of hair fell over his eyes, just as it always had when he bent his head over his books, studying. Reflexively, she reached to push it into place, the same as she had countless times as a teenager. He caught her wrist and pulled her gently against him. His lips hovered an inch from hers and his chest rose and fell under her fingers. Without warning, he released her and stepped back with a smile.

"I'm sorry, I forgot. Just friends." He grabbed the stack of dishes and headed to the kitchen, leaving Drea cursing that Danny always respected her boundaries.

Chapter Eight

"Someone's comin' up the drive." Gramps sat on the couch, his nose buried in a book. *Nothing wrong with his hearing.* Drea pushed back the curtains as a beat-up Bronco pulled in.

"It's Robert Moore." Drea slipped out and greeted him on the porch. "Chief Moore, it's nice to see you."

"Robert is fine, Drea," he replied. "We don't stand on ceremony around here. Have you got a minute?"

If Robert came out this way to talk to her, that meant it was likely about the fire. She pointed him to a chair then sat in the porch swing and waited.

"You know all about the fire." Robert frowned down at his hat and fidgeted. "I did a report, but with there bein' a body, the insurance company wants better cause than I was able to give. They wanted to call the State Police in on this, but I convinced them we could handle it. Bruce Talbot offered to complete the report, but he's no expert."

"Robert," Drea jumped in before he could continue. "It's been three weeks since that fire. There's been rain. How much evidence do you expect there to be left?"

"Oh, I know, I know," he said. "We shoulda done this sooner, and I'll tell you what, I feel terrible about that. But who knew the insurance company would be so stubborn?"

Drea could have told him they wouldn't accept that half-assed report Danny got. She reached into the porch cooler and offered him a bottle of water, grabbed one for herself and waited for him to get on with it.

"I hate to ask it of you," he continued, "and I wouldn't if I thought there was any better way. Would you mind takin' a look? See what you can see so we can properly close this thing."

The idea of going to another fire scene made the spit dry up in her mouth. It had to kill him to ask her to step in and clean up where he had failed.

"I'm a Certified Fire Investigator with the ATF. If I put my name on any report, it's got to be done right."

His eyes narrowed, and he sat back. "I don't think I like what that implies. It sounds like you're sayin' something wasn't done right to begin with."

Drea bit her tongue. No sense antagonizing the man with the fact that nothing had been done right. "All I'm saying is, I can't do this unofficially or off the record. If I go out there and look at that scene, there will be a full report made."

A shaky smile crossed Robert's lips. "Well, I wouldn't wanna ask you to do anything improper. Just take a look. I'm sure it's like I said, either a tragic accident or that damn pyro got up to her old tricks." He fidgeted some more with his hat. "I did question Penny, and her family. The girl has an alibi. Probably made up, but there isn't anything to say otherwise."

The fact that Robert had been so quick to blame the girl but unwilling to do anything about it raised a million red flags to Drea. Maybe it *was* Penny. Then again, maybe it wasn't. She'd never know unless she got out there and looked.

"I'll check it out tomorrow." She'd have to clear her involvement with Deputy Director Wilkes first. "Can you email me all the information you've got so far?"

"I can take you out there…"

"No, thank you," Drea interrupted. "It's better if I see it on my own. I don't expect to find much. The fire crew was all over that place. Plus Grace Kimmel, and you, and Bruce, and the county guys retrieving the body. And three weeks, including some heavy rain. All the more reason to do it by the book. Having another person there adds further complication."

Drea clenched her fingers in her lap. She also sure as hell didn't want Robert as a witness if she couldn't keep it together at a fire scene. Not to mention tap-dancing around his ego and not yelling at him for stomping all over whatever evidence might still be there.

Robert let out a long breath. "I don't like it. You've got your protocol, but you should at least have one of the fire crew with you. I want to be done with this sorry business. I'm sure the Parsons would prefer the insurance company pay up as well."

She was quite sure the Parsons didn't care about the insurance so much as the fact that they couldn't clean up until it was settled. A burned-out building was an attractive nuisance, leaving them open to more problems. "Do you want me to do this, or not?"

"Fine." Robert rose and crammed his hat on his head. "You give my regards to your gran'daddy. Call me as soon as you've got a report ready."

She watched him heave his bulk behind the wheel of his truck and waited for him to back out of the drive before she went upstairs to call Wilkes.

* * * *

Drea pulled down the gravel access road, thanking the powers that be for a bright sunny day. After Robert had left yesterday, she'd called her boss and gotten the go-ahead. She'd barely slept, worried about coming to a fire scene. Now, she was keyed up, her eyes darting, taking in every detail in hyper focus. The road ended in front of a pair of old stone cottages flanking a wide path that led to a handful of smaller wood and stone buildings.

Drea slipped on a disposable coverall and a pair of old rubber boots and pulled her kit from the back of her car, thankful she'd kept it there even though she wasn't active in the field. She remembered passing the little cottages while on rides with Danny. They didn't look any different today. She and Danny had stopped and kissed inside the bigger stone ones a time or three. Drea looked down the narrow path and swallowed hard. *Think clinically. It's just a black spot in the dirt. The fire is long since out.*

Even after the rains, the smell of burnt wood hung in the air. Acrid and unpleasant. Drea closed her eyes and heard the roar and crackle of flames, smelled burning drywall.

No! I can do this.

She took a deep breath, slowly letting it out, the way her psychiatrist had taught her to handle impending panic attacks. She focused on the building, the mud around it, the fire damaged tree nearby. The breathing was supposed to relax and calm her, but Drea never found that useful. Instead, she used the conscious breathing to narrow her focus, to block out anything but what she needed to see. After another deep breath, she was ready.

She walked around the building taking photos from every angle. The heavy rains had not obliterated the mess of boot prints on the ground. She pulled up the report on her phone and skimmed through the details.

Brian had smelled the smoke and called the fire crew and the police. The cottage had been fully engulfed, and they'd saturated the nearby buildings and let this one burn itself out. By the time Danny made it out to the site, there was nothing but a smoldering pile. It hadn't rained the day of the fire, but there had been rain earlier that week, and everything had still been wet. Grace Kimmel had been taking pictures and found evidence of the body. Plus, all the rain this week. There had been too many vehicles and people in and out to hope for any tracks or footprint evidence.

Drea stepped closer to the building remains. The body had been found along the back wall. The cottages had wood floors, with a pad of packed dirt or stone slab for a coal stove — though the stoves were long gone. Danny said some cottages had poured concrete instead of stone.

"Okay," she whispered. "Let's do this. Talk to me." She pulled on gloves and a face mask and got to work.

The crew had made an even bigger mess as they moved the body, apparently tossing everything this way and that. For the next two hours, Drea picked through the debris of the building, piece by piece, searching for the ignition point. She cleared a pile of wet ash and burned bits and hissed in a breath.

That wasn't a camp stove.

The concrete pad was damaged, and not from age. A shallow depression marred the center, surrounded by spalling and a blue-green discoloration. Spattered burn marks made a clear pattern around the divot. She sifted through the nearby ashes and turned up tiny blobs of what looked like molten metal.

She tried to put the pieces together with what she knew of Penny. The girl self-harmed. Not the same as pyromania. Penny didn't seem to like setting fires. She cut or burned herself. The fire was incidental. Plus, she didn't drive. Penny couldn't make it back on her own.

Drea stopped herself. She was overthinking. The scene would speak for itself, tell its story. If she let it.

She sat back on her heels. Could have been a firebug. Someone who lost control of their improvised incendiary device. But this wasn't a candle, or a lantern, or a camp stove gone awry.

She turned over more debris. *That's where the body was.* The floor next to the pad wasn't burned to a cinder, which meant that gal hadn't moved while the fire raged. Not one bit. She was unconscious. Maybe drugged.

Drea took pictures and collected samples. Not that there would be much to analyze after so long in the elements, but it was worth a shot.

She'd labeled everything and packed it all into her kit when another vehicle stopped behind hers. Robert came trudging up the path.

"Please stop there," she called out. "I'm finishing up here and I don't want to have to document any more footprints. You're welcome to tramp around once I'm done."

She took a last set of images, documenting what she had moved, stuffed the camera into her bag, and turned to Robert, who stood frozen in place and looking none too happy.

"Thank you," she said as she shouldered her bag. "I've got to document how the scene looked when I arrived and what it looked like when I left. And catalog any changes. You coming in would add to my workload."

"I don't like that you came out here by yourself." Robert's voice held a petulant tone.

She circled around him and tossed her kit into her car. "Why? We had this conversation. It's not like this is an active scene, or you're worried about someone hanging around to hurt people."

His face went from pink to red, and he pressed his lips into a hard line. "This is a crime scene, and you shouldn't be out here unescorted. You're not an officer of the law."

"Oh, so now it's not some tragic accident," she replied. "And you're wrong on that last point."

"You're an arson investigator," he retorted. "That's just a firefighter with some training."

Drea chuckled. "Wrong again. I'm an ATF Special Agent—which means not only am I an officer of the law, but I'm also a federal officer of the law. The fire investigator part? That's extra. Wanna see my badge?"

She nearly laughed at the comical expression on his face. Gramps was proud of her, and he talked to people all the time, but most of them assumed it was a grandpa bragging on his granddaughter. Most thought she was a firefighter, or a glorified paper pusher. A few probably had antiquated ideas of what a fire investigator did.

Robert shut his mouth and stammered something, then cleared his throat. "Even so, someone should have been here with you."

"You asked me to do this, and I told you I'd prefer to do it alone. No offense, but there's already been enough of a mess through here, and it's faster and easier if I don't have to explain what I'm doing every step of the way or worry about documenting someone else's presence. I'm sorry if you have a problem with that. What can I do for you?"

She was pushing his buttons and she knew it, but based on what she'd seen, this wasn't a camp stove mishap. Or any of Robert's other theories.

"Well… Fine. Do you have a report?"

"I have pictures. And evidence. And what I saw and documented. But no, it's not written down yet, and won't be until I can get home, shower, and sit at my computer for a few minutes."

"Why don't you come into the station and do it now?"

"Because I'm filthy. Even with the coverall and gloves, I reek of soot. This sat around for three weeks, it can wait three more hours."

He started sputtering as Drea pulled off her boots and the coverall, then tossed the disposable garment into a bag and labeled it as well. Just in case.

"You need to do that on an official computer… You can't just…"

"Let's stop this dance. Once again, you asked me out here." She turned to him and placed her hands on her hips. "When it comes to me working a scene, I report to my superior officer at the ATF, and I coordinate with the local police. You have no jurisdiction over my behavior or reporting methods. I am sorry you are clearly bothered by something here, but frankly, that is not my problem. If you would like to file a formal complaint, I will give you the name and number of my chief in DC and you can take it up with him."

Robert's face blanched as he drew himself up and mirrored her hands on the hips pose. "This is not the city, Drea. We don't do things the same here, and you'd best understand that if you plan to hang around. Otherwise, you're asking for bad things to happen."

Drea smiled, slammed the hatch closed and opened the driver's door. She turned back to Robert and batted her eyes at him. "I haven't been away so long that I don't recognize a threat when I hear one. But I know you wouldn't be foolish enough to threaten a federal agent, now would you? You have a nice day."

She'd regret goading him. Eventually. But not yet. For the moment, she was too busy fuming over Robert's attitude, and congratulating herself for keeping it together on a scene.

Chapter Nine

Danny slipped into a chair, squinting in the bright morning sun that filled the kitchen. His mother was already at work, laying out the makings of the day's lunches. A cup of coffee landed in front of him, and he looked up into Drea's dazzling green eyes. He still wasn't used to seeing her around nearly every day, but he liked it. Too much. She plopped down opposite him with a cup of coffee of her own, her head tipped back and her eyes closed.

Ma joined them at the table. "Robert came by yesterday afternoon in a pissy mood. Said you looked at the burned cottage. How'd that go?"

Drea sipped coffee. "It's been too long to tell much. I sent Robert the report, and I copied it to the medical examiner. I also sent a copy directly to the insurance company."

Danny leaned forward and tapped her arm. "Why send it to the insurance company? Won't the police do that?"

Her lips pursed, and he could almost see the gears turning in her head. All traces of the small-town girl he'd known disappeared behind a calculating, professional expression that gave away nothing, and that made him nervous.

"They probably will," Drea replied. "It's not uncommon for an investigator to submit the report independently. I figured you wanted it done quickly."

She wasn't saying something. Her guarded expression and careful tone said what her words didn't.

"Robert was mouthing off about you, ah...how did he say it...puttin' on airs, I believe." Annette winked. "Seems you went all high and mighty city girl on him."

Drea looked down into her coffee cup and mumbled something.

"What was that?" Danny poked her arm again.

Her head came up, and her eyes bored into his. "Don't you start." She looked back down into her cup. "I may have been a little brusque, yes. I can't say he didn't deserve it."

Danny arched an eyebrow at her and waited. Drea cracked a small smile and told them the story, though it was clear she was still leaving out details. When she was done, his mother threw her head back and laughed.

"Oh, I'd like to have seen that." She stopped when Danny gaped at her. "You have to admit, that boy's needed someone to smack a little humility into him since he first put on a uniform." She turned to Drea and refilled her coffee cup. "You ignore Robert and don't feel one mite of regret for giving him what for. Not one. At the very least, someone oughta figure out who that poor soul was and notify their family."

Danny rose and rested a hand on Drea's shoulder, the urge to protect her, to keep her safe was almost overwhelming, and wouldn't likely be welcome. He leaned down to meet her eyes. "Be careful about stirring shit."

"Daniel Parsons!" His mother's sharp rebuke echoed in the kitchen, and Danny smiled.

"Pardon my language." He looked back at Drea. "Catch me at lunch."

"What, for more of this pep talk?" Drea's eyes narrowed, and her chin lifted. That damn stubborn look. He knew better than to tell her what to do.

"I'm sorry. I was bein'…ungentleman-like. Can we talk at lunch?"

Drea shook her head. "Come over tonight after dinner."

"Okay." He didn't have time to dig into her reasons. While he couldn't blame Drea for getting pissy with Robert, that was a mess nobody needed. Robert had a petty streak about a mile wide. He was already useless, but if he felt he'd been insulted, his pettiness could turn vindictive, and Drea had set herself up as a perfect target. Still, Danny wanted to know what she'd found.

"Would you send me a copy of that report?" He waited for her to nod, then grabbed his hat, kissed his mother's cheek, and smiled at Drea. "See you tonight."

* * * *

Danny was exhausted after a long day at the ranch, but the idea of seeing Drea brought a smile to his lips. Even if the main reason for this visit was less than pleasant. He pulled up to the DeJarnet home and sat in his truck, staring down at the email from Drea, his eyes settling on the bottom line. Cause of fire — inconclusive. Movement on the porch caught his eye — Drea closed the front door and waved him over.

She put a finger to her lips as he reached the steps and beckoned him to follow, then she took off around the back of the house. He had a moment to admire the sway of her backside as she led him to the screened rear porch and pointed at a couple of chairs.

"Gramps had a hard day and he's resting, watching a little TV. I don't want to disturb him. I rarely use the front door anymore. I come and go through the kitchen. So, what can I tell you?" She tucked her feet under her legs and smiled at him.

Danny's breath caught. She was so beautiful. They'd spent hours studying or hanging out on this back porch, her curled up in a chair, just as she was now. He'd been smitten with her then, never able to find the right words to tell her how amazing she was. He didn't want to be talking about fires, and insurance reports. He wanted to pull her into his lap, wrap her in his arms and drown in her kisses.

He cleared his throat and pushed those thoughts aside. Work first. "I'm not sure what to make of this report. What are you not telling me? And why wouldn't you say any of this earlier, or talk at lunch?"

"This morning," she said, "we all had work to do — this wasn't a conversation to get into then. And it's definitely not a conversation to have with anyone other than you or your mother." She leaned forward. "Modern fire investigation isn't what it used to be. In the past, it was mostly guesswork based more on assumptions than science. That's all changed. The rest of the world hasn't caught up yet."

"Uh-huh. And this means?"

"That report says there's not enough evidence to determine cause, but there is no evidence of fraud. Basically, a bunch of long-winded, official language that says there's no fault on the part of the policy holder, and no attempt at deception." She took a deep breath before she continued. "Unfortunately, there was evidence that the fire didn't happen naturally, like lightning or via a traceable cause like faulty wiring. Which means..."

"The insurance company will likely deny the claim."

Drea nodded. "I'm sorry. You can appeal on a denial."

"I don't care about the settlement. I want to be able to clean things up. Why are you being evasive?"

She looked away and closed her eyes as if listening to some internal voice. She took a minute before she turned back to him and responded. "There was evidence of a possible incendiary device. Note I said possible? That could be someone goofing around and lost control, or it could mean arson."

Her words sank in slowly, and his eyes widened. *Arson.* It didn't make sense. It was an old cottage on the far side of the property that'd probably be torn down when they started building for the camp. But only a handful of people knew of those plans. Drea reached out and squeezed his hand, her touch electric on his skin, making it hard to concentrate on her words.

"Could also be some idiot decided to use magnesium, or a piece of an old Volkswagen engine to start the fire. I'm just a consultant on this and report my findings to the controlling agency. I could pull jurisdiction, but that starts a whole chain of events and pissing contests."

She gave him a cockeyed grin and continued. "I did send samples to the lab, and recommended a follow-up once the results are in. I also suggested a second autopsy, with a full tox panel. Whether that gets done or not is another story."

Drea bit her lip and a brief look of frustration crossed her face.

"Look," she said, "the damage to the concrete alone is suspicious. The extent of damage to the body, and the fact that it looked like the victim didn't budge? There are too many things that don't add up."

"Yeah, I get it. Not enough data to come up with a solid answer. And you don't think it was Penny?"

Drea shrugged. "Dunno. You said she was a self-harmer, not that she liked to play with matches. There are behavior patterns to a true pyromaniac. Arson's a different story. If I were investigating this, I wouldn't rule her out yet."

"I guess I understand that. Why arson?"

The corner of her mouth twitched up in a smile that didn't look cheerful. "Fires like that happen one of two ways — somebody doing something stupid and it gets out of hand, or somebody doing something intentional. If I'd gotten in there sooner, maybe I could have better answers. Arson is not well understood, and cases are rarely solved. Not all arsonists are firebugs, and not all firebugs are arsonists. Setting fires is a behavior. Pyromania is a psychiatric disorder."

The thought of an arsonist chilled him. The look on her face when she talked about it though...that was a different thing. All the passion and drive of her teenage self, tempered with age and experience. Like kissing her at Oak Bridge. Kissing the grown-up Drea was so much better than his memories of their explorations as teenagers. And he wanted more. To hell with the 'just friends' promise.

"Okay." He nodded. "Change of subject."

She raised her eyebrows at him.

"I'd like to take you to dinner tomorrow night, and I don't mean at Oak Bridge or any other place in town."

She tipped her head and gave him a side-eyed look that slowly changed into a tentative smile. "Uh-huh. This sounds suspiciously like a date."

"That's the idea, yeah." He'd never been this nervous asking a girl out. Maybe the first time he'd kissed Drea. Maybe. But never since.

She closed her eyes, her chest rose and fell on a long, slow breath. "Okay. It's been a busy week. The downtime sounds nice."

He resisted the urge to break into a huge smile. Instead, he slid forward on the chair, reaching out to capture her face in his hands. "Life is going to stay busy for a while yet, but I'll have more time after we get through the spring rush."

He leaned in and kissed her, barely brushing his lips against hers. Her lips parted, allowing him access. He tangled his fingers into her thick hair, and the scent of jasmine enveloped him. She tasted of honey and coffee, and he never wanted to stop.

She pulled back, abruptly breaking contact. "Just friends, huh?" Her words were a rebuke, but she was smiling.

"I guess I lied." Danny stood and pulled her up and into his arms. Her body fit against his like it was made to be there. *Still.* He'd been a rangy teen back then, and Drea as thin as a wisp. Now, his hands slid over firm muscles and lush curves. And he liked it.

"I'd call it more of a change of mind than an outright lie." Drea's words were soft, her breath a caress along his neck. Her hands slid up his back.

If he didn't leave now, he'd be spending the night in her bed. If she'd have him. As sweet as her kisses were, something had her nervous. Her fingers twitched on his back, and her entire body was tense.

He took a deep breath. This wasn't the time or place for what he wanted — she wasn't ready, her grandfather was in the living room and there was a possible arsonist running around town. That last thought was a dash of cold water. He loosened his grip and looked down into those stunning eyes.

"See you tomorrow night?"

She chuckled. "I'll see you before that at the ranch, but yeah."

He kissed her again, lightly, then left before the temptation to stay got any stronger. He had to adjust himself before he climbed into his truck. He couldn't remember the last time he'd wanted a woman so badly. Well, yes, he could. It was after a date with Drea. Parked on the side of the road, stealing kisses before he had to take her home.

Chapter Ten

Drea wiped her hands on a dish towel and checked in with Trish, the day shift home health aide.

"He's up surfing the internet," Trish said. "He had a good day. Jimmy is coming in an hour, so you'll see him before you go out."

"Thank you. I'll get dinner in the oven before I shower."

Drea stuck her head into the living room to check on Gramps. He was propped up on the couch, laptop in front of him. She kissed his forehead and went into the kitchen to start dinner.

Ten minutes later, she had *pastelón* in the oven, and Wilma's cheery hello carried in through the back door. She hugged Drea, then said hi to Trish and greeted Gramps.

"It's good to see you, Wilma." Gramps raised his head from behind the computer screen. "What's the occasion?"

She held up a tote bag. "Rescue mission for your granddaughter. Seems she's got a date tonight and nothin' to wear."

Gramps fixed Drea with a look that carried her back to her high school days and the times she'd gone out with Danny. "He comin' to pick you up?" That uncompromising tone said he'd damn well better be.

"Gramps..."

"If you're goin' out with Danny, he'll be comin' to get you and he'll come in to say hello as well. He wouldn't do less."

Drea rolled her eyes and leaned down to kiss his cheek.

"It's about time you went out with that boy again." Gramps looked back to the computer screen.

"Amen to that," Wilma chimed in.

"Oh, good grief!" Drea grabbed Wilma's arm and dragged her upstairs. "I'm sorry for calling you like this. I tried to find something in town, but there's nothing."

Wilma tossed the bag onto the bed and shushed her. "Friends take care of each other. Besides, we're still close to the same size."

She upended the bag full of clothes onto the bed. "I stuck with classic, nothing too flashy. And mostly black so it's easier to mix and match. These" — she waved at the pile of clothes—"are for you to keep. They're practically new, and they'll look better on your figure. I've gained a few pounds, and honestly, I've got way too many clothes sitting unworn in my closet. If you like them, you'll take them. End of story. Now, let's play dress up."

Wilma held up a slinky halter top and Drea cringed. "I need sleeves."

"How bad are the burns?" Wilma's unflinching look startled Drea and she sat abruptly on the bed. "I know you were in a fire," Wilma said. "And I know you were in the burn ICU. You don't have to tell me if you don't want to. But should I take out the short sleeve shirts as well?"

Her matter-of-fact tone made it easier. Even thinking about it was less painful than it once was.

"My back," Drea replied, "from my waist to my shoulder on the left. A little bit on top of my left shoulder and upper arm. It's not as bad as it was and not as good as it will be, but some of the scars will never go away."

The first time she'd seen her healing back, she'd cried. The puckered and peeling skin had terrified her. After months of skin grafts, silicone bandages, micro needling and other treatments, the worst of the scarring had lessened. The skin texture was still not right, and the coloration was definitely wrong. But she could look in the mirror now and not cry.

Wilma rifled through the clothes and tossed a few items onto the floor. The room was starting to look like it had when they'd had sleepovers as teens. Clothes strewn everywhere. The only thing missing was CeeCee's pompoms.

"I think I have just the thing in here. Sexy, a little revealing..." She looked Drea up and down. "Can you go without a bra?"

"What?" Drea sputtered. "Why would I...? Oh. No. Uh-huh. I don't know how I'm feeling about going out with him tonight. I don't think... I mean isn't that..."

Wilma shrugged. "A confident and beautiful woman dressing in a way that makes her feel good. At least try this on." She held up a scrap of silky black fabric.

Drea snatched the top and went into the bathroom. Talking about her scars was one thing. Stripping down in front of Wilma was something completely different.

"What brought you back here?" Drea called through the half-open door.

There was a long pause before Wilma answered. "I wanted to be the person I needed when I lived here."

Drea poked her head through the door. "I think maybe that's why I'm surprised you came back. You always seemed like a square peg in a round hole here."

Wilma sighed and leaned back on the bed. "And I had a good life. Good friends. My parents were great. But I didn't know myself. Not until college. After a few uncomfortable life lessons, I realized what I wanted to do was make a difference. What better place to do it?"

Drea slipped the top over her head and pulled on the slim-fitting cropped pants Wilma handed her. The top left her right shoulder exposed and draped beautifully down her left arm.

"That," Wilma said as Drea emerged from the bathroom, "looks fabulous."

It felt good. Drea wore practical, heavy-duty clothes for work, so she'd always liked dressing up. Looking feminine. She'd lost some of that after the fire. She lived in jeans and soft tees and sweaters.

"You don't think it's too much? Or sends the wrong message?" Drea cast a nervous glance at Wilma.

The other woman stood back and eyed her up and down. "I'd say this is just the right message."

"Which is what?" Drea laughed, but she had to admit, the outfit was flattering.

"Come hither but be careful." Wilma gestured for her to spin around and gave a low whistle when she did. "Yeah. That works."

Wilma's smile, her laugh, her uplifting attitude were infectious. Drea hadn't realized how much she'd missed their friendship. Her closest female friend was Gabe Mattix, but it wasn't the same. Drea leaned down and hugged Wilma.

"Thank you," Drea whispered. "For everything."

"Yeah, I've missed you, too." Wilma blinked away a tear and checked her watch. "You need to get showered. Promise me—makeup, nice hair. Be girly. You're on a date with a hot man. Enjoy it."

Drea rolled her eyes. She may have been so nervous she felt like tiny creatures were using her stomach as a trampoline, but she was also looking forward to the time with Danny. She waved at Wilma as she pulled out of the drive then headed for the shower.

Drea had finished putting on makeup and gone downstairs when Danny pulled up. She felt like a kid again, instantly transported back to high school and their stolen kisses on the back porch. His eyes went wide when she stepped out to meet him. He wrapped his arms around her waist and bent his head to kiss her lightly. She breathed in his clean, spicy scent and slid out of his arms before he could kiss her again. Kissing Danny made her knees go weak, not a good thing with Gramps in the other room.

"Is Paul up for a hello? I should at least pop my head in, or he'll think I wasn't raised right. And if Ma hears tell of that, she'll have my hide." The deep rumble of his voice sent pleasant shivers up her neck.

Drea pointed him toward the living room, and he talked with Gramps for a few minutes, then Drea went and kissed Gramps' cheek and said her good nights. He'd be sound asleep by the time she got home.

Danny opened the truck door for her, and she had the opportunity to enjoy the view. Around the ranch, he favored worn jeans and loose shirts. Tonight, he was in black jeans that hugged his body, and a crisp gray dress shirt that made his shoulders seem a mile wide.

"Where are we going?"

"I thought we'd do something special," he replied. "There's a nice place down in Charleston. The food's good, and I figured you might prefer something away from the local gossips."

He reached over and pulled her hand into his lap. The familiar gesture set Drea's pulse pounding. All the time they'd spent in his old truck, her sitting in the middle seat, hand curled against his thigh, her head on his shoulder. The memory brought a chuckle.

"Somethin' funny?" His fingers twined with hers.

"I can't lean on your shoulder like I used to."

Danny's lips curled into a smile. "Remind me my next truck needs a bench seat instead of buckets."

This felt good. Too good. She had a life to rebuild, a life she'd built on her own, without him. Still, being with Danny was... She glanced over at him. One hand on the steering wheel, corded muscles standing out on his forearm. The other hand curled around hers, resting on his thigh, rock hard from riding and working the ranch. Being with Danny was comfortable and exhilarating at the same time. Familiar and yet frightening.

His fingers squeezed on hers. Drea took a deep breath and willed herself to relax.

"No talk of fires or Gramps tonight," Drea said. "I don't care what we talk about, but not those subjects. Deal?"

He gave her fingers another squeeze. "Deal."

Over dinner, he told her more about the wind farm, and how it would generate not just revenue for Parsons Acres but needed jobs for the community. They carefully avoided any mention of the forbidden topics. Drea leaned back as the server brought dessert.

"Did you ever hear from Jake again?" she asked. "Your momma doesn't talk about your brother."

Danny paused, his fork hovering over the piece of chocolate cake. His mouth twisted into a grimace, and he set the fork down.

"Jake joined the Navy. Ma managed to get a message to him when Daddy took ill." Danny's voice was soft, his eyes focused on the tablecloth. "I don't know what was said, but Ma forgave him. I'm still workin' on it. The asshole didn't come home for Daddy's funeral." He looked up at Drea. There was no pain or anger in his eyes, just indifference, which seemed worse. "He settled in Norfolk. Went to college and law school. I don't know what was so terrible about his life that he had to do it like that. I used to care."

That last sounded like a lie. Something he told himself to make Jake's leaving, and continued silence, easier to bear.

"What about you?" he asked. "You were engaged. What happened?"

Drea nearly choked on her bite of cake. "Uhhh... Not an uncommon story. I found out shortly before the wedding that he wasn't the man I thought he was. And we broke up."

That was as much as she was willing to share on that topic. He didn't need to know that she'd found Frank in bed with another woman, nor did he need to know everything that came after.

"You should try the cake," she said. "It's delicious."

"Point taken." Danny laughed and scooped up a forkful of cake.

After dinner, back at his truck, Danny opened her door but stopped her before she could climb in.

His arms came around her waist and he pulled her against his body. His chest was like a brick wall beneath her fingers. He felt so good, so right. His hands slid up her back, and she jumped as his fingers traced her spine through the thin silk, grazing the edge of her scars, making her stiffen in fear. His body tensed, and he hissed in a sharp breath.

"You're not wearing..." His words whispered rough and low in her ear, and Drea shivered, relieved his response was to her lack of bra, not the puckered skin under her blouse.

She tipped her head back and reached up on tiptoes to kiss him. A soft moan escaped his lips as her mouth opened for him. His hands gripped her hips, then slid down her thighs and lifted. She wrapped her legs around his waist, and he pressed her against his truck, his body pinning her in place.

Drea gasped as his lips left hers and his teeth fastened on her earlobe. She pressed her hands against his shoulders and arched into him. A deep growl rumbled against her neck as he ground his hips into her.

"God, I want you." His breath rustled through her hair, and his hands wrapped around her hips, holding her close. Close enough to feel the hardness beneath his jeans. Drea's eyes snapped open, and she swallowed hard.

Sex. That meant getting naked. Being seen. Letting him touch. Her chest tightened, and her stomach heaved at the thought. Memories of Frank's face when he saw her back swam in her mind. His cruel words when he'd left — *"No one wants to look at that, touch that."*

"Put me down, please," she whispered. A confused look passed over Danny's features, but he let her slide gently down his body. He stepped back a bit, still keeping his hands lightly on her hips.

"Are you okay?"

Her breath came in shallow, grating gasps and the world around her went gray. *Not now. Please. Not now.*

The fire roared and crackled as it tore through the ceiling. Bits of flaming debris fell around her as she crawled along the floor, staying where the air was more breathable. The fire escape was ten feet ahead. She was almost there. Something heavy landed on her, pushing her down. Heat and pain flared. More burning debris landed in front of her. She pushed to her hands and knees and forced herself forward.

Pain seared, but there was no place to stop and roll. No way to put out the flames. She had to make it to the fire escape. Shattered glass dug into her skin as she dragged herself through the window. She couldn't see anything. She blinked, trying to adjust to the darkness outside. Trying to blink away the burning and the smoke. She rolled, praying she stayed on the fire escape and didn't fall off the edge. Cold wet metal hissed, and she screamed.

"Drea!"

She looked up at Danny. His handsome features were creased with concern. He guided her to the passenger seat then leaned down in front of her. His hands rested on her knees.

"You wanna tell me what's going on?"

"I'm sorry," she whispered.

He kissed her gently. "Let's go somewhere we can talk."

She wasn't sure she wanted to do that either. But Danny deserved some explanation. His hands still rested on her knees. His forehead pressed against hers. Protective, comforting.

"Okay," she whispered.

He drove past the main house and pulled up at his cottage. Drea had stayed silent the whole trip back. He didn't know what the hell had just happened, or where she'd gone in her head, but he had every intention of finding out.

She gave him a funny look when she realized they were at his place, but she didn't argue and followed him inside. She sat on the couch, he took up a spot on the coffee table, his knees touching hers. Something had hurt her, and bad. If the clenched fingers and mouth screwed up like she was trying not to cry hadn't given it away, the haunted, terrified look in her eyes would have. And the way she'd curled inward, as if trying to escape something, someone. After a few minutes of silence, she looked at him, her green eyes large and filled with pain.

"I'm sorry," she whispered again. "I don't know where to begin."

"You could start with where you went back there."

Drea chuckled, but it wasn't a humorous sound. It was cold and bitter.

"I was in an apartment fire last year. Not a work thing. It was the building where I lived. Sometimes I have…nightmares…flashbacks."

Paul had said something about an accident. He'd gone to stay with her for several weeks. Drea took a deep breath and continued.

"I was burned." The words came out in short bursts with no emotion. "Took a long time to recover, but I still have scars. Everything is better than it used to be.

But it's left me with some…issues. Intimacy issues, to use my psychiatrist's term."

"How bad was it?"

She grimaced and pulled away from him.

"I don't… I can't…my back was…is… I haven't…" She buried her face in her hands. "I'm scared." The depth of pain in her tone wrenched at Danny's soul.

"What do you mean, scared?" He leaned forward and caught her wrists, gently cradling her hands in his.

She raised her face, eyes hollow and wide. "I…" Her lips compressed into a tight line and her chin trembled, and she closed her eyes before trying again. "I'm afraid of everything. Of nothing. Of things I can't name and don't understand. But most of all, I'm terrified that I'll never…that I won't be able to… Uhhh…y'know…get naked with someone."

Realization hit him like a punch to the gut. She'd been engaged, about to get married. The local paper had run the announcement. "Your ex had a problem with the scars."

She nodded, her eyes still screwed shut as if she were afraid of what she might see. In that moment, Danny would have been all too happy to throttle the guy. "Drea, please look at me."

Her eyes opened slowly. Confused. Frightened. Hurting. But no tears.

"It's okay." He kissed her forehead gently. "I'm not your ex. Scars aren't going to bother me. Neither will nightmares or flashbacks." He smiled and shrugged. "I'll never push for anything you're not ready for. That hasn't changed, and it never will. But I can't promise there won't be any more kisses, unless you tell me no."

Her smile started small, lifting at the corners of her lips. The smile spread, growing, until she leaned back on the couch laughing. "I think you're a better kisser now than you were in high school."

"You weren't complaining at the time," he replied, laughing. "It's early still. What d'ya say we curl up and watch a movie?" An unmistakable ache pulsed and throbbed, reminding him that it had been a while. And unless he was very wrong, that wasn't going to change tonight.

"Okay." She smiled back at him, looking much the same way she had the day he'd first kissed her that summer so long ago. "I'd like that."

She scooted over on the couch and needed no encouragement to lean into him once he'd sat down. She tucked herself up against his side, and his heartbeat sped to double time. She felt so right, like she belonged there. He kissed the top of her head. His breath caught in his throat when she tipped her head and kissed him back.

"I'm not a prude," she said. "I'm just…"

"Scared. I get it." Danny chuckled. "And prude is never a word I'd associate with you. Cautious? Yes. Prude? No."

* * * *

Drea stifled a yawn while waiting for Gramps' prescription to be filled. She and Danny had watched movies late into the night, and he'd returned her home after two in the morning. True to his word, there had been more kisses. Lots more kisses. But he'd stopped there, leaving Drea in a mix of relief and desire.

"Here are your prescriptions, ma'am." The pharmacist's voice was a welcome interruption. Drea collected the meds and left — her face hot at the memories of Danny's mouth on hers.

"Drea, yoo-hoo!"

CeeCee slid out of a silver BMW, waving at her. Drea smiled and waved, though Wilma's warning about CeeCee's mean streak echoed in the back of her mind.

"I'm sorry about your granddaddy," CeeCee said. "What an awful reason to have to come back home. Poor you. You should get out more often."

Her sugary tones set Drea's teeth on edge. "It's tough getting out much." The excuse sounded lame, and Drea kicked herself for not coming up with something snappier.

"People will think you're antisocial," CeeCee cooed. "Everyone goes to Oak Bridge on weekends. Oh, that's right. You were there a while back. You coming out again soon, or is that place too backwater for you after living in DC?"

Drea shook her head. "I don't know. Life's a bit busy with Gramps."

"You've been helping out at Parsons Acres, too. This is a small town. Everyone knows everyone's business. Are you planning to move back home? I don't recommend it. I thought I could, but..." CeeCee heaved a theatrical sigh and linked her arm through Drea's. "Once you've been in the big city, this small-town life just ain't the same."

Drea extricated herself from CeeCee's grasp. The other woman's clinging and overly friendly tone set off alarm bells.

"I'm here to take care of Gramps," Drea replied, wishing CeeCee would get to her point.

"You and Danny started going out again," CeeCee continued. "Why are you bothering? He's not going anywhere. He just a plaything while you're here?"

Drea forced a wide smile and batted her eyes innocently. "You'll have to explain that one. I'm afraid I don't understand what you mean."

"You thinkin' maybe if you put out this time, things'll be different?" CeeCee's voice had lost all its charm. Her words were pure venom. "You never wanted to stay here back then and you sure as hell don't belong here now. I wouldn't be here if I had a choice. Why don't you pack your granddaddy off to a home like everyone figured you would?"

CeeCee didn't wait for a response. She turned and stomped off toward the pharmacy entrance. Drea swallowed the huge lump in her throat. Those words hit too close to home. She'd considered doing that — for about half a second. But she'd considered a lot of things. Wilma was right, the catty streak CeeCee had developed in high school had blossomed and grown.

Drea shook herself and headed to Wilma's, desperately in need of someone to talk to. Once safely inside, everything came pouring out in a rush. Watching her grandfather slowly dying, her fears with Danny, even CeeCee's pettiness. She choked on a sob and blew her nose. Wilma sat back and waited for Drea's tears to trickle down to occasional hiccups.

"There's more you haven't said." Wilma's voice was softer than she'd ever heard it.

Drea looked up at her friend. Behind the cat-eye glasses, the other woman's eyes were gentle and kind.

"Yeah. It's not something I've talked about with many people." Drea took a deep breath and blew it out. "I found my fiancé in bed with another woman two weeks before we were to marry. I moved out, called off the wedding. A few weeks later, we were trying to patch things up, but I was still in my own place. That's when the fire happened. At my apartment." Drea offered a shaky smile and took a shuddering breath. "I'd just gotten out of the hospital when he left me. He was repulsed by the burns. He couldn't stand to look at me anymore. Didn't want to touch me." She expected saying those words out loud to hurt. The only other person she'd told about that conversation was her counselor, and the half confession to Danny last night. She was surprised when she didn't feel pain. Instead, she felt numb.

"The first time I went back to the field after medical leave, I freaked. So, I got transferred to teaching. I was supposed to get final clearance to go back to field work when I got the call about Gramps."

Wilma let out a long sigh and chuckled. "Something tells me you're on the fence about going back."

Drea bit her lip. "No…yes…hell. I don't know. I want to get back to work. To the work I signed on to do. I want to catch the bad guys. That's why I pursued this career. But… If I get stressed, or smell fire, or…" She flopped back in the seat. "Gah!"

Wilma's fingers were cool and comforting on Drea's hand. "Let's see what I can whip up for dinner, and we'll crack a bottle of something and talk."

Drea shook her head. "I'd love to hang out, but can we go to Gramps' place? Jimmy gets off at seven, and we don't have evening help on Saturdays. I've got a bottle of riesling."

"Sounds perfect," Wilma said.

Drea rose and hugged her friend. "Think I'll take it easy on the drinking, though. Danny and I are going on a trail ride tomorrow, and I can't imagine being hungover on horseback."

Chapter Eleven

"This is Sheba," Danny said, handing the reins of a gorgeous bay to Drea. "Don't let her petite size fool you. She's a former racehorse, now retired, and she's given us two beautiful foals. You remember how to ride?"

Drea glared over the saddle at Danny, but he grinned back and winked. She slipped a foot into the stirrup, grabbed the pommel and swung up with ease. *Just like riding a bike. Thank heavens I didn't fall on my face.* She looked down at Danny and stuck her tongue out.

"It's been a long time," she said, "but I remember I used to kick your butt pole bending and barrel racing during the gymkhana every year."

He threw back his head and laughed. "You're smaller and lighter. You were riding that itty-bitty paint that used to belong to Mack Lawson's daughter and that horse could stop on a dime and give you nine cents change." He slung himself into the saddle. "Plus, you were a damn good rider with a serious competitive streak. One of many things I always liked about you."

A thrill went through her at his words, and Drea tamped it down, determined to keep things light between them. He led the way out of the barn, then along a narrow road up a grassy hillside before striking off on a trail that cut through the trees. The cool morning air smelled green and rich. Wind rustled the leaves into a whispering chorus. Ahead of her, Danny's broad shoulders rocked with the movement of his horse. His T-shirt stretched tight across his back, the short sleeves revealed deeply tanned, well-muscled arms.

She shifted in the saddle, loosening up, sinking into a more comfortable seat. It had been ten years since she'd ridden. The creak of the leather, the rhythmic clop of hooves on the path and the smell — sweet, grassy, musky, dusty horse smell. She'd forgotten all those things. Forgotten the feel of the reins in her hand, the chuff of the horse's breath. She ran her free hand along Sheba's neck and the mare twitched her ears toward Drea and gave a short nicker.

They crossed a stream and continued uphill until they reached a clearing. Drea exited the trees into the sunshine and gasped at the view. A broad meadow stretched at least one hundred yards, bright green with spring grass. Flashes of color from wildflowers dotted the lush landscape. The stream trickled along the edge of the trees until it pooled near a jumble of large rocks before cascading from their confines to flow back into the forest.

Danny dismounted and ground tethered his horse under a nearby tree. "Hop off. Figured we'd have lunch here." He pulled the saddlebags from his horse, then helped Drea tether Sheba. He spread a blanket on a flat rock near the stream and beckoned Drea closer.

She dropped down beside him, the heat from the rock already seeping through the thick blanket. He spread out a light lunch — sandwiches and fruit. Their voices and laughter floated in the air, joining the sounds of the wind in the trees and the burbling stream. Nothing had ever felt so easy, so right. She closed her eyes and sighed.

"You belong here," Drea said. There was no denying it. Danny looked at home on the ranch — easy, comfortable. He handled horses and people with equal ease, called everyone by name, and had maintained Parsons Acres as a thriving, growing business.

"I made the best of what life handed me," Danny said with a low chuckle. "That's all anyone can do."

"What did you wind up doing?" Drea asked. "After high school, I mean." She knew he'd chosen to stay because of the family needs, but not what he'd done otherwise.

"I got a business degree from Charleston." He looked down at his knees.

"That explains a lot around here." Drea smiled. "Did you keep playing football?"

Danny shook his head. "That was more than I could manage. Ma and Daddy wanted me to go to the community college. I insisted on Charleston. But I couldn't swing the ranch, full-time studies and football. Something had to go."

Drea understood that. She'd gone to George Washington University as they'd planned, and she'd barely managed her course load and part-time job. She couldn't imagine doing all of that and working the ranch.

"I keep tellin' Ma that the thoroughbred business isn't gonna be around forever." Danny rolled his eyes. "Finally got her convinced and now we're diversifying breeding and starting other projects — ways to make Parsons Acres more sustainable for the future. But I'm not out here to talk business or reminisce about the past."

"No?" Drea raised her eyebrows. "What should we be discussing?"

Rough, calloused hands cradled her face, gently tipping her chin up. His lips brushed hers, featherlight, as if waiting to be invited for more. She covered his hands with hers and pulled away, opening her eyes to stare into twin pools of confused blue.

"What are we doing here?" Drea asked. Danny's eyes widened and she tried again. "I mean, what's going on? I like spending time with you, but..." She trailed off and blew out a breath, frustrated at not being able to find the right words.

"You'd rather we ignore each other?" He cupped her cheek, and his gaze held hers. "Hell, I don't know for sure what we're doin' here either. I don't need to know everything. All I need to know is how much I enjoy being with you. How much I want you."

He leaned in and kissed her, and her world exploded. His hands, rough against her skin, the light stubble on his chin scratching her face. His lips pressing hard against hers, his tongue invading her mouth. Her breath caught in her throat when he rose to his knees and pulled her against his body. Drea tangled her fingers in his hair, torn between wanting him closer and the fear that reared its head at the slightest hint of physical intimacy.

He pulled back, his hands plunged into her hair as he pressed his forehead against hers, his heavy breaths mingling with her own. Her lips felt swollen from his kisses.

"You want me to ignore that?" he asked, his voice a near growl. "What we both feel?" He released her and sat back onto the blanket.

Drea's fingers itched to trace the hard bulge in his jeans. To undo his buttons one by one. To take him in her hands, then into her mouth.

"None of us knows what's going to happen in life." His soft whisper was almost lost in the sounds of the water flowing around the rocks. "I promised you I wouldn't push for anything you're not ready for, and I'm stickin' to that. I always have, and I always will. I know life brought you back here, and there's something pretty amazing between us. I'd like to enjoy that for however long we have. You know I'm not leaving here. And I know you're not likely to stay."

There it was. He wasn't going anywhere, and he expected she would leave. Drea scooted next to him, resting her head on his shoulder.

"I'm scared of so much," she whispered. "There's so much I don't know. I had everything planned out. Everything accounted for. And now, there's only one thing I know for sure." She swallowed, trying to ease the dryness in her throat. "I want you, too."

He crushed her to him, holding her body tightly as his lips claimed hers with a ferocity she'd never imagined possible. She traced her fingers up his arms and his muscles tensed and rippled, as she thrilled at the way his skin prickled at her touch. She wanted to touch every inch of him, to taste the salt of his skin.

His hands tangled into her hair and lifted her face to his. The kiss was furious, bruising, and he pressed her back until she lay pinned beneath him on the blanket.

He tugged on her shirt, but she grabbed his wrist. She wasn't ready for him to see her yet. She wasn't ready to fear his response. He shifted his body between her legs and pushed up on his elbows to stare down at her, then his mouth was on her again. His teeth nipped her lip, her earlobe, as his fingers squeezed her nipples through the thin shirt and bra.

As a teen, she hadn't known what to do with the way he made her body feel. There was none of that innocence now. And fear be damned, she knew exactly what she wanted to do with him.

Danny pressed up on his arms again, hovering over her like a Greek god, his hips grinding into her. He was stunning—she wanted to revel in the feel of his muscles beneath her fingers.

She arched against him, and he rolled, pulling her with him and settling her to straddle him. He gripped her hips, encouraging her to rock against him, then moved back up to cup her breasts. Drea lost herself in his touch, in the deep blue of his eyes, locked on hers.

The wind shifted, blowing her hair into her face and carrying a scent of something familiar. Drea sat up suddenly and sniffed the air.

"Do you smell that?" She looked down at Danny. His face registered confusion, then a scowl formed and he sat up with her.

"That's a fire." The words tumbled out of their mouths at the same time. She rose to her feet and scanned the horizon, focusing on the direction the wind was coming from. "There. Smoke. I don't remember what's out that way."

She kept her gaze on the wisps of smoke that quickly dissipated in the breeze.

"Old mine," Danny replied. "Abandoned company town. Not much."

Drea packed up their lunch and stowed everything back in the saddlebags, then turned to him with her hands on her hips.

"How far is the town? Can we get there on horseback? We're too far out to get back to the ranch and drive."

"Slow down." He captured her hands in his and held her gaze. "I get it, you want to go out there. Lemme get the horses. I'll call it in on the way. This is gonna be a rough ride. You up for that?"

She nodded, her eyes focused on the plume of smoke now clearly visible above the tree line. She needed to get over there. Needed to see the fire.

Drea swung into the saddle and followed Danny along a narrow path, listening as he gave instructions to Amos about the possible location of the fire.

"I'll keep you updated, but if it's where I think, there's not much we can do," he said to Amos, then hung up and reined to a stop. "The rest of the way is rough terrain. You're in a hurry, and we're gonna go quick, but we're not gonna go stupid. You got that? Stay behind me, and if you can't keep up, you'll turn around and go back. Clear?"

"Got it." She pressed her heels down in the stirrups, ready for a rough trail. She had no intention of turning back. Somewhere in the back of her mind came a nagging fear, but it was a whisper in the storm of thoughts in her head. Thoughts on the fire. And whether or not it was connected with the others.

The trail was rougher than Danny remembered, and it took them nearly an hour to crest the hill above the mining town. The closer they got, the more the air stank like a campfire made with bad wood. Danny wrinkled his nose at the tang of metal in the smoke. When they dismounted, the building was already swallowed by flames. Drea swore softly, then pulled out her phone and walked around taking pictures, muttering all the while. Danny hung back, keeping out of her way.

Drea was crouched in front of the building, taking pictures of something on the ground when the volunteer fire crew showed up and Amos Kimmel started shouting at her to get the hell out of his fire scene.

Her expression changed so rapidly, it looked as if someone had flipped a switch. One second, she had a slightly faraway look on her face and the next she was standing, hands on hips, body blocking the pathway between the buildings.

"Captain, I'm Special Agent Andrea Hidalgo, and…"

"Oh, for cryin' out loud, Drea, I know who you are." Amos gestured at the fire behind her. "And I know that right now you're in my way."

"Do you have a tanker? Retardants?"

He took a step back looking confused. "No."

"Unless you plan on beating out these flames with your bare hands, I'm not in your way."

"Tanker's on the way. Had some trouble getting up the first part of the road. This is my fire scene."

"I'm sorry, Captain Kimmel, but it's not—as a federal agent, I outrank you. Now, we can stand here and piss around each other's feet, or we can work together to figure this out. Your choice."

Danny had never seen Amos Kimmel at a loss for words. The man stood there, mouth agape, looking down at Drea. Danny tethered the horses and wiped his hands down his jeans. If Amos got ugly, he'd step in and deal with him. He didn't know what Drea had going on in her head, but she sure as shit was more qualified than Amos.

"You stand up to Robert like that?" Amos glared at Drea.

Her lips turned up in a sweet-looking smile and her eyes got big and round in a look of feigned innocence. "Oh, I was far less polite to Robert."

What Amos did next made Danny's mouth fall open in shock. The man stuck out his hand at Drea. "Well, all right. Good to see you back, and I'm sorry about your granddaddy. You tell me what you need us to do. I'll make sure this mess of guys who call themselves firefighters toe the line."

After a quick consult with Drea, the crew set about digging a trench in case the wind kicked back up. When the tanker arrived, they sprayed retardant on the closest buildings, but Drea asked them to hold the water for after the fire burned down. Then everyone settled down to wait. Drea typed frantically on her phone but kept glancing back up at the burning building.

"Everything okay?" Danny tapped her shoulder.

"What?" Drea looked up at him, her eyes wide and startled looking. "Oh. Yeah. Sorry. I was texting Emma Tanner. She'll sit with Gramps after Jimmy gets off." She plopped down into the grass next to him with a heavy sigh, her eyes glued to the fire.

"Why not use the tanker to put it out?" Danny asked.

"Waste of water," she replied. "That tanker holds three thousand gallons. It's big, but it's not big enough to put out that fire. Structure's too far gone to save anyway. Let it burn out."

"So, what are you planning to do with the water?"

"I don't want to wait for everything to cool down before I can get in there. Once the fire burns down enough, a little water will bring it to a workable temperature and kill any hot spots. Ever try to pour water on a campfire that's still burning?"

Danny nodded. "Doesn't work so well."

"Nope." She laughed. "But if you wait till the fire's down to embers…"

"A bucket of water will put it out." He smiled. "Smart."

"Hey, that's why they pay me the big bucks." She gave a theatrical wink. "How're we getting back? It's going to get dark before this is done."

"Already taken care of. A couple of guys are packing up a truck and horse trailer. Won't be able to get it all the way up here, but they'll bring my truck as well. They'll leave that for us, then ride the horses back down the road to the trailer. I'm stayin' right here with you."

Her eyes lit up with a smile. "Who's coming? Brian?"

"Nope," he said. "Couldn't reach him. I tried Lily, went straight to voicemail. So, I called Ma, and she chased down a couple of our crew."

Maybe Brian had to go out on a call or something like that. But even on a Sunday, the ranch manager should pick up his phone.

"Can you ask them to get my kit out of my Jeep?" Drea's words cut into his thoughts. "It's in the back, looks like a suitcase. Keys are in the barn." She didn't wait for a reply before turning back to the fire.

Danny sent a text, then shifted closer to her. He closed his hand over hers. She seemed calm on the surface, but her skin was pale with high dots of red in her cheeks. She was wound as tight as a spring and practically vibrating. This was what she did — every day. He knew the addictive rush of adrenaline, the excitement of solving problems and dealing with high-pressure situations. Breeding million-dollar horses and standing by when the result of that investment was foaled wasn't exactly a walk in the park. But it was nothing compared to this.

Danny squeezed her hand, and she squeezed back, never taking her eyes off the blazing building.

* * * *

The kitchen door closed softly as Drea slipped in and tiptoed to the stairs. The television flickered in the living room.

"Why do you smell like a campfire?" Gramps' voice was querulous and tired. Drea turned from the stairs and crossed the room.

He sat propped in his bed, watching late-night news with Emma Tanner. He should have been asleep long before now, but his glassy eyes and strained expression gave away what Gramps would never admit. He was in pain, and the morphine wasn't doing enough to tame it. She needed to shower, to get the smell off her, but Gramps needed her more. She said good night to Emma and pulled a chair up to Gramps' bed and sat, then reached for his hand and gave it a gentle squeeze.

"There was another fire." The words came out in a sigh. She closed her eyes and images of the burning building seared the back of her lids. She hadn't panicked at the scene. The old excitement was there. The tension, the feeling of discovery, and the drive to find the fire's secrets. But no panic. There had been a moment when her throat had closed up, when the sounds of the roaring fire called up things she wanted to forget. Then Danny's fingers had closed over hers and that little touch, the squeeze of his hand, had driven the visions away. She looked back to Gramps.

"Danny and I were out riding and smelled the smoke. A building in the old mining town was burning." This was her comfort zone. This she could do. Give him enough info to feel informed, but not too much.

"Was it like the last...?" Rough coughing erupted, and his chest heaved with the effort to pull in more air. He pushed himself up higher in the bed, the coughing fit doubling him over and making him seem small and frail. When he regained control and looked back to Drea, his eyes were red and runny, and his face looked tired. "Was there a body?"

She should avoid that subject. Should give a noncommittal answer. You didn't discuss open cases, didn't give details that weren't approved to give. But the volunteer fire crew had seen it, and the gossip was already across town by now. He'd hear it soon enough. Drea nodded.

"Do you think...?"

"I don't know what I think right now, Gramps." She interrupted him as gently as possible. "It's too soon to know anything, but I know that two fires, each with a body, is suspicious, never mind the first one up the hill. And I know that you don't need to be getting yourself all riled up. You need to be resting and getting better."

"Ain't no gettin' better from what I got, and you know it. But you're right, I need to be resting. Now kiss your gramps good night like a good girl."

She leaned in and kissed his cheek, then knuckled away the tear that slid down her own. "I love you, Gramps." She whispered the words in his ear as she helped him settle back into the bed. His eyes brightened and he smiled.

"Why I love you too, little one."

She bolted up the stairs before the tears could hit. She sank to the floor of her room and let them fall. She shouldn't have stayed away so long. Should have spent more time with him over the years. He was all she had, the only family she had left.

Chapter Twelve

Drea grabbed a shovel and trudged up the hill past the Tanners' new chicken coop, happy to see the berm she'd helped create out of fallen trees and old railroad ties had held. She scrambled over an outcropping of shale onto a flat stretch of earth. Rotted fenceposts and a few tangles of barbed wire marked the remnants of an old homestead. The early morning light revealed new green growth covering a rough square about the size of a small cottage, as if Mother Nature was trying to reclaim what was hers.

The mining town fire three days ago had signs of an incendiary device, likely thermite based. There was trace evidence of the same at the first Parsons Acres fire. If she was right, if the arsonist had used the fire above the Tanners' place as a test, there might still be evidence.

Two months was a long time. After all the cleanup efforts and nature itself, there might not be much left, but she didn't need much. It didn't need to stand up in court. She needed to know if her suspicions were correct.

Getting up the hill to start the fire would have been a tough journey. Possibly in the dark. Past two occupied houses.

"We all reckoned it was some vagrant's camp." Ms. Tanner's words echoed in Drea's mind. "There's still trains that go through back up there."

Drea pushed through the trees and heavy undergrowth behind the property. Tough going, but it was spring now. It would have been easier in late February. She came out on a grassy strip that gave way to gravel and a railroad track. A fire access road snaked over the hill on the other side of the tracks.

Hiking up the hill from the road below would have been a chore, especially while carrying a thermite device. But coming in from this side. Piece of cake.

Drea rushed back to the remains of the burned building. She leaned against the shovel and studied the charred earth.

"Talk to me," she whispered into the wind, willing the house to reveal some secret, some clue, to either prove her right, or very wrong. She walked around the perimeter, not yet willing to disturb the soft ground.

The fire crews had come in from above and below, concentrating their efforts on containing the fire and letting it burn itself out. Then came the cleanup. So many people left burned-out buildings to rot. Especially in a rural environment. But the Tanners had an egg business to think of, and neighbors took care of their own. Local folks would be quick to lend a hand.

Including Gramps. Especially Gramps.

Drea grabbed the shovel and picked a corner, carefully churning the earth, looking for anything that stood out. She worked methodically, a single shovelful at a time, going in a neat row to the next corner. She'd done three full rows and was halfway through the fourth when she turned over something shiny.

She knelt and scooped the metal blob into her hand, not caring about preserving evidence. There was nothing official about this dig. She pulled a hand trowel from her pocket and began turning smaller bits of earth. More metal blobs. A thin metal stick — sparkler maybe? She tucked everything into a bag and straightened up, brushing her hands on her pants.

She didn't need to see more. This was the arsonist's dress rehearsal. Someone testing their technique to ensure it worked before playing a very dangerous game.

First there was this fire. No one knew when it had started, but it had been burning merrily away by midday. Maybe set early morning. Then the first one at Parsons Acres. That had to be set in the middle of the night. That was easy enough to get to. That night had been a new moon, it would have been very dark. The fire in the old mining town had to have started after sunup. She and Danny had finished lunch when they smelled the smoke, and it was fully engulfed by the time they'd arrived. Again, remote but reasonably easy to access with a four-wheel drive vehicle. Little risk of any witnesses for either of those.

If this one was a test, then the fires at Parsons Acres were the main event. Maybe to hurt the Parsons or delay development. Maybe it was about the bodies, and the fact that both were on the Parsons' land was a coincidence. Not like there weren't plenty of abandoned mines around where it would be easier to dump a body. But maybe the arsonist didn't want to start a mine fire.

She was overthinking. There wasn't enough information to build a picture yet. But one thing she knew for sure — these weren't accidents.

* * * *

Danny propped his feet on the porch rail and cracked open a bottle of beer. Time to relax. After the fire last Sunday, and a long week dealing with horse owners, fussy mares and cantankerous stallions, he was more than ready for a break. Brian took a swallow from his soda and leaned his elbows on his knees.

"I want to start training Lily to take over as ranch manager," Brian said.

Danny nearly fell out of his chair. He kicked his feet down from the porch rail and set his beer bottle down before turning to look at Brian.

"It's the end of the day on Friday. We're sittin' here with cold drinks. You couldn't bring this up earlier?"

Brian gave a lopsided grin and shrugged.

"You're joking," Danny said.

"Nope," Brian replied. "I'm in my final semester of college. It's time to start thinking about someone. Lily's got a great hand with the horses, a solid head on her shoulders and she's good at keeping the crew in line."

Danny laughed. She oughta be. She was the eldest of the Elkins kids, and the ranch hands weren't all that different from a bunch of unruly teens. "I trust you to know your stuff," he said. "And I'm not ashamed to admit that a lot of my reservation comes from not likin' the idea of change. You live here, and that makes things awfully convenient. She gonna pack up her kid to move? Probably not."

"That's not a deal-breaker and you know it." Brian's tone was sharp, and Danny couldn't blame him. They had a deal, and Brian was more than living up to his end of the bargain. He was right, it was time to start thinking about someone, and if he felt Lily was the right choice, then she was the right choice.

"She gonna answer her phone better than you do?" Danny replied.

"Man, I'm sorry," Brian said. "That's one time in how many years?"

Danny scoffed. Brian had never missed a call before. And his half-assed excuse of his phone being dead didn't ring true. Danny suspected the truth was Brian and Lily had been with each other the day of the fire.

"Lily's phone dead, too?" Danny arched an eyebrow. Brian flushed bright red. "Like I said, I trust you to know your stuff," Danny continued. "Let's talk to her. See if she wants the job. Now can we stop talkin' business? Can't we sit on the porch in peace?"

He picked his bottle up and stuck his feet back on the rail, determined to do exactly as he'd said.

"What are you planning to do about that fire?" Brian would not take the hint.

Danny glared at the other man and slowly pulled his feet back down. *So much for a quiet evening.*

"I'm not plannin' to do much of anything. The whole building's a wreck. Don't know why my daddy ever bought that piece of land to begin with." He shrugged.

"Any idea who it was?"

"Nope," Danny replied. "And I'm tryin' not to think about it."

When the fire had burned out, Drea had directed the crew to hose everything down, then she'd borrowed a pair of boots and gear from one of the guys and gone tramping through everything. The wind had shifted as she'd lifted a large piece of debris, and the smell was not something he'd soon forget. Nor was the sight of the charred corpse. The picture of that claw-like hand he'd seen on Robert's computer was nothing compared to that. He had a strong stomach, but he'd still had to choke down the urge to vomit.

"Drea spent yesterday tearin' up the place that burned up the hill at the Tanners," Danny said. "Robert's comin' apart at the seams because she's doin' her job. And Amos Kimmel, of all people, is backin' her up."

"Amos has no use for Robert," Brian said. "Thought you knew that. Since Lawson retired, Amos has been fightin' tooth and nail to stay afloat."

Danny had forgotten about that whole conflict. That went a long way to explaining Amos' reaction to Drea at the fire. When he'd rolled up, he'd thought she was in Robert's court—the idiot had certainly blustered about town enough that sure, he'd brought in a consultant, but he was the one overseeing the work. Once Amos had figured out there was no love lost on Robert, Drea had become his new best friend.

"Who knows, maybe these fires will be what it takes to knock some sense into Robert. Or get him fired. I ain't holding my breath on that, but we can hope, right?" Brian's words cut into his thoughts, and Danny nodded absently.

"Town council ain't gonna get rid of him without a damn good reason. Incompetence is easy to ignore when everything's quiet," Danny replied. "Fuckin' politics and drama."

Chapter Thirteen

Heat and smoke. A heavy metallic taste.

Drea sat up in bed gasping, then coughed as the air seared her lungs. She blinked and looked around. This was her bedroom at her grandparent's place, not the apartment in DC. She shook her head, trying to clear the cobwebs of the dream, and coughed again.

But this was no dream.

"Shit." She grabbed her phone and dropped to the floor to rummage in her closet for shoes, then pulled the pillowcase off and dumped her water glass over a section of it. Holding the damp cloth over her face, she felt the door, then the knob. Warm. Not bad.

The fire had to be in the kitchen, or the back porch. No sound of the fire alarm. Weird. She needed to get Gramps out.

She eased the bedroom door open and crept into the smoke-filled hall, then down the stairs. Smoke drifted from the kitchen and up the stairs, and the living room was starting to fill as well. Popping and hissing sounds came from near the back door and the heat was getting intense. She looked around for the evening home health aide but couldn't find him. Then she remembered it was his night off. Panic welled up like bile, and Drea swallowed hard. There was no time for that.

She rushed over to the bed and got Gramps connected to portable oxygen before waking him up. "Shh, I'm sorry, Gramps. There's a fire. No time to explain more. You have to come with me now. Grab your phone and hold on to me, we'll get you into the car."

His eyes darted around the room and a look of fear crossed his features. He'd seen fires in the mines. He knew the drill. His watery eyes settled on Drea, and he nodded. She slid an arm under his and helped him from the bed. He was so light, not the strapping, strong man she'd known all her life. Together, they made it out the front door as the smoke detector finally started going off. Drea settled Gramps in the passenger seat of her car, thankful she'd parked far back in the drive.

"I'll be right back. Call in the fire."

His hand grasped her wrist, shaking, but still strong. "Where..." He cleared his throat. "Where are you going?"

"I've got to get some things. Don't worry. I'm a professional. You'll be safe in the car."

She grabbed the damp pillowcase again and hurried to the hose on the side of the house, dousing the cloth until it was dripping, then wrapped it around her face, wishing for her full gear and an air mask. She left the hose running, drenching the front porch with water.

Back in the house, smoke billowed from the kitchen and Drea moved quickly, forcing herself to keep going, keep focused on the tasks that needed doing. She didn't have much time. She gathered up meds and important papers, threw them into a bag then out into the front yard. She grabbed the extra oxygen tanks and carried them outside. She couldn't do much about the big tank.

She rushed upstairs and grabbed her purse. The smoke was blinding, and she stumbled as she came out of her bedroom. No time to go into her grandparents' old room and get the photo albums. Already, she was sweating and coughing, despite the wet cloth protecting her breathing. She ran on autopilot, not allowing herself to think, just doing what needed to be done.

Back downstairs, flames licked up the far kitchen wall and Drea eased her way into the room. Her breath came in short gasps as the heat assailed her. *Oh god, what am I doing in here? Get out. Get out. Get out. This isn't happening.*

Sparks flying by the back door caught her eye, she turned to see what looked like liquid metal spewing in the air. An unmistakable smell hit her — thermite.

She bolted out of the room and ran around the house. Flames engulfed the back porch, lighting up the night. Fire climbed up the side of the building, devouring the dry wood like a hungry beast. An upstairs window cracked in the heat. That was her room. Anger rose, red hot and raging. *Someone did this.*

She pulled her gaze back to the porch. There. Tucked against the kitchen door. A large canister still chugging molten bits into the air. Ingenious place to put it. Almost guaranteed to catch and move fast. Drea clicked a few pictures with her phone, hoping and praying they'd be clear enough to see the details.

Sirens pierced the air, and Drea came back around the house to find Amos Kimmel and his crew pulling into the drive. But there was no saving the little house. The rage flared again, along with an aching emptiness. Drea shoved it down. She had a job to do before she could indulge in feelings.

"Origin is the back porch." She greeted Amos without preamble. "I think it's thermite. You're gonna have some problems back there, but I'd like to preserve as much of the evidence as possible, so please be careful. And there's an oxygen tank in the living room."

Amos nodded at her, then shouted a few orders to his crew before turning back to Drea. "You wanna wait on the ambulance to take y'all to the hospital?"

Drea shook her head. "I'm not going. Someone get Gramps there, I'm staying here." She bent into her car and took Gramps' hand. "You need to be at the hospital. I'll be there as soon as I can, but I've got…"

The words dried up in her throat, and she hugged him, sobbing against his shoulder like a frightened little girl. Fear and grief and anger pouring through her, twisting, setting her whole body trembling.

His hands stroked her back, and his voice whispered in her ear. "Shh. It's things. It's sad, but it's just things."

Drea pulled back and wiped the tears from her face. "You're right. I know. I know. Still…" It was too much. Too much loss. This wasn't an accident. Still, Gramps was right, it was just things. She held that thought and leaned in to kiss his cheek. "Will you be okay?"

He patted her hand and gave her a tired looking smile. "I'll be fine."

"I'll take him." Grace Kimmel came up to the car and leaned down to greet Gramps. "No reason to wait on the rescue truck unless y'all think you need it."

Gramps shook his head. "I need a ride to the hospital, I guess. My granddaughter seems to think I need checking out." A fit of coughing cut his laughter short, and Grace smiled up at Drea.

"I'll pull up right next to you here so it's not too far to walk," Grace said. "You stayin' here for now?"

"Yes, and thanks." Drea grabbed her kit and scribbled a note before handing it to Grace. "The heat was bad, and I'm worried about smoke inhalation. It wasn't too heavy where his bed was." She swallowed hard. "Thank you."

They got Gramps settled into Grace's beat-up SUV, and Drea gave him another hug and kiss, then turned back to Amos as a loud thump sounded inside the house. Window glass shattered and the firefighters closest to the house stumbled back.

"There went the oxygen," Drea said. "What can I do to help?"

Amos shook his head. "I don't have extra gear, so I can't put you in there. But you can tell me what I need to know about...what was it? Thermite?"

"Pyrotechnic composition—basically burning metal powder. Not much you can do to put it out unless you've got access to a whole lotta foam. Water will just cause massive amounts of steam." Drea shrugged. "You'll have to let it burn. It'll go pretty quick. When we get to cleanup, let me take the back porch, and don't toss or tramp on anything that looks like metal, or melted blobs of stuff."

"So, this wasn't an accident?"

She shook her head and Amos swore.

"Drea!" Danny's voice carried over the crackling fire and pumping truck.

Hearing his voice set off an explosion of conflicting emotions—a sense of relief mixed with the urgent need to get back to work. She needed to keep going, not stop and cry. No matter how much she might want to. Amos turned to deal with his crew, leaving Drea staring at a very disheveled and upset looking Danny, and Drea couldn't think of anyone she wanted to see more.

"Are you okay?" Danny's fingers curled into his palms. All he wanted to do was pull her into his arms. Her hair was a tousled mop, and her pajamas were soaked, streaked with mud and soot, but she didn't look hurt. Relief flooded through him. "Is Paul okay?"

She leaned back against her car. "Yeah. He's..." She blew out a breath and tried again. "He'll be fine, I'm sure." She pushed her hands through her curls and looked over at the burning house.

"Grace called me," Danny said. "There's room at the house for y'all. Ma won't mind. In fact, she'd be insisting." He stuck his hands in his pockets. Drea looked so cold and distant.

"Oh." She sounded surprised. "Yeah. I'll probably... ah hell. Danny, someone burned the house."

The pain in her voice twisted him into knots. He wanted to comfort her, care for her, but he didn't know what she needed — what she would accept. Her fingers tugged at his shirt, pulling him closer, and he lost what little grip he had on his control. He wrapped his arms around her, felt her sag against his chest. He slid his hands down her back, stroking, soothing.

"What do you need? How can I help?" He spoke close to her ear, so she could hear over all the noise. She smelled of smoke, but he buried his face in her hair, thankful she'd gotten out safely.

Her body shook as she hauled in a breath. Then she was pushing out of his arms, standing back. Twin pools of green looked up at him—her gaze a mix of fear and anger. She sighed and gave him a shaky smile.

"I need to stay here until this is done." She took in a slow breath. "There are things I need to see. To record. Then I need to check on Gramps. Somewhere in there, I'll need a shower, and food, and sleep. I don't want to be a nuisance. It'd be easier on everyone involved if I take care of all that at the hospital, and I can't think of one good reason not to do it that way."

He opened his mouth, but she held up a hand and shushed him. "If you want to help, we need a place for Gramps that will work long term. Your mother's is great, but he can't handle stairs."

She slumped back against her car, and Danny chuckled. Drea was being herself—never mind that she'd just been in a house fire, that she could have died. She had a to-do list, ready to go.

"Ask for something hard next time, darlin'. That's an easy thing to fix. There's a guest cottage on the ranch. There's only three steps up the porch, and it's got two bedrooms all on one floor. It's nothing fancy, but it's enough space for you and Paul. You're welcome to stay as long as...well..."

Tears sprang to her eyes and overflowed. He reached out and wiped them away with his thumb.

"I can think of several good reasons not to do things your way," he said, then leaned down and kissed her gently. "But I understand. I'll get the cottage set up. Can I call Wilma and get you something to wear? Or were you plannin' on gallivantin' all over in your jammies? They're cute, but..."

Drea's lips twitched into a lopsided smile. "Yeah. That'd be...that'd be nice. Thanks. And coffee? Maybe?" The words were soft and almost lost in the sounds around them. She reached for his hand and squeezed his fingers.

"Whatever you need, darlin'." Danny squeezed back. Her asking for anything, even something as small as a coffee, was pretty unusual.

"Hey, Drea!" Amos' voice carried over the din. "Things are settling down back there. You might wanna come take a look."

She rose up on tiptoe and kissed Danny lightly, then turned and headed over to Amos. When Drea faced the fire, it was like she'd transformed into another person — tough, unflinching. A little intimidating. Danny fished his phone from his pocket. Five in the morning. He sent a text to Wilma, hoping she'd be awake on a Sunday. He could get coffee and a change of clothes for Drea, then drive home, get showered, join his mother for breakfast and let her know what was goin' on.

Chapter Fourteen

Gramps' overnight for observation had turned into a week in the hospital as the smoke inhalation had irritated his lungs and infection had flared. A bit of a blessing in disguise as it gave Drea time to get the cottage ready. The fire hadn't left much to salvage from Gramps' place, so it had meant replacing the bed, the shower chair, everything. Thankfully, the hospice program helped with getting all of that together.

Drea dropped the box of medical supplies in Gramps' bedroom at the Parsons' cottage and stretched to ease her tight back.

"You ready to take a break?" Danny came out of the bathroom where he'd been installing safety rails.

"Yeah. Sounds like a good idea."

"Grab a spot on the porch." He headed off to the kitchen. His faded, beat-up jeans clung to his thighs, and Drea couldn't help but smile, despite everything. He'd been her rock the last week. A strong pair of hands to help out, and a shoulder to cry on when she worried about Gramps.

She dropped into the porch swing. The view was nothing short of spectacular — a small grassy slope led to the mare's barn and paddock. Off to the side, a broad field stretched to the trees — and Danny's place. *So close.*

Danny came out with two glasses of iced tea and sat down beside her. He handed her a glass, then draped his arm over her shoulders. Easy. Casual. Comfortable. Except his touch felt like an electric current on her skin. And she liked it. She tipped her head back, resting on his shoulder.

"Thank you." Drea couldn't imagine where she and Gramps would have wound up without the Parsons' help. She'd have managed something, but this was better for Gramps.

"Seemed silly to have y'all worried about where you'd land when there's a perfectly good place here." Danny's fingers trailed over her arm. "I don't wanna bring up a sore subject, but, has Robert gotten back to you about the fire?"

"No," Drea muttered. And she wasn't happy about it. "He keeps telling me he's looking into it, then puts me off." She'd get there, eventually. The fire, and Robert's handling of it, sat simmering in the back of her mind — always present.

"You told him about what you found at the Tanners' place couple weeks back?"

"Yep. I think that one was a test," Drea replied. "And the one at Gramps' was meant as a warning. Back off, or else. I want to know what Robert's thinking. Does he still suspect Penny?"

"You don't?"

"I suspect everyone," Drea replied. "Penny would have to have help. So, who? Robert? Lily? Brian? Even you."

His entire body stiffened next to her, and she couldn't blame him. Here she was practically accusing him and his trusted staff, hell, his best friend, of arson and murder.

"I'll worry about that after I get Gramps settled," she said, wanting to change the subject. "I've been too busy to spend much energy on the fires."

"Focus on what's important, darlin'," Danny said. "You and Paul came out of it okay. Take care of people first, everything else can wait."

Drea chuckled. "Says the man with a business degree."

"Why do you think we feed our crew during the busy times?" He shifted, tucking her closer into his side. "The driving force at Parsons Acres has always been about taking care of our people." His chest rose and fell on a sigh. "I used to hate it here. Couldn't wait to get out. I hated Jake for leaving, for shirking his responsibility."

Ice clinked in his glass as he took a drink. Drea had never thought about things from Danny's perspective. She hadn't cared about Danny's needs. All she'd cared about was how he was abandoning their plans, and the impact it had on her life. A pang of guilt twisted inside her at the memory.

"I'm sorry." She'd been mad, hurt by his decision. She'd never stopped to think about him.

His hand tightened on her shoulder, squeezing, pulling her closer. "Water under a bridge, darlin'. We were kids, full of naive ideas and selfish needs."

He took the glass from her hands and put it on the rail next to his. His arms closed around her, cradling her, making her feel safe, comforted.

"You don't need to be sorry. You did what was right for you and look at you. You're amazing. Besides, I grew to love this place." He turned her in his arms, settling her back against his chest. "Look out there. All of that beauty and splendor. It's not better than what I thought I wanted. It's not worse. It's just different. Took a long time to reach acceptance. Longer still to get past the bitter. This place? It's part of me now."

There it was again. The reminder that this was home to Danny. He belonged here, and he wasn't going anywhere. Drea took a deep breath, not allowing herself to think about what that might mean.

"I've still got a bit to do," she said. "Gramps comes home tomorrow."

"You've got help," he whispered in her ear. "Break's not over yet. Speaking of which, you've been goin' non-stop, and that ain't gonna change this week." His hands stroked up her arms, igniting sparks everywhere he touched. "Next weekend is the Spring Carnival. How about it? Wanna go to the carnival with me?" His fingers caressed her cheek, and she turned her face into his hand.

"That sounds fun." Drea tipped her head back, and his thumb brushed her lips, making her crave his kisses and sending all her doubts and fears running into the shadows. She reached for him, fingers caught in his hair, tugging, pulling him into her. His lips were soft on hers, gently teasing. Drea gasped as he moved to nibble her neck, then her ear.

A whimper escaped her lips when he lifted his head. He didn't move away from her, and his arm tightened, holding her close to him. Drea was about to ask him what was wrong when footsteps sounded on the gravel path.

"Hey, y'all," Annette called out as she walked up, carrying a large picnic basket. "Figured you might like lunch."

Drea felt heat rising to her face. Danny's arm was still draped over her shoulder, and his face was calm. So different from when they were teens and they'd maintained a polite distance when adults were around.

Annette set the basket down on the top step and eyed the two of them for a moment, then smiled and started laying out lunch.

* * * *

"It's just three steps." Drea held on to Gramps' hand as he made his way up the porch. Danny held the door open, and they got Gramps settled into a big, comfy chair next to the window. Trish grabbed Gramps' bags and headed straight to his bedroom.

"Didn't I tell you the view was amazing?" Drea tucked a lap blanket over her grandfather's legs and slid the side table within easy reach.

"You were right. It's beautiful." Gramps nodded out the window. "Danny, I can't thank you enough for this."

Danny's face colored, and he looked down at his shoes. "You would do the same, sir." His voice was gruff, as if he were fighting back tears. He turned to the window. "Right down there is the mares' barn. You'll see plenty of activity in that arena over summer... Hey, uh, Drea... You expectin' Robert Moore?"

Drea shook her head, and Danny pointed out the window. Robert's Bronco pulled up behind her Jeep. Trish came back in with a nebulizer for Gramps' breathing treatment.

"I'm sure he's here to say hello to Gramps," Drea said. "I'll let him know to come back another time."

Gramps waved a hand at her, and Danny followed her onto the porch as Robert was climbing the steps.

"Hey, Danny," Robert greeted. "Andrea, I was hopin' you'd be here. Figured I'd save you a trip into town." He held out a sheet of paper.

Drea took the page and skimmed it — a police report on the house fire, listing the cause as unknown. Case closed. Drea held the sheet up and shook her head.

"It's been barely a week," she said. "How can you close this case? I gave you my report — there was a thermite device on the back porch. You've had four fires in this town now, and two bodies. I can point to clear evidence that the fire at my grandfather's place was intentionally set, and the previous three all show similar techniques. So, what is this?"

She ignored Danny's hissing intake of breath and arched her eyebrows at Robert.

"Look, I appreciate your help on that first fire here at Parsons Acres," Robert said. "I'm sure Danny agrees it was good to get closure. But you seem to have this idea that I've asked you to investigate every little fire that happens in this town."

Maybe Robert was trying to cover something up. Maybe he was the laziest cop Drea had ever laid eyes on. Either way, it didn't matter. "Why are you refusing to look into this? What happened to your theory that Penny was behind the fires?"

Robert sighed. "The question is, why are you makin' such a fuss?" He hooked his thumbs into his belt and shrugged.

"Drea has a point," Danny spoke up. "People have died, and she's saying there's evidence these aren't accidents. What's being done about that?" Drea wanted to kiss him for speaking up. Maybe if someone else started questioning Robert, they'd get somewhere.

Robert's face blanched. "This is a police matter," he sputtered. "I'll not discuss it with civilians. As for you" — he pointed at Drea — "I asked for your help once. Thank you. Great job. Now kindly stop tellin' me how to do mine."

He hitched his belt up and nodded. "Not that it's any of your all's business, but I questioned that girl every time. She has half-ass answers for everything, and her family swears she was never alone. I don't believe it. Now, if Little Miss Fire Investigator here thinks she can prove Penny did those fires, well, I'd welcome her help."

Danny opened his mouth, but Drea shook her head at him. She faced Robert. "It doesn't work that way, and you should know that. If I investigate, I look at all possibilities, not just one facet."

"Well," Robert said, "then I guess you're no use to me."

Robert nodded at Drea, then Danny and hurried from the porch. He'd barely slammed his car door when Danny erupted.

"What in the hell-kind of bullshit is that?" He pointed at the police report in Drea's hand. "A single page?"

"Welcome to my world," she sighed. "Robert isn't all that different from countless other small-town cops.

They have their way of doing things, and they don't like being questioned. Especially by a woman."

She dropped into a chair, and Danny knelt in front of her. "What are you going to do?"

"Right now," she replied, "I'm going to focus on Gramps." She reached for his hand, enjoying the warmth of his calloused fingers in hers. "And thank you."

He chuffed a short laugh. "For what? I wasn't much help there."

"You backed me up," she said. "And you let me stand up for myself. Not many men will do that."

"Hell, darlin', I figure you're more qualified in this stuff than Robert." His fingers squeezed hers. "You need to walk and blow off some steam, or you ready to go back inside and finish gettin' Paul taken care of?"

"Wow," Drea whispered. "You really are a remarkable person." She stood before he could question her on that. "Let's go inside."

Because she wasn't ready for the thoughts his support conjured up—thoughts of how nice it was to be with a man who not only believed in her, but who didn't feel the need to express his superiority in all things—even in areas where she had the education and experience.

"Lead the way." Danny held the door open for her.

* * * *

The smell of fried foods, popcorn and cotton candy hung in the air, and high-pitched squeals punctuated the throbbing music from the carnival midway. Drea's long hair was piled on top of her head and a few curls had escaped and twined about her face. The look in her eyes was one of pure joy and wonderment. Danny laughed as she tugged on his arm and practically dragged him to the Ferris wheel— a favorite of theirs when they were kids.

"Thank you for talking me into this." Drea smiled at him as they took their place in line.

He lifted a shoulder in a shrug. Robert's visit had had Drea fuming for two solid days. Danny had convinced her that she needed to take a break, let off some steam and reminded her of the upcoming carnival. That had finally got her focused on something other than the fires or Paul, and now she seemed to be having fun. The happy look on her face was more than worth the effort it took to put it there.

"I know you've seen a carnival before." He chuckled and handed two tickets to the ride operator.

"Not in years." She settled herself into the gondola and arched an eyebrow at him when he sat next to her.

"When have we ever sat across from each other?" He slipped an arm over her shoulders as the wheel moved up then stopped for the next gondola. "And, what? There aren't any Spring Carnivals in DC?"

"I'm sure there are. I never went to them. I think the last one I went to was here, during high school." She shifted in her seat, staring out over the gondola rail. "You did when we were kids. Sit across from me, I mean." She tipped her head back, looking over her shoulder at him. "Y'know, you're staring at me and missing the view."

He didn't care about the view outside of the ride. Danny chuckled and captured her chin in his hand. "No, ma'am. The view I like is right in front of me."

This was the first opportunity they'd had to get out since the day they'd gone riding and found the fire at the old mining town. The kisses they'd shared that day and since had caused him to take more than a few cold showers. Something he'd gotten very used to in high school but that hadn't been part of his life for years.

Having Drea back was a strange mix of nostalgia and discovering something entirely new, and despite the fires, he liked it.

He bent his head and brushed his lips against hers, lightly at first, teasing, waiting for her to invite more. Her lips curled into a smile, then parted. She always tasted sweet like honey and today was no different. He inhaled the jasmine scent of her hair and pulled her against him.

The gondola swayed as the wheel turned and the breeze tugged another curl loose from the knot on top of her head. Danny pulled back and gazed down at her upturned face, delighting in her smile. He wanted to see her like this always.

"There's your view," he whispered in her ear. The gondola was at the top of the wheel, and he pointed to their left where the countryside stretched away seemingly forever, and the setting sun glinted off the river. She shifted on the seat again, and he wrapped his arms around her, then leaned down and traced the curve of her neck with his lips.

She gasped at the first touch of his lips on her skin, then squirmed when his teeth fastened on her earlobe. He slid one hand up to cup her breast, and she arched against him, a soft moan escaping her lips, stirring an ache in him that was not entirely physical.

They alternated between kissing and looking out over the countryside as the wheel went around again and again. Danny could have stayed on the ride forever, reveling in the softness of her skin, the scent of her hair and the feel of her lips on his. The gondola wobbled as the wheel moved again and stopped to change passengers. Drea pushed away from him and rearranged her top, giving him a mock scowl as she did so. He flashed a wicked grin and winked, then helped her off the gondola when their turn came.

They walked hand in hand along the midway, winding between the rides and games, stopping for kisses every chance they got. Danny felt like he was back in high school. He hadn't been doing anything more than kissing her back then either. Later, everyone had assumed he and CeeCee were together, so there were no other girls. Later still, in college, there had been a few, but the one girl, the only girl, he'd ever really wanted had been long gone by then.

But here she was now, holding his hand as they strolled out of the carnival toward his truck. Kissing him lightly when he opened the door for her. Reaching across and laying her hand on his thigh when he got behind the wheel. It was everything he'd ever wanted with her, and it had his heart flying higher than a kite.

"Thank you," she whispered. "That was more fun than I've had in a long time."

Danny leaned over and kissed her quickly. "My pleasure."

He put the truck in gear and forced his mind to focus on his driving, not on the feel of her hand on his leg. Every now and then her fingers twitched, and it sent electric jolts through his entire body. He didn't want to take her home, didn't want to let her go.

Her hand withdrew as he turned onto the access road, and he had to resist the urge to grab it and pull it back.

"I don't want tonight to end." Her words were soft, barely audible over the sound of tires on the gravel road. She'd echoed his feelings so perfectly. He pulled to the side, threw the truck in park and turned to her.

"It doesn't have to. That's entirely up to you. I can drop you at home, kiss you good night, and we can go out another day. Or..." He let his voice trail off, not willing to put things into words that she could reject.

"What if...?" She paused, cleared her throat. "What if you don't like what you see? I haven't been with anyone since before the accident. I've got scars. Bad scars. And..." Her words trailed off as Danny's fingers curled under her chin, turning her face toward his.

Her worry tore through him, making him want to soothe it away. He leaned across the seat and lightly kissed her lips. "I'm not worried about any scars. You're beautiful, Drea. Always have been, and you always will be." He took a deep breath. "Would you like to come to my place? We don't have to do anything, and if we do, we stop wherever you're comfortable. Sound like a plan?"

A smile lit up her face. "That sounds perfect."

Danny sat back up, feeling more anxious than he had the first time he'd ever had sex. He put the truck into gear and drove on, bypassing the road that led behind the barns and heading out to his place instead.

Drea kept her eyes on Danny as he parked the truck, then came around to open her door. His smile was gentle as he took her hand and led her up the porch steps. Inside, she sat on the couch, twisting her fingers in her lap to keep them from shaking. Danny dropped down next to her, wrapped an arm over her shoulders and pulled her close to his side. Despite her nerves, she wanted him, wanted to touch him, feel him.

His lips caressed hers, teasing. It started out so gently, the barest brush of his tongue against her lips, his hands stroking her arms, setting off electric tingles everywhere he touched. She slid into his lap, facing him, her legs astride his thighs, his hands cupping her breasts as the kisses turned from gentle exploration to passionate demand that had her aching for more.

She pulled back and looked at him, his eyes half closed, his breath coming hard and fast. "What about condoms?" She kicked herself the moment the words came out of her mouth. There had to be better ways to do this.

Danny blinked, his lips curling into a small smile. "I probably have some still around. If not, we wait. There's plenty I can do to you that doesn't require wrapping anything." He leaned in close and nibbled on her neck, his fingers trailing along the side of her breast, sending delicious shivers up her spine. "I've got really good fingers, and a very talented…"

"I get the picture." The idea of what he could do with his fingers caused her nipples to tighten in anticipation. But first things first. "I uh… I had STI testing at the hospital. Negative. But I'm not on the pill or anything."

"I get it," he whispered, his fingers stroked along her ribs. "I got tested during my last physical—all clear. Any other pressing business?"

Drea shook her head. "Nope. Sorry for the interruption."

"Necessary evil," he replied, his words muffled against her neck as he kissed his way up to her ear, over her jaw, and back to her mouth. She didn't stop him when he moved to unbutton the top of her shirt. Instead, she shifted so he had better access to her lace-covered breasts.

"You're beautiful, Drea." He whispered the words against her skin as his mouth traced a line from her neck along the edge of her bra, then over the cups. Her nipples stiffened into hard peaks, and she gasped as his fingers brushed them lightly.

His hands cradled her face and his forehead rested against hers. "I want you." His voice was rough, breathless. Drea nodded. She wanted this. Him.

"Yes." It whispered out on a single breath.

He slid his hands down her body and cupped her ass, then stood, holding her against him. She curled her legs around him and let him carry her into his bedroom. He deposited her on the bed and reached to turn on a light. She put a hand on his arm, stopping him. Darkness would be easier.

"I want to see you," he whispered. "Let me show you that you're beautiful."

Drea removed her hand and nodded. He flipped a switch and a soft light glowed next to the bed, more like a candle than an electric light. He kicked off his shoes, then knelt to remove hers before pulling her up to stand. He unbuttoned the rest of her shirt and slowly slid it from her shoulders.

Drea's breath caught in her throat as the fabric slid off her left shoulder, exposing the burned skin. She braced herself for his response. For disgust. If Danny rejected her, she would shatter. But she had to know, had to risk it. She craved his touch, needed his kisses.

Danny smiled at her, his eyes unflinching as his gaze moved over her like a caress. He leaned down and kissed her gently. His hands were warm on her skin as they slid around her to unhook her bra. She tensed as they grazed over her back. The bra followed the shirt to the floor and Drea stood, naked to the waist, her entire body shaking.

Danny's hand closed on her right shoulder, warm, comforting.

"Are you okay? Do I need to stop?" His voice was soft and gentle, a warm murmur, soothing her frayed nerves and sending her fears scampering into the night. Desire tightened every muscle in her body.

"Please don't stop," she whispered.

He kept his eyes on hers as he lifted his T-shirt over his head, exposing rock-hard abs and a powerful chest with a slight dusting of fuzz. He was stunning.

"You are absolutely beautiful. I like what I see." His breath soft in her ear as he moved behind her. Danny's body pressed into her, the warmth of his chest against her back, and he reached around her waist to undo her jeans. He knelt as he pushed them off her legs, then stood. Soft sounds of a buckle and the swish of denim carried in the silence, followed by the feel of his bare body against hers. She hissed in a breath as his lips found her left ear, then he kissed, slowly, deliberately, down her neck and over her left shoulder. She stiffened again as his lips touched the edge of the scars.

His lips moved over her shoulder, and his fingers slid down her back. Her skin prickled at the unexpected sensations, and she gasped again as his tongue traced her collarbone. He took his time, slowly kissing every inch of scarred flesh. He was on his knees behind her, his hands on her hips as his lips covered the last lines of scar tissue along her lower back.

Tears trickled down Drea's cheeks, but she ignored them. She had not been touched like this since before the accident. No lover's hands had ever explored her burned flesh. But here was Danny, her friend, her first love, kneeling behind her, his touch as soft as a breeze, his voice soothing, telling her how beautiful she was. She reached for his fingers, needing to touch him, to know that this was real. Gentle pressure from Danny's hands directed her to turn to face him. He fastened his eyes on hers and smiled.

"Hold on tight." His smile turned to a wicked grin, then his fingers slid between her thighs and teased gently. Her hands settled onto his shoulders and held on as he slipped a finger into her wetness. The shaking started at her core, vibrating outward until her whole body was trembling and her breath came in panting gasps.

His other hand curled behind her knees, and she fell backward and landed on his bed. His mouth joined his fingers, his lips closing over her most sensitive spot as his fingers stroked inside. Her hands clenched into the blankets, then tangled in his hair as she arched against him.

"Please don't stop." The words came out as a plea, and his gentle touch got harder, more insistent. Drea's world exploded, and she cried out his name. Still, he didn't stop, and his fingers kept stroking until the last shudder, until she was lying flat on his bed, gasping for air.

"What...?" She sat up and looked at the man in front of her. "What did you do to me?"

He smiled. "I believe I mentioned good fingers and a talented tongue. What would you like?"

He kissed her legs, his hands stroking her thighs. This handsome, well-built god of a man was on his knees asking her what she wanted. She wanted him, simple as that.

"Stand up, please?" She crooked a finger at him, beckoning.

He gave her a lopsided smile and stood. Drea gasped as she caught sight of him. Long and thick, and throbbing hard. She reached out and traced a finger along his length and smiled at his hissing intake of air.

"Fair is fair," she whispered, and wrapped first her hands, then her mouth around him.

"Oh god, Drea." He gasped the words out as his hands closed on her shoulders. "Stop. I need... If you keep going, I'll explode."

"I thought that was the point?" She circled him with her hand, relishing the way he shuddered at her touch.

"Lemme go get..." He exhaled sharply. "Condoms." He disappeared for a moment and came back with a small box. "Wonder of wonders. Not expired."

She opened a wrapper and knelt in front of him, gently rolling the condom over his hard length. She wanted him. Nothing else mattered. She wanted to feel him, know every inch of him. She wanted his scent, his taste, in her memory forever. She tipped her head back and looked up at him, waiting. He grasped her shoulders and pulled her to stand, facing him.

"Are you sure, Drea?"

She nodded and his mouth closed on hers. His lips ground against her and she took them deeper, her tongue demanding entrance. He scooped her up and dropped her back onto the bed, then joined her there, his legs pressing between hers.

He lowered his head and took a nipple between his teeth. Drea's fingers clenched on his shoulders, her nails digging into his skin as he nibbled first one nipple, then the other, teasing them to hard buds.

"Please, Danny!"

She wrapped her legs around him, pulling him against her. The press of hot, hard flesh against her entrance sent jolts through her entire body. He pushed into her, then a brief spasm of discomfort followed by welcome warmth as he filled her. A few gentle strokes, and she was arching against him, digging her hands into his back, and urging him harder into her.

He rolled quickly, pulling her with him until she was on top and grinding against him. The soft light painted him in shades of gold, gleaming on his sweat slicked skin. Drea etched the sight into memory, never wanting to forget the look on his face — a mix of desire and tenderness, of barely restrained passion. He held her hips and thrust up into her. Her fingers clenched against his chest, and she came to a shuddering, trembling release. He rolled again, pinning her beneath him, her legs flat on the bed as he ground into her. The friction was delicious, and Drea was quickly on the verge of another orgasm.

His heartbeat pounded under her fingers, matching hers. Their ragged breaths mingled, filling the room with soft moans and gasps. His eyes, bright blue, bored into hers. The entire world faded, leaving just the two of them, in this moment. Drea drank it in, greedily filling herself with his touches.

Danny shifted and pressed her legs together, and Drea threw her head back at the intensity of it, crying out his name once more. His fingers dug into her hips, and his pace quickened before his entire body tensed, and he moaned softly against her neck.

A moment of stillness, then he withdrew. The sense of loss, of emptiness tore a whimper from her throat, and his arms closed around her. "I'll be right back," he whispered and rose from the bed. He was back in seconds, curling her into his arms and against his chest.

Chapter Fifteen

An insistent buzzing penetrated his brain, and Danny blindly reached for his phone. The weight on his arm pulled him wide awake, and he smiled down at Drea, still sound asleep. Seeing her there felt so right, so perfect, it hurt. He shifted her off his arm, careful to not disturb her, then slipped into the living room to answer Brian's call.

"It better be good," Danny muttered. He knew it wasn't, but it didn't stop him from hoping.

"Sorry, man." Brian's tone said as much as his words.

Danny groaned. Brian calling before sunrise was never a good sign. Danny padded into the kitchen to start coffee.

"We've got a mare showing signs of uterine infection," Brian said.

Shit. "I'll be there quick as I can."

Danny hung up and waited for the coffee to brew, poured two cups and took them into the bedroom. Drea sprawled in the bed, her dark hair fanned across the pillow and her face more relaxed than he'd ever seen it. He set the coffees down and scooped the empty condom wrappers into the trash. Three times last night.

It was the first time in his life a woman hadn't claimed exhaustion. Instead, Drea had bemoaned the lack of another condom, then knelt and taken him in her mouth. An act he'd happily returned in kind when she was done.

Yeah, that line of thinking had to stop. Much as he might want to, he didn't have time for that this morning. His cock was already at attention as he slipped into his jeans, buttoning them up before he woke Drea.

"Do you want coffee, or do you want to sleep?" he whispered in her ear. Her eyes opened slowly, and she turned to him, a smile forming across her lips, causing another twitch below his belt. And a corresponding increase in his heart rate.

"What time is it?" She glared at the window as if it had offended her. "It's still dark out."

He chuckled and kissed her, pulled her up and handed her coffee. "Early. I've got to get down to the barn. There's some problem with one of the mares. I didn't want you to wake up alone."

She blinked, looked around, and her eyes went wide, then focused back on him. She set the coffee down and dove back under the covers, yanking them up to her chin. Danny shook his head and laughed.

"Darlin', I've seen it all and then some." He tugged gently at the covers until she let them drop, exposing her magnificent breasts. "And I like what I see." He leaned down and kissed her, his lips pressing into hers until she yielded and opened to him. The throbbing thing in his pants thought it would be a good idea to get right back into bed with her, but he had work to do. *And no more condoms.*

"Go back to sleep if you'd like. Help yourself to breakfast. Shower. Whatever you need. I'm not sure how long I'll be gone."

The march of expressions across her face was almost comical. Her brow furrowed on a heavy sigh before her eyes popped wide again and her mouth made a perfect O.

"I never went home last night. I didn't call. Gramps will be going crazy! I've got to get back."

She shoved the covers off and made to stand, but he pushed her back gently.

"I'm sure he's still sound asleep. Take your time. It's too late for sneaking back home, and too early to come in lookin' like the cat that got into the cream. I'll call you later."

She nodded and pulled the covers back over her breasts before grabbing her coffee. Danny arched a brow at her, and she dropped the covers again.

"I like this look," he teased. He liked the sight of her in his bed even more. He tugged his boots on then gave her one last kiss and headed to the barn.

He found Brian outside the stall, wrapping up a phone call with the local vet. He hung up the phone and turned to Danny.

"Doc Jameson'll be out here later to see her," Brian said. "Meanwhile, you can give me a hand collecting samples."

"You got it." Danny moved around to the mare's head. Brian already had her halter secured, but he insisted that someone hold the head and soothe an animal when any procedures or testing were done. And Danny sure as hell wasn't going to argue — they'd had fewer staff kicked or bitten since Brian had taken over, and Brian himself was rarely on the receiving end of hooves or teeth. Danny stroked the mare's shoulder, whispering softly to her as Brian gathered his equipment and donned long gloves.

"Not as bad as it could be." Brian drew a vial of blood so quickly the horse didn't flinch. "But we won't know what's going on till we get these samples back from the lab. Meanwhile, we'll get this finished up and get her in quarantine, just in case."

Brian went back to work, and the only sounds in the early morning stillness were the occasional clink of an instrument on a tray, or the chuff of the mare's breath. Danny's mind wandered back to waking up with Drea in his bed. Maybe she'd still be there when he finished. Or in the shower.

Even in the barn, with the smell of horse, and hay and antiseptic, her scent wove through him. Starting every day with her in his arms would be pure heaven.

"All done." Brian's voice brought Danny rudely back to the present. "Let's get her moved." Brian untied the halter and led the mare to a box stall on the other side of the barn. By the time they'd got her settled, Lily had come in and was cleaning up after them.

"Hey, man, you've got a bite mark on your neck." Lily wagged a finger at Danny's throat. "Good times last night?"

"You're full of shit," Danny replied, though he made a note to check before he saw his mother today. That'd be a great conversation… "Hey, Ma. What's that? Oh uhh…a bite mark…"

"So, let's see the logs." Brian's words cut into those uncomfortable thoughts. "I want to see if this mare was covered by one of ours."

Brian turned and led the way to the offices. As they crossed the yard, Drea came out of the trees and down the trail to the cottage. Brian stopped in his tracks, watching until she got inside, then he turned to Danny.

"About time you pulled your head outta your ass and went after her. You two should never have broken up."

He resumed walking and Danny sputtered. "For the record, she wasn't exactly interested in hanging around back then. I'm not sure she's interested now."

Brian stepped into the office and rolled his eyes. "Whatever. Let's get to business."

* * * *

Jimmy came out of the kitchen as Drea stepped in the front door. *Dammit.* She'd been hoping to sneak into her bedroom and convince Gramps she'd gotten home so late he was already asleep. But Jimmy had a breakfast tray in his hands. Drea said good morning, then hustled to change before going to greet her grandfather.

Once showered, she knocked on his bedroom door and found him finishing breakfast. Jimmy smiled and cleared the tray, leaving Drea standing awkwardly at the foot of his bed, feeling like a wayward teen.

"How was the carnival?" His voice was strong this morning, and his color good. *Well, he got a good night's rest then.*

That didn't stop her from feeling guilty.

"I'd forgotten how much fun they can be," she replied. "We had a good time."

He looked up at her, those green eyes staring directly into hers, but she didn't see anger or upset. She saw laughter and something else. His lips curled into a slow smile.

"Figured you were having a good time when you hadn't come home by the time I went to bed." He winked. She took his hand and leaned down to kiss his cheek. "Not that it's any of my business, but you didn't come home last night at all, did you?"

Drea swallowed hard and shook her head. She never could lie to him.

"You always did have a sweet spot for that boy. He's grown into a good man." He stretched and pushed the covers back. "Well, no sense stayin' in bed all day. Help me up, little one."

Drea blinked and helped him up and into his robe. She'd expected the third degree. Or at least a lecture on being careful. Her own feelings on last night were all over the place—she'd certainly enjoyed it, and Danny seemed to. But she had no clue what it meant. And she wasn't about to dwell on it.

"I thought we might take a trip to the cemetery to visit your Abuela." He settled into the chair by the window. It had become a favorite spot where he could watch birds and other animals along the edge of the woods and see the comings and goings in the neighboring barns.

His eyes clouded with tears, but a soft smile formed on his lips. His left hand strayed to his throat where Abuela's wedding ring hung on a chain as it had since the day she'd passed. He probably wasn't aware he was doing it. Drea reached for his other hand.

"I'd like that," she said. "We should stop and get flowers. It is Mother's Day. I've got some unpleasant business to take care of tomorrow. The police report on the fire at your place is missing information, and Robert declined to investigate further, saying it was an accident. Which is bullshit. Pardon my language."

"So, you're going to talk to him?"

She nodded. "Robert's been a bit of a pill there. He keeps putting me off."

"Don't do anything foolish."

"I don't think it's foolish to ask what's going on and why he ignored the evidence I found." She shook her head at him. "I know I'm stirring shit, and Danny's been on me about that since the first fire at Parsons Acres, so don't you start. But this is ridiculous. There's something wrong here, and I think Robert knows it. That's why he's being such a jerk."

Chapter Sixteen

Danny put the truck in park and glanced over at Drea. She sat in the passenger seat, her eyes wide and her arms crossed over her chest. She looked adorable, but he didn't think she wanted to hear that.

She pointed out the window at Oak Bridge. "I don't know about this. It's Saturday night. Half the town is in there."

It didn't take a rocket scientist to figure out that Drea was stressed. Between Paul, and the fires, and the incompetent twit they had serving as chief of police, she was pretty much in a constant state of tension. Getting her out seemed to help, but they could only do so much riding.

Though wild horses couldn't drag the admission from him, he'd also figured coming to the local watering hole was a good idea. People mattered. Connections were important. Maybe those things would help convince her she wasn't alone.

"Brian and a bunch of the guys from the ranch, yeah," he said. "And probably Larry from the hardware store. Sure. Most of 'em folks we went to school with."

He grabbed her hand, stilling the fingers that were plucking at invisible bits of something on her pants. "C'mon, darlin'. It's gonna be fine. What's got you so worried?"

Her lips compressed into a thin line, then she took a deep breath and looked up at him. "When I saw them on the ranch, I was just another person helping out. Then senior year happened and now, with all the fires, and Robert, and you and me, and..."

Danny leaned over and kissed her softly. "Darlin', half the town is as worried about these damn fires as you are. Well, almost as worried. And nobody in there has much use for Robert. You ever seen him come in?" He waited for her to shake her head.

"And the rest?" he continued. "Everyone knows we're dating again. It's not a secret. And don't go sayin' we're not. I'm pretty sure we go out on a regular basis, we hold hands, we kiss...and lately, other things." He gave her a wink and was rewarded when a pink flush crept up her cheeks. For a woman who was so uninhibited in bed, she was awfully shy about it outside the bedroom. "If that isn't dating, I don't know what is."

Those other things had quickly become a source of equal delight and conflict. Though they'd seen each other nearly every night since the first time, Drea had refused to sleep over again. She insisted on getting up, showering, getting dressed and traipsing back to the cottage, claiming she didn't want to worry her gramps.

It frustrated him to no end. He'd liked waking up with her in his arms.

"We're gonna go in, say hello to Brian and the rest of the guys, have a bite to eat, maybe a couple of drinks and throw some darts."

"I suck at darts," she replied.

"I'm not tryin' to be an asshole," he said, "but help me out here. What do you want? Do you want to see each other on the sly, only go out where folks in town won't see us together, and spend our Saturday night in bed?" The hopeful look on her face almost made him laugh. "Scratch that last. I think I know the answer there."

"What's wrong with any of that?" She crossed her arms over her chest and raised her eyebrows in a wide-eyed, innocent look.

Danny took a deep breath and gripped the wheel for a count of five before answering. "I don't do on the sly. I know you're not likely to hang around for long, and I'm okay with that. I'm okay enjoying whatever it is we've got while we've got it. But I'm not okay with tryin' to keep it hidden like it's something we should be ashamed of."

He turned to her and cupped her face in his hands. "I…" He stopped himself, unsure if he was willing to admit what he was feeling, especially when she was acting so damn reluctant to be part of his whole world. He cleared his throat and tried again. "I like you. I like spending time with you. And I'm willing to take what I can get with you. But only so far."

"You have ex-girlfriends in there." Her eyes clouded and her lips pursed into a sour expression.

"I've got women in my past, darlin'. Same as you've got men." He took a slow breath. She wasn't being rational. Which wasn't like her. "What's really going on here?"

Drea flopped back into her seat. "I don't know. It's ridiculous. I know that. But you and I... Everyone knew we were together. And then we weren't. The difference between the women in your past and the man in mine is that you aren't face-to-face with my ex-fiancé."

That felt a little closer to the mark. Something in what she'd said nagged at his brain. It didn't ring right. Drea fussing over people in his past didn't make sense. Unless she was wanting more than a fling...and down that path lay emotional entanglement that he wasn't ready to admit. Because he didn't want to be nursing a broken heart when she left again.

CeeCee's silver BMW pulled into the lot, and Drea tipped her head at the car. "I don't want to be petty, but the last time I ran into her in town, she was pretty nasty. And there's a bit of history there."

Shit. Like most people, Drea assumed he and CeeCee had been more than they were. Drea probably thought they'd given it another go when CeeCee came home.

"You know she was dating that baseball player our whole senior year?" He kept his eyes on Drea, needing her to understand she had nothing to worry about. She never had. "I covered for her with her parents. Everyone thinkin' I was a slug for leavin' you and takin' up with CeeCee was easier than everyone askin' me about you all the time. Not the best way of dealing with things, but hell, we were kids."

He took her hands in his and kissed her knuckles. "Darlin', I don't know what she told you, or implied, or what you've imagined, but you know things about me that CeeCee does not." He let that sink in for a moment, then leaned over and kissed her lips. "You're with me now. That's enough for me. You ready to go in?"

Drea nodded, then grabbed his hand as he went to slide out of the truck. "I don't think you want me comparing notes with CeeCee in the middle of Oak Bridge. That could get a little embarrassing."

She held the straight face for a fraction of a second longer, then cracked up. Danny shook his head and slid out. When he helped her from the truck, he wrapped his arms around her and kissed her long and slow. She rose up on her tiptoes to meet him, her lips opening and her tongue sliding along his mouth. Honey. She always tasted of honey and smelled like jasmine.

He leaned down to whisper in her ear. "You've always meant the world to me, Drea. That's never stopped."

Heart pounding, he straightened and looked down into her face, her eyes were wide, and she gave him a shaky smile.

"Let's go inside," she said. "I'm hungry. But I'm warning you, I suck at darts."

Inside, it wasn't as bad as Drea had feared. Danny had been right—the group was almost entirely folks she knew from the ranch, so all the 'it's been so long' conversations had already happened. They all greeted her as if she'd been around forever. After they'd eaten, Brian, Lily and Larry convinced her to try darts.

"Danny, she's hopeless. I mean really hopeless." Larry shook his head and ordered another beer.

"How about pool?" Brian poked Drea's arm. "Think we can maybe try a game of pool?"

Drea swallowed a broad grin and gave a hesitant nod instead. Pool was much better than darts. Brian set up the balls, explained the basics and handed her a cue. Drea rolled the stick in her hands, nodding and pretending to listen while Brian finished going over the rules. Her brain churned over the things Danny had said in the parking lot. Especially the part about meaning the world to him.

"You want me to break?" Brian pointed at the table.

Drea nodded and stepped back to let him take the shot. The balls broke apart nicely, but none went into the pockets.

"Open table," he said. "That means you can take whatever you want — solids or stripes. See where the cue ball is here? You've got a clean shot into this pocket. Don't hit it too hard, or you'll scratch. If you do it right, you might have a second shot lined up."

Drea bent over the table and took the shot Brian showed her rather than the one she wanted. The ball dropped neatly into the corner pocket. She aimed wide and missed the next shot. Danny came over and handed her a beer before taking up a stool nearby. She leaned against him, enjoying the feel of his arms around her. Brian sank two balls and missed his third shot.

"How long are you gonna make him suffer?" Danny whispered in her ear. She smiled up at him and chalked her cue.

"So, looks like I can take this shot right here." She pointed at a ball lined up on a side pocket. Brian nodded, and Drea leaned over the table, rising up on her toes to reach across the expanse of green. She cast a glance back over her shoulder at Danny, whose eyes were glued to her ass. She whistled to catch his attention, winked at him and took the shot. The ball dropped into the side pocket and the cue ball came to a stop behind one of Brian's.

"Oooh, that's a toughie," he said. "You've got a couple of choices…"

Drea tuned him out and kept her eyes on Danny. He hid the smirk in his glass of beer. She nodded a time or two at Brian, then looked over the table again.

"Those all sound complicated." She bent over the cue ball and eyed the angle, then straightened and grabbed her cue. Crossing her fingers she could still make it work, she popped the cue ball, sending it sailing over Brian's before it tapped her ball right into the pocket. She dropped the rest of the solids, then lined up for the last shot and pointed.

"Eight ball, corner pocket." The black ball dropped into place, and the cue ball came to rest in the center of the table. Brian's mouth hung open, and his eyes were as wide as saucers. Drea patted his shoulder. "Shut your mouth, honey, you'll catch flies."

She settled onto the stool next to Danny and sipped her beer.

"Where did you…?" Brian sputtered. "How…? That was a jump shot. Then you cleared the table. What just happened?"

Danny chuckled. "I'd say you've been had by a pool shark. Paul taught Drea when she was a kid, and she used to kick everyone's butt when we played. You were a few years behind us, so you probably don't remember. Don't play ping-pong with her either. You'll lose spectacularly. She's vicious."

"Hey!" Drea retorted. "I'm not vicious. I like to win." Though Mattix had said pretty much the same thing the first time they'd played pool.

Brian shut his mouth and joined them on the stools. "I am so glad I did not put money on that game."

CeeCee ambled over from the bar, and Danny's arm curled around Drea's shoulders, pulling her more tightly against him.

"Should I run interference?" Brian looked to Danny, but he shook his head.

"You still remember how to play pool, Drea?" CeeCee stood pressing against Danny's other arm. Drea's stomach clenched into a knot as CeeCee leaned in closer. Drea didn't know what game CeeCee was playing, but she didn't like it.

"I dabble," Drea replied, feeling more than a little bit evil. "Wanna play?"

CeeCee's eyes narrowed, and she shook her head. "I know better. Too bad about your granddaddy's place." She looked up at Danny adoringly. "You gonna do any show ridin' in the gymkhana this year?"

Drea clamped her teeth into her tongue and forced herself to keep a neutral face, stunned that CeeCee would be so mean, so petty.

"You hadn't heard?" Brian leaned forward, breaking the tension. "We've got ourselves a new emcee this year. How about you doin' some ridin'?"

Drea nearly choked on her beer at the idea of CeeCee on a horse. She was terrified of them. But CeeCee smacked Brian's arm and laughed.

"Oh, I don't think so," she said. "I never could ride. Maybe Drea should. You'd have to borrow a horse, but hey, that's nothing new to you anyway."

Drea's head popped up at that. *Ride in the gymkhana? Oh hell no.* She was lucky to be keeping her seat in the saddle on trail rides. She wasn't about to make an idiot of herself out there.

"Oh, yeah!" Lily chimed in. "We need another lady for the opening ceremony. Missy had to back out. She's pregnant and her doctor put her on bed rest. That'd be great!"

Drea glared at her, then Danny chimed in.

"Not a bad idea." Danny looked down at Drea. "What d'ya think, darlin'? Think you could maybe handle showin' off a bit?"

"But that's in a couple of weeks..." Drea sputtered.

Lily waved a hand in the air. "It's easy. We're ridin' in with the flags. The kids come in behind and line up for the National Anthem."

Drea remembered. She'd participated in the thing every year from the time she was old enough to ride until her last year of high school. At least it was just the flag ceremony.

With Danny, Lily and Brian encouraging her, she couldn't very well say no. She finally agreed.

"Well, that's all settled!" CeeCee gave a big smile. "I'll be in the booth with Daddy. He's judgin' again this year." The door swung open, and a group of women came in. CeeCee waved at them, then turned back to Danny. "Excuse me, girls' night. Taa!"

Drea shook her head as CeeCee crossed the floor to join her girlfriends. At least now she understood what CeeCee's game was. She had ensured that Drea would be occupied for a good portion of the start of the event—leaving CeeCee free to be with Danny.

Danny wrapped his hands around her waist and kissed her, pulling her attention back to him. "That wasn't so bad. You okay doing the gymkhana?"

Drea sipped her beer and raised a shoulder. "Meh. I said I would. Though I think CeeCee played a bit of dirty pool there."

Danny gave a hearty laugh. "Yeah, she did. Joke's on her though."

Drea arched a brow at him, and he winked.

"I'm not emceeing from the judge's booth. We've got a different set up this year. Larry's putting finishing touches on a new sound booth."

She wrapped her arms around his neck and kissed him soundly.

"How about givin' me a go at pool?" His voice in her ear was low, seductive. Drea nodded. Danny had always been good — she'd have to work to beat him. She won the first round, and he won the second.

"Tiebreaker?" she asked and pulled quarters from her pocket for the table. He stopped her hand, his fingers circling her wrist in a way that had her sucking in a surprised breath as her nipples stiffened in response to his touch.

"I'm content to call it a draw," he growled in her ear. "After watching you prance around this table all night, I've got other things on my mind."

He grabbed her hand, paid the bill and they said quick good nights to everyone and headed for the door. Once in the truck, desperate to touch him, she rested her hand on his thigh, then stroked higher. His hissing intake of breath echoed in the cab. Drea let her fingers roam over the rough denim, teasing at the buttons as he throbbed to life.

At his cottage, he came around to her door and hauled her out of the seat and against his body, then carried her up the steps. She'd never felt a need like this before. It was a physical ache, gnawing at her. He felt so good. So right. She wanted him, all of him, always. She didn't want to ever let go, but knew she'd have to. That thought was chilling, but his lips on hers quickly shut off her brain.

They barely made it inside the door before he was unbuttoning her pants and sliding his fingers inside her.

"Yes, Danny, please!" she cried out, and he pushed her against the wall. Her pants came off with a few quick tugs. He didn't bother taking off his — he just unbuttoned and slipped on a condom. His hands gripped her thighs and lifted, and she wrapped her legs around him, eager to have him inside her. He pinned her to the wall as his delicious length slid into her.

"God, Drea, you are so fucking amazing!" His words were muffled against her neck. She echoed those feelings — Danny was everything, and she didn't want to imagine having to give him up.

Not a thought for right now. He pressed his hand between them and slid his fingers over her swollen clit, effectively driving all thoughts from her head — except how much she loved the feel of him. She arched against him, and her body tensed, then exploded in orgasm. He followed only a few strokes later.

Later, after they'd made it to his bed and enjoyed round two, she rose to shower, Danny caught her hand and tugged her back to him.

"Don't go," he whispered. "Stay, please?"

Drea's heart soared, then sank. The words she'd wanted to hear from Danny years ago, now uttered because he wanted her to stay the night. She gently pulled her hand away.

"I've got to get back to Gramps."

Chapter Seventeen

"Can you move it a bit to the left?" Gramps sat in the comfy chair by the big window — wide open, letting in the breeze along with the occasional sounds of whinnies and neighs coming from the barn. He gave her repeated, and contradictory, instructions on where to hang the hummingbird feeder.

"A little higher." A second later, "No, too high." She moved it again. "There. Right there."

Eyes rolling, she hung the feeder in exactly the same spot she'd had it when he'd said it wasn't right.

"Okay," Drea said as she came back inside. "You are to sit back and do nothing more strenuous than enjoy the view." He made a face, and she wagged a finger at him. "No arguing. Your color is gone, and the doctor said yesterday that you were not to be pushing yourself. What's the big envelope on the table?"

Gramps gave her an innocent look, and she laughed. The manila envelope was thick and lumpy. She opened it and dumped its contents on the table. Photos, dozens of them — of Gramps, Abuela, her... Drea gasped, even her parents.

"I made a few phone calls and texts." He reached and plucked a photo from the pile. "The photo albums were destroyed in the fire, but lots of people had pictures. I thought you might like the memories."

He handed her the photo he'd picked up. Her parents' wedding photo — a beautiful woman who could have been Drea, dressed in flowing white, standing with a handsome olive-skinned young man with a headful of jet-black curls. Victoria and Luis Hidalgo.

"That came from the newspaper. They ran the wedding announcement when your mother married Luis."

Drea sniffed back tears and sifted through the pictures. So many. "How? Where did all these come from?"

Gramps smiled, for a moment looking much younger than his years. "It's a small town. The paper runs a lot of stories about local people. And Grace Kimmel collects pictures of everything, and everyone."

Another photo. A much younger looking Gramps and Abuela, holding a wide-eyed girl, her legs bandaged, her hair short and curly.

"That was the day we got back with you. Your hair had singed from the fire, and you had mild burns on your legs."

Drea's vision swam. She remembered crying. The heat. And the monster that was her rescuer — it would be years before she realized it was just a man in fire turnouts. She didn't remember coming home with her grandparents. She did remember going to kindergarten that fall, and meeting Danny. And Wilma. And yes, even CeeCee. Drea missed the CeeCee she'd known in school.

As if reading her mind and conjuring something from her thoughts, Gramps slid another photo her way. The three girls. Teenagers, sitting on a fence rail at the annual gymkhana, all wearing wide smiles. Wilma with her faded blonde curls and classic red lips, CeeCee, bright blonde and dimpled, and Drea sitting in the middle, her arms over their shoulders, smiling straight into the camera.

"Gramps…" Her voice broke. All the memories. She had taken only one photo with her—one of her grandparents. Everything else she'd left behind, believing it would always be there for her. And then everything had been lost in the fire.

"Oh my god." She grabbed a picture from the pile, her eyes drawn to the swath of bright blue visible. Junior prom. Danny in his tux, the tie and cummerbund matching the electric blue of Drea's dress.

They were so young. And so naively in love. Believing they could take on the world.

"Remember that night?" Drea held up the prom picture. "Abuela had to show him how to pin on the corsage."

Gramps nodded, his smile a mile wide. "That poor boy was so afraid of sticking you with the pin."

Abuela had fussed that a wrist corsage would have been easier, but she'd stepped up and shown Danny how to angle the pin.

Drea shifted her chair over, and they went through the pictures one by one. Memories came flooding back, bringing smiles, and sometimes tears. Later, as she helped him stretch out on the couch for a nap, Drea kissed his cheek. "Thank you. You always know exactly what I need."

Drea gathered up the pictures, she'd have to put them into an album later. Maybe that was something she and Gramps could do together. She glanced back down at the picture of her with Wilma and CeeCee. She dropped the envelope back to the table, grabbed her keys, and headed for town to see her friend.

The high school lot was nearly full as Drea pulled in and parked at the back. Inside, she waved at Mabel and went straight through to Wilma's office, greeting her friend with a tight hug.

"Wow, what's the occasion?" Wilma's eyebrows shot up her forehead.

"I had a reminder today about how wonderful friendship is. And I wanted to thank you for that."

Wilma shut her door and plunked back into her seat. "Always happy to help. Meanwhile, what did you say to Robert that has him in a snit? I ran into him at the grocery last night, and he more or less suggested that I encourage you to go back to the city. So, what happened?"

Drea sighed and leaned back in the plastic chair, shaking her head. "I stepped on his toes a little too hard, apparently. And I may have sent copies of all the reports to a colleague at the ATF. And copied my boss."

"Uh-huh." Wilma chuckled. "And...?"

Drea shrugged. Technically they were in a gray area here. The local police had asked for a consultation, which she'd given. They were free to do with that information as they saw fit. The ATF wouldn't get further involved unless there was cause—the local authorities asking for help, evidence of criminal activity at a federal level, or if after a consultation, the investigator felt ATF involvement was warranted. Drea had not requested ATF involvement...yet.

"Mattix, my colleague, called the police station yesterday afternoon, said she'd gotten copies of the incident reports, but that apparently the report was incomplete. The CFI's entire report should be included, not just cited." She shrugged again. "A call like that isn't uncommon. It's sort of a shot across the bow that gives folks a chance to straighten up and fly right."

Wilma nodded. "Makes sense. He's having a hissy because you went over his head. Way over his head."

Drea shook her head. "I don't think that's it." She leaned forward, resting her elbows on Wilma's desk. "Robert had to get me involved — it makes him look good. Unexplained fire with a fatality and people are upset over the minimal investigation? Well, we had a Certified Fire Investigator take a look. See? No problem here. So, why is he so upset now? The only possible reason is that I'm not willing to rubber stamp something being swept under the rug, or his bullshit version of what happened. And that has me wondering why."

The window rattled and a loud boom echoed in the room. Drea leaped out of her seat and sped through the front office, past the confused looking Mabel and out of the front door. Across the parking lot, Drea's Cherokee sat in a ball of fire, sparks spitting skyward as smoke roiled.

A high-pitched scream pierced the air. A jumble of voices, someone wailing, another person yelling about getting a hose, or a fire extinguisher. A bunch of people pulling out their cell phones, taking pictures, video. As far as Drea was concerned, the more evidence the better. Robert wanted to keep something quiet? *Too late. Someone's blown up my car.*

"What the hell was that?" Wilma's voice came from her elbow. The crowd swelled as students poured out of the building and low-grade panic ramped up. Drea saw it in their faces, heard it in the tone of people's voices.

"Please stay on the steps, or go back inside," Drea called out, and was gratified when all eyes turned to her and the murmuring stopped. Incident command voice, Mattix called it. It was the voice that said 'don't worry, I'm in charge here, everything will be okay.'

She turned to the school security officer. "Keep the students back. What's your evac point for a fire? The football field?" He nodded, his eyes wide and staring. The guy wasn't a cop—he was just a young man in a uniform and he looked overwhelmed. Drea grabbed his elbow and got close, speaking right into his face. "Start your evac protocol. Now."

That seemed to get through to him. He blinked once, then started barking orders at the teachers, herding students toward the football field. Drea looked around and grabbed Miss Mabel, who was standing there with her mouth hanging open.

"Mabel," Drea said her name sharply and the woman turned to look at her. "I need you to call the fire department and tell them there is a vehicle fire in the school parking lot." Mabel nodded and pulled out her phone.

Drea turned back to Wilma. "Can you call Gramps and Danny? Let them know what happened, and that I'm okay?"

"Sure, but why don't you...?" Wilma stopped and looked up at the fire, then back to Drea. "Oh no, you are not going near that."

"Just call them."

Drea walked down the steps and across the lot. The heat hit her like a living thing, and she paused, sucking in a harsh breath and forcing the nightmare images from her head. She had to take pictures before it burned too far. The boom had been the gas tank going. It might not have left enough to get pictures.

She walked around the car, then crouched down and looked under the back end. There, right where she suspected, was the culprit wedged beside the right rear tire. She snapped a few images, then crawled closer to get a better angle. The smell of burning gas and oil and car parts stung her eyes, and she pulled her shirt up over her mouth and nose to filter out the worst of it. Sparks still spurted from the can, clearly the source of ignition. She moved again and saw the second can, behind the front bumper. The flames hadn't yet ignited it.

She needed to get that thing.

The fire crackled and popped, and she squeezed her eyes shut as she edged around to the front of the car. Something hot singed her hand, and she pulled back with a hiss. Broken bits of glass covered the ground.

Glass pierced her hand as she grasped the window ledge and pulled herself over the sill. Cool night air rushed into her lungs and a cough racked her body. Got to roll. Careful. Careful. Stairs. Stay near the stairs. Cold metal under her hands. Glass digging into her legs. Pain and heat searing her back.

Drea blinked those memories away and focused her attention on the car. She shoved forward and kicked at the can. Fire licked along her leg, and she gritted her teeth against the images flashing in her head. *Dammit. Not now.* She had to do this. One more kick sent the can rolling away from the car. She scrambled back, away from the heat and flames.

A hand closed over her shoulder and hauled her upright and backward. Drea whirled. Shock, fear and anger painted a strange mix on Danny's face. His mouth moved but the only sound she heard was the roaring of the fire. She squeezed her eyes shut then opened them and focused on his lips.

"What the hell are you doing?" His voice penetrated the fog as he shook her. Drea pushed out of his grip and glared at him.

"I'm doing my job." She waved her hand at the fireball that was her car. "*That* doesn't happen on accident. Parked cars don't spontaneously combust."

She turned, searching for the can, but his grip on her arm pulled her back. "Where are you going?" His tone was softer, more worried than angry.

"There is evidence over there, and I'm going to retrieve it before it's destroyed, contaminated any more than it already is, or lost, or anything else. If you want to help, find me a shovel."

She tugged her arm away and went in search of the second can. She found it ten feet from the car, resting against the curb. A trail of gray-black granular material showed the path it had taken after she'd kicked it.

"Here." Danny handed her a stall scoop. "Best I could do on short notice. It was in the back of my truck."

"Thanks." She started with the can, scooping it up and carrying it a safe distance from the fire. It hadn't caught. Small favors. Inside the can, there was still plenty of the gray-black stuff, plus a lump of something similar, and what looked like a strip of thin metal mesh. *Standard thermite device. Lovely.*

She took more photos and sent them to Mattix and Wilkes along with a quick note. "My car got blown up.

One of these under the gas tank, one under the engine. Managed to retrieve this one before it caught. Full report to follow. I'm okay." With business taken care of, she looked back to Danny. "How did you get here so fast?"

His face was creased with worry and a short, humorless laugh came out. "I was at the hardware store, workin' with Larry, gettin' things ready for the gymkhana this weekend. Then Wilma called. Are you okay?"

Drea nodded. He needed more. Deserved more. Then the fire crew pulled in. "I've got to talk to…"

"Go," Danny replied. He shoved his hands in his pockets, and the concerned look on his face tore at Drea. But she had to do this first. She grabbed Amos, giving him direction on dealing with the possibility of thermite, then she got out of their way. It was time to let the hose jockeys do their job. Flashing lights and a blaring siren announced the arrival of the police. Robert stormed up to her, a scowl etching ugly contours into his face.

"Get off the scene, Andrea. Now." He pointed his arm toward the crowd of onlookers still gathered on the steps. "You, too." He waved a hand at Danny. "Get back."

Drea's hands clenched into fists, and she counted to ten before responding. "There were two cans under my car. This was not an accident. I managed…"

"I don't care what you think," Robert interrupted. "I told you to get off the scene. Just leave that…" He waved at the can. "Leave whatever it is you claim you found."

"What in the hell?" She managed to keep herself from yelling. Barely. "What I found is evidence. That's an incendiary device. I'm trying to help here."

Robert walked over to the can, looked down at it with a scowl, then glanced back up at Drea. "Looks like a bucket of sand to me."

Oh, screw counting to ten. Drea took two steps closer to Robert, then thought better of it. If she was within arms' reach, she might deck him. "Are you really that...?"

"Drea." Danny's voice whispered in her ear. "Not now. Let's go." His fingers wrapped around her arm, and she looked over her shoulder at him. "Later." That whisper in her ear again. "Let him strut and posture."

He was right. As much as she hated to admit it, now was not the time for this discussion. There was an active fire scene, and no matter how much she might disagree with him, Robert had a job to do, even if he was a total fuck-up at it. She pressed her lips together and turned back to Robert, smiling sweetly. "I'd like to file a police report."

He stuck his thumbs in his belt and smiled. "Of course, as soon as we've got time. As you can see, we're dealing with a big fire right now. Why don't you come into the station next week? We are comin' up on a holiday weekend, and I'll be a bit busy."

Drea didn't bother smiling at that. "Fine. I've got pictures of the scene, and that can is evidence. I've also sent a note to my boss at the ATF. He'll want a copy of the police report as well." She turned to Danny. "Think I can talk you into a ride home?"

* * * *

Danny dropped Drea off at the cottage, then pulled around to his place to find his mother standing on his porch, arms crossed over her chest, her foot tapping out a rhythm on the deck. Looked like the gossip chain was in full swing.

"Ma." He nodded as he came up the steps. "I can guess what brought you over here."

"You smell like a gasoline fire. Why didn't you stop on the way in?"

"Drea wanted to get to her gramps. What was I supposed to do? Tell her no, we had to see you first?"

"Don't get smart with me."

"Yes'm." He shut his mouth and waited. She had something to say, or she wouldn't be here. But she'd get to it in her own sweet time.

"Can I come in?" She looked from him to the door.

Danny pushed open the door, holding it so she could enter. He flicked on the light and pointed to the kitchen table, then started a pot of coffee. Something told him this wasn't going to be a short talk.

"Can we make this quick?" he asked. "I'd like to shower and change."

"Before Andrea gets done with her granddaddy and comes over for the night." Her tone was matter-of-fact, no judgment or condemnation. Just simple truth.

Danny blinked in surprise. The thought of denying it crossed his mind. "Yes'm." Not that Drea ever stayed the night.

She sat, tapping her fingers on the table until the coffee maker beeped, and he rose, poured them both cups and placed hers in front of her. She took a sip, then sat back and fixed him with a stare that as a teen would have had him quaking in his shoes.

"I heard about the explosion," she said. "Robert's likely to say Andrea's stirrin' up trouble. Most won't listen to him, but a few will. And they'll be noisy about it, given the chance."

Her fingers tapped on her coffee cup, and Danny waited. She was letting her words sink in. It was her way. She'd beat around the bush until she felt she had you cornered. He didn't think she'd say anything he wasn't already feeling himself.

"Those folks need to mind their own." She said it firmly, with a nod of her head, as if that was the final say on the subject. "She's doin' right by her granddaddy. And she's doin' right by this town, pushin' to find out what happened with all these fires." She looked up, directly into his eyes. "She belongs here, even if she doesn't think so."

Well, at least he wasn't the only one who thought that. She shifted in her seat and a trace of what could have been discomfort passed her features. *Here it comes.* She was about to get to the point.

"Y'all are playin' house. Don't think I don't know that." She leaned back in her chair. "You don't believe she's plannin' to stay after Paul passes, do you?"

He swallowed past the lump in his throat. "No, ma'am. I don't." He'd seen Drea dealing with fire. She was right, she was doing her job. He had no idea what he could offer to make her want to give that up. To choose him over her career. He didn't have the right to ask it of her.

"Well then, you need to give her reason to stay." Another nod. As if it were that simple.

"I don't think it's that easy," he replied. No matter how much he might wish it were.

"Of course it's not that easy, Daniel." She sighed, pushed her empty coffee cup toward him, and waited for him to refill it. "I'm no more blind nor stupid now than I was when you were a teenager. Andrea is the only girl who's ever really turned your head, despite how much tomcatting around you did after high school. You gave up your hopes and dreams to stay here and take on the family business. You think I don't know that? You think I don't appreciate that you did that?"

She shook her head at him. "I want to see you settled, and I want to see you happy. I'd also like to see a grandchild someday."

She reached across the table and covered his hand with her own. "What I'm saying is Andrea's fixin' to have a heaping helping of reasons to leave. Maybe you oughta be working harder on giving her reasons to stay."

"What did you have in mind? I'm not exactly sittin' on my ass ignoring her." Danny pushed back from the table and paced the kitchen.

"You're in your own home, you can cuss all you like, but I'll ask you to watch your language when I'm present."

"Yes, ma'am." Danny muttered the words, and she gave him a sharp look. She finished her coffee in silence, gathered both cups and rose to drop them in the sink. She put a hand on his arm, stopping his pacing.

"You might try telling her how you feel," she said. "You're expecting her to take an awfully big risk — give up a career and make a move, for what? A possibility?"

Her words dug deep. The kicker was, she was right. Except Danny wasn't ready to risk the heartbreak if Drea said no.

His mother nodded again and glanced around the space as she headed for the door. "You've done wonders with this place, but it could use a woman's touch here and there."

He waited until she was out of sight around the barn, and there was no danger of her turning around for one more jab. Sure that he was alone, he stripped and headed to the shower, cranking the water up as hot as he could stand. The smell of the fire was everywhere. He could only imagine how Drea felt. She'd been in the middle of it all.

He ducked his head under the spray to rinse and jumped as the shower curtain flapped against his leg. Cool fingers slid over his chest, making him jump again and sputter as he got a face full of water. He opened his eyes to see Drea, still dressed in the clothes she'd had on earlier, still covered in soot and dirt, standing next to the shower.

"How long have you been there?"

She looked shell-shocked. Hell, she had a right to be.

"I just got here. I needed... I need to shut off my brain. The door was open. I hope it's okay."

He grabbed her around the waist and lifted her into the shower, ignoring her squeal of protest. He knew one sure-fire way to turn off her brain. Luckily, it was the same thing that could shut off the nagging in his own thoughts. He turned and got her under the spray, then started peeling her clothes off. Thankfully, she'd kicked off her shoes at some point before she came in, and it was quick work to get her out of the thin top and capri pants she was wearing.

Once she was naked, he handed her the shampoo and leaned against the wall, enjoying the rise and fall of her breasts as she washed and rinsed that glorious mane of hair. When she was done, he reached for the soap and lathered every inch of her skin. She stiffened as his fingers grazed the scars on her back, but he pulled her closer against his chest and whispered in her ear.

"Let me be here for you." He trailed his fingers along the edge of the scar as he rinsed the soap off, all the way down her back, then cupped her ass and pulled her tight against his body. His hard cock pressed against her belly, and she moaned softly as his lips grazed her neck.

Her fingers tangled in his hair, pulling his head up to kiss him, hard, demanding, needing, driving everything from his head except for her. The way she smelled, tasted, the feel of her. She lifted her leg and wrapped it around his waist, shattering any sense of control he had. He didn't need further encouragement. He slid into her silky heat. Her fingers gripped his shoulders as he pressed her against the tiled wall, lifting her so he could slide all the way home. She shuddered around him as he ground into her.

Drea lifted her other leg and locked her ankles behind his back. She pressed her hands into his shoulders and shifted, lifting her breasts up. He didn't miss the hint and lowered his head, closing his mouth around a nipple and sucking until she cried out in pleasure.

"Oh god, yes! Danny!" Her cries echoed on the tiled walls. He raised his head to watch her as he thrust into her again and again. Her head was thrown back, an expression of pure ecstasy on her face as her body trembled against him. He didn't want to stop. He didn't want to ever stop. He wanted to be the source of her pleasure, always. She made a little sound of complaint when he pulled out, then her eyes went wide as he stroked himself, spilling out onto the tub floor.

He wrapped his arms around her from behind and pulled her against him, grabbed the handheld shower and directed the spray between her legs. She gasped, then wriggled, then spread her legs and her fingers dug into his thighs. He held her up as the tremors spread through her entire body. She pushed the shower head away and leaned against him.

They were toweling off when she turned to him with an odd expression. "You weren't... We didn't... I mean...umm...shit."

"Yeah." He hung his head. He'd been so caught up in her that he'd entirely forgotten a condom. "Not exactly the best method of birth control. I'm sorry. Got a little carried away there."

"My fault as much as yours," she whispered. "At least you had the presence of mind to... Well... y'know?"

He didn't think an unplanned pregnancy was what his mother had had in mind when she said give Drea reasons to stay. He dropped his towel and pulled hers off, then lifted her in his arms and carried her to the bed.

"I just... What if...?"

He quieted her with a kiss.

"It happened," he said. "And I don't regret it. If there are consequences, we'll deal with them. Together. Always. But right now, I'm not done."

Chapter Eighteen

The arena looked bigger than Drea remembered, and the seats were filling up for the annual gymkhana. She shifted in the saddle and cast a nervous look down at Danny. "I still don't understand why Cisco." The beautiful palomino was Danny's old horse, now retired from regular work. Seeing him took her right back to high school. "I thought I'd ride Sheba. I'm used to her."

Danny patted her knee and smiled. "Sheba's too competitive. She's easy enough on the trail, but here? In an arena, with so many other horses around? She'd be wound up tighter than you'd want. Cisco's perfect for this." He stroked the gelding's shoulder, and the horse turned his head into him.

Cisco was stunning, with a coat the color of golden wheat and an almost white mane and tail. He was also so mellow that nothing fazed him. She wished he didn't bring up so many memories of all the rides she and Danny used to take together.

Lily rode up on her gray appaloosa along with the other two ladies making up the color guard. Danny greeted them all by name, then turned back to Drea. He grabbed her hand and gave a gentle tug.

"Lean down." There was a not-so-innocent gleam in his eyes that made Drea wonder what he had in mind. Still, she leaned down to him.

He cupped her chin and kissed her, long and slow, eliciting hoots and applause from the three ladies next to them. When he finally let Drea up for air, there were more than a few smiling faces looking their way.

"Everyone saw that." The kiss left her breathless and wanting more.

"Yup." There was no shame or apology in his look. His smile was so wide it dimpled his cheeks and crinkled the corners of his eyes. "I gotta get into place. C'mon up when you're done."

He ambled off, saying hello to folks as he moved slowly through the crowd.

"That man really does have a fine backside." Lily reined in next to Drea and elbowed her. "Not that I'm lookin', of course."

Drea chuckled. "Look all you'd like. It's true. He does." She wasn't about to regale Lily with everything else that was oh-so-fine about Danny. Drea cleared her throat and looked away, hoping she wasn't blushing.

"Okay." Lily addressed the group. "Let's do this. I've got Old Glory and Kelly's got the state flag. Drea to the left, Georgia to the right, half a length behind. Nothin' fancy — let's leave the showin' off to the kids. We'll ride out the center gate, take it at a walk to the middle of the arena. Face the judge's booth. The participants will come in behind us. Once everyone is assembled, they'll play the anthem, and we ride out. I've got the lead in and out."

They'd taken their places when Danny's voice came over the loudspeakers announcing the color guard, and Lily rode out. Drea took a deep breath, gathered her reins and followed, terrified she was going to fall off. She shook herself over that silly fear and looked around as they reached the center of the arena.

It seemed like half of the county was there, or more. The gymkhana happened every Memorial Day weekend and attracted pony clubs and agricultural groups from all over. She'd participated most of her life—pole bending and barrel racing mostly.

Drea tipped her head, watching the last of the participants riding in. She knew some of the older ones, well, had known them. She'd babysat a few of them when she was a teenager. She shifted her attention back to the front. They were right in front of the judge's booth, and she spotted CeeCee's blonde hair off to one side. Probably next to her father. He'd been a champion rodeo rider back in his day and had helped with the gymkhana as far back as Drea could recall.

"Folks, please rise for the National Anthem." Danny's voice over the loudspeakers again.

Drea sat up straighter, eyes on the flag Lily held, blinking away tears brought on by a pang of nostalgia. This had been a good place to grow up. She'd had a happy childhood, good friends, a loving family.

But still she'd wanted out. She'd felt stifled by the small town. Eager to do something more. Be part of something bigger. And she had. She'd done exactly what she'd set out to do. Finished college, got into the ATF, became a Certified Fire Investigator, and helped solve arsons. She'd been all over the country with the

National Response Team and testified in more trials than she cared to think about. She'd helped bring bad guys to justice.

Even if she never went back to the field, if all she ever did from now on was teach, she was an ATF Special Agent. A CFI. She had a good job, a good life. But she wasn't happy.

The anthem ended, and Lily led the color guard out of the arena. Drea wiped her eyes and sniffed. She didn't want to be red eyed and pensive when she got to the emcee's booth.

The first demo event was wrapping up by the time she finished untacking Cisco. Drea turned him into a stall and forked hay into the feeder.

"I'll take care of the rest." Lily rested her hand on Drea's shoulder. "You get on up to Danny."

Drea made her way to the new booth, above and behind the judge's booth. She opened the door and found Danny sitting in the front, microphone in hand as he watched out the window, and Gramps in a wheelchair next to him. Jimmy sat in a chair off to the side.

"What is going on?" she whispered the question to Jimmy, who smiled and pointed to Danny. Drea hugged Gramps, then turned to Danny, waiting for an explanation.

He finished announcing the next event, hit the mute button and rose to wrap Drea in a big hug.

"Surprise, darlin'." He kissed her quickly and pulled out a chair, placing her between him and Gramps. "CeeCee was teasin' at Oak Bridge the other night, but after Lily talked you into ridin' with the color guard, everything else seemed to fall into place and I figured you'd like your granddaddy here. Lily and I worked it out with Jimmy."

Gramps had a wide smile on his face as he watched the riders on the field below, but he turned to Drea. "Do you remember the year you talked Wilma into riding?"

Drea laughed. She did. Vividly. It was the year she'd turned sixteen. The organizers had decided to have an opening parade with the flags from all fifty states. Drea had tried to convince CeeCee and Wilma both to ride that year—CeeCee was absolutely terrified of horses and refused. Wilma could ride, just not well, but she'd agreed.

As they'd rode out, a dragonfly landed on her horse's nose, setting the gelding to shaking his head and prancing around. Poor Wilma could only hang on and hope she didn't fall off. Annette Parsons had run out onto the field, snagged the horse's reins as it zipped past her, and managed to calm the horse and get Wilma safely dismounted. As far as Drea knew, Wilma had not been on, or even near, a horse since.

"Yeah." She nodded to Gramps. "Good times." He turned his attention back to the field where a group of boys were tackling the keyhole race. She leaned over to Danny. "Thank you."

"My pleasure, darlin'." His hand rested on her knee, squeezed. Drea sat back and enjoyed watching the show. Even more, she enjoyed the easy way Danny touched her as he went about his work.

After the last event, Jimmy took Gramps home, but Danny and Drea stayed for the annual picnic. They ate hotdogs and walked, hand in hand, and Drea felt like she was a teenager again. Though Danny was a lot less shy about kissing her in front of everyone now than he was back then. As teens, they would slip away to quiet places, tuck themselves behind a tree or alongside a barn. Now, Danny leaned down and kissed her as they walked along.

Mack Lawson talked Drea into playing cornhole — which she lost — then she and Danny won at horseshoes against Larry Gable and his girlfriend. They stayed until the end, talking, laughing.

"Have a good time?" Danny opened the truck door for her and kissed her as she settled into the passenger seat.

"Yeah. I did." The realization surprised her a bit.

"Think I can talk you into comin' over?"

She didn't need to see the gleam in his eyes to know what he had in mind. And she liked the idea. She waited for him to slide behind the wheel and start the truck.

"Lemme check in on Gramps, and sure. But I need to shower."

He put the truck in gear. "I think that can be arranged. I promise I'll behave this time."

Drea laughed. She didn't believe that for an instant.

* * * *

Danny walked over to the cottage the next morning and found Paul sitting on the porch with Jimmy, who took off inside right after saying hello, leaving Danny feeling a little like he'd done something wrong.

He'd once brought Drea home late after a date. Isabel and Paul had been standing on the front porch, waiting. Isabel had ignored him and marched Drea straight into the house amid a slew of Spanish that he didn't have to understand to know that Drea was in hot water.

Paul had shaken his head at his wife's outburst, then looked at Danny and beckoned him to sit. The conversation had been uncomfortable, as Paul talked of respect, and boundaries, but it had also left a lasting impression. His own father would have yelled, had a few choice words, and left the rest of the conversation to his mother. Paul had spoken firmly, but with kindness and gentleness. And Danny had vowed then and there to grow into a man that Paul DeJarnet could respect.

"Thank you for coming over, Danny. Figured we'd have a talk while Drea's out with Wilma. Sit, have an iced tea." Paul pointed at the pitcher on the little side table.

"Thank you." Danny took the seat next to him and poured them both a tea. "So, what are we chatting about?"

Paul closed his eyes and tipped his head back, his fingers tapping on the chair arms. "I always thought you and Drea would end up together."

Danny nearly choked on the first swallow of tea. He wasn't sure he liked where this was going.

"The second half of senior year was hard for her." Paul's voice was strained, tight. The hiss of oxygen a constant rhythm. "I'm not blaming you for that. Never have. You were both young, too young, maybe. You were faced with hard choices. You did what was right for your family, but you sacrificed your own happiness."

"And Drea's." The words came without bitterness. Danny had gotten past that long ago. But he still felt guilt.

"Do you think she would have stayed if you'd asked her?"

The directness took Danny aback. At the time, he had. He believed that had he asked, she would have stayed. And eventually resented him for asking her to give up her dreams.

"Back then? Yes. I believed she would. Now? I'm not so sure." He sighed, sat his drink on the table and pushed his hands through his hair. "She was so determined. She might have refused. But there's no real way to know."

Paul shook his head. "You made the right choice." Those words hit Danny like a punch to the gut. Though supportive, they were not what he expected. Not what he'd told himself for years.

"What?"

"You both needed to grow," Paul said. "To learn more about yourselves. And to accept your place, your role. You have. Drea has had some challenges."

Danny knew that. Recognized that. It had taken him a long time to reach acceptance. Drea was still struggling with her own sense of self, and where she belonged in the world.

"Thank you. That means a lot to me." He meant it. He loved his own father. He'd been a good man. Rough around the edges, old-school tough-love type. And Danny had always strived to live up to his dad's expectations. After his dad had passed, it was Paul who'd served as an example of the strong, gentle, loving man Danny wanted to be.

"Drea knows what she wants." Paul spoke softly. Slowly. "Deep down. But she's afraid to admit it. Afraid of what it means."

"I don't suppose you're gonna tell me what it is she wants?"

Paul chuckled. "Tellin' ain't what you need. You need believin', and I can't give you that. But I can maybe help you along the way. You'll have to do the figurin' out on your own."

Any pointer was better than nothing. At the moment, Danny felt like he was dealing with two Dreas—one who smiled and held his hand, and warmed his bed, and gave him every impression that she loved him still. And the other made him feel like she'd leave in an instant, taking his heart and soul with her.

He settled back in his chair as Paul pulled a chain from around his neck.

"I met Isabel at a USO dance when I was still in the service," Paul said, his eyes closed and a soft smile played on his lips. "Drea calls our story a fairy tale. Isabel was visiting her cousin, and I was smitten with that raven-haired girl. I wrote a letter every week."

Paul's eyes opened and fastened on Danny's. Even nine years after his wife had passed, Paul's eyes still shone with love. His fingers toyed with the chain he'd pulled off. Danny had heard bits and pieces of this story from Drea. Hearing it from Paul was different—almost magical.

"I saved every penny," Paul continued. "When I got discharged and came back home, well, there wasn't much work to be had, so I worked the mines. I didn't want to bring that pretty little thing into this backwater, but I couldn't imagine life without her. And the world didn't have too much to offer anywhere else. Coal company offered me a good job. I had enough saved up I could afford a house and a ring. I wrote Isabel and asked her to come."

Drea had shared this part. Isabel had packed her things, left Puerto Rico, and married Paul at the courthouse the day she arrived.

"Isabel was my reason for being," Paul said. "My everything. Then we had Victoria. And when she was taken from us, we had Drea to care for."

Paul reached out and grasped Danny's fingers, his grip surprisingly strong and sure. "Drea is very much like her grandmother. Strong and stubborn. It will take work." Paul sighed and sat back. "Why don't you tell me what you want, Daniel Parsons?"

The question came out of nowhere and Danny blinked in surprise. So many things crowded for attention, but one thing stood out above all else. One thing had been consistent for longer than he could remember.

Drea.

"Don't you two look comfortable." Drea stepped onto the porch, eyeing the empty pitcher of iced tea, and equally empty pair of beer bottles. She gave Gramps a pointed look.

"The beers are mine." Danny swept his hands through hair that looked like it had already been through the wringer. "It's a gorgeous Sunday to be out on the porch, and we've been sitting out here shootin' the breeze."

Gramps used to have an occasional beer. He was a grown man and could certainly make his own choices, but alcohol and his meds weren't a good mix.

"Mack Lawson not coming by today?" She bent to clear the beer bottles, but Danny scooped them up first. He grabbed the pitcher and glasses as well and headed inside.

"He'll be by for an early dinner tonight." Gramps gave a little shrug. "I guess I shoulda told you the change in plans so you could figure out dinner."

Drea wasn't too worried about dinner. Gramps barely ate anyway and there were plenty of vegetables around. It was hot — a salad with a little chicken would make a good dinner and could easily feed an extra person. Or two.

"Danny's joinin' us as well." Gramps looked at her apologetically. "If you can make that work."

Before Drea could answer, Jimmy came out and started fussing over Gramps — getting him up and moving him into the living room. Drea found Danny in the kitchen, washing the pitcher and iced tea glasses.

"Figured I could help with dinner, if you'd like." He dried the glasses and put them away without asking where they went. An odd little reminder that this cottage was more his space than hers.

"Uh...sure." Something was off. Danny seemed subdued somehow. Quiet. She wondered what he and Gramps had talked about. Wouldn't do her any good to ask. Neither one of them would be very forthcoming. "You can rinse the lettuce. I'll get the chicken started."

Danny turned out to be surprisingly helpful in the kitchen. He made a huge salad and whipped together a vinaigrette from things he pulled out of the fridge and pantry all while Drea got the chicken prepped.

Danny slid a hand around her waist as he went behind her or leaned in and kissed her cheek when she reached past him for a paper towel. It felt as if they'd been sharing a space for years. He grabbed silverware and set the table and Drea stood transfixed — those big hands carefully laying out napkins, utensils just so.

And his arms... He had on a short sleeve tee that stretched tight across his biceps.

"You're gonna burn the chicken." Danny laughed and pointed at the stove.

By the time Mack Lawson arrived, Drea was arranging slices of chicken breast on top of the salads. A few shavings of parmesan and a handful of homemade croutons, and dinner was on.

"Have you heard anything else about your car? Or the fire that took the house?" Chief Lawson speared a piece of lettuce as he spoke.

"That's a bit of a sore spot." Drea didn't want to get into unpleasant conversation at the dinner table, but the chief had worked with Robert. Trained him. Though she'd never had cause to remark on whether Lawson was good or bad at his job, everyone else seemed to think things had been better off when he was around.

"What's been done?" he asked.

Drea, Danny and Paul all spoke at once. "Nothing."

The laughter broke the sense of tension Drea felt and she sat back, sighing. "Robert has indicated he's unwilling to put any effort into these fires."

Lawson looked confused until Danny leaned forward and explained everything, far more concisely and politely than Drea could. She would have included a few not-fit-for-polite-company phrases.

"How do you feel about this?" Lawson directed the question at Gramps.

"We all know Robert has been useless since you retired. I'm not happy he's ignoring the fact that someone burned down my house, and Drea's car." Gramps shook his head. "I'm less thrilled that he's got someone right here who's been asking questions, pointing out evidence, and he's ignored it."

"I'm going to talk to him, or at least try. He's not answered my calls." Drea lifted her shoulders in a shrug. "After the car, he told me to come in if I wanted a copy of the police report. I still haven't gotten that."

Lawson nodded. "Do you believe he may be responsible?"

Drea shook her head. "He certainly had the opportunity, and I suppose he could have motive, but I don't think he's the planning type. I do believe he knows more than he's letting on though."

Lawson sat back. "Don't let him bully you."

Danny let out a short burst of laughter. "Have you been around Drea? I don't think she can be bullied." He dropped her a wink, and Drea stuck her tongue out at him.

"Town council appointed Robert after you retired, Chief. His term is up next year." Jimmy gave a small smile. "Seems that's where this is likely headed."

"Has the town council ever voted against an incumbent chief of police?" Drea couldn't recall. As far back as she could remember, it had been Lawson. She was sure there was someone before him, but she was too young to remember.

"No, they haven't." Lawson offered a sad smile. "But there's a first time for everything."

After Lawson had left, Jimmy said he'd take care of the cleaning up before he went home for the day. Drea sat running her finger around the rim of her glass, wondering how best to deal with Robert.

"Don't go doing anything foolish." Gramps tapped her hand as Jimmy came to help him shower. "Tell her." He kissed Drea's cheek and said good night.

"He's right." Danny sat back, his expression gentle, apologetic.

"Oh, don't you start." Drea leaned back in her seat and rubbed her eyes. "I don't know what I'm going to say. Or how I'm going to deal with him. I'll see what he's done first. This is my car we're talking about. And before that, it was Gramps' house."

Danny covered her hand with his, his skin warm against hers. "I know. And I'm sorry. All I'm sayin' is don't go stirring shit unless you absolutely have to. Robert can be a petty bastard if provoked. Can you promise me you'll at least think about that?"

"Yes." Drea mumbled the word but glared up at him.

His fingers slid under her chin. Those eyes. Those amazing blue eyes. And that smile. She could lose herself in him.

"That's all I ask," he said. "Think we can sit on the porch and steal a few kisses? Or should we take an evening stroll for that?"

"I like the idea of both." Drea leaned over the table and kissed him. She loved the prickle of his ever-present stubble, the feel of his lips against hers. And how he responded to her touch, hungry, demanding more.

She closed her eyes and pulled back. "Let's take a walk."

Danny took her hand and led her out the door and into the night.

Chapter Nineteen

Drea dropped the single-page police report onto the counter and glared at Robert. He glared right back, legs wide and arms crossed over his chest, making her want to reach out and slap him. She wouldn't lose her temper. She wouldn't.

"What is this?" Drea pointed at the paper.

"It's a police report," he replied. "Exactly what you asked for."

Drea gritted her teeth. Danny had asked her to behave. Gramps had asked her to behave, and he was having a rough day of it. She needed to wrap this up and get back to him. She was going to behave if it killed her.

"There is no mention of any sign of an incendiary device—the cans I found, the one that still had what looked like thermite and a magnesium fuse. This report says the cause of the fire is unknown."

Robert picked up the report and scanned down the page. "Well, ma'am, it's all right here. Seems there was a vehicle fire in the high school parking lot. Coulda been any number of things that caused it."

Drea took a deep breath and blew it out. She needed to keep it together, not bite his head off. "Why isn't there anything in here about the potential evidence I found? I sent you the images."

He crossed his arms over his chest again. "Look, Andrea, I'm sure you mean well, but the simple fact is, your car caught fire. Doesn't mean there's a crime that happened. Now before you go gettin' all upset, maybe you oughta think things through." He pushed the page back across the counter at her. "If someone did set that fire, and I'm not sayin' they did, I'm sayin' if... Well, folks who go meddlin' often find the cost can be a bit high, don't you think?"

He stared at her, blinking innocently and smiling. Drea picked up the report and slid it into her bag, then pulled out her badge holder. She flipped it open and laid it on the counter.

"Perhaps I need to reintroduce myself. Hi, I'm Special Agent Andrea Hidalgo, Certified Fire Investigator with the ATF. I have reason to believe my home was burned, and later my car was set on fire via two improvised incendiary devices, possibly thermite based..."

"Let me stop you right there." He pushed her badge across the counter at her. "I don't want to see you in this station again. I don't want you near any fire that happens in this town. You've been stirring shit with your meddlin' and it's time to stop. You can't barge in here and call the shots. You've got to go through channels. Or we have to ask you. Well, we asked you to do one thing and now you think you can run free with it."

He lifted the divider and stepped through, scooped up her badge and handed it to her, then escorted her out the door. "Consider this us un-asking you. Your jurisdiction has been revoked. Have a nice day."

He slammed the door shut, turned the lock and waved at her through the glass.

Oh, no way was she going to behave when an asshole pulled shit like that. She picked up the phone to call Mattix, knowing what the other woman would say—start an investigation. Drea stuck the phone back in her pocket. No. She needed to focus on Gramps. She shot one last look at Robert, still standing at the door, glaring at her, so she waved and flashed him the brightest, most plastic smile she could muster, and climbed into Gramps' old truck.

Gramps was having lunch when she came in. Propped up in the cushy chair near the window, he was looking sickly again, pale and shaky, struggling to breathe.

"You get your business dealt with?" Gramps' voice was raspy and thin, and a stab of fear pierced her. Despite the good weeks he'd had, he was sick and slowly dying. Her digging had already cost him his home.

"No," she whispered. "And I don't know that I can deal with it. Not without a lot of cost."

"Everything costs." He took a shuddering, wheezy breath and let it out on a laugh. "What are your options?"

Drea shrugged. "I can drop it. Let it be. Whatever happened in the first fires, and the one that burned your house, and my car...just happened." That idea didn't feel good. It didn't feel right. Every part of it grated against her and made her uncomfortable. She had taken this career path to solve fire crimes. She wanted to chase the arsonist and catch them. Preferably before they could do it again. And here she was, uncertain what to do about a series of fires in her own hometown.

"I can keep arguing," she continued, "nagging and trying to get something done around here. But I don't think that'd get me anywhere. Fact is, I think it'd be about the stupidest thing I could do."

Gramps laughed, then the laughter turned into a coughing fit, and she fetched his inhaler from by the bed. "Does this thing help?"

He coughed some more, then finally managed the inhaler. A moment later, his breathing was back to normal. "A bit. It's not magic, though. Doesn't sound as if you like either of those choices."

She shook her head. "The only other thing I can do is call in the cavalry." He looked confused, and she rubbed her forehead before continuing. "If I make a full report on this, including everything I suspect but can't prove, the ATF will be here in a heartbeat."

He seemed to consider the idea. "What's stopping you from doing that?"

"I don't want to make our last bit of time together about work." She pushed up from the chair and paced the room. "I don't want to make people here hate me."

He grabbed her hand as she passed by, his grip still surprisingly strong. He gestured at the chair and Drea sat.

"Some folks will always be hateful, you know that. You're worried about Danny." It was a statement, not a question. "You have to do what's right for yourself, little one."

Tears pricked her eyes, and she sniffed them back. "Yeah, I know. I know." She stared out the window, the rolling green hills, the trees in the distance. It was beautiful here. Every morning, the rising sun took her breath away, making each day feel like a gift. "If I do that, if I call my boss, it starts a chain of events that I can't stop. If I make that report, it feels like I'm making a decision I'm not sure I want to make."

"You're thinking of staying." Gramps always had a way of getting to the heart of what was bugging her. Two sides waging war — one struggling to reclaim the life she thought she'd wanted, the other missing the things, and the people, she'd left behind.

"I don't know what I'm thinking," Drea said. "I thought I knew what I wanted with my life, and sometimes I still do."

"Then you came back here, and you're findin' you're fittin' in, and folks are taking a liking to you." His smile was gentle, knowing. She nodded and he continued. "Then you and that young man."

The tears crept down her cheeks, and she knuckled them away. "Yeah, then me and Danny." That snuck up on her. They were supposed to be just friends. Then somehow, they'd been dating. And the sex. That was amazing. The most amazing thing she'd ever experienced. But it wasn't supposed to mean anything.

Then she'd fallen back in love with him. Her stomach flip-flopped, and her heart felt like it was about to pound its way out of her chest. She loved Danny. Maybe she'd never been out of love with him. Either way, going back to DC meant giving him up. If she chose her work, she'd be shutting the door on this town. Ten years ago, that was all she wanted to do.

Now, she wasn't so sure. Loving Danny only complicated things.

"You underestimate yourself, and him." Gramps reached out and patted her arm. "If he would turn away from you for doing what you feel is right, then he's not the man I believe him to be."

* * * *

"We're going to be a mosquito feast if we stay out here much longer."

Drea's words drifted through the air, joining with the wind whispering in the trees and rustling the early June grass. She was right, but Danny didn't want to move. Sprawled naked on a blanket with her tucked under his arm, skin drying from the dip in the stream after lovin' seemed like the perfect place to be as far as he was concerned. Nope. He didn't want to move at all.

"You start snoring," she threatened, "I swear, I'll punch you."

She would, too. "Lucky for me, I don't snore. This is too nice to give up just yet."

She rolled, tucking her back against him, then pointed at the tree where the horses were tethered.

"I remember our first kiss. Under that big pine right there."

"Yeah." He'd been head over heels in love — or as in love as you could be at fourteen. They'd been on a trail ride, just the two of them. Something they weren't supposed to do anymore. Drea had complained bitterly, not understanding the new restriction. But Danny understood it all too well.

Standing in the shade of that big tree, pressing her back against the rough bark. His hands on her hips, uncertain if she'd accept his kiss, or punch him. He knew the ache he felt, the urge to do more than kiss, was why they weren't supposed to ride alone anymore.

She hadn't punched him.

"First kiss, but not our last, not by a long shot." That kiss had exploded his world, forever searing Drea into his heart. They'd managed to still ride together — Danny's parents were too busy to enforce their own rule. There had been many, many more kisses, yet they'd always stopped there. Even then, Drea had been determined. Focused on a goal that she was going to achieve.

Oh, he'd wanted more — any boy would — but he wasn't foolish, nor was she. She couldn't very well go to the local doctor to get on the pill, and the idea of buying condoms at the drugstore where the pharmacist had known him since he was in diapers had terrified Danny. And her grandmother — that woman was sweet and terrifying, and very Catholic. Sex waited until after marriage. It was as simple as that.

So, they'd waited. Then their well-planned world had come apart and Drea was gone.

Not this time. He curled his arms around her. His lips found her ear, and he planted kisses along her neck, his fingers stroking her skin.

"Did you ever miss this place?" He'd often wondered if she thought about him, the town, the ranch. Their plans.

She shook her head. "I didn't have time. I know that sounds terrible, but it's true. At first, it was all about school. I was young and hurting. I lived that entire last semester watching you and CeeCee together. Realizing I'd have to do everything we talked about on my own. After that came internships, and working, and busting my ass to get into the ATF. I missed some of the people, and I missed what we had, but..." She grabbed his hand, stilling it, holding it to her chest. "Maybe if I'd allowed myself to think. But I didn't. Couldn't."

"I'm sorry." He whispered the words in her ear. Knowing they weren't enough. Could never be enough.

"It's long past. You did what you had to do, and I understand that. I understand why you stayed. I didn't at the time, but looking back? I get it and I respect it." She took a deep shuddering breath. "But I never felt I had a place here before."

"And do you now?"

Her fingers trailed along his arm, tracing patterns up and down. She shifted again, rolling to face him. Until he was staring directly into those emerald eyes.

"I don't know. Maybe."

His heart skipped a beat. *Maybe. Maybe is not a no.* She wrapped her fingers into his hair and pulled him in for a kiss.

"I don't want to talk about that right now."

Her invitation couldn't have been more clear. He rolled onto her, pinning her to the blanket and fastened his lips on hers. She sighed as he pushed his thighs between hers. He couldn't get enough of her. Her legs clenching his waist, the silkiness of her hair, the feel of her surrounding him. He pushed up onto his arms, holding himself above her.

"Open your eyes, I want to see you."

Her eyelids fluttered up and twin pools of deep green stared up at him. She was so beautiful. So amazing. Everything about her fit. She belonged here, if only she'd see it.

The afternoon sun painted the world in shades of gold as he slipped a condom on and slid into her. As far as he was concerned, this was bliss.

Drea rose to meet his next thrust, her fingers digging into his shoulders. She threw her head back, the little gasps she made getting lost in the wind. She was his world. He belonged to her, body and soul, heart and mind.

He wanted to see her lose control. To feel her lost in everything, conscious only of their two bodies. As if by loving her right, he could convince her to stay. He rolled to his back, pulling her with him. He stroked her body, cupping her breasts, then gliding his hands down until his thumb rested against her clit and she shuddered at the first stroke.

He took his time, until her gasps became cries, echoing over the hills, then his name on her lips as her body shook with tremors, sending him over the edge. He wrapped her tightly in his arms as his world came shattering apart.

Pulling away from her was the worst, like leaving a part of himself behind. He wanted to stay there, to feel himself going soft inside her. He wanted her in his life, now and always.

She sat fingering the tangles from her hair, then gave it a shake and let it fall in a riot of curls and frizz. She was magnificent. He could get lost in her eyes, drown in her kisses.

"I don't know what to do." Her voice was soft, her tone serious, and it took Danny a moment to switch gears. "About the fires. About Gramps' house. My Jeep."

He took a deep breath and slowly blew it out. "I know you don't. I can't tell you what to do, darlin'."

She rose and crossed to the stream, disappearing into the water with barely a splash. She surfaced and twisted her wet hair into a rope down her back. "Why can't it be easy?"

"I dunno. You figure that one out, let me in on the secret." He sat on a rock, dangling his feet into the water. After the things she'd just said, he was pretty sure she was considering staying, and pretty damn determined to help ease that decision along. If her only reason was finding pleasure in his bed, he'd accept that. For now. He was also sure if she pushed harder on the fires, she was going to stir up a major shit storm, and there was nothing he could do to dissuade her. He didn't think he wanted to.

Drea hauled herself out of the stream and plunked down next to him. She laid back on the rock, beads of water on her bare skin turning her into a sparkling, bronzed goddess.

"Robert isn't willing to do much of anything about the fires." She sighed and turned her head toward him. "I know what I should be doing. But I've got Gramps to think about."

Danny took her hand in his. "I know you're torn. I can feel it. What's got you so tied up?"

Drea swallowed hard. "The most difficult thing to consider. Opportunity."

Not the response he'd expected. "You wanna explain that?"

"I believe the fires here were about covering up the bodies. But the ones at Gramps' place and my Jeep were meant to scare me off." She took a deep breath and sat up. "Any crime, you have to look not just at motive, but opportunity."

He pushed his hands through his hair, slicking it back from his forehead. "I get it. Just because someone has a reason to do something, doesn't mean they have the chance to do it."

Drea nodded. "Basically, yeah. The one that gets me is my car. Someone was either carrying around two buckets of thermite, waiting for the right chance, or they figured I'd be there."

"In all fairness, you are at the school a lot." Danny shrugged. "Visiting Wilma."

"Sure, but not regularly enough to plan that I'd be there. Maybe on a Friday. But this was a Wednesday."

Danny arched an eyebrow at her. "Another reason to not believe it's Penny. Someone had to have a car."

"Right," Drea replied. "The first fires are the key. And they both happened here. Which could mean it's less about the bodies and more about someone trying to damage Parsons Acres—maybe stall the development, considering the locations. That points to a disgruntled ex-employee, or a current employee with an axe to grind."

He shook his head. "Why would anyone do that? Those plans are going to benefit half the town, not just the ranch. Look, I know this is your job. You're trained to see things other people miss. But what do you have to go on here?" He reached out and snagged her hand again, holding it lightly in his own.

"My experience. My training." Her words were a sharp rebuke, then her face softened, and she smiled. "Intuition. This is what I do. It's who I am. If I were running this investigation, I'd be picking apart Robert's approach, maybe even wondering if he was involved. I know you don't like the idea, but I'd be looking at Brian, first and foremost, and Lily a close second."

"What?" She was right. He didn't like that idea. Not one bit. "Robert I get, but why Brian? Or Lily?"

Drea shrugged. "Opportunity."

"What about motive?" Danny replied, trying to keep his tone neutral.

Drea shook her head. "I know you don't want to think about someone on your crew doing something like this. Motive isn't clearly understood. What makes sense to one person is a complete mystery to another. I'm not saying I suspect either of them, just that I'd be looking at them. And asking to see your employee records. And talking to ex-girlfriends. But I'd be starting right here at the ranch."

"Well," he replied, "not telling you how to do your job, but I'd lay money on you bein' wrong on that one." He shook his head and smiled. "That's all mechanics. It's not what's diggin' at you. Can't be."

Drea pulled her hands from his, gently, and squeezed water from her hair. "In DC, it's easy." She fingered her hair into a rough braid, her actions an easy tell — she was about to get to what was bugging her. "It's work, nothing personal. I know everyone here. And they're all connected. Plus, in DC I've got the backing of the entire ATF. Here? Now? I'm at the mercy of the local law enforcement. And Gramps, and... Well, it's frustrating."

Danny slid over and curled an arm around her shoulders. His fingers played in her hair. He kissed the top of her head. "How can I help you?"

Even after her practically accusing two of his employees of arson, his first concern was taking care of her. Same as it had been when they were kids, and same as it would be for the rest of his life. No matter what she decided to do.

"If I knew the answer to that," she said, "this would be easy."

"What do you want, Drea?"

Her head rested on his shoulder. When she spoke, her voice was soft, quiet. "I want Gramps to not be sick. I want the fires to have never happened. I want my life back... No, I want myself back." She took a deep breath. "I want you."

She lifted her head and kissed him, then slid into his lap, her legs wrapping around his waist.

"Why do I get the feelin' that was a request to change the subject?" His fingers curled into her hair.

"Because that's exactly what it was." She kissed him again, and his body responded, in spite of his brain's desire to keep digging and get to the bottom of whatever was bothering her.

"Do you need me to sit back and listen?" He slid his hands up her thighs, held her hips still. "I can do that. I'll bite my tongue till it bleeds if I have to, but that's not who I am. You talk to me about a problem, I'm gonna look for a solution."

Drea shook her head. "When it comes to these fires, I don't like any of the available solutions. They all suck. And I don't want to think about that, or anything else right now."

She curled her fingers behind his neck and pressed her lips to his and his brain gave up the battle.

"Point taken," Danny murmured. "Less talk, more action."

Chapter Twenty

Heat shimmered and the air smelled of rich green things and damp soil. It was a smell from childhood. Summer days spent outside with friends. Drea handed two glasses of fresh lemonade to Jimmy, then carried the pitcher and two more glasses to the porch. Wilma sprawled in a chair, her feet up on the rail. Drea sat the tray down as memories came unbidden—the first weekend after school let out. CeeCee eager to don her latest bikini and start on her tan. Danny and his football buddies at the swimming hole. Drea, slathering on sunscreen so she wouldn't get darker, even more different than her classmates.

"Hey. Yoo-hoo!" Wilma's voice penetrated her reverie, and Drea looked up to see her spraying sunscreen on her bare legs. Wilma maintained a creamy-pale complexion without so much as a freckle. "You kinda disappeared there for a minute."

"Sorry." Drea laughed and waved away the sunscreen Wilma offered. "A little trip down memory lane."

"Paul seems to be having a rough day," Wilma said.

Drea offered a sad smile. "He has good days and bad, but he's holding up." The truth was, the good days were fewer and farther between, and the bad days were increasing. "Thanks for coming over today. Gramps loves his Sunday visits with Chief Lawson, but they wear him out. And even though Jimmy is a saint, I don't like always being gone."

Wilma took a lemonade and sat back. "This is perfect." She waved a hand at the expanse of green in front of them. "We're on a shady porch, enjoying some of the most amazing scenery this county has to offer. Which reminds me, what's up with you and Danny?"

A short laugh burst from Drea's lips, and she settled into a chair next to Wilma. "We uh…spent yesterday together." She shrugged again.

"Uh-huh." Wilma leaned over and poked her. "And?"

"As much as I enjoy spending time with Danny, I don't know where it's going." She sipped her lemonade. "On top of that, and my sick grandfather, there are these suspicious fires that the local law enforcement won't investigate. I can't do anything about them without risking alienating everyone I care about, especially since the strongest suspects are so closely tied to Danny. Oh yeah, and my career has taken a left turn, and I don't think I care anymore."

Drea shook her head. She hadn't planned on unloading on Wilma like that. But after yesterday's conversation with Danny, her head was swimming.

"What would you do normally?" Wilma asked. "About the fires. If this weren't your hometown? If you didn't have your grandfather or Danny or anything like that."

Drea's eyebrows drew down into a scowl and she pursed her lips. She'd never thought of it in those terms. What would she do, absent all these other things?

"Well..." She sat forward and wrapped her arms around her knees. "Probably ignore the very first fire. Possibly ignore the first one at Parsons Acres. No reason to get involved with something that's a local matter. If an investigator is sent to consult, we make a report and we leave. That's it. No follow-up unless we feel there's a reason."

And therein was the problem. "The mining town fire changes things a little. There was clear evidence there, but it's still a local matter. I was a witness on that one. So..." Drea shrugged. "Could go lots of ways at that point. Maybe we get involved, maybe not. The house fire and the car fire? Different story entirely."

"Because they were clearly intentional?"

Drea nodded. "Yeah. No getting around it, those weren't the work of a firebug, or someone being careless. And that warrants an investigation. Simple as that. That's why I called my friend Mattix this morning. I need to bounce all this off someone. She'll be down next week. Speaking of which..."

"Of course she can stay in my guest room." Wilma adjusted her sunglasses. "It'll be nice to meet someone from your work. Will Mattix stay through that weekend? You should take her to Oak Bridge."

Drea shot Wilma a horrified look. That would cause a hell of a stir. Gabe Mattix stood nearly six feet tall, with lean muscles and a lot of tattoos covering skin the color of polished mahogany, and her idea of going-out wear often included tight leather and high heels. She raised eyebrows in DC. Drea didn't want to imagine taking her to Oak Bridge.

"I think we'll skip the local watering hole," Drea replied, "and thanks."

Wilma waved a hand, dismissive. "So, what would you do? If you were in DC, and your house was torched... Oh, I'm..."

Drea shook her head. "The apartment fire was an accident, not arson. Not even a kid playing with matches, or a firebug losing control of his fun. It was bad wiring and faulty smoke detectors, plus neighbors on vacation."

"Okay, so if it had been deliberate? Or if your car had been blown up?"

"Half the department would be so far up Robert's ass that we'd be able to tell you what he had for lunch." A bitter chuckle escaped Drea's lips. "It's also possible he would have been cuffed, at least once. And Brian brought in for questioning. Lily, too. Possibly even Danny. Or Annette." The smile she turned to Wilma was not a pretty one, and she knew it. "We're not always nice people."

"In other words, the only things holding you back are Paul and Danny?"

"Pretty much." Drea drew circles in the condensation on her glass. "Gramps because I don't want to ruin our time together, and Danny...huh... Danny because..."

"You're thinking of staying around."

"No..." Drea shook her head, then nodded. "Yes... I don't know..." Her head thumped to her knees, and she blew out a breath. "I feel so stupid. Pining over some guy, because maybe he might like me enough to ask me to stay. When I'm not sure I want to." She flopped back in her chair. "Maybe I should pack up Gramps and move back to the city. There're better doctors there. He'd be comfortable. He could stay in touch with everyone by phone — the FaceTime thing has been great. Then I wouldn't have to think about any of this shit."

"You could do that. What would you go back to?"

A light breeze stirred the windchime, scattering sparkling notes in the air. "When I go back, I'll be reporting to the Fire Research Lab. But the classroom or the lab would be better anyway, I mean, while, y'know..." She shook herself and cocked her head to look at Wilma. "I'd have to get a different place. Move into something bigger for a while."

"Is that what you want?" Wilma gazed at her over her sunglasses, and Drea was transported back to high school. It was Wilma's signature glare, and Drea was sure she put it to good use these days with the students.

"Are you encouraging me to leave?" She laughed, a little uncertain. Wilma whipped her glasses off and gaped at her.

"God no! I'm not encouraging you to stay either. I'm suggesting that you might consider what you want, rather than thinking about what you used to want. What do you really want? Right now. Today."

"I don't know." But that was a lie. She wanted Danny. And that scared the living crap out of her.

* * * *

Danny switched off the pressure washer and pulled the mask off his face. The smell of disinfectant wasn't pleasant, but it was preferable to the suffocating feeling of the mask. Brian rinsed his broom and hung it to dry.

"Where's Lily today?" Danny prodded.

Brian's mouth turned down. "She and the family are at Prestera. Penny's been hurtin' herself again. Started up after Robert questioned her about the first fire at the cottages." He shoved his hands into his pockets and looked down at the floor. "Lily's mad as a hornet. Robert's been over to their house after every fire, and he's got a handful of people thinking Penny's responsible. But I can't believe it."

Drea had said similar things. Penny didn't have the opportunity. Of course, then Drea had pointed out that Brian did. Or Lily. "Shit, man, I'm sorry to hear that. She seemed to be doin' well hangin' around here with Lily." The girl was quiet, but she was good help, and like her older sister, she was good with the horses. He'd considered finding a way to offer her work.

"Lily was hopin' maybe bein' around the horses would get Penny out of her shell a bit," Brian said. "Maybe she could get to be more independent. Lily's got Kyle, and when Penny's home, a lot of that falls on her, too."

"You think Lily will be able to take over when you finish school?" Danny asked.

Brian's frown instantly transformed into a goofy grin, then quickly morphed into a more serious expression.

"Uh, yeah. She's...uhh..." Brian cleared his throat and offered a sheepish-looking smile. "Speaking to my boss, you know I'd never steer you wrong when it comes to company business. She's solid."

Danny nodded. "You're a lot more than an employee, and you know it." Drea may have been suspicious of Brian, but Danny didn't see it. Couldn't believe it. Brian was like family. He wouldn't do anything to hurt Parsons Acres.

"Yeah," Brian replied. "Lily's got a lot goin' on, but she's good. Speaking to my friend, well…" He stopped, the goofy grin back on his face. It was clear to see Brian was smitten.

"No shenanigans in the barn," Danny said, laughing. "What d'ya think about hangin' around after you've graduated?"

Brian leaned back against a stall door, his eyes wide. "That wind farm isn't gonna need a vet. And even if you keep branching out, diversifying breeding, you don't need an in-house vet here. So, what's in your head?"

"Equestrian camp," Danny replied. "The big stretch out by the old hayfield, where the cottages are. Facilities won't be that tough to build. It'll have to run as its own business. How many foals do we get that can't cut it as racehorses? How many retired horses wind up being sold for pleasure riders? We'd need a small staff year-round—the rest would be seasonal work."

Brian shoved his hands through his hair, his eyebrows furrowed in concentration. "You talked to the bank yet?"

"I don't plan on doin' any of it with loans. The wind farm isn't costin' us anything. That's all on the energy company. The breeding program is already in place and payin' for itself. We need to keep up the good work. The only investment is the camp, and we've got the capital for that."

Brian pressed his fingers into his eyebrows. "Jesus, you're serious. And you want me to take that on as manager?"

Danny shook his head. "As the vet. I've got the offer all drawn up. I'll email it to you tonight. It's already a hassle to not have a vet on staff here. We get a camp goin', it's gonna be damn near a requirement. It's a contract job, year-round, and you'd be free to take on other clients."

"What about Doc Jameson?" Brian shook his head, as if trying to clear cobwebs inside his brain.

"He's fifty miles away, older, wantin' to retire, and currently has no one lookin' to take on the business, unless you buy it from him — and I'm willin' to bet he'd float you a loan himself. There is no other large-animal specialist in the area."

Brian's mouth hung open then snapped shut. He mumbled a thank you, and Danny nodded and left before Brian's emotions caught up with him. Danny had promised his mother he'd be there for dinner. He sighed as he climbed the steps and glanced up at the Parsons Acres sign above the porch. The family business. Moved to West Virginia to get away from the Confederacy during the Civil War, the Parsons family had been on this land, in this house, since 1862. Things he'd taken for granted until recently. All the fires brought home just how much he had at stake here. And there was Drea.

He reached up and tapped the sign, gently. One day, it would be his kids, stretching their hands up, trying to reach. A life he'd never wanted back in high school was now the thing he cherished. Family. He could picture Drea here, sitting on the porch, hand in hand with him, watching the sunset together. He pushed those thoughts aside. He wasn't living in a daydream.

"Somethin' smells amazing." He closed the screen door gently so his mother wouldn't fuss, then bent and kissed her cheek. "What's for dinner?"

"Fried chicken sounded good," she replied. "Go wash up. It's almost ready. You talk to Brian today like you said you were gonna?"

Danny went to the kitchen sink, pumping soap from the same glass frog dispenser that had been there since before he could recall. The hand towel hung to the side, plain white with a faded red border. He wiped his hands and set the table before she could ask.

"Yes'm." He poured iced tea for both of them and sat down.

"And?" She scooped coleslaw onto his plate, then a big, fluffy looking biscuit, and finally a pile of still steaming fried chicken. Danny inhaled and smiled. Just the smell was enough to take him back to summer days as a kid.

"And nothin'," he replied. "He wasn't all that shocked at the idea. We've talked about it before, and he's got a good head on his shoulders."

"Will he take the job?"

Danny shrugged. "Don't know." He bit into a piece of chicken and rolled his eyes in pleasure. "Ma'am, this is a bit of heaven."

"Don't change the subject," she snapped, but smiled at the compliment. "What do you think?"

Danny chewed and swallowed, then took another bite, deliberately taking his time while she sat watching him with an expectant look on her face.

"Ma, I don't know for sure. Brian's got no reason not to take it, especially since he and Lily seem to be hittin' it off so well. So, yeah. I think he will, but there's no tellin'. Maybe he wants to move on. What I do know is we're making him a fine offer, and he won't do better anywhere else in this area. Now can I eat? You haven't made fried chicken in forever, and I'm plannin' to stuff myself."

She bent her head to her food and a few minutes passed in merciful silence. Too good to last. She was being too agreeable. She finished her drumstick, wiped her hands on her napkin and sat back. Danny braced himself for whatever was about to come out of her mouth.

"Wondered how long it'd take you to figure out Brian and Lily have something between 'em." She took a sip of tea. "What's between you and Andrea?"

Danny nearly choked on a bite of chicken. "Can't we have dinner without goin' down this road?"

Asking wouldn't make it so. She'd have her say, no matter what. He pushed back from the table and rummaged in the refrigerator for a beer. She always kept a few stashed in the back. Beer in hand, he returned to his seat and glared at her.

"Fine," he muttered. "Drea is torn up over these fires, and I can't blame her. We've been lucky, despite two of them bein' on our property, it's only caused minor delays. And a bunch of insurance nightmares."

His mother rose and cleared their plates, whisking away the tea glasses and starting a pot of coffee. "You already grabbed a beer, so I'm guessing you don't want a cookie, or a coffee?"

"If you made chocolate chip cookies, you'd be guessin' wrong."

She pulled two cups from the cupboard and leaned against the counter. "You're worried that Andrea's digging will make things worse," his mother said. "That whoever is doing this won't stop until she quits—one way or another."

He pressed his lips together and looked down at his half-empty beer bottle. Yep, that was exactly what he was worried about. "Yeah." The word came out as a whisper. "She leaves? Well, that's her choice." He shrugged. "It'd hurt, but it'd be nothing I didn't expect. But if she got hurt?"

His mother slid a full coffee cup and two cookies in front of him. So like her. All the times he sat there, fussing over something, eyes on the worn tabletop, and a glass of milk and two cookies would appear. As if there were magic in those little treats. Maybe there was. He was telling his mother things he wouldn't talk to Brian about.

"Live life for today, Daniel. And let Andrea do what she needs to do." She reached over the table and patted his hand. "This ranch is your job. Fire investigation is Andrea's. You can accept that or not. Now eat your cookies, then help me with the washing up."

"Yes, ma'am." Danny smiled at her. As much as she drove him nuts sometimes, she was right. And she only drove him nuts because he was more like her than he cared to admit. He shook his head and bit into a cookie.

Chapter Twenty-One

"Company's here," Wilma called out.

Drea threw the door open and stood on the porch as Gabe Mattix unfolded her tall frame from the rental car. Drea smiled. Mattix didn't bother owning a car — she lived and worked in DC and rented when she needed a vehicle.

"What the fuck have you gotten yourself into, Hidalgo?" Mattix greeted Drea with a hug. "And why the hell did you drag me out to this podunk town?"

"Same shit, different day." Drea laughed.

"I suggest you take the greetings inside," Wilma piped up from the door. "You two are gonna give the neighbors fits if you keep standing there jawin' on the steps."

Wilma stepped back and held the door wide for Drea and Mattix to enter. She shut the door and stuck her hand out at Mattix.

"Wilma Davis, since this rude person hasn't seen fit to make introductions."

Mattix smiled and shook Wilma's hand. "Gabrielle Mattix, but friends call me Gabe. Or just Mattix."

Drea's eyebrows went up. Mattix never introduced herself as Gabrielle. Never. They followed Wilma to the living room and sat.

"How're things at the lab?" Drea asked.

"Up to my ass in a whole bundle of new trainees." Mattix sat with her elbows on her knees, leaning forward. "Nothin' new there. Remember Adams? He may make a damn fine investigator, but he's a lab rat in disguise. Who knew?"

Drea couldn't imagine the go-get-'em Peter Adams content with the relative predictability of the FRL. Still, stranger things. She made a noncommittal sound and waited for Mattix to continue.

"Down to business." Mattix gave a pointed stare at Wilma.

"She's fine," Drea said. "This isn't official or anything."

"Okay." Mattix shrugged and leaned back. "Wilkes asked me to go through everything you sent, covering our asses and all. You've got a mess on your hands, kid, and I'm not afraid to say it. Why aren't you calling this?"

Drea took a deep breath and sighed. There it was. With one word, Drea could pull in the ATF. She'd probably be taken off the team because of her involvement, but it would still mean CFIs and other Special Agents crawling over everything Robert had done, or not done, with the fires, and the bodies.

"I'm not willing to go there at this point." She bit her lip. "It's good to know, and maybe in the future, but for now I don't think I need to stir up any more shit here."

Mattix's sharp exhale sounded harsh in the cozy room. "What the hell? Since when do you give a fuck about that?" She shot a glance at Wilma. "Sorry. I guess I should watch my mouth."

"Have you heard the mouth on this one?" Wilma pointed at Drea. "Besides, I'm a high school counselor. Profanity isn't gonna curl my hair."

Mattix gave a hearty laugh. She had never been one to mince words. And she was right. Drea had never cared about whose feathers she ruffled, or how many boats she rocked. She had one goal — catch the bad guy. She couldn't pursue this one with the same single-minded determination. She had Gramps to think about. And Danny.

"Talk to me," Mattix demanded, fixing her with a piercing gaze.

Drea knew what Mattix would advise. Set that personal shit aside and investigate. Mattix continued to stare, her eyes scanning Drea's face.

"Fine," Drea breathed. "But I know what you're going to say."

Mattix leaned an elbow onto the armrest, her expression softened, and Drea knew she was all ears. Mattix wouldn't open her mouth until Drea was done talking. So, she talked. She couldn't hide anything from the other woman anyway, and Wilma had already heard most of this. Mattix could always see through any attempt at bullshit. Drea told her everything: Her worries over her career, her grandfather, and Danny. Especially Danny. She braced herself for Mattix's unflinching opinion.

"You think I'm going to say screw everything, go after the arsonist," Mattix said. "How's it feel to be wrong?"

Drea shook her head and sputtered. She thought she'd had Mattix pegged. "You're funny. What do you suggest?"

Mattix looked down at the couch, her fingers twirling invisible designs on the armrest. "The hardest thing to do. Follow your heart."

Drea's stomach did a flip-flop. That was the last thing she'd ever expected to hear from the always practical Gabe Mattix. Wilma let out a short laugh and smacked Drea's leg. Wilma code for I told you so.

"Your grandfather takes priority," Mattix continued. "He's your family. You won't be good for anything if your mind is torn from thinking about him. So, you take care of him first." She looked at Drea, her eyes soft and kind. "His time is short, cherish it. You can kick ass and take names later."

Her words lifted a weight from Drea's chest, so much that a relieved laugh escaped. "Thank you," she whispered.

"That's the easy one," Mattix replied. "The fires are easy, too, though. Unless something changes, like another body, or more fires aimed at you, take care of your family first. When it's time to deal with the fires, it doesn't matter whether you come back to DC or stay in West Virginia."

"But, I don't know... What if I piss too many people off by investigating?" Drea heard the whine in her own voice and didn't like it. The fact that Mattix had nailed her conflict so succinctly left her nearly speechless. Drea cleared her throat. "Pursuing this could ruin some relationships."

"Not if they're worth having in the first place," Wilma said.

"Exactly." Mattix shot Wilma a big smile.

Their words hit like a punch, knocking a sharp breath out of Drea.

"Hypothetical," Mattix continued. "You ignore the fires. Let the idiot cop here in Podunk Orchard have his way. You go back to your high-school sweetheart and get everything your heart desires. Would you be satisfied? Could you live every day knowing that justice wasn't served?"

Drea shook her head. She couldn't. She knew that much about herself. It would eat at her, dig at her, until she had to do something.

"Do you really want a relationship with a man who would expect you to deny the very thing that drives you?" Mattix whispered the question, but the words cut Drea sharper than a knife.

"No," Drea replied. "You know me better than that."

Mattix nodded. "I'm not hearing you say he's asked that of you. You fear it. But that's on you. Be true to yourself. If he cares for you, truly cares, it won't matter in the long run. I didn't say following your heart wouldn't hurt or require tough choices."

Mattix was right. Drea had been tying the fires and Danny and everything all together into one big problem. She needed to prioritize and think about each problem on its own. Make the most of whatever time she had left with Gramps. Enjoy spending time with Danny—without worrying about where it was going, or what it meant. She'd decide on the fires later.

Drea hugged Mattix. "Thank you," Drea said. "I don't think I've ever been so happy to be wrong."

"Wait." Wilma sat back, fanning herself theatrically. "Did you just say you were wrong?"

Mattix grinned at Wilma. "It does happen, every now and then. She's even admitted to needing help a time or two."

"Ha-ha," Drea replied. "Can we stick to business?"

Wilma rose. "Why don't I fix dinner? Y'all can talk fires, then come set the table."

Mattix's eyes followed Wilma as she left the room, then she shook herself and turned back to Drea. She should have realized Mattix would find Wilma attractive. Wilma was totally her type — tall, curvy and girly, but blunt as a spoon. She didn't know what Wilma's type was — she'd never dated during high school, and Drea had only just learned that her childhood best friend identified as queer.

"Before you ask," Drea said, "maybe? I don't know for sure. Now put your eyes back in your head."

* * * *

"You wanna tell me what's goin' on?" Danny traced his fingers up Drea's arm, reveling in the softness of her skin. She sighed and turned toward him, her green eyes dark and clouded.

"You first," she whispered. "Your mind's been a million miles away most of today."

He huffed a short chuckle and shifted to his back, pulling her with him so she nestled into his shoulder. He liked her right there. Her hair tickling against his ear, her breath warm against his skin. He considered outright asking her to stay, but the thought of her refusing stopped the words from forming.

"It's Father's Day. Almost seven years and it still hits hard." He took a deep breath and let it out on a sigh. "Energy company is comin' in next week to complete the bases for the windmills. All the environmental stuff checked out. Had to get some bird study of some sort done."

Her fingers trailed up and down his chest, sending little shivers through his entire body. Her lightest touch could take his mind straight to sex. To what he wanted to do to her, with her. And how good she made him feel. He caught her hand and stilled it, then bent and kissed her forehead.

"You keep that up, I'm gonna stop talkin'. Should be able to start hiring folks for those jobs by the end of this month—only a couple weeks behind because of the mining town fire. That's most of what's happening right now. It's hittin' the quiet season, still, there's all the day-to-day stuff. Brian gettin' Lily trained up. He's finished his classes, but he's havin' to do rounds with Doc Jameson and that takes him off the ranch a lot. Puts a lot back on me."

He shrugged. This was ranch life. This was his life. It never stopped. There might be slow times, and sometimes you could get away for a bit, but there were never really days off. He slipped a hand under her chin and tipped her head back. Her lips parted as if in anticipation of a kiss, but he stopped a breath away from her mouth.

"Your turn. Your friend headed back to DC yesterday?"

Her lips pursed and she stretched, distracting him with the view of her curves fully on display. "Yep. It was good to see her."

Danny chuckled. Drea had adamantly refused to go out Friday night, instead, she and his mother had fixed dinner, and everyone had converged on the house. It had been a long time since there'd been a crowd like that at the big table, and Danny was surprised to find he'd missed it. He'd also quickly taken a liking to Gabe Mattix. She was tough and no-nonsense, and she treated Drea like a kid sister, with obvious love and respect.

"I can see why you admire her," he said. "She must've been a tough teacher. And a good one."

Drea laughed. "Nailed it in one."

She curled into him, her lips pressed against his neck, sending shivers of anticipation over his skin. "Aside from that, you know my world – it's all Gramps, all the time. Do the cookies every week. Help your mother out when she needs a hand with something. And I've been spending time with Wilma. And you. That's about it." Her fingers went back to tracing up and down his chest, and this time he didn't stop her.

Her hand dipped under the sheet, tracing lower on his belly until her fingertips stopped above the half hard-on already throbbing between his legs.

"What about the fires?" he asked. They'd been avoiding that subject lately, but he knew it had to be weighing on her. It sure as shit was weighing on him – they'd escaped the first fires with only minimal delays to the expansion plans at the ranch, but the latest ones targeted Drea, and the idea of her getting hurt tore him to pieces. "You decided what to do about all of that?"

Cool fingers encircled his cock, stroking gently and half grew to full in about two heartbeats. His breath hitched as she squeezed gently, then lowered her hand to cup his balls. Goddamn she was gonna kill him this way. *But what a way to go.*

"Mattix and I talked about options while she was here," Drea replied. "There's not much I can do if the local police want to be stubborn. Sure, I could pull rank, but I don't see that'd do me a whole lot of good. Oh... I am going to the city for a week at the end of the month. Pick up some more clothes. That sort of thing."

Her fingers wrapped around his shaft again and slid up, then back down, making it very hard to concentrate.

"Why a week?" That felt like a long time to pick up clothes.

"When I realized I'd be here a while, I sublet my place, fully furnished, but my lease is coming up. I've got to get my stuff moved into a storage unit. No sense keeping that place or getting a new one yet. And I have an appointment with my counselor—just a formality, but it's got to get done if I want to be eligible for field work."

All of that made it sound like she was planning to go back to DC. That thought twisted cold fingers into his heart. He opened his mouth to ask about her plans when her other hand joined the festivities, and there was the unmistakable feel of a condom rolling down.

She slid on top of him in one fluid move, then he was inside her, surrounded in her warmth and wetness. She leaned down and tangled her fingers in his hair. She shifted above him, her hips rocking then lifting, and he groaned at the exquisite feel of her.

"God, I love..." Danny gasped as her mouth closed on his, cutting off his words. Her teeth nipped and her tongue invaded. He wrapped his hands around her hips, but she sat up and pushed them away. She grabbed his wrists and held them to the sheet next to his head. A nipple pressed against his lips, and he opened his mouth, licking and sucking until it tightened into a hard bud. She pulled away and replaced it with the other, demanding the same attention as she ground herself onto him.

He liked when a woman took charge, demanded what they wanted and took their satisfaction from him. He'd never seen Drea do it. She was an enthusiastic lover, and a good one, but she'd never taken control like this.

She sat up and pulled his hands to her breasts, then leaned back, resting one hand on his thigh while her other went between her legs. He almost lost it as her finger stroked against her clitoris, and she moaned, shifting on him, speeding up her rhythm.

His view was the most spectacular thing in the world. Drea, straddling him, lush breasts filling his hands and her body arched back, legs wide, grinding on his cock as she stroked herself. He brushed his fingers over her nipples and was rewarded with a low moan. He circled the tight buds with thumb and forefinger, pinching lightly. She hissed in a breath through her teeth and trembled.

"Yes!"

That was all the encouragement he needed. His fingers closed over her nipples, and Drea cried out again. She clenched around him, tightening as her body arched farther back. Then suddenly she was leaning forward again, her eyes locked with his before she tangled both hands into his hair and pulled him up to her. She shifted and her breasts were in his face, her fingers tugging at his hair until his teeth sank gently into her skin.

Drea exploded. A rush of wetness, and her entire body shook as a high, keening wail erupted from her lips. Still, she didn't stop grinding against him. She held on, riding him until the tension of his own release built. She brought her lips to his and kissed him deeply, then let her lips travel to his ear, where she nipped the lobe.

"Come for me, Danny."

With her breath on his ear and those words from her lips, Danny's body clenched and he saw stars. Then a rush of blood in his ears as he emptied himself with another quick thrust. He rolled her to her back and thrust into her again and again, until another orgasm ripped through him, and he fell back, exhausted and breathing hard.

Minutes later, Drea rose to shower. He had the distinct impression she just used sex to avoid a more serious conversation. He shifted and pulled the sheet up over his hips, not caring at the moment. It was time to get over his fears—he wanted her here to stay. But they could talk about that later.

Chapter Twenty-Two

The hot water stung, causing Danny to wince and hiss in pain. It had been a long time since he'd been kicked by a horse and he'd forgotten the discomfort. Damn hoof had nearly caught his knee. The whole thing was a stupid accident that wouldn't have happened had his brain been fully engaged and not worried about what Drea had been doing all week in DC.

They'd brought in new stock, a mix of older, fat and happy mares destined for the camp side of things, and one young and very ornery stallion. The son of a bitch had gotten rambunctious coming out of the trailer, reared up and clipped a stable hand a good one. The kid had gone down and lost his grip on the lead rope. It had taken both Danny and another hand to get the animal under control, and in the process, he'd taken a hind hoof to the thigh hard enough to tear the worn-out jeans he had on and break skin.

He toweled off and got dressed, wincing again as he pulled on his boots and straightened up. He'd be walking with a limp for a day or two. Tonight, he might go over his usual one or two beer limit. He grabbed his keys and headed for his truck.

Once at Oak Bridge, he pushed open the doors and the noise hit him like a wall. He made his way across the floor to Brian and the other guys gathered around the dart boards.

"What the hell happened to you?" Brian looked down at his leg. "You walked in like some broke dick cowboy."

Danny rolled his eyes at the joke, ordered a beer and waited until he'd taken a long pull from the frosty mug before answering. "If my damn ranch manager, or his trainee, had been around, I'd be walkin' just fine."

Brian's eyes went wide, and his mouth worked. Danny didn't have the heart to leave him scrambling for an apology. He laughed and clapped Brian on the shoulder.

"Nothin' new. New stallion pitched a fit comin' outta the trailer, and I didn't get outta the way fast enough. Hurt like a bitch and took a bit of skin with it." He settled onto a stool and took another pull of beer.

"You're gettin' old, man." Brian chuckled. "Where's Drea? Figured I'd see her and Wilma out tonight if she wasn't with you."

Danny drained his beer and ordered another. "Drea's been in DC this week. Said she's gotta deal with her old apartment." He shrugged. They'd been texting all week, and she'd been evasive any time he'd asked questions about the trip and the only reasons he could come up with were not good. She was due back late tonight. He'd tried to talk her into coming over, and she'd refused. But they'd made plans to go to the Fourth of July picnic together. "We're spendin' the day together tomorrow. Can we play, instead of talk?"

"Sure," Brian replied. "If you think you're up to it, bein' injured and all."

"The horse kicked my leg, not my arm, and I'll still beat the stuffin' out of you."

Danny won the first round but lost the second by a few points. They were setting up for round three when a cool hand closed over his biceps, and he looked down into CeeCee's big, round eyes.

"Hey, handsome," she greeted. "Been a while since you came in here. Drea finally let you off the leash?"

"You're in the line of fire." He pointed at the line on the floor.

"I'll play you next round." She leaned into him and planted a kiss below his ear.

He dropped the darts to the table and picked CeeCee up around the waist. She squealed and kicked her feet in mock protest but rested her hands on his shoulders. When he carried her to the bar and deposited her on a stool there, her smiles and giggles turned to a pout.

"No offense." Danny forced himself to keep his voice light and low so only she could hear, not wanting to make a bigger scene than he already had. "You know damn good an' well I'm seein' Drea, and I don't fool around. I'm here to hang out with the guys and what you're offerin' doesn't interest me. Stay outta my game."

Her pout turned to a scowl, and he tipped an imaginary hat in her direction before turning back to his dart game. Brian was busy hiding a big grin behind his glass of iced tea but pointed down when Danny limped over.

"You might wanna get that looked at."

A spot of blood bloomed on his thigh, and Danny swore softly. He wasn't about to drop his pants in the bathroom here to check things out.

"Later. If it's that bad, you can stitch me up when we get back to the ranch." He needed to shut off the swirling thoughts clouding his brain. Worrying about Drea wasn't gonna change the facts.

He won another two games and lost the third. Then sat out a few rounds while Brian played some of the guys.

Brian settled into the stool across from him. "It's last call. You havin' another?"

Danny shook his head. "I'm at my limit." Danny tipped the last of his beer into his mouth and set the mug down.

"You're past it, if you're plannin' on drivin'," Brian replied. "We're taking my truck."

Danny started to argue, then thought better of it. Brian was right. Danny might not be drunk, but he had no business driving after more than a couple of beers. He settled his tab with the bartender and looked around as they left. The place had mostly cleared out. A few guys sat around the tables near the darts, nursing their last beers, but the rest of the place was empty.

"You'll have to come back tomorrow to get your truck." Brian slid behind the wheel and pulled out of the lot. "What the hell, man? You usually stop at a beer or two. Not that anyone would have noticed, you're so damn mellow when you drink. Still…"

"Seemed like a good idea at the time," Danny replied. He wasn't about to admit he was worried Drea had spent the last week making plans to move back to the city and he'd lose her all over again.

Brian took the hint and drove the rest of the way in silence. Once at the cottage, he insisted on looking at Danny's leg. It took soaking the denim to peel it from the cut on his thigh and Danny hissed in a breath as Brian's fingers dug into the tender skin.

"Just some torn skin. You don't need stitches. You shoulda put a decent bandage on this thing. You might wanna have it looked at though, in case of infection." He rummaged around in his truck for a bit, then came back in with a bandage and gauze. "Take something for the pain and swelling and get some sleep. It should be scabbed over nicely by morning. If it looks like shit tomorrow, or hurts, you go to urgent care. I can dress a wound, and I'd stitch you up if I thought it needed it, but I can't prescribe human meds. And you might not wanna wear shorts at the picnic tomorrow."

Danny flipped him off. "Wasn't plannin' on goin' swimmin'."

After Brian had left, Danny downed some ibuprofen and a big glass of water, then flopped down into bed, still half dressed.

* * * *

Drea circled the barn as she came down the hill and headed up the grassy path for Danny's place. He'd said he'd come over at ten, but that had come and gone with no sign of him, and no text or phone call. That wasn't like him at all. Danny was nothing if not punctual and dependable—if he was going to be late, he'd text. She stopped in her tracks as she got to his place. No truck. Maybe he got pulled away on some business…

"He left it at Oak Bridge last night." Brian's voice interrupted her thoughts. "I gave him a ride home. You wanna be nice? Call him. Me? I'd be bangin' on his bedroom window. Good to see you, Drea."

He ambled back down the path to the barn. Drea made her way up to Danny's porch and stood there for a full minute, debating. Finally, she knocked on the door and waited. No answer. She called his phone — straight to voicemail.

"Oh, to hell with this." She tried the door, unlocked. She tiptoed past the kitchen, vaguely noting a pair of bloody jeans and a pile of bandages on the table. In the bedroom, she found Danny sprawled on the bed, still in a T-shirt and boxers, covers twisted around one leg. A large bandage wrapped around the uncovered thigh. That explained the mess she'd seen. Sort of. She shook her head and made her way back to the kitchen.

She started a pot of coffee, cleaned up the trash, and tossed the jeans into the washer in the hall before heading to the bedroom with a cup of coffee. She sat on the edge of the bed and shook Danny. He mumbled and shifted, kicking at the covers. His hair was a tousled mess and coarse stubble covered his chin. *Still damn sexy.*

A bit of bright pink lipstick smeared under his ear, and Drea leaned down, looking for more. She'd been out of town, and it looked like he'd found someone else to keep him company. Images of Frank swirled in her head, and she forced them back. Not that she should care about what Danny did. It wasn't like they'd ever agreed to be exclusive.

Her eyes shifted to the bandage.

"Think I'll live?" The deep rumbling voice made her jump back in surprise. His blue eyes were a bit bloodshot, but wide-awake looking. He stretched, exposing a swath of rock-hard abs above his boxers, then sat up with a groan.

"Interesting night?" Drea leaned back against the wall, her arms crossed over her chest.

Danny blinked at her, then looked around the room and back to her. "How did you get in?"

She turned her wrist and glanced at her watch. "It is now nearly eleven thirty. Last I heard, you were coming over at ten so we could go for a ride before heading to the Fourth of July picnic. You didn't answer your phone, or my pounding on the door...which, for the record, was unlocked. There's coffee on the bed table. Call when you're feeling human."

She turned to go, but his hand closed over her wrist and pulled her down to the bed. Scratchy whiskers rubbed her skin as Danny nuzzled into her neck.

"You smell amazing," he whispered in her ear.

"That's because you smell like stale beer and yesterday's clothes." She didn't like the stab of jealousy that twisted like a knife. She liked the thought of another woman in his bed even less.

He sat back and pulled the sheet up, hiding his growing erection. "Point taken." He grabbed the coffee and took a slow sip, eyeing her over the cup. "I'm sorry. I overslept. Gimme a bit, and I'll shower and get dressed, if you're still up for the day."

She looked down at her hands, twisted together in her lap, rather than into his eyes. "Not that there're any promises between us, but I'd like to hear what got you into this state before I make up my mind on that."

His eyebrows knit together in a frown. "What state? I went out and had a few drinks with the guys. Same as I've been doin' for years."

"Your truck is still at Oak Bridge," Drea said. "I realize I've been back about four months, but this is the first time I've heard of that happening. You've got a big-ass bandage wrapped around your leg, and I tossed a pair of bloody jeans in your washer and cleaned up the mess in the kitchen." She cleared her throat and gave him a sweet smile. "Again, not that we have any promises, but our time together usually includes sex.

252

There's a smeared kiss mark on your neck. I've no intention of jumping into bed with you if you've recently been there with someone else. So, I'll ask again. Interesting night?"

He finished his coffee in silence. Not looking angry or reacting defensively. Just sitting in his bed, looking as sexy as hell, drinking his coffee as if she'd said good morning. The calm quiet was unexpected, forcing her to take a deep breath and wait. He set the cup aside and pushed up from the bed, stripping off his shirt as he went.

Drea stood transfixed by the rippling muscles along his back. He pulled off his shorts and she was treated to the sight of his well-muscled backside as he made his way into the bathroom. He took time to brush his teeth and wipe the offending lip print off his neck before fishing a pair of scissors from the medicine cabinet, snipping the bandage off his leg. Purple bruising went from above his knee to halfway up his thigh.

He straightened up and leaned against the bathroom door. "I got kicked yesterday and yeah, maybe had a few too many beers as a result. The cut's not as bad as it looks. I didn't bother dressing it before I went out. And Brian got a little over enthusiastic with the gauze later."

He cranked on the shower, then turned back to her. Even scruffy and hungover, he was the sexiest thing Drea had ever laid eyes on. But he still had to answer for that lipstick smear.

"The lipstick was CeeCee's, but don't go gettin' any wild ideas." The words came out of his mouth, and Drea fought the urge to walk right out the door, but instead, bit her tongue and glared at him. He gave her a crooked smile. "Hell, darlin', she didn't interest me then, and she doesn't interest me now. She was at the bar makin' her usual offers. I didn't take her up on it. Talk to Brian or ask half the guys around here. Ask Wilma. She's always up on the town gossip."

He crossed the room and cupped her face in his hands. "I'm sorry. Truly. I need to shower. You wanna wait here, or should I come get you when I'm done? Or are you gonna tell me to go to hell?"

The debate raged. Seeing that lip print called up memories of coming home to find Frank in their bed with another woman. Knowing it was CeeCee's was worse. Danny's calm, measured response and complete lack of self-righteousness brought the comparison to Frank to an abrupt halt. The bottom line was simple, she trusted Danny.

"Do I need to go get the bandages for that thing?" she asked.

"I don't think so. Drea, I hate to ask…"

"We'll get your truck once you've showered and eaten something."

He leaned in and kissed her neck, his lips moving slowly over sensitive skin. His whiskers prickled, raising goosebumps all along her body. His teeth grazed her ear and her nipples tightened. Then he straightened up, his erection sticking up like a flagpole.

"You could join me in the shower…" He was already tugging her top off. She rose and kicked out of her shoes, shucking her pants and underwear in one move. The water was hot, and she washed him first, letting her soapy hands glide over his tense muscles. His mouth closed on hers in a tender kiss. His fingers gripped her waist, holding her hips tight against his.

"I'm not a tomcat," he whispered against her neck. "And you may think there aren't any promises between us, but I'd like there to be. You are everything to me, darlin'."

His words sent Drea's heart into double time.

Chapter Twenty-Three

Danny took Drea's hand as they passed under the branches of the tall oak behind the main house. He figured it was as good a place as any to have this conversation. Drea saw the tire swing and shot him a smile that sent his heart into cartwheels.

"It's still here?" Her hand slid down the rope to rest on the black rubber.

"The old one was long gone," he replied. "I put this up earlier this week."

After her trip to DC, they'd settled into a routine of avoiding any difficult subjects — he didn't ask about the fires, and she didn't offer what her plans were after Paul died. They lived and loved in the moment, treating each day as if it were their last together. Her near refusal to talk about it the last ten days had him worried she was planning to leave.

Drea leaned into the tire and pulled him against her. His cock twitched in anticipation, but it would have to wait. Her head tipped back, those green eyes staring up at him. *She belongs here. Beside me.* Danny shook himself. He hoped she felt the same.

"Talk to me about your trip to DC," he said. Not the best conversation starter.

"I told you," she replied. "I needed to deal with my apartment. And storage."

That was all she'd said, all she'd been saying. He swallowed against his fear. "I'd kinda hoped that maybe..." The words stuck in his throat, and he swallowed hard. *This shouldn't be so difficult.* He was twenty-eight years old, not some teenager stumbling over how to tell a girl he liked her.

He lowered his head and kissed her gently, slowly. The thought crossed his mind of taking her there, sitting in the swing, legs hiked around his waist, under the heavy canopy of the big oak. The dappled shadows and swaying branches of the big tree were cover enough, but he wanted leisurely. He wanted to spend as much time with her as possible before she took off again. No, he had to take the risk.

"You make me happy, Drea." He cupped her cheek in his palm. "It's as simple as that. I've been waiting for ten years to feel like this again. You came back into my life and shook up my world. And I like it. I like you here."

Her eyes went wide, and her mouth popped open as if she were searching for something to say. Her fingers clenched on his and a strange-sounding laugh escaped her lips. When he thought about her leaving, he could taste the panic. Forget a broken heart — if she left again, he'd be a broken man.

"Danny," she whispered. "I..."

A loud boom thundered through the air, cutting off whatever she was about to say. Danny whirled around, and Drea ran past him and into the front drive before he could get her name out of his mouth. She stood on the rise, shielding her eyes from the sun.

"There. Smoke." She pointed to the plume billowing from near the mare's barn. His stomach lurched. Another fire.

"Get in the truck." He grabbed the keys from the floorboard of the old Harvester as Drea jumped into the passenger seat. He slammed the truck into gear and sped toward the barn. A raging fire covered the back half of the building and the trees behind it. Drea flung herself out of the truck before he'd come to a stop, running flat out for the cottage where she and Paul were staying.

Brian appeared at his shoulder, shouting in his ear, but Danny didn't hear what he said over the roar of the flames. He coughed at the stench of fuel in the air. Brian shook him, and he turned to face his ranch manager.

"Propane tank blew." Brian's shout carried over the crackling flames. "Lily and I have the barn under control. Already called fire. You take care of Drea."

Danny ran after Drea. He rounded the corner, and she was gone. Where the hell...? Movement at the cottage caught his eye. Flames licked the cottage roof and down the side of the front porch. The door burst open, and Trish stumbled out with an armload of bags and supplies.

Immediately after her came Drea, half helping, half carrying Paul out the door. With a sigh of relief, Danny rushed up the steps and took the man from her arms. Her face was set in a grim mask, and his heart seized. Then Paul coughed and wheezed.

"Get him someplace safe, please." Drea didn't speak loudly, but her words carried all the same. She rushed back into the cottage and came out with an armload of items that she dumped on the grass before going back up the steps.

"Drea!" Danny shouted after her. "You can't go in there. The roof is on fire!"

She shouted something about getting the oxygen tanks and disappeared into the cottage. Paul coughed again, and Danny scooped him up, carrying the man down the porch steps and loading him into the pickup.

"Can you drive a stick?" he asked Trish. She nodded, and he tossed her the keys. "Take him up to the main house. My mother will get y'all settled into a room."

Flames crackled and roared, tearing Danny's world apart. He hauled in a breath filled with the stench of fire and forced himself to focus. Lily's voice drifted up from the barnyard as she shouted orders, and Brian had every hose running full blast, dousing everything in sight. A stable hand led a mare up the hill, and Lily nodded and waved at him. "That's the last one."

Danny waved back and hurried to the cottage. He skidded to a halt as he rounded the barn. Damn, that moved fast. The entire front of the cottage was in flames. He looked around, frantic to find Drea — no sign of her. Jesus, was she still in there? He moved along the side of the cottage, looking for a clear window.

"Hey!" The shout came from behind and he whirled. Drea crouched near the propane tanks, phone in one hand, the other waving frantically at him. She duck-walked around the tank, snapping pictures, then retrieved what looked like a broom handle that she poked into the center of the blaze. A flaming bit of something rolled out, coming to rest in the bare dirt. She quickly stomped on the fire trail it left behind.

"You gonna let that burn?"

She nodded. "If it's what I think it is, I couldn't put it out if I tried. Water won't touch it. It's safe there. Nothing around it to burn. Gramps okay?"

"Trish is taking him to the house," Danny said. "Ma'll make sure he's taken care of. Speaking of which, that's where you should be goin'."

She shook her head, her mouth set in a harsh line. When the fire crew arrived, Drea morphed into non-stop action. At the previous fires, there had been an undercurrent of fear and tension. Today, she was like a force of nature. She conferred with Amos, then suited up in turnouts and fought the fire alongside the rest of the squad.

Shock and dismay warred with anger as Danny watched the crew battle the blaze. A strange sense of pride bubbled up when he caught sight of Drea, legs braced wide, directing a spray of water onto the cottage and shouting something at one of the crew members.

Danny stayed out of the way, feeling useless at first. He needed to do something other than watch his business burn to the ground. He called Lily and had her bring a cooler full of water bottles. She showed up with that and a pile of snacks his mother had thrown together, then she headed back to deal with the displaced mares, and Danny made sure the fire crew was taken care of.

Dusk was creeping in when Drea and Amos declared the scene done and the guys packed the hoses and gear back into the trucks. Drea gave Amos a big hug and the crew pulled out. Her tee clung to her body and black soot smeared every inch of visible skin. Despite all the dirt and grime and the horror of the last several hours, he still thought she was the most beautiful thing he'd ever seen.

She pushed her hair out of her face and gave him a grim smile. "Propane fires suck. I don't think any of the mares' barn is salvageable. Or the cottage. Sorry."

"We didn't lose any people, or animals. I'll call it a win." He'd worry about details later. Right now, all that mattered was Drea. And Paul. Danny cupped her cheek. "How are you?"

She tipped her head into his hand, then straightened. "I'm holding up. Someone set that thing. They had to come here, put that can under the tank, and light the fuse. Hopefully someone saw something."

The thought sent a shiver down his back. "I'll check with Brian and Lily. Right now, let's get you back to the house so you can see your Gramps."

Drea nodded. "Ask them separately," she said. She still had her eye on finding who was responsible. And this time, Penny was back in residential care, so Robert couldn't blame her.

Dread coiled in his stomach when they strode up the walk, and he saw his mother standing on the porch, arms over her chest like she was hugging herself. Drea must have sensed something off because she stopped short of the first step and looked up at his mother, shaking her head.

"Trish drove Paul to the hospital." The words came out gently, but Drea reacted as if she'd been punched in the gut. "They got up here, and we were gettin' him in a room, and he...well... Oh, honey... He had a heart attack, or something."

Danny dropped the armload he was carrying and slid his arms around Drea just in time to catch her as she sank to the ground. She was out cold.

"Is he alive, Ma?"

"Yes, but doin' poorly."

The tears stung and Danny sniffed. He didn't have time for grief or worry right now. He scooped Drea into his arms and climbed the steps. "Call Wilma Davis. Drea's gonna need clothes. All her things from the cottage are ruined."

* * * *

Drea's hands shook around the paper cup as she chugged the last of the cold, bitter coffee in one swallow. She paced the hospital floor, jittery from lack of sleep and too much caffeine.

She'd woken up on a couch in Annette's living room, with Danny, Annette and Wilma hovering nearby. She'd showered and changed into clothes Wilma had brought, then Danny had driven her here. And she'd sent him away. She'd refused Wilma's offer of company as well.

The raging thoughts spinning through her head didn't need any other input. She'd tried to nap, but every time she closed her eyes, images of fire pulled her awake. *Fire is my life. It's claimed too much around me. First my parents, then my body and mind, my career, and now this.*

The doctor said Gramps had indeed suffered a heart attack. Not unexpected, all things considered. Probably brought on by the excitement and exertion, made worse by the cancer eating his system. They'd done what they could to stabilize him. Now it was wait and see. Then Dr. Jarvis had delivered the news that Gramps had signed a DNR after his previous heart attack—no intubation, no breathing machines, no defibrillation. She tossed the empty cup and headed back to the ICU. Knowing what was coming didn't make it any easier to face.

Drea made her way to Gramps' room. The oxygen mask had been replaced by the nasal cannula she knew so well from home, but the gray, withered body in the hospital bed did not look human, much less like her grandfather. She sat by his bed and reached for his hand. The skin was warm and dry, like a brittle leaf on a fall day. His eyes cracked open, and the ghost of a smile crossed his lips.

Drea leaned down to kiss his forehead. "I love you, Gramps." She whispered the words into his ear, and a tear trickled down her face.

His lips pursed and a shushing sound came out. "Little one..." It was the voice of age, of a dying breeze that no longer had the strength to rustle the trees. "I love you, too." The words were barely audible amid the hiss of oxygen and the beeping of the heart monitors. But Drea heard them, and more tears coursed down her cheeks. She knuckled them away and gave him a smile.

"Hush now and rest, Gramps."

He nodded and closed his eyes. She held his hand, carefully watching the rise and fall of his chest. She kissed his forehead again and rose, looking for the floor nurse. There had to be a place for her to sleep here.

* * * *

Danny bent over the nurse's station, doing his damnedest to charm the nice lady behind the desk into giving him some information, but getting nowhere.

"What... When did you get here?"

The relief in Drea's voice was evident. Danny turned and gave her a gentle smile. She looked like hell, but that was to be expected. He glanced down at his watch. It had been early evening when he'd dropped her at the hospital. He'd bristled at her insistence that she go in alone, but he'd done as she asked. Now it was two in the morning. The cotton dress Wilma had brought over was rumpled, and Drea's hair was a tangled mess. Her eyes had a haunted, hollow look he didn't like, and he was pretty certain she hadn't eaten anything since breakfast.

"About an hour ago," he replied. "And I never should have left in the first place. You don't have to go this alone, darlin'. You need some sleep."

"There's a family lounge. I can stay there."

Danny nodded and pressed his lips together. Yeah, he remembered that family lounge from when his daddy was sick. A place of plastic-covered recliners that were about as comfortable as airplane seats. Bad coffee, stale pastries, and glaring lights did not make it a comfortable place to stay.

"Why don't you come back to the ranch to get some real sleep? Or stay with Wilma if you want to be closer. I'm sure she'd have you."

Drea shook her head and stalked off down the hall. He gritted his teeth and followed. She turned into the lounge, and he sucked in a harsh breath. Damn place hadn't changed one bit over the years.

Drea settled into a chair and glared at him. "I want to be here. You don't have to stay. I'm fine."

He pulled a chair up next to hers. "I'm sure you are, but indulge me, would ya? How long has it been since you ate?"

She blinked at him and frowned. "I…umm… I…had something at…while we were…"

Her words stopped on a dry, racking sob, and she buried her face in her hands. Danny reached out and put his arms around her, then gently tugged her into his lap where she sagged against his shoulder. Her ragged, hitching breaths slowed into hiccups then a deep, even rhythm. She'd fallen asleep.

He shifted as gently as possible, leaned the chair back and reached for a blanket to cover her up. The position wasn't exactly comfortable, but he'd be damned if he was going to risk waking her to move her.

Chapter Twenty-Four

Drea woke curled in the chair, a blanket tucked securely around her, and Danny nowhere to be seen. The taste of bad coffee and sleep clung in her mouth, making her wish for a toothbrush. The door swung open, and Danny came in, sending her heart soaring before memories of last night's tear fest hit the pit of her stomach like hot stones of shame. Danny had a tote bag in one hand and a tray in the other, and the smell of bacon wafted across the room. And he looked surprisingly well rested, damn him. The man was a saint.

"Before you ask," he said, "Paul's unchanged. Still sleeping. Wilma and Ma rustled up a few things for you." He set the bag down next to her and pulled up a small table. "I grabbed what passes for breakfast around here. Didn't know what you might eat, so there's a bit of everything." He placed the tray on the table, then reached into the tote bag and pulled out a foil-wrapped package that he added to the tray. "Ma sent a muffin."

Drea heaved a sigh of relief, grateful he hadn't brought up her breakdown last night. She poked at the eggs, then the oatmeal, and finally settled on toast and bacon, then polished off half of Annette's huge blueberry muffin.

"Aren't you eating?" She glanced up at Danny.

He shook his head. "I had a muffin and some bacon. The rest of it looks too scary for words. Oh…" He bent to the tote bag again and pulled out a thermos. He grabbed disposable cups from the kitchenette and poured them both coffee. "Made fresh at home this mornin'."

She took a swallow and let out a low moan. "Heaven. I don't know what swill they're brewing here, but it's the worst ever." She sipped her coffee and eyed him over the cup. He was still in yesterday's clothes, but somehow, he looked fine. A little scruffy from the lack of a shave, but she wasn't about to complain about that. In fact, she kinda liked it. And she kinda liked that he was here. Hell, she more than liked it.

That brought up the conversation they'd been having when the fire started. He wanted her here. In his life. She shook her head. She couldn't deal with that right now. She had to focus on Gramps. And those fires. Enough was enough. She finished her coffee and peered into the tote. A change of clothes and a small bag filled with a toothbrush, toothpaste, a hairbrush, and a few other necessities.

"I'm gonna… I gotta…" She pointed at the bathroom. On impulse, Drea leaned down and kissed his cheek. "Thank you." She hurried into the bathroom, too shaken to do much more. She wasn't used to letting people help. It was a strange feeling.

Twenty minutes later, she was nodding as Dr. Jarvis explained Gramps' condition wasn't improving. "He's still breathing on his own, but at this stage, that could change at any moment. When that happens, we will not resuscitate. Do you understand?"

Drea nodded. She knew what he meant. The thought wrenched her insides, tightening and clawing until her stomach threatened to reject her breakfast. The idea of losing Gramps hurt, but he was fighting a battle he couldn't win. If he had another heart attack, or stopped breathing, and they brought him back, the rest of his life would be miserable. He'd made his wishes clear — he didn't want to live a life like that.

She nodded again and slipped into Gramps' room. His breathing came in irregular bursts, and the nurses came in to check on him every fifteen minutes. One explained they'd up the morphine if he appeared to be in distress, but that right now, he seemed comfortable.

At a brush of papery dry skin against her hand, Drea looked up. His eyes were open a tiny crack and a tremulous smile crossed his lips. His fingers twitched, and she took his hand in hers, sniffing to hold back the tears that stung her eyes.

"So…like your Abuela."

If only. Abuela had been strong, fearless. Drea feared everything these days — even her own feelings. The smile faded and Gramps' face went slack. His eyes widened, then closed. Drea stopped fighting the tears and let them fall as she watched the light slowly fading from him.

"I love you, Gramps. Tell Abuela I miss her. *Via con Dios*." She whispered the words just before the incessant beeping of the heart monitor changed to a solid alarm.

Alone. She was alone.

Everything became a blur as a nurse rushed in, checked for a pulse and breathing, then silenced the monitor. They gave her a few minutes to say goodbye. With her heart breaking, Drea kissed his forehead one last time.

She felt ready to fly apart, shatter into tiny pieces. She made her way back to the family lounge where Danny was waiting. His strong arms wrapped around her. No words passed between them, but he was there, a rock to cling to, lean on. She looked into those blue eyes — she loved him. She always had. No matter what happened, she always would.

Danny tightened his arms around her, holding her as she sobbed against his chest.

* * * *

Sitting in the cramped family counseling room making funeral arrangements, Danny was in awe of Drea's ability to keep going despite the fact that she had to be exhausted and emotionally drained. She gathered the pile of paperwork and slipped it all into an envelope, then nodded at the priest. The man rose and excused himself, leaving the two of them alone. She turned to Danny and shouldered her bag. "That leaves one last thing. Can I stay with you tonight?"

Danny caught his breath. Drea rarely asked for anything. "You know the answer to that," he replied. "Of course. Whatever you need."

She took a deep breath, and the pain in her eyes ripped into him. He wanted to soothe it all away, but he couldn't. She had to walk this path, but she didn't have to walk it alone. He'd be right there with her if she'd let him.

"We can't get the funeral scheduled before the weekend, so it's on Monday." Drea's words were tight, and she hauled in another shuddering breath. "I need to do what I should have done as soon as Gramps' house burned — get to the bottom of these fires."

Danny's heart twisted at the barely restrained anger in her voice. If she went back to the ATF, to DC, she might not come back. Still, this was who she was.

"You know I'm here for you, whatever you need. I told you before you don't have to do this alone. I want to help." He wanted her to stay, but he was terrified she'd get bored and leave. He needed her to stay because she wanted to — for herself, not just for him.

"You know when I ask for an investigation, the ATF is going to look at everything here, including the ranch." Drea spoke slowly, as if she were choosing her words carefully. "Three of these fires were on your property. They're going to pick it all apart. Everything."

Even now, torn up with grief over her grandfather, Drea was being her practical, focused self. So far, none of the fires had caused much more than a hiccup in their plans. They'd been lucky there. The first fires had seemed different, like they were more about the bodies. The later ones had targeted Drea. If she continued digging, they could get worse. He couldn't ask her to stop — to not investigate. If she left, maybe they'd stop. But then she'd be gone. That thought dredged up every bit of pain and anger and frustration he'd felt when Jake had left. When he'd had to say goodbye to Drea the first time.

He wasn't going to make that mistake twice.

"I know," he replied. "I think you're wrong about Brian or Lily, but I understand."

He took her hands in his, caught her eyes, mentally crossing his fingers that Paul had been right — that Drea knew what she wanted, but she was afraid of it. He wanted to erase her fears. "We can get through this, Drea. Together."

The small smile that curved her lips sent his heart skyrocketing.

Chapter Twenty-Five

"I'm sorry about your grandfather, Hidalgo." Mattix greeted her as Drea climbed out of Gramps' truck. Mattix didn't give Drea a chance to respond before she wrapped her in a crushing hug. When Mattix finally let go, Drea caught her wiping a tear from her eyes.

"Now, tell me why you dragged us to the middle of nowhere," Mattix said.

"The Medical Examiner's office in the county seat hardly qualifies as the middle of nowhere," Drea retorted. "And who is us?"

Peter Adams unfolded himself from the passenger seat of Mattix's rental car. "Hi."

Drea looked from Adams back to Mattix. "I'm confused. I called Deputy Director Wilkes and asked for a team to take a preliminary look at this series of fires."

Mattix smiled and spread her hands wide. "And that's what you've got. You, me and him." She nodded at Adams.

"But…" Drea sputtered. This was not what she'd expected. "You're not normally in the field. And what the hell is Adams doing here?"

"Hey!" Adams cried out. "I'm shadowing Mattix. Part of training."

"Wilkes went outside the lines on this one," Mattix replied. "Since Adams is stuck to me like glue, he's along for the ride. Besides, he's brilliant in the lab. And Wilkes agreed, the place to start is the records — see what's been done, what's still waiting. You know how slow lab results can be."

"Going through all the data and samples might help shed a little light on one of the victims. If not, I'm at a dead end." Drea shrugged. "After this, we'll have to go back to the Deputy Director for additional warrants."

Mattix nodded. "You won't have any problem there. I didn't have any trouble getting this warrant. Wilkes starts fuming every time you send a text or email. You know how much he hates when local cops don't cooperate."

"One thing at a time. I'm trying to focus on these fires. I've had a weird feeling since the first fire at the ranch. I'm missing something. I know it."

Adams leaned his lanky frame against the car. "Did anyone on the ranch see anything the day of the last fire?"

"Not really," Drea replied. "The power company folks were on the far side of the property, and there was a crew out where they're planning to build an equestrian camp. A couple of hands saw someone in an orange work vest traipsing around, but they didn't think anything of it. Robert, of course, thinks there's nothing to investigate. As far as he's concerned, the culprit in the earlier fires went back to the residential unit at Prestera, so this one must've been an accident."

Mattix let out a string of expletives. "Because propane tanks are so well known for spontaneously blowing up and thermite devices spring out of the ground like weeds? Who've you got eyes on?"

Drea shook her head. "I don't have enough to go on. If the point was to hurt Parsons Acres, the bodies could be anyone, and mean nothing. I don't like to think it could be Brian or Lily, but that remains a possibility. Could be an ex-employee, too."

She took a deep breath. "If the point was to hide the bodies, the location could be a coincidence, or maybe the arsonist thought it out and figured they'd get two birds with one stone. Whatever. That opens it up to half the town. Anyone who might be inclined to not only murder two people, but to set a bunch of fires, destroy a lot of property, and threaten a lot of lives in the process. That's why I need to do this."

Mattix hauled out her keys and pulled a suitcase from her trunk. "Stopped at your storage unit like you asked. It's all work clothes, that's pretty much all you had left there. Hope that's okay?"

Drea hugged her and tossed the suitcase into Gramps' truck. "Thank you. For everything."

"I've always got your back, kid. You know that." Mattix squeezed back. "Funeral's Monday, right?"

Drea nodded, swallowing hard. Focusing on work kept her mind off Gramps. And Danny. She could throw herself into this investigation, figure out what was going on, and worry about where she and Danny stood later. Or she could wallow in self-pity.

Anger and action were easier, and she'd never been very good at wallowing.

"Hey, can we get inside and get out of this heat?" Adams gestured toward the building's door.

Drea laughed and led the way. In minutes, Adams was up to his eyeballs in lab reports while Mattix combed through missing persons reports, and Drea dug through the rest of the records.

"Aha!" Adams jumped up from his stool. "I'm gonna go check with the lab, see if they still have samples. They didn't do complete tox screens yet. I can run those right now, get results in hours instead of weeks or months."

He took off at a brisk pace, and Drea rolled her eyes at Mattix. "I suggested they do those."

"You know how it is. Unless law enforcement is hollering for results, they'll get to it eventually." Mattix turned back to her computer.

Drea wasn't finding anything—aside from more reminders of how Robert had botched every step of the investigation. Though seeing the timelines laid out side by side was interesting.

She'd already figured the first fire in February had been a dress rehearsal—someone testing their technique. Then the next one in late March—three and a half weeks later. It had been a new moon—dark, easy to avoid being seen on an unused rural road out in the middle of nowhere. The fire she and Danny had seen came four weeks after that in an even more remote location.

"How are you doing on missing persons?" Drea leaned back in her seat.

Mattix stared at the computer, her hands dug into her hair. "This is infuriating. There's no communication between agencies. It's insane."

"Welcome to field work," Drea replied. "Any luck?"

"I'm compiling a list," Mattix said. "We'll have to cross-check to find closed cases. This is a mess."

"Are you ready to say thank you?" Adams came back in waving a printed sheet. "Both vics were processed by a worker at the county level," he said. "Not uncommon. The police report cited accidental fire. Neither vic had sufficient fingerprints for identification. Dental images were taken, but you know how that goes. Without some idea who they might be, it's a crap shoot at best."

"Nice summary," Drea said. "Now tell us something we don't know."

Adams slapped a printout onto the desk. "They still had blood samples. I was able to run tests. Ketamine, rohypnol, telazol and xylazine."

Mattix scanned the results, but Drea leaned back. "I know the first two. What are the others?"

"Ketamine and rohypnol make up the classic date rape cocktail," Adams replied. "And would fool most techs on a standard tox screen. Hell, most of them would miss the ketamine on these vics, if they even tested for it. Telazol doesn't show up on standard tests, and xylazine is usually seen with heroin."

He held his hands out a bit and smiled. "Hey, c'mon. This is cool stuff, and it's hard stuff to find."

"Yeah, you're awesome," Mattix intoned. "Now tell me what the fuck it means. Aside from the fact they'd been roofied."

"It means you've got something to chase," Adams replied. "Aside from the rohypnol, these are all veterinary drugs. Usually used in equine surgery."

Drea's ears perked up at that. Veterinary drugs. Equine surgery. There were only two places around she could think of where those drugs would be available.

Doc Jameson didn't make any sense, but someone could have taken drugs from him. Penny Elkins had certainly been around Parsons Acres all summer, but she wouldn't have had access to the drug cabinets. But her sister would have. And so would Brian. It still didn't make sense, and she didn't like it.

"Adams, great job!" Drea's stomach churned as she grabbed the printout. "Let's call Wilkes and get some warrants."

"You wanna tell me for who or what?" Mattix raised her hands in the air, questioning.

"These aren't exactly things you can buy at the local store," Drea replied.

Mattix nodded. "You're thinking maybe the local vet? Or that vet student you said was working at the ranch?"

Drea shook her head. "Hey, who taught me to never go into an investigation with preconceived notions? I'm simply following the evidence. It's time to talk to a few people, starting at Parsons Acres, and Henry Jameson, the local vet. And Robert. I want access to everything he's got. Then we'll see where things go. And we need to check in at the Charleston field office. That way we're not having to go all the way back to DC."

* * * *

Drea threaded through the mess of cubicles that took up the front of the field office. Mattix had somehow commandeered a tiny conference room in the back for the three of them. Adams was nowhere to be seen — presumably in the lab running still more tests. Work and sheer rage were the only things keeping her going.

Gramps was gone, and she still had the funeral to get through. Her stomach flip-flopped at the thought.

And Danny. Serving a warrant at Parsons Acres wasn't going to be a good time. When she'd talked to Danny about the investigation looking into Parsons Acres, she hadn't expected to be personally involved. What she was about to do could cause a rift between them that couldn't be healed. She crossed her fingers, hoping it wasn't anyone at the ranch.

Mattix waved her over and hit the button on the speakerphone. "She's just walked in the door, sir."

"Mattix laid it out for me." Deputy Director Wilkes' voice rang through the room. "Hidalgo, normally, we'd pull you from this case because of your connection with the subsequent fires, but the damn locals did everything they could to undermine you and that needs to stop."

He cleared his throat and continued, "Putting any investigator on this could make the perpetrator run to ground. If it's you, their emotions may outweigh their brain and they'll make mistakes. That could work to our advantage. You're taking the lead on this. Start with the bodies. Getting an ID is top priority. That will point you to your suspect. Who are your top contenders right now?"

Drea hauled in a deep breath. Moment of truth. "Well, sir, the local police would like me to believe all but the last fire were done by Penny Elkins. She's eighteen, has a history of self-harm, including burning herself, but as far as I can tell, she's not a pyro."

"Not a viable suspect?" Wilkes asked.

"On her own? No, sir. She's very small, doesn't drive, and is never left alone. I can't see how she would have gotten out to the remote locations of the first fires or to my grandfather's house or my car. She was around Parsons Acres with her older sister who works there, but Penny was never out of Lily's sight on the ranch. And she had checked back into a residential care facility prior to the latest fire. But that does leave Lily Elkins as a possible suspect."

Drea paused. She didn't want to think about the next possibility. But she had to. "Recent evidence points to veterinary drugs, which makes me wonder if one of the ranch employees might be involved. Lily, and Brian French, the ranch manager are both worth looking into. They both have the access, and the means. But not the motivation."

The sounds of papers shuffling, then Wilkes said, "That you know of."

"True," Drea replied. "Outside of that, I don't have a good suspect. I'm suspicious of Robert Moore because he's been ridiculously uncooperative, but I can't put two and two together yet. I want to dig into the veterinary drug records, and rattle Robert's cage a bit. Maybe we'll get somewhere."

Silence for a moment. Wilkes would be sitting at his desk, fingers laced, staring out the window as he thought things over. Many people made the mistake of filling the silence with chatter. Drea knew better.

"I'll have the warrants for you by Tuesday. Take care of this after the funeral. Keep it small and tight," Wilkes said finally. "You, Mattix and Adams. That's it."

"Thank you, sir."

"Hidalgo." Wilkes' voice echoed in the little room. "Keep it quiet in house, but the time for walking softly in the field is over. You're going to piss a lot of people off on this. It's your hometown and your grandfather just passed. Are you sure you're up for it?"

Drea smiled, but it felt brittle and hard. "This is who I am, sir. I'll do my job and deal with the fallout. If folks can't handle that, well…they don't belong in my life, do they?" And no matter how much it might hurt, that included Danny Parsons. She wanted him in her life, but not at the cost of losing herself. She'd already lost everything else. She needed to find the arsonist. Period.

She turned to Mattix. "Let's do this."

Chapter Twenty-Six

The day was hot and clear — the bright sun painting everything in stark colors that felt too garish. The white rose in Drea's hand trembled as she placed it on the headstone. She traced the smooth marble, following the lines of the names — Isabel and Paul. The masons would be out next week to carve in the date of Gramps' death. She took a shuddering breath and pushed herself up. Her wedges sank into the soft earth, and she grazed her fingers along the top of the double headstone.

She looked away from the patch of green, too bright and artificial, not wanting to think about the pile of dirt covered with fake grass, or the cemetery workers, patiently waiting for her to leave. The casket had been lowered into the ground and the ceremonial earth dropped in. The unpleasant work of filling in the grave happened after the bereaved were gone.

Grass changed to gravel as she reached the path and made her way to Danny's truck in the parking lot, her mind churning over practicalities. Anything was better than the gnawing grief tearing her apart any time she stopped for a breath. The fire at the house had destroyed so much, and the one at the cottage had taken everything else.

She didn't have much here. A suitcase of clothes, her laptop and Danny. He reached a hand out to her, curled her into his arms. He'd been there for her all day, right beside her during the service, holding her hand. Rock steady. She'd asked him to give her a few moments, after everyone else had left. He hadn't questioned. He'd squeezed her hand and gone back to his truck, leaving her staring at the headstone.

"Saying goodbye is tough, darlin'." Danny's breath ruffled her hair, and his hands cradled her, firm, comforting. She rested her head on his chest then sighed. Every muscle in her face hurt from holding it together. She wanted to curl up somewhere quiet and forget the world existed.

"Can you manage the wake?" he asked. "Even for a bit."

Drea sniffed, raised her head. "Will you...? I don't want to be alone."

"You won't be." He squeezed her hands then got her settled in the passenger seat.

She'd been focused on Gramps all through Abuela's wake, kept going by taking care of him. She didn't know how she'd make it through this one. She understood it. People needed to share. It was the way they began grieving. It was connection. But she didn't feel it. Didn't want it.

She made it through an hour, with Danny or Wilma by her side the entire time. The scent of flowers grew heavier, sweeter by the minute until Drea never wanted to smell another lily or carnation in her life. Until that cloying sweetness made her want to gag, and she could no longer open her mouth when someone talked to her for fear she would vomit from the smell.

"Why don't you let Danny get you out of here?" Wilma looped an arm through Drea's and steered her toward the door, dragging Danny along with them. At the door, she hugged Drea, whispered how sorry she was and kissed her cheek. Drea's heart clenched and tears threatened to overflow. Again. She sniffed.

Then Danny was leading her down the steps, into his truck, and before she knew it, they were at his place, and she was on his couch.

"You want a coffee?" Danny asked. "Or would you prefer the hard stuff?"

Drea shook her head. "Coffee, please."

"Do you want to talk?" His voice carried in from the kitchen, along with the blessed sounds of coffee brewing.

"I don't know." Drea didn't want to do anything. She didn't want to think. Tears burned as they spilled over her eyelids. "I'm not ready to say goodbye."

Danny was beside her in a heartbeat. His hands holding hers. Ever since she'd come back to town, he had been there for her every time she'd needed him. She'd been waiting for him to ask her to stay, and he'd been showing her, time and time again, that he wanted her with him. She hadn't believed the clues. Now he'd said something and tomorrow she'd be back here with a warrant, throwing all of his trust and caring right back in his face.

"Maybe I will go for the hard stuff," Drea said. "Just a splash."

* * * *

"How's the head?" Mattix handed Drea a cup of coffee as she settled into the uncomfortable office chair. Drea flipped her off. She'd had one too many whiskey-laced coffees yesterday.

"That good, huh?" Mattix gave her an evil-looking smile. "Well, how about some good news?"

Drea sipped coffee. "That'd be nice. But I'm not holding my breath."

"Adams and I narrowed down the missing persons reports."

Drea groaned. "Great. Anything promising?"

Adams slid a laptop in front of them. "So, missing person reports are kind of a mess. Hard to search. We've got some info on our vics — sex, approximate age and height, stuff like that. And we can make a reasonable guess that they weren't missing long before each incident. Geographically, I figure they've got to live or work fairly close by. Good place to start, anyway."

Drea scanned down the list on the screen and whistled. "Twenty?"

"You should have seen it before," Adams replied. "We cross-referenced with other cases, removed entries where the person was found — one way or another."

"The real break came when we filtered by gender and date," Mattix chimed in. "That brought it down to thirteen female and seven male, all from within a reasonable distance, all missing in the right time frames, and all matching the data we have."

Drea pushed back from the table. "Great work! Mattix, start running info on those names. It's twenty. That won't take too long. Meanwhile, Adams and I can go antagonize the local law enforcement. Robert's dropped the ball on this so many times it isn't funny. If he'd done his job, we wouldn't be here. Nobody can be that incompetent without reason. I wanna rattle his cage a bit and see if he responds."

Drea smiled. "I've already got a strained relationship with Chief Robert Moore. If it comes down to a game of good cop-bad cop, Adams can play the guy card as well."

"You're evil." Mattix was practically grinning with glee.

Drea shook her head. "Sadly, no. I know the territory and frankly don't care about pissing Robert off. C'mon, Adams, we've got an hour's ride, and I want to get to Parsons Acres today."

Drea didn't want to believe it was anyone at the ranch, and she wanted that possibility wiped off as quickly as she could. They passed the drive in silence until Adams whistled as they pulled into the lot at the police station.

"Jesus, you told me you came from a small town, not from a pimple on the ass-crack of nowhere."

"Bite me," Drea muttered. "Let's do this."

Drea grabbed her bag, then led the way to the glass doors. Robert looked up from his desk and immediately stood as she came up to the counter.

"Andrea, I told you to stay out of here…"

Drea pulled her jacket open to reveal the badge on her waist and slapped the warrant onto the counter. "Chief Moore, I'd like you to meet Special Agent Peter Adams. We have some questions for you regarding two fires and unidentified bodies your department reported."

"What the hell is this, Drea?" Robert's voice rose half an octave. "They were vagrants. Or druggie friends of Penny's. I told you that."

"Yeah, you did. And that really makes me wonder why you're so determined to not properly look into things." Drea slid the warrant closer to him, barely resisting the urge to smile at the sick expression that crossed Robert's face.

"This is a federal investigation," Drea continued. "It doesn't matter what you think about those two victims. And it's Special Agent Hidalgo. Or Agent Hidalgo will do."

She caught Adams rolling his eyes and glared at him. He shrugged and smiled over her head at Robert.

"I'm sorry, you are Special Agent..." Robert was looking to Adams with a hopeful expression.

"Adams." He took Robert's hand and gave it a hearty shake. "As my uh...colleague was saying, we're trying to take care of business here. The warrant covers, umm..." He slid the warrant back over so he could read it, and Drea almost laughed out loud. He'd typed the thing.

"Oh, here it is. All reports, evidence and records pertaining to these two cases. Huh. Pretty inclusive. You closed these cases, right?" He looked at Robert, when the other man nodded, Adams smiled. "Right. So, we need all the case files. Simple really. Professional courtesy and all."

"Who were they?" Robert's eyes flicked from the warrant, to Adams, then Drea and back again.

"Federal investigation, Chief Moore," Drea replied with a brittle smile. She sure as shit wasn't about to admit they hadn't ID'd the bodies yet. "I don't need to give you anything. I'm trying to be nice here."

Robert guffawed at that, and Drea's smile widened. He really was falling for this whole routine. If she was wrong on this, if Robert wasn't hiding something, this would all blow up. Badly. And she could kiss any future with Danny goodbye.

"Fine." He spat the word at her and went to his desk. "I'll release all the records. We don't keep evidence. There isn't space."

"What happened to any evidence collected?" She leaned across the counter and glared at him. He took his time, clicking around on the computer and finding a USB drive.

"We photograph everything and send any samples to the lab, the county, or the state. It'll all be in the reports. If we don't feel anythin' needs analysis, then nothin' is sent and the only thing we keep are the photos. Digital, of course." He drummed his fingers on the desk, waiting for the drive to finish, then handed it to her. "That's everything."

"Why, thank you." She gave him a sweet smile and waved as she and Adams left.

Once in the car, Adams turned to her with a horrified look on his face. "You grew up around that shit? Is that guy for real?"

"Sadly, the answer to both of those questions is yes. Let's get to Parsons Acres and check their med records before going back to the field office. We can tackle Jameson tomorrow."

Drea's stomach churned, and her hands clenched on the wheel as they turned down the road heading to Parsons Acres.

Danny's heart leaped into his throat when he saw Drea standing in front of the ranch office talking with Lily, Brian, and some guy he didn't know. He stopped himself from rushing up to her. The expression on her face was strange — lips pressed tight, as if something were causing her pain.

She gave a shaky smile when he stopped next to her, bit her lip and took a deep breath. "Danny, this is Special Agent Peter Adams. I'm sorry. We have a warrant to search your veterinary supplies and records."

Well, she'd told him this would be coming, but he'd expected someone he didn't know. Not her.

"Sure," he replied. "Whatever you need. But what's going on here?"

"Just covering all our bases." She shifted her feet and looked uncomfortable. Then she sighed and fixed her green eyes on him. "When a piece of evidence points in a particular direction, no matter what I believe personally, I have to follow all possible avenues."

She'd hinted at this before. Told him the victims were likely roofied. She must have found something, or they wouldn't be here. "Let's go inside."

Danny pulled in extra chairs so the five of them could sit at Brian's desk.

Drea leaned back in her seat. "Do you use ketamine on the ranch? And do you keep a supply of ketamine on site?"

"Well, sure, we use ketamine here. We're a horse ranch," Brian replied, then turned to Lily. "Pull the paper records. Take it back through January, please."

"Some of the physical stores were destroyed in the fire, but we've never had anything missing," Danny added. "We don't keep a lot in stock right now."

Lily came back with a stack of papers and handed them to Brian. He didn't look at them before he slid them across the desk at Drea. Adams picked up the pile, then ran his finger down the list.

"Impressive record keeping." He tapped an item. "So, these are visits from the veterinarian. Looks like in addition to whatever prescription he gave, he also restocked anything you keep on hand?"

Brian nodded and Drea scanned the records. "And this" — she pointed at a new page — "is the pharmacy cabinet? Wait, cabinets? Kept locked at all times. Who has the keys?"

"Currently?" Brian spoke up. "Me, Lily, and Danny. Back then? Me and Danny. And yeah, two. Though one got ruined in the fire, you're welcome to check the main cabinet if you'd like."

The five of them walked through the office to the storeroom in back. Drea was acting as if she'd never met them, never spent time on the ranch, and it had him twisted into knots all over again. Danny directed them to the big, locked cabinet that held the ranch's pharmacy supplies. Brian produced a key and opened the cabinet, and Adams checked the contents against the list, then handed it to Drea.

"It all checks out," he said.

"May I keep this?" She held up the list.

"Sure." Brian shrugged. "You didn't need a warrant for that."

She slipped the papers into her bag and smiled. "I'm following protocol. Brian, Lily, thank you." She turned to Danny. "I appreciate your willingness to help. Just a couple more questions, then."

She gave Danny an apologetic look, her eyes wide and sad looking, then turned to Brian and Lily. "Brian, could you please go with Agent Adams to the office? He has a few questions he'd like to ask about your whereabouts and activities on the dates of the fires. I'd like to ask the same questions of Lily."

Brian took a step back, as if stunned. Lily looked like she was ready to explode. Drea was being so cold. Distant. Professional. The only reason Danny could think of was that she'd either found hard evidence linking the fires to someone here, and he couldn't believe that. Or she'd made up her mind to go back to DC.

Either way, this had gone far enough. "Your questions can wait until we get an attorney here," Danny said. Doing her job was one thing, but coming in here like this, acting like a stranger, and accusing his staff of these crimes was something else entirely.

"It's just preliminary questions," Drea replied. "I'm not charging anyone. I'm not accusing anyone. I'm following leads. That's all."

"If your leads pointed you here, either you're confused, or the leads are wrong." Dammit. Getting angry was the wrong thing, but he didn't know what was up with her. Yesterday, he'd been sure she was determined to stay. Now this. "And preliminary or not, they have a right to an attorney."

Danny shoved his hands through his hair. He needed to talk to Drea. Not this professional robot standing in front of him. "Could y'all give us a minute here?"

Brian and Lily were out the door before he could take another breath. Adams waited until Drea nodded at him, then he followed suit. Danny breathed a bit easier. Maybe now he and Drea could really talk.

"You wanna tell me what this is all about?"

She shook her head. "You know I can't."

"Really? You can't believe anyone here had anything to do with this? For what purpose?"

She turned cold eyes up to him. "It doesn't matter what I believe. I have to explore every avenue. Read between the lines all you'd like, but please stop jumping to conclusions."

He caught her arm as she turned away. "Can we talk?"

She glanced pointedly down where his hand circled her wrist. She was practically vibrating, barely holding herself together. He released her, his hands clenching and unclenching by his side. He didn't have the slightest clue what to say.

"Arson is a crime," Drea said. "A federal crime. Adding bodies kinda ups the stakes a bit. That propane explosion wasn't an accident. If the wind hadn't shifted, the cottage would have gone up faster, and there might've been more deaths — human and horse. I don't like coming here and asking these questions. But I have to."

The pain in her eyes gave him a moment's pause. He ran his hand over his face. She'd go after this, find the answers, no matter what it cost her personally. She had nothing left to lose.

"Ah, hell." He leaned back against the wall with a sigh. "Take what the warrant covers, but you're not talking to me, or my staff, without an attorney present. And I can't believe you put me in the position to say that. A little more warning would have been nice."

Her eyes shot to his, anger flaring. Somewhere along the line, this conversation had gone horribly wrong, and he couldn't figure out how to fix it.

"That would have been unethical," she snapped. "The things I shared with you could compromise this investigation. That's why Adams is along. I'm too close, too involved."

"Not involved enough," Danny muttered.

"I will not compromise who I am, or what I do for anyone." Drea faced him, hands on hips, her expression hard.

Danny scoffed. He had always followed her rules. Her limits. "I have never pushed you — even when you refused to talk about your week in DC. I've never asked you to compromise anything or to give up what you wanted."

The anger in her eyes changed, morphing back into pain, hurt, confusion. "No," she whispered. "You never asked anything of me. Except to get into my pants."

Her words sliced into him. He had wanted her — still wanted her. And she'd wanted him. He'd thought there was more to it than that. He'd never stopped loving her and had hoped maybe she had come to love him again. It looked like he was wrong.

"You were pretty enthusiastic about it at the time. Nothin' wrong with just sex," he replied. "Always happy to oblige. It's been long enough since our little shower indiscretion. No unpleasant surprises? Or would you even tell me if there were?"

Her lips twisted and her expression cycled from pain through hurt and into cold fury. She didn't say another word to him. She turned on her heel and stomped off, calling for Adams as she trudged across the yard. Danny didn't bother calling after her or trying to apologize. He'd opened his mouth and stuck his foot in, and she wouldn't listen right now.

Brian and Lily came back in looking confused.

"Don't worry about anything." Danny shook his head. "But if I find out later I was wrong to defend either of you, jail will be the least of your worries. Now let's get back to work. We've got an over-crowded barn to clean up."

Danny spent the rest of the day shoveling and sweeping until his arms were sore and his back ached. Space was tight after the fire took the mares' barn, but all the horses were doing well. It was a pain, but it could have been much worse. He checked on Raphistra and her foal before turning off the lights. He tugged the barn door into place and wiped his hands down his jeans. The heavy physical labor had kept him from thinking about Drea. His gut wrenched. Jesus, he'd handled that badly.

"You comin' out to Oak Bridge tonight?" Brian finished hosing out the wheelbarrow he had and propped it against a fencepost.

Danny shook his head. Brian and the guys would play darts. That wasn't the crowd he needed right now.

"Not tonight," he replied. "You and Lily okay?"

"Yeah," Brian replied. "I get it. She's a little pissed, but she gets where it's coming from. Seems like she was almost expecting it." He shrugged. "Hey, Cisco is in the winter shed in the lower field. He seems to like it there, and I'm bettin' he'd enjoy some company."

"Thanks," Danny replied. Cisco. The horse he'd ridden all through high school. He'd put Drea on Cisco for the gymkhana in part because he was still a beautiful horse, and completely unshakable no matter what happened, and he'd hoped seeing Cisco would bring back happy memories for her.

A trail ride sounded like a good way to get some time to think. And Cisco was the perfect companion for it. It was coming up on sunset, but that old horse knew the trails at Parsons Acres so well, he could navigate in the dark. Danny grabbed a lantern and a saddle and headed to the lower field.

An hour later, he tethered Cisco and unlocked the door to his daddy's old hunting cabin. The place was a bit dusty, but otherwise clean and dry. Alone in the quiet, he pulled a bottle of water from his bag and climbed the stand out back.

Perched in the trees, he let his thoughts wander. Maybe he was stuck. At one point, he'd had a choice, but now, even if he could take a different road, he wouldn't. The ranch was his life. A life he'd foolishly imagined sharing with Drea.

Well, he'd certainly screwed that up. Wallowing in self-pity and coulda-beens wasn't gonna do him any good. He had a business to run. Drea... He heaved a sigh and let his head thump back against the tree. *Fuck. Drea.* The thought of her made his stomach clench and his face turn hot with shame and anger. No matter what she said or did, it didn't excuse his behavior.

His mother would have read him the riot act for the way he'd acted. *I didn't raise my boy to speak to women with such disrespect.* Her voice echoed in his imagination. *If your daddy were alive...*

The old man would have tossed him from their property for that. *You don't say such things to any woman. Let alone the woman you say you care for.*

"Dammit." He thumped his head against the tree again. How could he ever apologize to her for that?

Chapter Twenty-Seven

Dr. Harry Jameson looked like he'd stepped out of a Western set at the turn of the century, right down to the cowboy hat hanging in the corner of his office. He'd been around as long as Drea could recall, and he'd always seemed old.

He peered over the warrant and sat back. "We had some stock go missing in January. Had a young man workin' for us. He took money from the till a time or two, and that I can forgive." He raised his head and gave Drea a kind smile. "You need money to eat or make bills? Well, it's hard times. But drugs missin'? I can't look the other way on that."

Drea nodded. "You got a name?"

"Oh, sure." Jameson tapped a few keys on his aging computer and scribbled the info on a notepad. "Charlie Phelps. Lives in one of those trailer parks out in the middle of nowhere. Rough places." He handed Drea the paper.

Drea looked at the address. Phelps lived in the county. *Well, that'll make things easy.* Agents at the field office said they had a good relationship with county law enforcement. She thanked Jameson and called Mattix on her way out the door. "Can you get on with the Sheriff and ask them to bring in Charlie Phelps." She relayed the information. "Let's have a chat with this kid."

"You got it." A flurry of clicking and Mattix's mumbling filled the phone. "While you've been out charming the local vet, I narrowed the missing persons down a bit more, we're down to seventeen. I fuckin' hate this. Adams took it on himself to run backgrounds on Brian French and Lily Elkins."

Drea's fingers clenched on the phone. Mattix bringing it up meant Adams had found something. She didn't want it to be anyone at the ranch. She didn't want to have to go to Danny with that. What she wanted was to be able to go to him with the guilty person caught—someone who had no connection to the ranch—and see if they could salvage their relationship.

From the moment she'd run into him at the hospital, Danny had been there for her. Even when she'd pulled away—he'd given her space, always respecting her needs. And she'd repaid him by acting the bully. It didn't matter that it was her job, there was no reason for her to be cruel. The fact that he'd responded in kind didn't excuse her behavior. She crossed her fingers that it wasn't Brian.

"What did Adams find?" Drea braced herself for the worst.

"French is off the hook for at least one of the fires—he was in class when your car blew."

Drea breathed a sigh of relief. Off the hook for one didn't mean off the hook for all, but it took a little suspicion off Brian. "Anything else?"

"French had a DUI," Mattix replied. "He was underage. Slammed his car into a tree. Right before he started working for the Parsons. The job at the ranch kept him out of deeper trouble—Danny Parsons went to bat for him, insisted that French living at the ranch would reduce his risk—which I can picture him doing. This was years ago, though."

Brian was looking less and less likely. He had every reason to be grateful to the Parsons, and zero reasons to cause any harm there.

"Lily Elkins is harder," Mattix replied. "We'll have to get witness statements for specific dates. She's either at the ranch, at home, at her parents', or she's with French."

"What about Lily's ex?" Drea asked. "Kyle's father. Is he in the picture?"

"No clue," Mattix said. "No name given on the birth certificate. But I called your favorite neighborhood gossip, Wilma Davis. Best anyone can figure, Lily had a summertime fling with a carnie and didn't realize she was pregnant until they'd left town. It was a bit of a scandal. Small towns are so full of this backwards shit."

Drea wasn't sure what to make of the idea of Mattix calling Wilma. And she didn't think she wanted to ask about it either.

"Here's the kicker," Mattix continued. "That first fire in February? Penny Elkins was released from Prestera one week prior."

Huh. Maybe Robert had it right all along. Maybe Penny did have something to do with it. She'd have to have had help.

"Thanks. Keep at the missing persons," Drea said. "I'm headed to County. I don't think it's going to take long to round up Mr. Phelps."

Drea got the text as she was pulling into county lockup. "Got Phelps." The officer in charge directed her to an observation room. On the other side of the glass sat Charles Phelps, age nineteen, glaring at the two-way mirror.

"I dunno nuthin'," Phelps muttered at the glass.

Lank brown hair hung over his eyes and a patch of adolescent acne marred an otherwise good-looking face. The kid was tall and well built, but he was also a high school dropout with a record of arrests for petty theft, breaking and entering and a list of other mostly minor offenses.

"You goin' in there?" One of the deputies pointed as the kid flipped his middle finger at the glass. Phelps surged out of the chair, pacing, his fingers jittering and twitching at his sides.

"Yep. He's been read his rights?" Drea asked, she waited for the deputy's nod before continuing. "He's nervous and I can't tell if he's high or in need of a fix. Maybe we can get him to talk before he asks for a lawyer."

Phelps flopped back in the chair, drumming his fingers on the table. Drea smiled at the deputies, grabbed an envelope full of images from the fires and the autopsy reports, then headed into the interview room.

The smell of pot and sweat permeated the space, and as she got closer, an underlying odor of ammonia suggested he was doing meth as well. Drea walked in front of the table slowly, then sat down. The kid's eyes never went above her chin.

"Mr. Phelps," she began. "My eyes are up here." His eyes darted to hers, then back down. *Attention span of a hyperactive squirrel.* In that brief glance, she'd seen what she needed to see. She'd nailed it — nervous and itching for his next high.

She took her badge out and sat it on the table in front of him. "I'm Special Agent Andrea Hidalgo, and I'm going to give you one chance to talk to me."

"I don't have to say nuthin' to no cops." The kid spat on her badge.

So much for nice.

"No, you don't. Mr. Phelps, you are the primary suspect in two arsons. Those are felonies." She dropped pictures in front of the kid. The burned buildings, body parts visible. The most gruesome shots she could find.

"Plus, I've got two dead bodies." She flipped the final picture in front of him. She'd snapped that one of the second body — the charred layer had peeled away, leaving a wet red hole. Phelps dry heaved twice, then turned and threw up on the floor.

"You're here for questioning. Here's the choice. You can keep silent, but I've got clear evidence that points to your involvement in these cases."

She shifted the photo again, slid it closer to him. He turned his head, looking up at the ceiling, away from the pictures spread out on the table.

"That's not a choice," he mumbled.

"See, Charlie, there is a brain in there." She gathered up the pictures and placed them face down on the table. "Your alternative is to tell me all about the drugs you stole from Dr. Jameson's office."

"Somebody paid me."

"Well, that's incredibly helpful." Drea needed to know who that somebody was. Brian had direct access to veterinary drugs—it didn't make sense for him to pay a petty thief. Lily might have thought it less risky to steal from Jameson than from Parsons Acres. Drea needed a name.

"You can do better than that," she said. "Is this somebody so important to you they're worth going to federal prison over?"

Phelps swallowed hard. His Adam's apple rose and fell and his eyes went wide. Drea flipped the pictures back over and spread them out.

"All's I know is I got paid to get the stuff." He blurted the words, not looking at the pictures.

"Uh-huh. Paid by who?"

"How the fuck should I know?" Phelps replied. "Someone gives me cash, I don't ask questions."

"See, I think you're feeding me a line of bullshit," Drea replied. "Let's try again. I'll read the autopsy reports." She picked up the report. "Says here the body of the male victim was burned so badly there were no external sex organs. Huh…" She looked up at Charlie with wide eyes. "This guy's dick got burned off in the flames. That's horrific."

Charlie heaved again, but nothing came up. He coughed and wheezed, then looked at her with watery eyes. "You can't fuckin' arrest me for this shit. I'm in…in… I got invisibility." He wiped his eyes and glared at Drea.

"I think you mean immunity." That didn't point to Brian or Lily. Drea heaved a sigh of relief. Though Phelps could be lying. "Who promised you that?"

Phelps shook his head and crossed his arms. His legs jittered under the table, and his eyebrow twitched in time. Drea picked up her badge, spit and all, and held it up.

"Remember the federal agent part? Talk to me now, or we'll haul your ass away today." A little white lie, but not far from the truth. It took a minute to sink in, then all the fight went out of the kid and he collapsed back into his seat.

"I can't go to jail. I can't." He mumbled the words, over and over, as if they would protect him.

"I've got you on four felony charges." Drea pitched her voice soft and low, speaking slowly, giving Phelps time to process her words. "You start talking, and maybe the judge will drop any accessory charges, and you can walk with just another theft on your record."

"He had a list. Paid me cash up front, then more on delivery. But I don't know shit 'bout what he was doin'." His head hung low and the jitters had died down. Before, he'd looked tense, keyed up, now he looked like a limp dishrag. *Definitely in need of a fix.* And Phelps had said "he."

"Very good, Charlie. Let's keep talking."

"Jesus. He's a cop. Don't you understand? He's a cop."

A thrill went through Drea. Right about now, every cop in the observation room would be bristling, worried one of their own had crossed the line, but Drea knew better. She needed Phelps to say the name. Without any prompting.

"Yeah. I get it, Charlie. I do." She'd played hardball and managed to put a chink in his armor. Time to be nice. Gramps always said you catch more flies with honey than with vinegar. She leaned across the desk, trying to catch his gaze. "You give me a name, and I'll go after him. If what you've said is true..." She let that hang there.

Phelps looked up. His face had gone pale, sweaty. His eyes drooped, and he looked exhausted. Withdrawal had well and truly set in.

"Pulled me over for speedin'. I had...stuff on me. He said he'd look the other way, y'know. He had a job he wanted done. Paid cash. Hey, I'm tired, all right? I gotta..." Phelps shifted in his seat. He wanted, needed a fix. Or sleep. He wasn't going to get either.

"I need a name, Charlie. Without that, this is all on you."

His head rolled back on his shoulders, and he groaned. "Fuuuuuuuck." He sat up, sniffed, wiped his nose on his sleeve and leaned his elbows on the table. "Fuckin' cop out in Orchard Creek. Last name's Moore. I dunno his first. Okay? Now lemme go."

Drea nodded at the glass. "Thanks, Charlie. You did good." She turned to the deputy who'd just come in. "Sorry about the mess on the floor. My fault. Take it easy on him, okay?" The man nodded, and cuffed Phelps, then helped him stand. Charlie shot her an accusatory glance, but he was too strung out to do much more.

"You are one cold-hearted person, Hidalgo." The second deputy looked shaken, but he was smiling.

"I do what needs doing." She grabbed her phone and texted Mattix. "We need a warrant for Robert Moore. I'll text details but get it in the pipeline."

Her phone chimed with a response from Mattix. "Warrant in process. You're gonna enjoy this, aren't you?"

Drea smiled and typed a reply. "Arresting Robert? Maybe a little."

It took less than an hour to get the paperwork in order. Drea asked Mattix to come along this time. If

Robert got nasty, she knew Mattix could hold her own. She wasn't sure about Adams.

"I don't get it." Mattix glared at Drea from the passenger seat. "Why are you not marching right into the police station and arresting his ass?"

Drea winked at her friend. "Because I'm playing small-town politics for once in my life." She pulled up to the curb and shifted into park. If she arrested Robert, it put the town in an awkward place. No chief of police.

"Most of the town thinks Robert's useless as a cop," Drea said. "But there aren't too many problems around here, and folks tend to mind their own, so he gets by. Like him or not, he is a local boy. Arresting him is going to raise a stink."

"Yeah, I thought that was the point." Mattix waved out the window at the pretty little house they'd stopped in front of. "This isn't Robert's address."

"Nope." Drea smiled. "It's Mack Lawson's—the retired chief of police. And everybody loves Mack Lawson."

Mattix's eyes went wide. "You're… Oh! You figure he'll offer to step back in as chief and help everything go all smooth and nice." Drea winked and Mattix shook her head. "I'm not sure if you're brilliant or evil."

Drea laughed and got out of the car. Lawson was on his porch by the time she and Mattix made their way up the walk.

"Why do I get the feelin' this isn't a social call? Y'all may as well come in. Don't wanna give the neighbors any more reason to gossip."

He held the door and directed them into the small living room. After she'd introduced Mattix, Lawson sat in his cushy-looking chair, his eyes on Drea.

"You have a suspect in these fires." It wasn't a question. Drea nodded and Lawson pulled his chair closer to her. He leaned forward, elbows on his knees. "It's not Penny Elkins."

Drea sighed. "No, sir. It's not. I never liked Penny for this. At least not on her own."

Lawson tipped his head to the side. "And it's not anyone at Parsons Acres."

Of course he'd heard that she had questioned folks at the ranch. No matter how quietly she'd done it, people still talked. Especially in this town.

"I had to follow the leads, sir," Drea replied. "I had passing moments when I thought Brian or Lily might have been involved. But that didn't sit right."

"That young man owes a lot to the Parsons," Lawson said. "He wouldn't do anything to harm that family, or that business. Not even if it cost him everything."

He was right there. But she'd had to look into it. Lily had been the unknown. She was as sweet as they came and head over heels for Brian, but she was also as tough as nails, and her life was far less complicated when her little sister was hospitalized.

"Why don't you tell me why you're here?"

Drea took a deep breath and blew it out. "Well, sir... I'm about to arrest the local police chief, and I thought it might be a good idea to talk to the man who was his boss." She looked up at Lawson. If he was surprised, he didn't show it. "I'm going to make a big mess here, one that can't be avoided. And it'd go more smoothly..."

"You want me to stand behind you," he interjected. "Support your decision to cut off any tongue waggin'."

He'd about summed it up. "Yes, sir. I know you still serve on the town council. Someone's going to have to act as chief until this all gets sorted and the council can appoint a new chief."

Lawson's eyebrows went up at that. "I see." He sat back in his chair, nodding at her. "Paul and Isabel did a right fine job raisin' up one helluva young lady. And Daniel Parsons is a very lucky man."

Those words twisted into Drea's heart. "Thank you, sir. I'd like to think my grandparents would be proud," Drea replied. "As for Danny, well...we'll see if he'll have anything to do with me after this."

Lawson sat back, blinking and looking shocked. "Why on earth wouldn't he? Because you're doin' your job?" Lawson shook his head. "Relationships take work, on both sides. Don't go makin' insurmountable problems outta hurt feelings." He glanced over at Mattix. "You're a quiet one."

"I'm trying to keep this one out of trouble, Chief." Mattix gave a broad smile, and Lawson threw his head back, laughing.

"Good luck with that. Y'all go do what you have to do and don't worry about the town council."

Back in the car, Mattix gave Drea an odd look. "Did he encourage you to pursue law enforcement?"

Drea pulled away from the curb and pointed the car into town. Robert ought to be at the station, or the bakery next door. "Not really. Mack Lawson was always tough, but fair. Community minded. He did encourage me in that. I think that's why he gave Robert the job to begin with—he saw a young man with no direction and thought to mentor him."

Mattix chuffed a short laugh. "Yeah, that worked out well. What'd he mean about Daniel Parsons?"

Drea's stomach twisted. Despite Lawson's reassurance, she was worried Danny would never speak to her again. That choice hadn't been easy. But in the end, she had to be true to herself and hope that later she and Danny could make up. "I'm not thinking about that, or him, right now."

"So, relationships are only about the good times?" Mattix shook her head. "I don't know where you got these fucked-up ideas, but it's time to give them up."

Drea glared at her but didn't respond as they pulled into the lot. Robert's Bronco sat parked in front, and Drea wiped her hands down her pants, suddenly nervous. Mattix had been right—she was going to enjoy arresting Robert. But she was also worried about what he might say—she didn't believe for an instant Robert was working alone. She and Mattix walked up to the station together. Robert jumped when the door opened and came barreling up to the counter. He stood in front of the entrance to the office and shook his head.

"I told you not to come around here."

Underneath the bluster, he looked nervous. His eyes were too wide, his face a little too pale. When Charlie Phelps had been processed, the deputies had found a burner phone in his pocket, and a recent text to an unknown number. One word—busted. Drea smiled at Robert and leaned back against the wall as Mattix stepped up to the counter and stood face-to-face with him.

"Robert Moore," Mattix said, a little louder than necessary. "Place your hands on the counter. You are under arrest."

Robert's eyes went wider. "What? For what? You don't have the authority, Andrea! What do you think you're doing?"

"Funny, here I was thinking a warrant for your arrest, and this little badge thingie I wear did, in fact, give me that authority. But what do I know?" Drea joined Mattix at the counter. "I'm doing my job. Now are you going to listen to Agent Mattix, or do you want this to get ugly?"

His eyes flicked to the side, and Drea could almost see the wheels turning as Robert considered his options. Had she been alone, he might have believed he could overpower her and run. Drea would have been more than happy to prove him wrong. But with Mattix standing there, he had to know there was no way out.

Robert sighed, came around the counter and placed his hands flat on the surface as instructed.

Mattix held up a pair of cuffs. "You wanna do the honors?"

Drea shook her head. "Nope. I'll call County for transport. They'll be quicker than our guys. I want to get to searching this office and his house."

They could hold Robert based on Phelps' testimony, but not for long. She had to find something to connect him to the drugs, or the victims.

Chapter Twenty-Eight

The big bulldozer crunched over burned wood, and the smell of diesel fuel filled the air. A pang of frustration tore through Danny as the charred remains of the mares' barn came down. Thankfully, in late July, they didn't have much going on. But the repairs were going to put a dent in the camp plans. He couldn't afford to wait for an insurance payout that might never come. He shoved his hands in his pockets and turned away. They might have to take out a loan or put off the camp for a year.

The remains of the cottage still stood. Its blackened windows looked like eyes — reflecting the emptiness he felt. He pushed his hands through his hair. Brian walked over and leaned against the fence.

"It's hot as hell out here and these guys don't need babysittin'," Brian said. "Lily's got most of the horses down in the lower paddocks to get away from the noise and smell. We're gonna take a break and grab lunch with your ma. You comin'?"

Danny shook his head. He didn't want his mother's opinions right now. He didn't need reminding how he'd fucked up with Drea. She was doing her job, and he'd been an asshole about it. He'd said shitty things to her, things that never should have come out of his mouth.

She'd been completely silent since their disagreement two days ago, and it stung. He should call or text instead of sulking and waiting for Drea to make the first move. He'd find a way to apologize. Maybe they could start over.

"Think I'll grab a burger at Oak Bridge," Danny said. "I need to get away from this."

"And you'd rather be alone," Brian replied. "I get it. You're messed up about Drea. She was doin' her job. You of all people oughta respect that. When are you gonna call her?"

"When she's solved this thing," Danny snapped and immediately regretted it. Drea had practically accused Brian and Lily of having something to do with all the fires, and Brian was defending her. Danny had told her to get a warrant, to do what she needed to do. He had no reason nor right to get pissed. But all he'd seen was her pulling away, preparing to leave.

"I'm sorry," Danny said. "I don't see the point of tryin' to talk to her when she's got her head set on chasin' the bad guy." He sighed. He'd find time. Find a way. When all this was over, first he'd apologize, then he'd tell her, again, how much she meant to him. Repeatedly, if he had to. "I'm headin' for lunch."

Danny hopped in his truck and drove to Oak Bridge. It was after lunch hour, just past two, and he had the place to himself. He ordered a cheeseburger and skipped the beer in favor of iced tea.

* * * *

Drea flopped into a chair at the field office and grabbed her phone. She pulled up Danny's contact info and her finger hovered over the call button for a moment, then she hit the message button instead. A text would be easier than hearing his voice.

Her fingers flew over the screen. "I am sorry. I acted like an ass and said some hurtful things. I can't tell you much about the investigation, but I can say I'm sorry for the way I handled it. My goal was to quickly rule out anyone at Parsons Acres. I should have talked to you more. Trusted you." She took a shaky breath before adding. "I miss you. And I'd like to see you to say all of this in person." She hit send before she could change her mind and turned her attention back to her notes.

Robert had immediately asked for a lawyer and been silent ever since. Searching the police station, Robert's house, garage and Bronco had turned up enough evidence to link him to Phelps and the drug theft, but nothing else. Drea glared at the whiteboard where all the case information spread out in a seemingly random mess.

Mattix strolled in, coffee in hand. "You don't think Robert did this?"

Drea shook her head, staring at the board, even though she'd committed every detail to memory. "Oh, he had a part in it, that's obvious. But Robert wouldn't know an original idea if it smacked him in the face. And what's his motivation? I think he's hoping his attorney can wrangle a plea in exchange for testimony against the real perp."

Drea's phone buzzed, and she snatched it up and looked at the screen, hoping for a response from Danny. Instead, it was a failure to send message.

"You trying to send a text?" Mattix asked. "The signal in here is shit. May take several tries. Or go to the front office."

Drea muttered a few curses and stuffed her phone into her pocket. She'd deal with that later. Right now, she needed a break in this case.

"Hey!" Adams ran into the room. "I've got an ID on the female vic."

Drea sat up and Mattix raised her hands. "Well?"

"I was able to get DNA from bone marrow, and her family submitted to NamUs — the missing persons DNA database."

Drea glared at him. "Any time now."

"Jane Doe is Vivian Privet," Adams declared. "She's on our list."

"Mattix, see what you can get on her — the report, news stories, anything. Adams and I will keep working on the rest of this mess." Drea grabbed her laptop and started typing. Mattix and Adams both did the same. In minutes, Mattix crowed with success.

"Got her!" She spun her monitor around. "Vivian Privet was reported missing by her boyfriend, baseball player Reggie James. I've got the report and some news stories."

Drea's head popped up. That name rang a bell. She leaned over Mattix's shoulder to read the news reports. He looked familiar, too.

"It gets better," Adams chimed in. "Reggie James was reported missing when he didn't show up for court-ordered rehab."

Drea swiveled to look at his screen. James was supposed to report to rehab on April 18. The second fire was April 19.

"Why is he not on the missing persons list?" Drea scanned the list again. "And why in the hell does his name sound so familiar?"

"Are you a baseball fan?" Adams asked. Mattix let out a bark of laughter, and Drea flipped them both off.

"Uh, no," Drea replied as she clicked through pictures, waiting for something to connect. She opened his rookie picture. Ice water hit her veins and she gulped in air. "Pretty sure that's the guy CeeCee was dating in high school."

Mattix and Adams both stopped what they were doing and turned to her. Drea stared at the screen in horror, then turned to Mattix. "Find out if Ohio's marriage and divorce records are public. Maybe Reggie James isn't his legal name."

Drea pulled up more news articles on Reggie James. "Looks like he retired last year after a drug scandal where he was caught using steroids — third time's the charm equals a lifetime ban from the game." Drea's head spun. She'd been looking in completely the wrong direction. *Jesus.*

A few minutes later, Mattix turned her screen for them to see. "Well, hello, James Starcher. Married to, then divorced from, Cecelia Cobb. And, incidentally, on the missing persons list."

Drea gave her a thumbs-up and pulled up a calendar. "Reggie James — Mr. Starcher — went missing right before the second fire at Parsons Acres. The one that killed John Doe. Did CeeCee complain about him failing to pay spousal support? He's had to have missed at least two, possibly three. If she filed a complaint, it would be in the court records."

"On it," Mattix replied.

Drea wanted to throw up. While it didn't look like anyone at Parsons Acres was connected with the fires, it did look like her childhood friend was. She sat back after twenty more minutes of digging and surveyed the additional details the three of them had added to the board.

"I think we can break this down," Drea said. "This has been a cluster fuck of communication nightmares from the get-go. Let's run with what we've got and see if it makes sense."

She pointed to the list of fires, including the first one behind the Tanners' place, and all of the subsequent fires.

"We know this side of the story. We've seen this picture and it didn't make sense. But we weren't looking in the right place."

She pointed at the new information as she talked, glancing between three laptop screens and the big whiteboard.

"Vivian Privet went missing while James — Starcher — was out of town. Ms. Privet went out to dinner with a few girlfriends. Witnesses say she had a minor altercation with a woman at the bar — a woman who was described as petite and blonde. Ms. Privet complains of a headache and gets an Uber home. That's the last her friends heard from her. The Uber driver reports dropping her at her address and watching her go inside."

Adams sat up. "No one interviewed CeeCee?"

Drea shrugged. "No reason to at that time, I'd guess. These were Ms. Privet's friends. It's possible they'd never seen CeeCee. Ms. Privet disappeared the night before the first fire at Parsons Acres. That fire was in the early morning hours. The timing is perfect."

Drea took a deep breath and continued. "According to the missing person report, Ms. Privet's boyfriend called this in when he couldn't reach her via phone, and her coworkers said she didn't show up for work the next day."

Adams tapped on the dates. "His failure to check in at rehab coincides with the second fire at Parsons Acres. I don't get it. Why didn't anyone connect the dots?"

Drea shrugged. "Because the dots are all over the place, seemingly unrelated, and several of them were missing."

"I think I found a few more dots," Mattix said. "CeeCee was awarded two thousand dollars a month in spousal support, and no complaints on file about missed payments. Mr. Starcher's attorney did file paperwork indicating CeeCee picked up her car in Cincinnati the day before Ms. Privet disappeared. That was the final transfer of property."

Drea bit her lip. "CeeCee has been living in an apartment over her parents' garage—I think she'd holler if she was suddenly not getting two thousand dollars each month unless she's the reason it's not coming in. We can point to her as a suspect in Ms. Privet's disappearance. Which means she's also a prime suspect for James—Starcher."

Drea's stomach turned over. She owed Danny an apology. She'd known CeeCee had turned petty and vindictive, but she'd never imagined her capable of murder. She fired off another text to Danny, hoping it would go through this time.

"You've got to hand it to her," Adams said. "It's pretty damn near perfect. There's no reason to associate a couple of fires in a rural West Virginia town with missing persons in Cincinnati, Ohio."

Mattix laughed. "Except one of the missing has an ex-wife who lives here."

Drea shook her head. "That's where local law enforcement comes in." She closed her eyes. "That's why Robert was so determined to include as little information as possible. Nothing to tie-in to the missing person reports. Nothing to raise any suspicion."

"Until you came along and started asking questions," Mattix added. "Not enough, mind you, but you still rocked his boat."

Drea smiled. "Yeah. I think I just capsized his boat." She tossed the marker on the table and glanced at her watch. "It's two thirty. Can we get a warrant on Cecelia Cobb pushed through before the end of today? I wanna serve this to her for dinner."

* * * *

A full beer glass slid in front of Danny, and CeeCee plopped into the stool next to him with a glass of her own.

"I'd like to apologize." She shook her head and looked down at the bar. "My life's been fucked up ever since Reggie left me, and I've been a complete shithead. I treated Drea badly, and I shouldn't have come on to you when I knew y'all were dating." She raised her glass and gave a little chuckle when he sat there staring at her. "Okay, fine. I get it." Her glass clunked to the bar and she slid off the stool.

"Hang on." Danny picked up the beer in front of him. *No sense in bein' rude.* "My momma didn't raise me to be an asshole."

CeeCee returned to her stool and picked up her glass, clinking it against his. He took a slow sip and sat the glass down, then shook his head. "Guess we've all been a bit off-kilter, what with the fires, and Paul bein' sick and Drea…" He'd checked his phone about a million times, waiting for a text from her, and was still trying to work up the courage to text her first. CeeCee took a sip, then stood.

"Thanks for understandin'." She nodded toward the pool tables. "I'm no Drea, but I can play. Fancy a round? I'll behave, I promise."

He pushed up from his seat and followed her to the tables. A game of pool would get his mind off things — the ranch, Drea, the fires, Paul. It was all too much. He racked the balls and chalked his cue for the break.

Halfway through the round, he started feeling dizzy. He leaned over to take a shot and the floor shifted beneath him. He couldn't focus on the cue ball and the stick wavered in his vision. He straightened up and took a deep breath, then leaned down to try again, over-corrected and caught himself on a bar stool. The expanse of green on the table rippled like water and the balls glowed, floating above the surface.

Danny shook his head and the room spun. Cool hands closed over his arm, and he looked down to see CeeCee's concerned face staring up at him. She helped him to a stool, then called for the bartender to give her a hand. Danny tried to focus, but everything was blurry, and her words all jumbled together.

"Gongetyooohooom." Her mouth was moving and sounds came out, but it made no sense to him. He stumbled as he stood, and the bartender slipped an arm under one side while CeeCee grabbed his other arm. Together, they tumbled him into his truck, and Danny's head lolled against the window. He cracked his eyes open and saw CeeCee in the driver's seat, with a worried look on her face.

Something was wrong. He opened his mouth, but no sound came out. The world was spinning like a Tilt-a-Whirl, and CeeCee's voice turned into something from a cartoon. *Minnie Mouse. No – Bettie Boop. Maybe they had a baby, and that was CeeCee's voice.* He laughed, but it sounded like a snort. Maybe he was turning into a horse. That would explain the snort-laugh thing.

This wasn't right. His eyelids drooped and his face felt heavy. Rest. He needed rest.

Chapter Twenty-Nine

Drea stood in the driveway as Mattix, Adams and a team of Sheriff's Deputies climbed the steps to CeeCee's apartment over her parents' garage. Drea was left with the task of informing the Cobbs their daughter was wanted for murder and arson. Marla sobbed in her husband's arms, while Stanley glared over the top of his wife's head as if this whole thing were Drea's fault.

"I've no idea where she may be," Stanley Cobb snapped. "She doesn't check in with us. We've been providin' a roof over her head after that philandering druggie dumped her for another woman. It broke CeeCee's heart."

I bet it did. Drea gave up trying to talk to them. They didn't know anything. Instead she went to find one of the county officers.

"I need to find CeeCee Cobb," she said as she came up to him. "I don't care how at this point. I want her found."

"What about the local police, Agent?" The man looked confused.

"I'm afraid the Orchard Creek police are a bit understaffed at the moment," Drea said. "Their only officer is in custody as an accessory in this case. I know we're already pressing our luck here with y'all, but..." She'd fallen into colloquial speech patterns of the locals, but it seemed to do the trick. The man smiled and nodded.

"We'll put out a call. I think we can spare a man or two from here, don't you?"

Drea thanked him and tried calling Danny again. She'd been trying ever since they'd put in the request for a warrant. It went straight to voicemail. Again. That wasn't like Danny. Unless he was avoiding her calls. Drea called Wilma and left a message for her to call back ASAP, then she headed upstairs. Mattix caught her eye as she came in and shook her head at the mess. Bags of aluminum powder, iron oxide, and strips of magnesium ribbon littered the dining table, along with printed instructions taken from some website.

"Make sure we capture that web address. We may be able to prove she visited the site." Drea bent and hauled a box of plaster from under the table.

"Why bother?" Mattix scoffed. "There's enough evidence here to nail her for all of it. Drugs are in the kitchenette, with dosage notes. There's a printout showing the gas tank location of a Jeep Cherokee. The list goes on. But if all of this isn't enough?" She waved her hand around the room, then nodded toward Adams, who held up a handful of evidence bags.

"Cell phones." Adams grinned. "One's a burner. The other two belong to Starcher and Privet."

Drea scowled at him. "And we know this how?"

Adams winked at her and smiled. "Not that hard to trace a phone, especially when that person was reported missing and their phone records flagged and searched. We got the cell tower records as well. Oh, and video of a thermite device being lit in some building. Uh...not one of the ones in your report."

"That would be the test run." Drea turned to Mattix. "You're right. We've got her for everything. Question is, where the hell is she?"

* * * *

Danny turned his head to the side and groaned. Jesus, he had a headache. He hadn't drunk enough for this hangover. He shook his head and groaned again, then rose but was yanked back by something on his wrist. He glanced up, forcing his eyes to focus.

Handcuffs locked onto his right wrist, holding his arm over his head. Panic surged, clearing some of the fog.

He blinked and shifted to sit up. This wasn't his bed. The soft thing he'd mistaken for his mattress was a sleeping bag. And his wrist wasn't handcuffed to his bed, but to a metal stair railing. He strained to focus in the dim light. Strange shapes swirled in his vision, making him dizzy. He gagged and forced himself to breath slowly, trying to fight the wave of nausea. He knew that smell—metal and wood, oil and... *The basement.* He was in his own fucking basement.

He had no memory of the afternoon. Foggy pictures danced at the edge of his consciousness.

"You're awake. Good."

He whipped his head around at the voice, then blinked as a light flared in the dark. CeeCee bent down and peered into his eyes, then straightened back up.

"Wha' fuck we doin' down here?" His brain couldn't get the words right, but his voice was stronger than he expected.

"Ooo, feisty!" CeeCee giggled. "You know what they say? Hell hath no fury like a woman scorned." A foot lashed out and connected with his thigh. Danny grunted in pain and gritted his teeth, willing himself not to cry out. "Well, you scorned me. All for that tart who shouldn't have come back here in the first place."

She set a can on a shelf along the far wall and turned back to him with a smile. "I believe your kitchen is above there. Propane stove, isn't it? Gas lines." She gave a theatrical shudder. "So exciting!"

She flicked a lighter and held what looked like a stick of incense to the flame. Sparks flew from her hand. A sparkler. A little kid's firework. Something nagged deep in his brain, stirring an inkling of fear.

"Hey, uh...you don't..." Danny scrambled, trying to string cohesive thoughts together. "You don't hafta do this."

CeeCee smiled and shrugged. "Drea didn't have to go digging. She knows everything by now. Poor Danny, still in the dark." She stuck the sparkler into the can and turned back to him. "Thermite. Magnesium wire. The sparkler will catch the wire, which will burn into the thermite. Your cute little house will burn. Oh! And you'll be in it. So sad."

She gathered her things and crossed to the steps. Danny scrambled in his pockets, feeling for his phone. He had to call Drea. Had to tell her it was CeeCee.

"I only act like a dumb blonde." CeeCee squatted in front of him, waving his phone in her hand. "I turned it off as soon as I got you in the truck."

She sighed and stood, then heaved her foot back and kicked him again, pulling a groan from him.

"Buh-bye now."

She clicked the light out, and her footsteps echoed on the stairs. Danny yanked on the cuffs, trying to pull loose, but she'd cinched them down tight. Across the room, the sparkler sizzled, burning closer to the magnesium fuse. It was actually kinda pretty.

That inkling of fear surged again. *Fire. Shit. Fire.* CeeCee had killed twice already. She might go after Drea. Or the farm.

He looked away from the burning can and closed his eyes, hoping to regain some vision in the darkness. Grogginess tugged at him, lulling him. It would be easier to sleep. Just lie down and rest.

Dammit! No!

Danny stretched out as far as he could, feeling around with his free hand and his feet. Searching for anything he could use to break free or make a lot of noise.

Chapter Thirty

Drea leaned against the door as the crew finished processing CeeCee's apartment. She glanced at her watch — nearly seven. They'd been at this for hours, and she was dying of hunger. Plus, Danny still hadn't called back. Mattix leaned in the doorjamb next to her.

"Y'know, I think I may be starting to like this field work thing. Relax, Hidalgo. We've got Robert and we'll get CeeCee."

Drea glared at her and took a deep breath. She needed to find CeeCee. "Hey, Mattix, how about a bet?"

"On what?"

"CeeCee claims it was all Robert's idea. She came back home after the divorce, and Robert filled her head with these thoughts."

Mattix's face screwed up as she mulled the idea over, then nodded for Drea to continue.

"Robert'll say the opposite. CeeCee came to him. Begged him to help her. She manipulated him — either with sex, or by convincing him he could get back at all the people who'd laughed at him through the years. Maybe both."

Mattix scoffed. "No bet. I think you nailed it. But which is the truth?"

Drea's smile spread slowly. "No contest. Robert's a follower, not a leader. CeeCee, on the other hand, always has a plan, and a bit of a mean streak. Speaking of her…"

Drea's phone rang, and she punched the answer key without looking at the screen.

"I got your message and made some calls." Wilma's voice sounded concerned. "The bartender at Oak Bridge says CeeCee and Danny were playing pool earlier this afternoon, and Danny was drunk. CeeCee said she'd drive him home. What's going on?"

Drea's insides turned to ice. "Adams! I need CeeCee's phone info."

"On it," Adams replied. He beckoned them to the table where he sat with his tablet. "I was just loading that up. Give it a second."

A map page popped up on his tablet, and he zoomed in. "A little cell-tower magic," Adams explained. "I can't give you exact locations, but her phone pinged these towers. We can triangulate. Aren't you glad the bad guys don't think to turn off location services when they decide to do illegal stuff?"

Drea glared at the screen. She didn't need to triangulate. There was one thing that sat in the middle of those cell towers — Parsons Acres. She lifted her phone.

"Wilma, did you hear all of that?" She waited for the affirmative before continuing. "Call Annette. Or Brian. Try Lily. See if they can find Danny." To hell with protocol. Drea took a deep breath. "CeeCee is the arsonist and she was at the ranch. Thanks!"

Drea hung up without waiting for a reply. Wilma wouldn't let her down. Drea turned to Adams. "Call the fire department and get them out to Parsons Acres. I don't care if they're eating dinner or bathing their kids — tell them to get their asses in gear. Mattix and I are going there. Tell the county guys if they let CeeCee slip through their fingers, I will personally hurt them."

She turned and yelled for Mattix, "I'm driving."

They peeled out of the drive, and Drea sped down the road, swerving around any cars that got in her way and going fast enough Mattix's fingers showed white on the dash. She couldn't lose him, not after everything else. The sick feeling made her palms sweat, and she gripped the wheel tighter, her foot mashed on the pedal, willing the car to go faster.

"You never said you were related to Mario Andretti... Jesus, don't get us killed."

"I learned to drive on these roads, relax." Drea didn't take her eyes off the road as she navigated another turn. "We'll get there in one piece."

"You wanna explain what's going on? Why send a fire crew?"

Drea didn't answer as she whipped around the corner and slowed to make the turn into the Parsons Acres drive. A thick column of smoke rose from Danny's place — still early, from the looks of it. Brian pelted out of the barnyard with a fire extinguisher in hand.

Cold dread pooled in her stomach as she sped around the barn and pulled up with Amos Kimmel and the fire truck not far behind. Amos' crew jumped out of the truck and started rolling out hoses.

Brian diverted his path and stopped in front of Drea.

"What in the hell is going...?" Brian's words were cut off by a popping sound coming from the house. "Get down!" Drea yelled at Amos and the fire crew, then grabbed Brian and Mattix and pulled them both to the ground as the popping turned into a roar and a loud boom shook the ground. Glass shattered around them, and Drea's ears rang with the noise.

No, no, no, NO! She was not going to lose Danny, or anyone else. Mattix stumbled upright and tugged Drea to her feet. Brian pushed himself up and scanned the yard.

"Anyone in there? Danny's truck ain't here." Amos shouted at her.

"I..." Drea swallowed hard, glaring at the building as if the flames were monsters trying to consume her life. "Probably." Panic surged through her as crackling sounds filled the air, but she shoved it down. Fire had claimed too much from her already.

"Brian, grab Annette and make sure everyone is someplace safe. I don't know if this is the only incendiary device."

She didn't wait for his response. Instead, she closed her eyes and pictured Danny's place. The explosion was near the kitchen. The stove. But from below. The laundry room in the hall. The back door. Stairs to the basement. Danny kept his tools down there.

"There's a side access to the basement over here." She grabbed an axe from the truck and gestured for Mattix to get the big extinguisher and follow. Around back, she found the double doors, padlocked from the outside, flames and smoke creeping over the top edge. The doors thrust outward, straining the hasp, then fell back. A loud thump and the doors bulged again.

Mattix sprayed the doors with the extinguisher and Drea leaned close, raising her voice above the crackling fire. "Step back! Step back!" She hefted the axe and swung for the padlock. Another swing and the hasp fell to the ground. She and Mattix grabbed the big doors and hauled them open. Smoke billowed out and the most wonderful sight in the world greeted her. Danny stood on the step below, sledgehammer in hand and his shirt wrapped around his face. He stumbled coming up the steps and collapsed at her feet. Drea sank to her knees, nearly sobbing in relief. His hair was singed, and he stank of smoke and fire, but he was alive.

"You take care of him," Mattix said. "I got this. Whatever blew was down here." She lifted the extinguisher and sprayed the entrance again.

Drea looped an arm under Danny's. "Can you stand?"

His eyes were wide and staring, but he nodded. Drea rose, hauling him up with her. He stumbled on the first step but leaned on her, and they made it around the house.

Drea cast a glance at the propane tank — one of Amos' crew had already disconnected it and it was venting nicely. There would be no second explosion. Still, his home was gone. CeeCee must've opened the gas line in the house for the fire to move that fast. An ambulance pulled up, and she helped Danny into the rig.

"Hey!" Drea called to Brian. "I'm riding with the medics. Tell Mattix." Drea swung into the back and slid into the jump seat, nodding at the paramedic who'd already hooked Danny up to oxygen.

She looked down at him — covered in soot, hair a mess, oxygen mask covering his face. She stroked the hair back from his head. Her heart soared when those blue eyes focused on her and crinkled into a smile. The idea of life without him wrenched her soul.

Drea leaned down and spoke near his ear. "You look like crap, Dan-the-man."

He coughed and muttered something, but between the oxygen mask and his raspy voice, she didn't understand him. And she didn't care. He was alive, that was all that mattered.

"I don't know what to say first—I'm sorry, or I love you." Drea snagged his hand and squeezed but got no response. He was out cold. Anything she wanted to say would have to wait until he was conscious again.

Chapter Thirty-One

Danny plucked at the IV snaking out of his arm, trying to recall how he'd got into a hospital bed. The last thing he had any clear memory of was watching the bulldozers tear into the mares' barn. Then it was all a haze of disjointed images, fire and smoke and Drea. She was as clear as a bell—in a shaft of light, smoke billowing around her, an axe in her hands, looking like an angel.

He shook his head. Ridiculous fantasies. Her smiling face swam in his vision and cool hands closed over his.

"Quit messing with the IV." *Drea's voice. Warm and wonderful and here.* "Welcome back."

Danny blinked. This was real. Drea was real. He curled his fingers around hers. Forced himself to focus. She was here. Beautiful as ever. Beside him, holding his hand. He coughed, struggled to sit up. Her face creased into a frown, and her hands left his, settled on his shoulders, pushing him back.

"Easy there." Her voice soothed, caressed. "You've had a rough twenty-four hours. Best not to push things."

More disjointed images flashed in his mind. Oak Bridge. CeeCee. His basement. Danny sucked in a breath and tugged at Drea's hands.

"What...?" His voice came out hoarse, raspy. He cleared his throat. Tried again. "What happened?" Better. Not quite right. "What day is it?"

Drea's soft smile faltered, for the briefest second she had a murderous look on her face that struck fear into him, then her smile was back.

"It's Friday afternoon. What do you remember?"

She wasn't saying something. He was in the hospital, hooked up to an IV, an oxygen tube in his nose and bandages up his arms. And no goddamn memory of how he got here. He shook his head.

"Fractured bits," he said. "At best."

Drea nodded. "Do you remember your mother coming to visit? Or Brian? Lily? Anyone?"

Danny shook his head. All he felt was confusion and a vague sense of panic and fear. He tried to sit up, but she pushed his shoulders down and handed him the bed controls. He fumbled with the buttons, finally getting himself into a sitting position, fighting the wave of nausea that hit. Drea handed him a bottle of water.

"Drink," she ordered. "It's important to stay hydrated. You have some minor burns on your arms, and a seriously abraded wrist. Your throat and lungs were damaged by heat and smoke. That's why you're in the hospital." She flashed a small smile. "Good ole observation. That, and you were semi-conscious. Kinda goes with the territory of being roofied."

Fire. He remembered fire. And a wheelbarrow. Hiding under a wheelbarrow while flames roared over him. He drank. The water was cool, delicious, soothing. The fog in his brain lifted a bit. The last day might still be a complete mystery, but there was something he remembered clearly. He snatched Drea's hand, held it tightly.

"I'm sorry," he murmured. "I'm so sorry. I said some shitty things to you."

Tears pooled in her eyes and spilled over. "I wasn't exactly all sunshine and roses myself." She sniffed. "I'm sorry, too. I could have, should have, handled this whole thing better. I thought I'd lost you. Again."

His heart jumped to his throat, pounding so hard he imagined it echoing in the room. Drea stared out the window with an odd, faraway look on her face.

"Do you remember the ambulance ride?" Her voice said he should.

Danny closed his eyes and tried, but there was nothing. "No," he said. She turned to him, the odd expression morphed into something he recognized — soft and sweet. It was the look on her face when he held her in his arms after sex. He had the horrible feeling whatever he was missing was important.

Her fingers rested on his arm, stroking gently, then she cleared her throat and the moment was gone. Back to all-business Drea.

"You want to know what happened?" Drea asked.

A vague sense of fear circled and swirled and he almost said no. Instead he nodded.

"It was CeeCee," Drea said, and her words felt right. True. "With a little help from Robert. CeeCee confessed some of it — the rest we put together from evidence."

Drea's voice was flat, emotionless. She stared down, not looking at him as she spoke. "CeeCee slipped a cocktail into your beer. Rohypnol and ketamine, most likely. Those account for the fuzzy memory, and a lot of the other charming symptoms, by the way. Bartender helped her get you into your truck. That was about three thirty yesterday afternoon."

Drea glanced up at him, a questioning look on her face. He nodded. He needed to hear this. And he'd rather hear it from her than anyone else.

"Under the influence of roofies, you'd be pretty suggestible. Mentally out of it, but capable of following simple commands, moving, walking with help. CeeCee handcuffed you to the stair rail in your basement."

Danny rubbed his wrist. The ache and the bandages suggested he'd done more than sit passively the whole time.

"I don't know what she said to you, or did, or all the details in there. She used a sparkler as the ignition for a thermite device. She'd disconnected the propane from the kitchen stove, so the upstairs was filling up with gas. Add heat and flame, the welding rig... You get the picture."

"How'd I get out?" Danny said. "I... The basement door. I remember you. But I wasn't..."

"Best we can piece together? You somehow grabbed a pair of bolt cutters and cut the handcuffs. Probably doused your shirt in the work sink and wrapped it around your face. Then you took a sledgehammer to the basement doors."

She paused before continuing. "If Mattix and I hadn't come along, you might've managed to get out. A couple more hits like that and the doors would have splintered. But the place was filling with smoke and the flames were getting heavier."

"You were there. With an axe."

"I..." She cleared her throat. "I had to get you out." She looked down, color high in her cheeks.

"CeeCee and Robert were arrested?" he asked.

"Yes," she replied. "Mattix and I picked up Robert. County guys got CeeCee last night." Her face clouded with a look that made Danny cringe. "I'm kinda glad I wasn't there for that one."

The door opened and a doctor came in. Drea squeezed Danny's hand and sat back.

"Time's up," Drea said and the doctor nodded.

"I'm sorry," the doctor replied. "One visitor at a time. I'll let your mother know she can come in."

The doctor slipped out the door, and Danny's chest tightened at the thought of Drea leaving. "Don't go." He clasped her hand. "Stay, please?"

She smiled, leaned down and kissed his cheek. "One visitor at a time, those are the rules. Besides, I've got a meeting with Mack Lawson this afternoon."

She squeezed his hand again and headed for the door. She stopped, one hand on the door and looked at him.

"You said something to me, right before the fire." Drea's eyes closed and her face colored pink. "Do you remember that?"

"The drugs CeeCee slipped me didn't fuck me up that badly," he replied. "I told you I liked having you here. That you make me happy. And you do."

Drea opened her eyes, her gaze unflinching and Danny's breath caught in his throat at the warmth in those green depths.

"I love you, Danny Parsons."

For a split second, Danny forgot how to breathe, and the world froze into perfect stillness. Drea's smile, her bright eyes, the tumble of curls, her expression open and unafraid — he wanted to capture this moment and hold it forever.

Then the door closed behind her and before he could catch his breath, Annette Parsons whisked into the room.

* * * *

Drea came out onto the porch as Annette and Danny pulled up to the main house at Parsons Acres. Danny let himself out of the passenger side, eliciting a glare from Drea, but seeing him steady on his feet turned the glare into a smile.

Drea braced herself on the steps, just in case, but Danny made it up the porch without holding the rail. He reached up and tapped the Parsons Acres sign and flashed a triumphant smile at her.

"I made up your old room last night." Annette turned to Danny. "That package you asked about is on the coffee table. I'll see y'all tomorrow."

"You're not staying?" Drea asked.

"I think you two need some space," Annette replied. She hugged Danny, then surprised Drea by hugging her. "I'm headed to my sister's in Charleston. We're due for a visit."

As soon as Annette was back in her car, Danny's fingers closed around Drea's. Wordless, he opened the door and led her to the living room. Something had him nervous. He swallowed hard and his chest rose and fell on a shuddering sigh. Butterflies bounced in Drea's stomach and her tongue felt too big for her mouth.

"I'm surprised your mother didn't stay." She stopped as Danny's hands cupped her face.

His lips covered hers in a slow, languorous kiss that had her toes curling. She whimpered as he broke the kiss, and he rested his forehead against hers.

"Darlin', I want you here with me." His voice was soft, low. "And I mean here on the ranch. Sleepin' in my bed. Our bed. Wakin' up next to you. Every day."

The butterflies ceased bouncing and soared around in great circles. Danny was smiling broadly, those amazing blue eyes wide open and staring into hers. Drea's breath caught. He took her hands in his, his fingers trembled a little, but his eyes were steady.

"I love you with all my heart and soul and I want you by my side for the rest of our lives." Danny paused and took a slow breath. "Will you marry me?"

Forget butterflies, this is an entire circus thundering around my chest.

"Yes!" The word left her mouth in a whoosh, taking Drea's doubts and fears along with it. Danny's kiss seared her soul. He felt so good. He felt like home.

Danny sat, pulling her into his lap, his fingers still laced tightly in hers.

"This isn't how imagined doin' this," he said with a laugh. "Not exactly fairy-tale romance here." He reached for the little box on the table. "I ordered somethin' for you in early June. After I talked to your grandfather." A nervous sound escaped his lips. "After you and I had that little…uh…shower…" He cleared his throat. "The weekend of the gymkhana."

Danny pressed his lips together. "Paul was a good man, and he thought the world of you. That day we talked…" His voice broke and he paused then sucked in a deep breath. "That day we talked, your grandfather pulled this off a chain he had around his neck. Said he'd worn it there since the day your grandmother passed. He'd planned to give it to..."

Danny stopped talking, his eyes sparkling, and Drea's throat tightened. After getting out of the military and putting his dog tags away in his top dresser drawer, there was only one thing Gramps had ever worn around his neck.

"He said he'd always planned to give it to a man who deserved you. And then..." Danny stopped. His eyes filled with sadness and joy. "Then he gave it to me and told me he knew I'd make you happy." He opened the box, and Drea's heart thundered.

One ring was Abuela's — the tri-color braided roses were unmistakable. Gramps had worked extra hours and done odd jobs to save up the money, then had a local craftsman make the ring. It was one of a kind, simple, but stunning. She reached out a shaking finger and traced the delicate lines, then plucked both rings from the box.

She'd never seen the diamond before.

Danny pushed his hair back from his forehead, a nervous gesture reminiscent of his teenage self. "I had a jeweler design the engagement band to go with it. I hope that's okay."

The second band mimicked the original, but instead of an endless circle of braided roses, the braid came together on a single rose, in the center of which sat a large diamond solitaire. Drea bit her lip, fighting back the tears.

"It's... Oh my god, Danny, it's beautiful!"

He took the solitaire from her shaking hands, then slipped it onto the third finger of her left hand. She tugged at his shirt, desperate to feel him, touch him again. Clothing came undone in a flurry of hands and buttons, then Danny stood and led her to his old bedroom.

His touch electrified her, sent her soaring to heights she'd never known. He gave as much as he took, and she could never get her fill of him. Drea lost track of where her body ended and his began.

"Drea." His voice was a growl against her ear. "I don't have condoms."

"I don't care."

His broad shoulders hovered over her, his thighs pressing against hers, his mouth on her neck. He raised his head up to her and a wicked grin crossed his lips. "Hmm...should I stop?"

"Don't you ever stop." She took his head in her hands and kissed him.

"Darlin', those words are music to my ears."

Epilogue

Drea sat on the porch with a mug of herbal tea, making faces over the taste—she wanted coffee, but she'd already had her one cup today. The sound of hammers and power tools carried up the hill. It was early September, and in the two months since the fire, they'd finished a new cottage and construction on the mare's barn and veterinary complex was coming along nicely.

She stared down at the email on her phone. Danny strode up the porch, tapping the Parsons Acres sign before he leaned down and kissed her, sending shivers up her neck.

"Y'know," he said with a big smile, "I've pictured you sittin' here more than once." He settled onto the swing next to her, his arm over her shoulders and nodded at her phone. "Mack Lawson again, huh? He's not givin' up."

Drea rolled her eyes at him. She got a new email every week. Annette came out and dropped into a chair. "You made up your mind about takin' over as chief of police?"

Drea shook her head. When Mack Lawson had suggested it, her first reaction was horror, but the more she thought about it, the more she liked it.

"That's a talk I'll have to have with the town council, I guess," Drea replied. "Deputy Director Wilkes refused my request to transfer to the Charleston field office—no openings, and in a way, I'm glad. That's still an hour away."

Unless she wanted to go back to DC, the ATF wasn't an option. And her heart wasn't in DC. It was here. With Danny.

"It's not like you don't have choices," Danny said. "What about the teaching job? Or workin' with Amos?"

"Teaching fire science at the local college could be interesting," Drea replied. "I'm not a hose jockey—I've got no interest in working on the fire crew, especially now. But, Amos and I did give the council a proposal for revamping the fire department. We'll see how that goes."

Drea finished her tea. "Much as it surprises me, I think I'll take the chief position. It isn't catching arsonists, but it's still going after bad guys. Sort of." She leaned back and sighed. "Besides, maybe I can undo some of the damage Robert did. Do something good here."

The construction foreman came up the steps. "We got everything connected in the cottage. Power's on, propane, water, and septic all hooked up—figured y'all would want to move in over the holiday weekend. I'll have the guys clean it up before we leave today."

"Wow, that was fast." Danny rose and went down the steps to talk with the man.

"Y'all sure you don't mind me bein' so close?" Annette said and nodded at the pretty cottage on the other side of the drive. She gave a soft sigh and looked around the porch. "It'll be nice having a smaller house to clean, and it's about time a new generation moved into this place. It's too big for just me. This is a home meant for children." She leaned back and cleared her throat. "What did you find out at the doctor's today?"

Drea took a deep breath. The sun caught Danny's hair, turning it shades of gold and bronze and the scent of sawdust mingled with late-summer grass. Trees swayed in the breeze. Soon the deep green would give way to bright fall colors. Danny had been right. There was beauty and splendor here. It wasn't any better or worse than what she thought she wanted—only different. And it was part of her now.

"I'm due mid-April." The words slipped out. Effortless. Comfortable. Like coming back home, the idea had taken a while to grow on her.

"What about the wedding?" Annette pressed. "You gonna move it up?"

"We're figurin' middle of October," Danny replied as he stepped back onto the porch. "Just family and a few close friends."

He sat next to Drea and his arms slid around her waist, his hand pressing against her still flat stomach. She didn't have all the answers, but she knew they'd find them together.

Want to see more from this author? Here's a taster for you to enjoy!

Logan County Love: Scorched
Roxanne Blackhall

Coming November 2024

Excerpt

Katie
September 8, Friday

Twenty screaming five-year-olds broke from their orderly line and ran across the playground.

"Walk, please!" Katie Tilman laughed at herself. Getting her students to comply was a lost cause, but she had to try. She couldn't blame them for being excited. The big red firetruck had all its lights flashing and several crew all geared up. Still, she had to try.

"Oh, come on. What kid can resist? Public Safety Day is always a fun event." Cinda Gable pointed to her first grade class, gathered around the police car.

Katie pushed a lock of hair behind her ear and smiled. She knew she should remember Cinda — they were only a year apart in school — but Katie had left Orchard Creek just before she turned fourteen. Twelve years had passed.

She dutifully laughed at Cinda's comment and hurried to catch up with her kindergartners. Half of her students joined the line waiting to play with the truck's sirens. The other half stood behind a firefighter who was training a hose on a target that looked like flames painted on a piece of plywood with a hole in the middle.

She did a quick head count—hard to do with everyone moving around—but she managed. One of the playground monitors caught Katie's eye, then pointed her finger at the group waiting to play with the sirens. Katie shot the woman a relieved smile and refocused on the guy with the hose.

He'd shut the flow of water off and was squatting, telling the kids how the truck could hook up to a fire hydrant so they could pump water on a fire.

"That's why you should never park in front of a hydrant," he said.

"Because 'mergency trucks are big!" A little boy with blond curls stood with his arms crossed over his chest and a wide smile on his face. Katie was pretty sure he was from the first grade class.

The firefighter tipped his head back and laughed. He turned to face her and Katie caught her breath. Even in the shadows cast by his helmet and visor, she couldn't miss those bright blue eyes, or the wink he dropped.

"I'm sure they'll all remember that in ten plus years when they start driving." Well, if that didn't make her sound like a complete stick in the mud. "Please tell me you're showing off and not letting them play with the hose. I'm not sure they all have changes of clothes here, and…"

She stopped as the man rose to his feet. From across the playground, he'd seemed big, and now she had to keep looking up and up to see his face. Or attempt to. Between his height, the angle of the sun and his helmet, his features were cast in shadow, but she couldn't miss those eyes.

His hands were still wrapped the hose nozzle in a way that at any other time might have sent Katie's head into not entirely polite places. Now, she was at work, and instead of sexy thoughts, her brain imagined a bunch of soaked children and the inevitable angry parents.

"Awww, bet me they all do." Another wink. A scruff of a beard covered his chin and framed a full mouth, but the rest of him was a mystery. "Everybody knows kids are gonna get wet and messy today. We usually let them have a go—with help, of course. Don't want anyone knocked on their...ahhh...bottom. What d'ya say? You go first?"

He held out the hose nozzle to her and Katie backed away. "Oh... Umm... No... I couldn't. I'd get all wet."

His lips curled up in a smile and heat rose in her face. He gave a shrill whistle and shouted something to another firefighter who sat on top of the truck. An instant later, something hurtled toward them. He caught it one handed and held it out to her.

"We have smaller ones for the kids. This one will be too large for you, but it'll keep you from getting doused. C'mon, teach, give it a try. That's what today's all about."

Her students were staring at her. She couldn't very well refuse—how would it look to them? She hefted the beat-up yellow coat, then shrugged into it, sure she was putting it on wrong.

"Okay. How do we do this?"

He cracked another grin as he helped fasten the coat, giving her a glimpse of his face. Good grief, the man was handsome under that helmet. Then he straightened up and faced the students.

"All right y'all, pay attention. Your teacher and I are gonna show you how this works. Then you're going to line up and see Cadet Wilkes right there who will get you into a coat. You ready?"

A chorus of squeals and giggles and shouts of "yes" filled the air. He had the students' full attention, and the crowd was growing as some of the other children finished with the sirens and joined them at the fire target.

"When it's your turn, you'll stand right here." He pointed to a spot about a foot from where Katie stood. She took a step forward. "Good job. I want you to put your feet a little wide—not too wide, just about shoulder distance."

He looked back at Katie until she moved her feet apart. "Perfect. Now, the water comes out of the hose really hard. There is a lot of pressure there. It takes a lot of strength and practice to handle it. So I'm gonna be your buddy. That means I'll stand behind you, like this."

He stepped behind Katie and she held her breath. He leaned in so close his visor brushed against her hair, then spoke softly near her ear. "I'm going to have to put my arms around you for this. Are you okay with that?"

Her brain whirled in so many directions she couldn't find words. All she could do was nod. This man had asked consent to touch her instead of assuming. He was remarkably good with children. She missed the next thing he said to them, but caught something about how he would show them where to grip the nozzle.

"This is a one inch hose," he continued. "It's the smallest we have, but it can still be hard to handle. The nozzle is a straight tip—which is what we use to hit specific spots, like the hole in our target over there."

He shifted the hose to one hand and stepped a little closer. "Here we go."

His other arm came around her and Katie was surrounded in the smell of smoke and a clean, crisp scent that had to be his cologne. He pointed to the nozzle and guided her hands. This guy could make a mint doing this at a bar or someplace like that. On her school's playground, with her students watching, Katie was struggling to keep her mind out of the gutter.

Then his hands tightened over hers and the hose jumped as he opened the nozzle. The stream soared over the target and the children laughed.

The man's chest rumbled with his own laughter and he leaned down to her, bringing the scent of his cologne even closer. "It's stronger than you think, isn't it? Use your core, it'll make it easier to control."

In a complete fog, Katie tightened up and found he was right. Instead of feeling like the hose was trying to lift her arms away from her body, she was able to bring it down and get the stream right into the target.

"That's it!" His breath was hot on her ear, but that had to be her imagination. "Just like that. Hold it steady. Now count backwards from ten."

Everything in Katie was at war as she mentally started a countdown. This felt like flirting. Serious flirting. If she were anywhere but at work, she'd be flirting right back.

She got to one and his hands twisted, the flow of water stopped, but the hose still felt like a live thing in her hands. "There's always tension in the hose," he said. "Great job. Thanks for being such a good sport."

Her class cheered as she stepped away. One of her students, nearly swimming in even the children's size coat, rushed forward for his turn. Cadet Wilkes helped Katie out of her borrowed coat.

"We've got three kid-size coats," Wilkes said. "If you help, we can get the next two students ready while this one takes his turn. Then we'll just kind of assembly line it from there."

Katie watched as Cadet Wilkes demonstrated how to fasten the coats. Everything went quickly after that. The firefighter kept up a steady stream of encouragement that was always cheerful. The playground monitor brought the rest of her class over and took the ones who had already had their turn up to the front of the truck.

"I'm next!" The boy with the blond curls took his place in front of Katie and held his arms out for the coat. Cadet Wilkes took over and thanked Katie with a smile. She did a quick check — all her students were in the care of a playground monitor. She could relax for a minute and process whatever the hell had happened between her and the firefighter.

"You look like you're in a daze." Cinda gestured to the picnic tables under the trees and the two sat. "You okay?"

Katie forced a smile. "Yeah, that was just..." She didn't have words for whatever that was. Even if she did, she didn't want to be sharing them with the first-grade teacher.

"Amos is a bit like a big kid himself," Cinda replied. Katie's stomach did a flip flop and she swallowed hard.

"Amos? As in...Kimmel?" She looked back at the tall man now squatting next to the little blond boy. "That is Amos Kimmel?"

Oh no. No. No. No.

Amos had been best friends with her older brother, Miles. She'd had the most crushable crush on the boy with intense blue eyes and a laugh that had rung in her dreams for years after she'd left. She'd kept those feelings to herself, mostly, but it wouldn't have taken a genius to see it.

How did Amos of all people become a firefighter? Miles had been staunchly anti-establishment — police, fire, it didn't matter. Just like their father. If they wore a uniform and worked for the "gov'ment", he didn't like them. And neither did his friends.

The Amos she'd known had been thin and a little awkward. His firefighting gear might make him appear larger than life, but the arms around her earlier, and the wall of chest she'd felt behind her, said he was not skinny now.

"Didja see me, Miss Cinda? Didja see?" The blond boy jumped up and down in front of them, talking rapid fire about Mister Amos and how he was going to grow up to be a firefighter someday. Or maybe police, like Miss Drea. Or maybe he'd become a vet like Papa Brian. Or a ranch manager like his mama.

"Yes, Kyle," Cinda replied. Katie recognized the patient teacher voice and took the opportunity to make some polite comments before going to gather her class. Unsurprisingly, none of the students were interested in the police cars or the road equipment after the excitement they'd already had. They were thirty minutes from the half-day pickup time and many of them were getting tired.

She herded everyone back to class and encouraged them to take turns talking about their favorite part of the day while they gathered their things and got ready to go home.

After her last student had gone, Katie went back to the playground, now filled with the older children. She looked toward the fire truck and tried to tell herself it had nothing to do with catching another glimpse of Amos.

It took her a minute to spot him. He'd taken off his coat and removed his helmet and now sat perched on top of the engine. Katie's mouth went dry. His blue uniform T-shirt pulled tight across his shoulders and heavy lines of tattoos coursed down both arms. His dark hair was cropped close — she remembered him with longer hair that flopped into his eyes, he'd always been flicking it back.

She'd spent enough afternoons doing her homework at one end of the kitchen table while Miles and Amos had hunkered together at the other end, supposedly working. She pushed those thoughts away. Miles was the last person she wanted to think about. Well, the second last. Their father took first place in that category.

She hadn't chosen to move away. She had just graduated eighth grade and Miles had barely passed tenth. That summer, without any warning, their mother had packed Katie and her brother's things and the three of them had left Orchard Creek. For the next several years, they'd moved around whereever their mother could find work and cheap housing.

Jan Tilman's intentions may have been good, but the reality was, nothing changed with Miles. No matter where they moved, he found the same crowd and fell into the same habits. Miles' behavior had gotten worse, not better, and Katie needed to stop this little trip down memory lane. She hadn't talked to her brother in years, and didn't want to. After college, she'd never imagined she'd move back here, but in all the time away, she'd never found a place that felt like home. She'd missed the mountains and the woods.

When she'd seen that Orchard Creek had an opening for a kindergarten teacher, she'd jumped at the chance. In the four weeks she'd been back, she'd found a few familiar faces and a lot of familiar names. She never imagined that Amos would still be here. Or that he would have grown up so fine.

* * * *

Amos

It was nearing five by the time the crew got the rig packed back up and ready to return to station. Amos Kimmel stretched, trying to ease the cramp in his back from spending so much time bent over talking to the kids. Public Safety Day was always a fun time, even if it was draining.

He glanced back at the school. She'd have left by now. Most of the teachers had. He'd heard there was a new teacher. He had not expected a tiny woman who looked like a goth fairy with an edge.

From the streak of blue in her hair to the chunky pink Doc Martens on her feet, she tripped every happy button he had. Which went a long way to explaining why he'd gotten a little flirtatious when he'd shown her how to handle the hose. He didn't think he'd crossed a line, but he'd had his toe on it for sure. The way her cheeks had turned red when he'd talked about controlling the hose had him wishing they were someplace he could flirt for real.

He shook his head of those thoughts and turned his attention to his crew. They were still a bunch of volunteers, but he and Drea had put forward a proposal for a paid department. She remained confident the town council would approve the plan for next year. If he was proud of anything in his life, it was this.

He'd been a major fuck up in high school and he'd gotten lucky that Chief Lawson had seen something good in him and turned him around. The fire department had done the rest.

If the proposal went through, and he could get paid for the work, it would mean he could finally leave his old man's garage. Speaking of which... *Shit.* He'd promised he'd come straight over to help with a transmission job.

"Hey, Shawn! You mind getting everything situated? We're a little later than expected."

His second in command shot him a thumbs up. "Surprised you didn't bug out earlier. Just figured you were hoping to catch that Miss Katie on her way out."

Amos flipped him a middle finger, but he didn't miss the woman's name. He'd been so busy with the garage, the fire department, and the whole proposal to the town council that he'd not paid any attention to local talk. Not that he ever really did. He could ask his sisters. One of them always seemed to know the latest. Small town gossip spread like wildfire.

He grabbed his gear from the truck and took off at a brisk walk. The garage was only a few blocks away. He was starving, but it was a safe bet his big sister Leah would have a pot of soup or something going, just like their mother had whenever the shop got busy.

He bypassed the garage and went around the corner to the house. A page from a yellow legal pad sat stuck in the screen door at his eye level. Leah's tidy printing filled only a couple of lines.

There's soup in the microwave. Your coverall's in the mudroom. If you wanna get on Pop's good side, grab the six pack that's in the fridge before you come out and tell him to take a load off.

Amos hit the button to heat his food then kicked off his uniform boots. It took less than ten minutes to gulp down a meal and change clothes. A lifetime of experience told him what his sister's words did not.

Their dad was only in his sixties, but wasn't in the greatest health and should have retired years ago. He figured Amos would take over the garage and Leah and their kid sister Grace would do the part their mother always had—keep the books, keep the place clean, and handle customer service.

Trouble was, Leah was the better mechanic. Amos had no real interest in the garage, and once the department started paying for his time, he'd barely be around. And Grace? Well, Grace wanted to leave their small town behind. The kid had dreams.

Amos fished around in the fridge find the six pack. In the shop, Leah was elbows deep in an old Ford—probably the Tanner's by the looks of it—and their dad was hovering so much he was getting in her way.

"'Bout time you showed." Roy Kimmel had lost whatever softness he may have had when his wife died seven years ago. He looked older than his sixty years thanks to a lifetime of smoking, a terrible diet and, Amos was convinced, just being a general pain-in-the-ass grouch. He dropped the beer on a tool cart and pulled up a rolling stool.

"We got this, Pop. Siddown."

Maybe not quite Leah's words. She was usually nicer than Amos was. But Pops expected girls to be soft and boys to be tough. Surprisingly, the old man didn't complain. Amos rolled up his sleeves and turned to Leah.

"All right boss. Let's finish this thing."

For the next few hours, he and Leah worked side by side as they had most of their lives—the only words exchanged were short requests and comments related to the job at hand. Amos looked up once when their dad rose from his stool, grabbed the half-finished six pack and headed into the house.

By nine, they had the old truck humming along just fine. They cleaned up in the shop sink, silently following their mother's longstanding rule — don't track garage dirt into the house. Inside, faint sounds from down the hall said Pops was watching TV in his room.

"The second you show up, he can relax." Leah sank into a kitchen chair, then made a face at the full ashtray sitting in the middle of the table. Amos emptied it before she could get up and do it herself. It was Leah who'd held the family together after their mom passed. Grace had been in her senior year of high school, hellbent on going to university. A dream she still hadn't realized. Amos spent more and more time at the fire department because it got him out of the house.

Leah had stepped into their mother's shoes as if she'd been doing the work all her life. She'd also started picking up the slack at the garage — first because Amos was rarely around, and then because their dad's work had started slipping.

Roy Kimmel didn't see any of that. He never truly saw any of his children. Grace's brilliance and thirst for knowledge. Amos' passion for helping people. Leah's skills as a top-notch mechanic. All were things their father couldn't — or wouldn't — see.

"Grace's been making noises about moving again," Leah said. "End of this semester, she'll have finished all the classes she can take locally."

Amos wiped a hand over his face. Grace had passed on going to university because of their mother's death. Then she'd lost the chances at scholarships that made college affordable. Once she'd turned twenty-four and no longer needed a parent's signature on the FAFSA forms, she'd started talking about school again. Each time, Pops talked her into taking part time classes at the community college in Logan.

"If you think I'm gonna try talking her out of it…" Amos stopped when Leah's mouth dropped open, then snapped shut.

"More like I figured you'd tell her to get her ass in gear and submit her application and start picking up extra work so she can save up and make this happen next fall. Maybe even take a class or two in spring, if she can get in at Charleston."

A flood of relief surged through him. As much as he loved Orchard Creek, Grace was never going to be truly happy here.

"That, I can do," he replied. "And gladly. What about Pops?"

He didn't want to lie to the man, but if he found out Grace was thinking of leaving, he'd start in with the guilt trips.

"That's my department," Leah said. "I'll deal with him. How was the school thing?"

Typical Leah. Address a problem head on and as soon as you make a decision, you move on.

"You know I love those days. It's fun letting the kids see all the emergency services when there isn't something bad going on. Makes their parents happy, too. And since parents are voters…"

Leah threw her head back and laughed. "I never thought I'd see the day when my brother was thinking about politics."

He scoffed at her. "Robert Moore kinda cured me of keeping my head in the sand. That man nearly ruined the department."

Leah cursed under her breath. "He did a lot worse than that, but I understand your take."

"Did you know there's a new kindergarten teacher? Like new, new—not from here." *Why the hell did I say that?*

Leah's expression shifted to something he couldn't read. One eyebrow arched up and she crossed her arms over her chest and smiled.

"Kinda surprised you hadn't heard." Grace leaned in the kitchen doorway.

Her tone set Amos on edge. There was a hint of something he was missing. It wouldn't do any good to ask directly. Grace would never spill until she wanted to. The kid had learned long ago to keep her thoughts to herself.

"Like a new kindergarten teacher is news." Amos rolled his eyes and looked away, hoping the old trick of blowing it all off might get her talking.

"Nope." Grace crossed to the fridge, pulled out three bottles of pop, then stuck two on the table in front of Amos and Leah.

"I'm friends with Lily, and her son is in first grade. Of course I knew."

Amos didn't see what that had to do with anything. He cracked open a bottle and took a sip. Leah's eyebrows furrowed, then she turned to their kid sister.

"I think your head is fried from working too hard. You're not making sense."

It was Grace's turn to roll her eyes.

"Also, she's not new. Not like that." She pointed at Leah. "You were too busy being the big sister, already working full time in the garage. Then dealing with Mom and Dad when Amos got in trouble."

Grace turned to him and smiled. "Who were you hanging with back then? Doesn't surprise me that you somehow missed that your best friend's little sister had a major school girl crush on you. Or that you didn't recognize her today."

Amos nearly choked on a mouthful of soda. *Miss Katie. Katie Tilman. Fuck me.*

"Have a good night!" Grace threw a wave over her shoulder as she flounced toward the stairs.

Leah's laughter rang in the small kitchen. "The look on your face is priceless. If I didn't know you better, I'd think you did something like try to put the moves on her."

There was no point in lying to his big sister. She'd spot it a mile away. "Uhh…well…" He rose and tossed his empty bottle into the recycling bin. "I flirted a little. Okay, maybe more than a little. I'm goin' home. 'Night."

He hurried out the door before Leah could say something else.

Miles Tilman. He hadn't thought of him in years. His best friend since childhood and the reason he'd gotten in trouble back then. His little sister Katie had always been around — sitting at the table while they did their homework or hanging on at the edge of their crowd. She'd worn her hair in pigtails and had braces. He'd never thought much about her. She was his buddy's bratty kid sister.

He pulled in a breath of the cool night air. The stars seemed extra bright tonight and the walk home might help clear his head. It was only a few hundred yards to the group of tiny cottages that used to house coalminers.

For the first few years after he'd come back, after graduation, Amos had lived in an apartment above the extra garage bays. Then their mom had passed and

Leah had returned home. He'd moved out to give her the apartment.

He liked his cottage better. It wasn't fancy, but having his own space was a good thing. Right now, he needed it. He sure as shit didn't want to be talking to his older sister about how right Katie had felt in his arms.

About the Author

Roxanne Blackhall is a former magazine and newspaper editor from San Diego, California, now living in the heart of Baltimore, Maryland. When not at her desk coming up with new ways to torment her characters, she can often be found in the kitchen, glass of wine in hand, cooking a meal for friends.

Roxanne loves to hear from readers. You can find her contact information, website details and author profile page at https://www.totallybound.com

Home of Erotic Romance

Sign up for our newsletter and find out about all our romance book releases, eBook sales and promotions, sneak peeks and FREE romance books!